GENE RODDENBERRY'S

EARTH
FINAL CONFLICT™

LEGACY

GENE RODDENBERRY'S

EARTH
FINAL CONFLICT™

LEGACY

GLENN R. SIXBURY

TOR ®

A TOM DOHERTY ASSOCIATES BOOK
NEW YORK

GENE RODDENBERRY'S EARTH:
FINAL CONFLICT—LEGACY

Edited by James Frenkel

A Tor Book
Published by Tom Doherty Associates, LLC
175 Fifth Avenue
New York, NY 10010

www.tor.com

Tor® is a registered trademark of Tom Doherty Associates, LLC.

ISBN 0-765-30039-7 (hardcover)
ISBN 0-765-30040-0 (trade paperback)

First Edition: June 2002

Printed in the United States of America

0 9 8 7 6 5 4 3 2 1

For Brenda,
My wife,
My friend,
My love.

ACKNOWLEDGMENTS

Many thanks to Pam Poe, Tay Ledford, and Susan Frankenberg from the University of Tennessee at Knoxville. The mistakes contained in this novel are mine, not theirs. Susan is a much better archaeologist than I am.

Also, my appreciation and respect to Wendy Despain for her wonderful Web page and her thoughts on the change of seasons.

Most of all, I thank Ziporah, Stacey and Ron, Marie, Linda, Juli, David, and Brenda for their time and their wisdom. Thanks also to Char, Jean, Kim, and Stacy. Finally, my thanks to Chris (for the free samples, among other things).

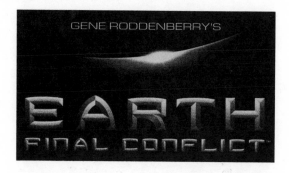

LEGACY

Dr. Waneta Long uncovered the rim of the vessel. Horizontal, intact, priceless. She knew how rare a find this might be, especially for a site so old. The few shards of pottery already found dated from the Woodland period, two to three thousand years ago. Long before her ancestors had come to these mountains. Long before Dr. Waneta Long was born.

As a child, she had lived in the nearby town of Cherokee, North Carolina, tourist capital of the Eastern Band of Cherokees. The town provided a reasonably good museum, a way for casual drifters to touch the past on their way to the casino or a weekend of camping near the Great Smoky Mountains National Park.

But the town had not been kind to an unmarried woman with a young child. Waneta and her mother moved away when Waneta was only five, and she had never looked back. Not until this summer. Not until an anonymous donor awarded a grant to the University of Tennessee at Knoxville to explore this site.

The grant was unusual not only because it was anonymous, but also because no one seemed to care about doing fieldwork in the United States anymore, not since Taelon artifacts were discovered in Ireland and Peru. More unusually, the donor of the grant specifically requested that Dr. Waneta Long be placed in charge of the dig.

The request was not made because she was the most qualified—Waneta earned her doctorate only five years ago and had yet to receive tenure. More likely, the donor specified her name at the top of the project because she was Cherokee, not realizing this could complicate matters with the local tribal government rather than improve them.

In general, Cherokees did not look kindly on archaeologists, especially women archaeologists who were fullblood Cherokee and therefore supposed to know that one did not dig in the ground to find the secrets of the past.

Waneta's mother had taught her differently. She claimed that Cherokees did not know the facts of their own history, regardless of their rich oral tradition. Although a fullblood Cherokee herself, she nevertheless urged Waneta to think independently, to examine the world with a critical and logical eye. She encouraged Waneta to reject the traditions, the mythology, and the narrow-mindedness of the Cherokee cliques that protected the bones of their ancestors. She always wanted her daughter to be a scientist.

Until the end. Until the sickness took away her mind.

Waneta forced away those thoughts. Her mother had been dead five years, but the pain of her passing had never lessened.

Pulling herself back to the dig site, Waneta focused on the late afternoon sunshine and the pine-scented air, on the rustle of trees in the soft breeze and the color of changing leaves. A glorious day atop Rattlesnake Mountain. One for which she had waited a very long time.

She leaned forward and peered into the vessel. What little fill existed appeared as nothing more than a shadowy mound of dust, which might be exactly what it was. If she wanted, she could have reached her hand inside—the mouth of this pottery jar was a full ten centimeters across—but she forced herself to wait. She would need to weigh the vessel's contents and possibly run them through a water screen, either the temporary one they had built on site or the custom-made tank back at UT.

This site had originally been the interior of a dry cave whose roof had recently collapsed. Although sediment had surrounded this jar since the cave-in, its interior had remained untouched, perhaps for thousands of years.

During the next forty-five minutes, Waneta troweled around the vessel to a depth of twenty-five centimeters, careful to stay away from its sides to avoid scratching it. The dirt went into a white plastic bucket, and like the fill, it would be water-screened to reveal tiny fragments of the past.

Most days she pulled her hair back, but today she had forgotten. Spiral-permed, it fell in black waves to her shoulders and clung to the top of her sweater as she worked. She refused to grow her hair long, in part because that made it easier to take care of while in the field, but also because it made her look less traditional. In other parts of the country, she had often been mistaken for Asian or Mexican. That never happened around here, but no one mistook her for a conservative Cherokee, either.

When the bulk of surrounding material was cleared, she removed the soil immediately next to the vessel using bamboo picks. Similar in appearance to giant pencils, the bamboo picks were homemade, cut by one of the grad students who had a knack for it. Bamboo worked best for this kind of excavation. The tips did not mar the pottery surface—important because early North American pottery was fired but not glazed and so tended to scratch easily.

As she worked, the grad students arrived. She heard the sound of the old van—it must be Jason's turn to carpool—then the rustling of grass as three sets of footsteps neared, their approach curving away and back as the students skirted the string-bounded squares of the site. They gathered around her, but she did not stop to greet them and they did not interrupt her work.

She could have chased them off to sift through the wheelbarrow of dirt they had flat-shoveled yesterday, but opportunities to watch a vessel like this being uncovered were rare and should be savored. They would all learn more in the next thirty minutes than they would from days spent screening for potsherds.

Gradually the shape of the jar emerged. It resembled a spherical bowl topped by a columnar mouth. Waneta scraped away the surrounding material until only a layer of caked dust remained, then paused in her work and greeted the three grad students for the first time. Ashley and Denene smiled at her, but Jason's gaze never left the vessel.

"How much longer?" he asked. "Are we going to water-screen the fill today?"

Waneta glanced at the shadows. The sun was already deep behind the mountain. "I'm guessing it'll be sunset in thirty minutes. Let's just record the context and get the vessel packed for the trip back. I'll run the fill through the water tank back at UT."

Jason frowned.

She stood up and stretched. "Don't worry, Jason. I'll let you know what I find."

Jason was a tough one to figure out. Most of the time, he acted as if he was here only for the small stipend she paid the grad students from the grant money, but today, staring at the uncovered outline of the vessel, he seemed more animated and interested than she had ever seen him. Perhaps, like many students, he did not see the importance of the fragmentary evidence. He was impressed only with vessels, figurines, pipes, and jewelry—intact objects he could hold in his hand and marvel over.

Waneta took the first round of pictures that would verify the vessel's place within the grid and demonstrate the context of how it had been found. She allowed the students to take the next round while she walked several paces away and stretched. Her muscles were sore from sitting cross-legged and bending over her work.

The evening was cool and crisp, but not yet cold. The sun no longer warmed her back, but the trees around the site blocked the wind. Unfortunately, they also hid her view of the surrounding mountains.

Fall was the only time of year when someone could tempt

her to move from Knoxville back to Cherokee. Mountains surrounded the small town like bright sponge paintings, the kind she used to do in Sunday school when she was only three.

Funny, the moments she could remember. Her small fingers dipping the sponge into the bright primary red, giggling as she stamped it across white paper.

Other moments, too: pine needles beneath her feet as she walked through the forest, holding the hand of someone she could not see; her stomach uneasy as her mother's old car twisted and turned, crawling its way up the mountain—this mountain.

Silly. She could not know which mountain. She had been too young to remember.

But since June, when they first mapped out this site in two-meter squares, more and more memories had slowly found their way into her conscious mind. She tried not to think about them. Most, like the walk in the forest, she did not understand.

She glanced back at the site, at her students hard at work, fascinated by their discovery—an incredibly important discovery. When Waneta had been asked to lead this dig, she had a hunch she would find something remarkable, something unique, but as work on the site dragged summer into fall with no stone artifacts and only a few potsherds found, she lost her initial confidence. She began to question why anyone would award a large grant for such an unproven site and worried that all the time spent here would provide her with nothing she could publish, jeopardizing her chances for tenure. Only in the past few days had her optimistic feeling returned, steadily growing day by day, as if she were getting close.

Today the hunch had finally proved itself. The vessel provided the first evidence this site had been occupied rather than a burial site. Many times, pottery vessels placed in graves were ceremonially "killed." No holes had been knocked in the piece uncovered here, which gave Waneta hope that the vessel had once served an entire community and was not part of a grave. She expected to find more pottery, refuse, and perhaps some worked flakes within this and the adjoining grid, but to have her first meaningful evidence be an intact piece was remarkable.

She returned to the vessel and continued her work.

Her first sign that something was wrong came when she brushed the dirt away from the top of the jar and saw the pattern impressed in its rim. It looked remarkably familiar. She quickly brushed the sides of the vessel. As she revealed each new millimeter of the pattern incised on the pottery, she grew more anxious, more certain that everything had gone terribly, irrevocably wrong.

When she uncovered enough of the pattern to make out the design, she stopped and the brush fell from her fingers. "Oh, God. Oh, no."

"What's wrong?" Ashley asked.

"It's a snake," Jason said.

"Snake." Waneta gripped her throat, struggling to breathe.

The word *snake* conjured up horrible memories of her mother in the last month before she died. In those final days, as she grew thinner, wasting away, she had become obsessed with snakes—terrified of them. She spoke constantly of her Cherokee heritage, especially as it related to snakes and how she was dying because she had offended one.

"It's my fault," she would claim, rearing up in bed and grasping Waneta's sleeve. "I should have buried it. Now I'm too weak. I can't do it. You must go to the mountain. Tame the snake before it escapes and destroys the world."

Waneta hated it when her mother spoke that way. Her mother had been so proud, so logical. To see her reduced by illness and fear to the point that she quoted ancient myths was in some ways more painful than her death.

Now Waneta could not look at a snake without thinking of her mother—and this snake disturbed her more than most. Portrayed in the classic two-dimensional Cherokee style, rows of fangs protruded from both upper and lower jaws and tentacles or horns sprouted from the top of its head. An impossibly long forked tongue extended from its mouth—or perhaps the long tendrils represented twin flames, like those from a fire-breathing dragon. An unusual pattern of lines radiated from a circle on the creature's forehead, and lines decorated the long, thin body asymmetrically, as if the front half of the beast served a different function from the back.

Waneta recognized the drawing. She had seen many similar works before. It was an *Uktena*, a mythical serpent common in Cherokee artwork.

Cherokee. That meant Mississippian, not Woodland.

She stood up and backed away. "We can't dig here."

The students looked at her, dumbfounded.

"The Native American Graves Protection and Repatriation Act," she said irritably.

Denene shook her head. "This site's too old for that, isn't it?"

"It's a mixed site," Waneta said. "We can't continue work here until I contact the Cultural Resources Office in Cherokee."

"What does that mean?" Ashley asked.

Waneta did not answer. She stormed a few steps away, then stopped and pinched the bridge of her nose between her thumb and forefinger. Desperately, she wanted to find a way to keep digging, but the law was clear on this. This artifact belonged to a living, identifiable aboriginal group. She had no choice but to surrender control to them.

"Damn," she said. "Damn it, anyway."

Denene took a step forward. Her voice trembled as she spoke. "We haven't found any bones. This isn't a grave site."

"It doesn't matter," Waneta said, pacing now. "Look at the serpent incised on the pottery. That's an *Uktena*. It means this bowl may have been used for ceremonial purposes. It certainly means we can't proceed without permission from the Eastern Band of Cherokees."

Ashley was staring at the vessel as if it were a dissected rabbit. "That's still okay, isn't it? We can just ask, can't we?"

Waneta laughed for several seconds, then pressed her hands to the sides of her face and groaned. "We can ask. We can always ask."

Jason bent low and reached for the vessel with both hands. Waneta watched, unbelieving, as he lifted it off the ground. She croaked several times before she managed to get the words out. "What are you doing? Put the vessel down, Jason. Put it down now!"

Jason lifted his head and looked at her, his expression cold, unfeeling, then his lips turned up in the slightest of grins.

For Waneta, that instant remained frozen, forever clear in her mind. Jason's hands were tight around the vessel—she saw the pink of his fingernails, the tension in his wrists—then his grip loosened . . .

. . . and the pot slipped free. Waneta lunged forward. She was five steps away. Much too far. Helpless, she watched it fall.

The vessel shattered against the ground and the fill inside exploded in a cloud of dust. Pottery fragments sprayed across the loose earth and bounced on the green grass next to the grid square. One large, dark object rolled free of the rubble, something from inside, something that had been buried beneath the dust.

Waneta's mouth worked silently and her fingers clenched and unclenched in dying spasms. A groan escaped her lips as she lifted her face and stared at Jason.

"What the hell are you doing? Have you lost your mind? You've just . . . shattered a piece of history. It's gone. Forever. I can't believe it."

He said nothing.

"What were you thinking?"

"You startled me," he said. "I didn't mean to drop it."

"The hell you didn't. You did it on purpose. Your days in this department are over. You're out. You're gone."

Waneta started toward Jason. To poke a finger in his chest or to pummel him, she never knew. Before she drew close enough to touch him, movement to one side attracted her attention.

Ashley had bent forward and was reaching for the object that had rolled free of the destruction.

"Ashley, no!"

Waneta said the words the way she would scold a dog or a small child.

Ashley did not stop. She picked up what looked like a round ball of dusty rags—and started to unwrap it.

"No!" Waneta tried to grab it from her, but Ashley jerked away at the last instant. Instead of taking it away, Waneta only knocked it from her hands. Ashley kept a grip on part of it and the rest unraveled. A shiny crystal fell free, sparkling, its red surface catching the light as it dropped to the ground with a thud.

Waneta shoved Ashley away and reached for the sparkling red stone, but Denene was already there, her hand outstretched.

What was going on? It was like a scene out of a horror movie.

"Stop!" Waneta growled. She slapped Denene's hand away and grabbed the gleaming gem.

It burned, and she almost dropped it, but it cooled so quickly that she questioned her senses. She transferred the gem to her other hand and looked at her palm. No red marks. No sign that her initial impression of heat had been real.

Puzzled, she stared at the stone. It filled her small hand. Clutching it tightly, she spun to face the students. "Which one of you wants to explain what's going on?"

Ashley and Denene lowered their chins and stared at the ground. Jason met her gaze at first, but after a moment even he looked away.

"You could all be thrown out of the department for this. You've tampered with a site that I just told you was protected by NAGPRA, you've ruined the context of the find—hell, you've destroyed the artifact itself. All of you know better, especially you, Denene. You're one of the best students the department has."

Waneta fought to keep the tears from her eyes and her voice even as she spoke. "Why didn't you stop when I asked?" She held up the stone and shook it. "Why did you even touch this in the first place?"

"I'm sorry, Dr. Long, I—" Denene paused, swallowing hard. "I didn't want to, it's just that, well . . ."

"Well?"

"It made me."

Waneta frowned. "What do you mean—it made you?"

"The crystal."

Waneta held up the gem. "Are you saying this rock forced you to pick it up?"

Denene lowered her gaze and nodded.

Waneta sighed and shook her head. "That's the worst excuse I've heard in a long time. What about you, Ashley? I suppose the crystal made you unwrap it, too? Is that what happened?"

Ashley folded her arms protectively across her chest. Her eyes, wet with tears, glinted in the fading light. "No. I don't know why I picked it up."

"That much I believe." Waneta nodded and turned to Jason. "What's your story?"

"It slipped."

Waneta put up her hand as if to ward off a blow. "Let's not get into that. We both know better. Just tell me why you picked it up at all."

"We had our context pictures. We measured and recorded its position within the grid. What else did we need to do? Or are you mad only because *you* weren't the first one to hold it?"

"It has nothing to do with that. An archaeological artifact is not a toy."

"Isn't it? Isn't that why you got into this business in the first place?"

"It's not a business."

"Really? Then who's paying for us to be here? Who spon-

sored this dig? You think they did that out of the goodness of
their hearts? You think you're going to get to keep anything
you find here?"

"Don't even go there, Jason. That's not the issue. The point
is, you don't pick up an ancient artifact just to look at it. Even if
you do, you need to understand that holding a piece of the past
is like holding a life in your hands. You certainly don't drop it."

"Maybe it's better I did," Jason said smoothly. "What we've
dated so far says this is a Woodland site. There's no law that
says you need to date every potsherd you find, and without the
design on the vessel, no one can claim we aren't allowed to dig
here. We can pretend none of this happened."

"The hell we can."

Waneta's whole body shook. She tried to control the tone
and volume of her voice but failed. "Get out of here! Get off
this site! If you aren't gone in the next minute, I'll do more than
throw you out of the department, I'll have you dismissed from
the university for ethics violations!"

"You can't do that."

"The hell I can't. Now get out of here. All of you. Now!"

Waneta took a step toward them, still holding the crystal in
her hand. They scattered and regrouped at Jason's van, climbing inside without looking back. The old Ford rumbled to life
and its headlights snapped on. With creaks and groans, it
slowly rocked over the rough ground to the trail. After a
moment, it disappeared into the trees on its way back to the
main road.

Waneta was alone.

She swallowed. Tears ran down her cheeks as she turned in
a slow circle, looking at the devastation, knowing the full ruin
of what had happened.

Not only would she need to convince the Cherokee nation
that she had *accidentally* disturbed what she now believed was a
ceremonial site, but she also faced the long ordeal of proving
that Jason had acted inappropriately. She was sure he would
deny his comments about ignoring what they had found.

Although Ashley and Denene were witnesses, they were also Jason's friends. Would they tell the truth?

No matter what, she could not allow a person with Jason's lack of scruples to graduate with an advanced degree in archaeology. He was nothing more than a modern grave robber. It now made perfect sense why he showed interest only in intact objects. It was hard to sell a flint flake or a fragment from a figurine to the highest bidder.

How had he ever made it this far?

She knew the answer to that, at least the simple answer. Dr. Messmore, her department head, had forced her to hire Jason for this dig. She did not know why, but assumed the boy's family had money.

Ashley and Denene were a different story. She felt especially bad about Denene, but the girl's excuse was maddening. It was like saying, "The devil made me do it." Not that Denene had done anything wrong—Waneta had grabbed the stone before she could. That was Waneta's mistake. It was just that by the time the crystal rolled free, all the students were acting crazy. She was merely trying to regain control before any more damage was done.

Waneta covered the site using thick black plastic, which she anchored with heavy stones. Perhaps she had chased off the students a bit too soon. Darkness came quickly in these mountains. Night had already fallen before she managed to secure the site and put away her tools.

The work went more slowly than it might have, because she carried the crystal in her free hand, stubbornly refusing to put it down or put it away, even after she retrieved a jacket and a flashlight from her SUV. She was being silly, she knew, but the crystal was the only good to come from today. If she let it go, it seemed she would lose everything.

Fortunately, the flashlight was unnecessary. The nearly full moon provided more light than many of her friends in the city would ever believe it could. Low in the sky, just over the eastern trees, it cast long, eerie shadows across the small clearing as she located the largest pieces of the vessel and placed them in a cardboard box lined with tissue paper. Tears formed again on her cheeks as she thought about what had been lost.

All she had left were pieces of the past. Memories. Like those of her mother.

Waneta finished packing everything into the back of the SUV, then made a final pass, walking around the site and shining the flashlight across the black plastic that covered the squares. The white strings at their edges stood out in the beam of the light. Normally, she removed the strings from the squares they were working on so no one would trip over them, but she had been distracted by the discovery of the jar and the idea of what might be inside it. She would remove the strings tomorrow.

As she turned to go, she spotted the dark, rumpled mound of wrapping that had contained the crystal. It still lay in the grass where Ashley had dropped it. Waneta retrieved it but did not bother to look at it now. It felt soft and slick with dust. She would examine it tomorrow in the lab.

As she walked to the SUV, the beam of her flashlight darted among the vegetation like a frightened rabbit. At the vehicle, she turned off the light and shut it and the dusty wrapping in the back with the cardboard box. Keeping the crystal with her, she walked around the side and reached for the driver's door.

Suddenly she stopped, frozen, her heart pounding. In the window, the reflection of a face hovered above her left shoulder.

Waneta let out a small cry and spun to face the stranger. She backed against the SUV, ready to fight or flee, depending on who it was.

She did neither.

A stocky old woman stood a step away, the moon bathing her in milky light. She wore a simple print dress. A red kerchief bound her white hair behind her head and a corn-bead necklace arced across her upper chest. Wisdom had worked its way into her bronze face, visibly etched in the wrinkles along her forehead and imprinted at the corners of her eyes, which were deep-set and kind. She had high cheekbones, a shallow, wide nose, and fleshy skin flanking a small, rounded chin—a face like many Waneta had seen in the nearby town and along the roadways leading to the dig site, a face Waneta might see in the mirror forty years from now.

Waneta's heart quit pounding, but her words still came out more quickly than she would have liked.

"Who are you? What do you want?"

"Do not be afraid, *Sgilisi*. I have come to help."

The woman's speech bore a heavy Cherokee accent. Waneta had heard stories of people who spoke mainly Cherokee, preferring to live out their lives clinging to the past. They resorted to English only when necessary. This woman sounded like one of them.

"Help who? I don't need any help."

The woman smiled indulgently, the way old people do at young children. "You must put *Uluhsati* back."

"Oola-what?"

The old woman stepped closer. Her brown eyes, hazy from cataracts, focused briefly on Waneta, as if studying her. She held out her hand at a height just above her waist.

"The last time I saw you, you were only this high. My, what a woman you've become. Your mother is so proud of you."

"My mother's dead."

Waneta said the words without thinking. The woman probably thought she recognized Waneta and would now believe that one of her good friends had died.

"I'm sorry," she said, wanting to repair the damage, "I'm Dr. Waneta Long from the University of Tennessee at Knoxville. I'm in charge of the dig site behind you. I was surprised to see anyone, especially after dark. This place is very hard to find."

Waneta scanned the clearing and the trail leading back to the main road. She had not heard a car and could not imagine someone walking around on this mountain at night.

The woman stared at Waneta, and her eyes seemed to clear

somewhat, a trick of the light. "You have removed *Uluhsati* from his resting place. You do not understand the danger that lives inside him."

Waneta shivered and folded her arms. In her hand, the crystal felt like ice. She closed her eyes long enough for a deep breath. This was more than mistaken identity. This poor old woman sounded confused, perhaps senile.

"Please. Let me give you a lift somewhere. It's late, and it's getting cold."

Waneta opened the door of her SUV. The dome light popped on, creating a small brightly lit square that pooled at her feet.

The old woman shuffled quickly backward, and Waneta spoke in a soft voice, trying not to alarm her further.

"It's all right. I'll take you home."

The old woman clucked softly to herself. "You have the power in your blood to control *Uluhsati*, but you do not have the experience—or the desire, just as your mother never had the desire. That is why she left."

"My mother's dead," Waneta repeated coldly.

The old woman spoke quickly now, the voice sharp-edged and scolding. "When she took you away in the night, she had not yet found her faith in the old ways, just as you have not. I was wrong to force them upon her before she was ready. I know that now."

Waneta swallowed. She recalled a flash of memory: her mother, almost in a panic, rushing around their small house, packing boxes, loading them into a U-Haul trailer. She could remember later being carried to their old car, a blanket wrapped around her, stars twinkling in black velvet overhead.

"Who are you?" Waneta asked. She backed up until the door frame of the SUV pressed against her legs.

"You must decide," the old woman said sternly. "I cannot protect you once you leave this mountain."

"Decide what?"

"Decide if you are ready to take my place."

Waneta paused, torn between confusion, anger, and apprehension. Something about this old woman was familiar. The words she spoke made no sense, but deep inside, a part of Waneta recognized them, knew the choice—and was terrified of it. Boundless, uncontrollable fear welled up within her.

Without a word, she scrambled into the driver's seat and slammed the door. Quickly, she switched the crystal to her other hand and turned the key in the ignition, then stepped on the gas even before she threw the SUV in gear. The truck lurched across the clearing, bouncing and jerking over the rough ground. After Waneta's head hit the padded ceiling the third time, she slowed down, but she did not stop until she reached the old trail that led to the gravel road and back to the highway.

Waneta glanced in her rearview mirror, ridiculously expecting some kind of chase, but the old woman had hobbled out of sight and back down whatever mountain trail had brought her to the dig site in the first place.

Even so, Waneta did not feel safe until she was completely off the mountain and back on Highway 441, twisting north through the Great Smoky Mountains National Park toward home. Only then did she feel guilty for leaving the crazy old woman stranded on the mountain.

She should go back, she knew, but she could not force herself to turn around.

"You must decide," the old woman had said.

Waneta could not understand why those words terrified her, but she had no energy left to think about them tonight.

The crystal had finally warmed in her hand. She cradled it while she drove, already starting to theorize what it may have been used for and why the ancient Cherokees might have kept it buried in a cave on the mountain. She would have to surrender it to the Cherokee Cultural Resources Office and wondered if it would end up in their museum.

Until then, she would have the chance to study it and perhaps publish a paper. But for now, holding it in her hand would have to be enough, its secrets beyond her reach until tomorrow.

TWO

Traditional Irish music, accented by the lively stamping of feet, filled the old Ford's Theatre in Washington, D.C. Liam Kincaid saw the dancers but not the dancing. He was not here for entertainment.

Da'an, whom Liam had sworn to protect, sat in the center seat of the third row, main floor. Liam, the only other person in the audience, stood one row back, watching for movement away from the stage, his caution encouraged by the flag-draped presidential box to their right.

Liam recognized the irony: Da'an, the Taelons' North American Companion—survivor of more than one assassination attempt—was attending a performance in the same theater where President Lincoln had been shot in the back of the head while watching a comedy. Despite that morbid bit of history, Liam would have preferred that the Taelon sit in the president's old chair rather than here in the open, an easy target for a sniper in the balcony behind them or hidden behind the gold curtains of the luxury boxes that loomed above to their left and right.

Too many people wanted Da'an dead. Liam knew some of them, had worked with them as leader of the Resistance. A time existed when he had staunchly defended Da'an to them, believing Da'an was their best hope for reaching a peaceful equality with the Taelons. Now he was not so sure.

Da'an had betrayed him more than once. People had died because of that betrayal. Even so, Liam knew that killing Da'an was not the answer.

Like John Wilkes Booth and his failed conspiracy to throw the Union into chaos, many renegade cells of the Resistance would leap on the chance to implement a similar plan against the Taelons. It would be the worst move they could make. Not only would such a round of murders make the Resistance no better than the Taelons, but it also would condemn both races to eventual extinction. The only chance either had to survive was to work together.

As for Da'an, the Taelon dismissed all notions of danger. "That is why I have you to protect me," Da'an told Liam before they left the embassy.

When they arrived at the theater, Da'an insisted on sitting center stage, where the performance would be most aesthetically pleasing.

Now he seemed consumed only with the spectacle before him, his hands flowing through the air in slow, graceful patterns—a stark contrast to the rapid heels of the dancers as they tapped out their precisely controlled rhythms on the stage.

Under other circumstances, Liam might have enjoyed the performance, but today he viewed the synchronized clattering of feet as a problem. Too much movement and too much noise. With such an effective diversion, an assassin would not need stealth to sneak into position. To complicate matters further, the boisterous activity kept luring Liam's attention to the stage. He refused to repeat the mistake Lincoln's guard had made and forced himself to conduct a constant surveillance pattern that included the balcony and dress circle as well as the luxury boxes.

At first consideration, an attempt today on Da'an's life seemed highly unlikely. This visit had been arranged around four o'clock this afternoon for a show that started at six-thirty; it was now only a few minutes after seven. What had been planned as a dress rehearsal had become a private showing. No publicity. No advance warning. Beyond the dancers and the orchestra, few people even knew this performance would take place.

But Liam was the only bodyguard.

No time existed to put together a complex plan, but a lone killer who had been patiently waiting for an opportunity would find this one too tempting to pass up. Liam had tried to talk Da'an out of coming, but the Taelon's interest in human culture and art overwhelmed his reason. This was not the first time Da'an had allowed his curiosity to overcome concerns for his personal safety.

Liam watched the dancers for any hesitation, any falter in their steps that might indicate they carried a weapon, but his gaze was repeatedly distracted by the darting violin bows in the narrow gorge of the orchestra pit. He gripped the hard back of Da'an's chair and shifted uneasily, his weight pressing into the red carpet at his feet as he continued to scan the theater.

Suddenly the music stopped and the stage darkened. Instantly Liam widened his stance and tensed. His hand slipped beneath his black jacket, his fingers resting on his energy weapon, but the interruption was planned—a preparatory pause before the climatic finale.

The music began again, slow and soft, and a red-haired boy, no more than five or six, danced onto the stage, twin spotlights tracking his every move. Head down, he seemed intent on each step, but the grace of his movements set him apart from the dancers who had come before. Liam had never seen the boy but knew him by reputation: Daniel Shaunessy, a young prodigy who astounded audiences wherever he went. Reviewers claimed that he already danced better than Michael Flatley, the man who a decade before had pushed traditional Irish dancing from its stiff roots into the popular mainstream of entertainment.

Liam did not know if the boy was that good, but certainly he did not dance like a child. His steps were precise and powerful, and yet restrained, as if he held back some greater energy that longed to burst forth.

The beat of the song quickened.

The boy twirled once and stamped his heels against the hardwood beneath him in an ever expanding pattern that carried him across the stage. As the music crescendoed, he spun toward his small audience and snapped his head erect. The young dancer's eyes burned a bright, fiery green, sparkling in the stage lights with what looked like an inner glow.

Liam flinched, then relaxed as he recognized the effect. Adult patrons wearing weird contacts often haunted the Flat Planet Café, but it seemed a mistake to have a child wear that kind of lenses on stage. The intensity they produced disturbed rather than excited. They made Liam feel as if he were looking at a hungry wolf instead of a small boy.

Da'an leaned forward in his seat. His hand motions increased in speed and frequency, losing some of their grace, becoming erratic.

On the stage, the young dancer hopped in place, slashing and kicking with his legs, faster and faster, the music staying with him. One by one, other instruments joined the mix to create a climatic fusion of sight and sound and energy. The stage lights snapped on at low intensity, then gradually brightened as dancers bounded onto the stage and formed lines of blurring motion that flanked the show's star.

The program listed the boy's mother as Triss Shaunessy, but Liam had no way to know which of the shadowed faces might be hers. What tricks and enticements had she used to teach a child so young to dance better than most adults? While all prodigies had enormous innate talent, the ones who realized their potential this early usually did so with a great deal of help and recognition from a driven and domineering mother or father.

In sync with an upbeat to the music, the boy suddenly hopped straight into the air, the top of his head reaching above the adults around him. When he came down, the lights flashed full on and he skipped across the stage in an explosion of rhythmic energy that carried him in a zigzag pattern between the other dancers. All of them fixed their eyes forward, their feet moving in unison, pounding out the accompaniment. Together they provided a giant human backdrop to the boy's bounding ability as he ran and danced and twirled among them.

The tempo of the music doubled. The dancers matched the change, and the boy released the energy he had been holding back, his small legs moving faster than Liam's eyes could follow. He circled the stage in a final quick burst before stopping in the center of the other dancers, his movements instantly matching theirs, then increasing beyond them as he danced to the front of the line, his kicks taking him higher and higher. With each leap, it seemed he would take off with a Peter Pan laugh and fly about the theater in youthful enthusiasm.

Instead, all movement and music stopped in a defining instant. The stage went black, leaving the boy trapped in a circle of light. One knee bent, he sucked in great gulps of air, his chest heaving, his gaze on Da'an.

Liam started to applaud, then realized that Da'an had collapsed forward. The Taelon's body glimmered a soft blue, and rainbow lines danced across the glowing skin as if Da'an were about to transform to an energy state.

Liam let out a breath and jerked the weapon from inside his jacket. He examined the balcony, the dress circle, and the boxes, but saw no one. He glanced across the narrow gulf of the crowded orchestra pit and scanned the stage and the shadowy faces of the motionless dancers. He stared into the fiery green eyes of the small boy. Nothing.

Da'an groaned. His body brightened in shimmering pulses, rays of light blasting from his skin like hundreds of tiny spotlights.

Liam vaulted the row of chairs and landed beside the Taelon. Keeping his body low, he scanned the theater but found no threat, no explanation for what had happened.

Ozone filled his nostrils. Normally Taelons smelled like

week-old babies, fresh skin with an earthy undercurrent, but in
their energy states they were more like bottled lightning.

Liam helped Da'an to his feet. The touch caused Liam's
skin to prickle, and the hair stood out in bumps along his arms.
"*Sorack'path'ta!*" Da'an roared. After pushing Liam away,
the Taelon grabbed the back of a chair, as if in pain.

Staring at the stage, Da'an completely reverted to an
energy state for several seconds before regaining a human
facade and slumping forward.

The stage lights came on. Dancers relaxed out of their final
stance, and members of the orchestra stood up to peer quizzi-
cally out of their pit.

For Liam, none of them existed. Only the boy remained.
He had yet to move from where he had stopped, still bent on
one knee, his arms outstretched, as if waiting for applause that
would never come.

Liam and Da'an struggled down the row and into the aisle,
but the more Liam tried to hurry, the slower he seemed able to
guide Da'an from the theater. They curled around the balcony
pillar and paused beside the emergency exit.

Still the boy remained, his green eyes aglow. Calm. Quiet.
Harmless. Somehow he had caused this to happen, had injured
Da'an—but that was impossible. Taelons might appear effemi-
nate, but Liam knew better. A grown human had no chance
against one of the aliens in hand-to-hand combat—and this was
just a child, a little boy who had danced. While he had glared at
Da'an just before the collapse, looks did not kill, despite the old
cliché.

When they were outside, Liam thought back over the few
seconds just before the dance had ended. No one had fired any
weapon. He would have seen and heard an energy blast, and a
bullet would not affect Da'an this way.

Perhaps Da'an had just taken ill. The Taelons were not
invincible—they could be affected by viruses, such as the
pesh'tal—but Da'an's collapse had occurred so suddenly. His
initial symptoms were similar to what would happen if he were

separated from the Commonality, but if that were the case, he would have transformed into an Atavus by now, and Liam would have sensed the separation.

No, the boy was responsible, but how? The child had no weapon, no way to hurt the Taelon. The explanation must lie elsewhere. Something Liam had missed. A mistake he had made.

Da'an shimmered again and Liam's palms glowed softly, his shaqarava active. Although Da'an knew the truth about Liam's alien-human parents, Liam closed his fists to hide the signs of his Kimeran heritage. He remained uncomfortable with his alien DNA, despite the fact his human genes dominated his body most of the time.

After Da'an was safely on board the shuttle, Liam settled behind the pilot's controls. Since his elevation to Da'an's personal Protector, he had often shielded the Taelon from danger, sometimes acting against the desires of Renée Palmer and others in the Resistance to do so. They thought he betrayed humanity through his actions.

He certainly betrayed Da'an today by losing focus. He would not do so again. As he guided the shuttle upward and in the direction of the Taelons' North American embassy, he tried to relive those last few seconds of the performance, to discover the critical detail that would allow him to understand, but all he saw were the burning green eyes of the young Irish dancer.

THREE

Zo'or walked to the virtual glass of the viewport and gazed out from the Taelon mother ship. Earth rotated slowly below, not as a complex and beautiful world, but as a foreign entity—complete and controllable as a whole.

After years spent studying the planet, Zo'or's fascination went beyond its link to the future of the Taelon race and his own ambitions as leader of the Synod. Its inhabitants, with their casual approach to life and their easy deaths, intrigued him. They provided distraction as well as being a valuable resource.

Of late, he had become especially fascinated by their notions of sexuality. Not their crude animalistic mating rituals, but the way even their children instinctively understood the differences between male and female, boy and girl, strong and weak. Some women on the planet proclaimed themselves equal to men in all things—but he cared nothing for their meaningless babble.

Zo'or knew the truth. By taking control of a man whose consciousness had been lost to a coma, he had wielded the raw physical power of the male human animal. He knew the rage that could be produced by the flood of testosterone in his blood and he had relished the blind fury and feeling of invincibility provided by that primitive hormonal secretion.

On rare days, Zo'or could also appreciate the feminine qualities of the human species, but his race was engaged in a war of attrition with the Jaridians. For that agenda, he preferred to adopt a masculine mind-set for himself and his fellow Taelons. It gave him an added edge of strength, another level of understanding. It was why he often looked at the blue sphere below not as the complicated resource it was but rather in the way an ancient human warrior would have surveyed a conquered domain.

Taelons were rarely so crude or so absolute in their judgments, but he enjoyed adopting the human male's simplistic viewpoint. He relished it in a way his parent Da'an would have said was unnatural . . . and unwise. It gave him pleasure to stare out at the blue world, knowing he would have it for his own.

Except that the conquest of this planet was not yet complete, a situation with which Zo'or had grown increasingly impatient.

Footsteps clicked across the living floor of the mother ship, but Zo'or did not turn to see who approached. He liked maintaining an air of omnipotence, even with his protector, Agent Ronald Sandoval.

Zo'or glanced at the human as it stopped a respectful step away, beside the virtual glass of the viewport. Agent Sandoval wore a business suit, a ritualistic garment intended to convey power and virility. The broadness of the padded shoulders accented an impression of strength; the tie pointed directly to the concealed genitals. Da'an had described earlier human garments from which the modern suit descended, many of which had strength and virility features that were much more pronounced. Zo'or imagined Agent Sandoval in a codpiece and moved his fingers in a graceful pattern of amusement. While Taelons lacked the passions and zest for life so many humans possessed, they retained vestigial feelings that resembled emotions, and it pleased Zo'or that none of the humans had yet decoded the subtle differences in hand gestures that revealed too much of a Taelon's inner sensibilities.

As Agent Sandoval stopped beside Zo'or, he placed his hands behind his back and looked out the viewport. Zo'or watched the agent's eyes as they focused on the planet below. No recognition. No appreciation. This human no longer saw the beautiful blue orb as home. To him, it mattered only as it related to the Taelons and their future needs.

He understood.

But with that understanding, he had lost the edge that made so many of the humans below more interesting. He no longer functioned as an animal in its natural environment. Instead, he had become a valuable tool to be guided—but also to be watched, because all tools wear out.

Agent Sandoval spoke. "Doors International has stepped up its purchase of ancient artifacts—not only in Peru, but around the world. It's becoming increasingly difficult to track their activities. I need more Volunteers."

Zo'or had grown weary of human interference in his plans for Earth, especially the meddling of Joshua Doors, and before him, of his father, Jonathan Doors. He had finally come to terms with the elder Doors, rendering him virtually harmless, but shortly thereafter, the human had interfered in the Taelon's control project at One Taelon Avenue and had been killed.

Zo'or moved his fingers in a pattern of impatience. "Do not think, Agent Sandoval, that I do not recognize these transparent attempts to strengthen your own position by increasing the number of people you command. Regardless, you shall have the men you need. I will not be surprised again by Doors International as we were—"

Suddenly Zo'or stopped. He grunted, convulsed once, then threw his head back and straightened his fingers in alarm.

An unfamiliar sensation flowed through him, growing stronger, surprising in its intensity, unknown in origin. He closed his eyes and stepped away, needing to be alone, not wanting the human to see him in this moment of weakness.

Zo'or concentrated on the sensation and allowed his face to relax. His hands halted their graceful movements and slowly lowered to his sides.

He felt energy, unpleasant, tinged with malice and greater

in power than anything he had experienced. It called to him in a way he did not understand: tempting, alluring. He had never felt anything like it before. As he sought deeper inside himself, he shimmered, his physical body losing its tight cohesion as he edged closer to his energy state.

In his mind, he saw images viewed through red prisms: a feminine human face surrounded by dark, wavy hair, a hand reaching for him through a backdrop of distant trees and dimly lit sky, then a flash of light and the eyes of a young boy.

"Zo'or?" Agent Sandoval touched him.

Zo'or snapped his eyes open and moved his fingers in several quick, expressive patterns of agitation. Agent Sandoval backed away.

The images vanished. A moment later, the sensation dissipated, fading the way a wave breaks on a beach, then races back toward the sea. Zo'or soaked up as much of the passing energy as he could. He would digest it later when he could concentrate fully on its exact flavor.

Agent Sandoval stared at him with wide eyes, obviously wanting to speak but afraid to do so. Anger flared inside Zo'or and his body brightened before he willed it to solidify into its uncomfortable humanoid facade. He wanted to reprimand Agent Sandoval, but the human was doing his best to act on the guidance provided by his Cyber-Viral Implant, and CVIs, by design, were impossible to ignore.

As Zo'or spoke, he accented the words with precise, flowing gestures. "I feel a shift in the Commonality. It is not a lessening. Nor is it an increase. A separateness—unwelcome, unsettling. I must know it better."

Agent Sandoval straightened. "What do you wish me to do?"

Zo'or paused, sampling the residue left from the strange energy pattern the way a connoisseur evaluates a new wine. His eyelids fluttered as he recognized a familiar mental signature among the patterns received.

"Da'an," he breathed.

"Excuse me?"

Zo'or glared down at Agent Sandoval, knowing he had chosen such a short human protector partly because it allowed him to assume exactly this gesture of superiority.

"I feel the mark of Da'an in this. If he is not the cause, he is near the source. Go to the planet. Track his movements. Report all his actions, no matter how insignificant."

Agent Sandoval puckered his lips, then nodded. "I'll talk to Major Kincaid. Perhaps he'll reveal something."

"No. Da'an must not learn that I suspect he is linked to this disturbance. Not yet. If he is truly part of . . . what I feel, he is not to be trusted."

Zo'or again considered the sensation he had experienced. He would need to meditate on it to fully understand all he had felt, but for now, he knew that this intrusion into the Commonality represented a force much greater than any single Taelon could generate. It was a raw, unpolluted power, the kind he had always dreamed of obtaining.

Agent Sandoval assumed a wider stance and clasped his hands behind his back. "What about our investigation of Doors International?"

"It is unimportant now. We must not delay in discovering the source of what I felt."

Zo'or turned to the window and stared down at the blue planet again. His fingers traced an elegant pattern as he considered the possibilities.

"This new energy presents a unique opportunity. Whoever is first to embrace it will have an advantage not easily offset. Perhaps Da'an intends to use it to regain leadership of the Synod, but I will not allow that to happen. I will bring this force under my control. When that is done, I will bring our original plans for this planet to fruition. Nothing will stop me."

Agent Sandoval stood for a moment, awaiting further instructions, then turned and strode from the room.

FOUR

Joshua Doors stirred at the chiming of his global. He fumbled to wake from sleep the way a drowning man struggles to reach the surface of a cold and unforgiving sea. His hand snaked across the nightstand and grabbed the plastic case of the noisy device as he pushed himself up in bed and checked the time: ten minutes past one in the morning. Just once he wished he could get a good six hours of peaceful slumber without an emergency somewhere in the world requiring his attention.

"Ya," he said, and coughed, his throat scratchy with sleep.

The display brightened, but only enough to show the control icons. Like most people, he turned off his global's video each night before going to bed. He considered keying it on now, but he looked like hell, his brown hair tousled, his hazel eyes bloodshot and weary. Besides, while the built-in cameras on globals were good, especially on the ones he owned, they were not good enough to pick up much beyond dark shadows unless he flipped on the light. If he did that, it would take forever to fall back to sleep.

When the voice on the other end spoke, it ruined his chances anyway.

Joshua came fully awake and listened carefully, knowing the signal was tainted, a disruption carrier making it impossible to record. Without even an old-fashioned pencil and paper, he relied on the software inside his head to remember every word.

At the end of the call, Joshua switched off his global, then paused to gather his thoughts. During the conversation, he had asked the same question he had been asking for months: What was so special about this artifact? He was again told he did not need to know. His only information about the object had come months ago from specifications provided for its duplicate. Under orders, he had directed his labs to manufacture a replacement—a red-tinted gem—but he felt certain that while the look-alike might be similar in appearance, it was otherwise nothing like the original.

Joshua had inherited one of the biggest corporations in the world from his father and did not like being told what to do. He was used to being the puppeteer, not the marionette, and he especially did not like who was pulling his strings.

Clenching the bedsheet in his free hand, he twisted the smooth fabric into a tight wad. He had yet to recover from the loss of his father, or the guilt over playing a part in his death, regardless of how little control he had actually exerted that night.

But this was different. Tonight, he did have a choice. He could lie down and go back to sleep. Or he could do as he had been told.

A great deal, financially, rode on what he decided in the next few minutes. The Taelons giveth—and the Taelons taketh away.

Too many people, both in the Resistance and among the ranks of the stockholders, depended on him to make the right decision. He could not please everybody.

Not even himself.

The Taelons' arrival on Earth had heralded a new era of peace and cooperation, but money still set the world in motion. Without it, he had nothing.

Only now, holding the reins of power in his hands, could he understand why his father had made some of the choices he did, and why he had devoted so little time to worrying about his growing son. The man had been overstretched, trying to do too much in too little time. Something—someone—had to suffer. Joshua wondered whether, if he ever had children, he would be able to do any better by them. He had sworn he would.

Joshua sighed, then flipped on the lights. After pulling on a dark blue turtleneck shirt, he combed his hair, then settled onto the bed again. One thing he had learned from his father: In business, impressions were everything.

"You can't be in control, Son, unless you look the part."

Good advice.

Joshua took two deep breaths, then keyed on his global's video. Speaking to the device, he said, "Renée Palmer."

His global connected with hers. As he listened to it chime, he wondered if she would look at the caller ID before she decided whether to answer.

She damned well better answer. Her importance to Doors International could not be overstated, but he was still the boss.

Renée's image appeared on the display, but she did not speak. Blond hair hung in a tangle around her face and straps of white lace bit deliciously into her bare shoulders. In the background, the brown grain of a headboard stretched off the screen in all directions. He was not the only one to lose sleep tonight.

Joshua smiled. Misery loves company.

"The excavation at our North Carolina site has progressed to the next level. The artifact we've been waiting for has just been discovered by the professor in charge. We need to make sure we retrieve it before the Taelons do."

Renée's face wore its typical expressionless mask. "Do the Taelons know it's been found?"

Joshua thought about the phone call he just received. "Definitely. We don't have much time, so I need you to take whatever steps are necessary to make sure this deal goes through as planned."

"I'll start on it first thing in the morning."

"You'll start on it now. I don't call people at this time of night for my health."

She paused, probably considering whether she should tell him to go to hell. "Of course."

"That's my girl," he said, partly because he knew it irritated her, but also because she needed a reminder that while he was younger than her, he was higher on the food chain.

She grimaced, fatigue allowing her irritation to show through her iron-jawed mask. For a moment, he thought she really would tell him to go to hell.

Instead, she asked, "Is there anything else?"

"No." He smiled then. "I really do appreciate your help, Renée. You know I wouldn't ask you to do this, but you're the only one I can trust to do it right."

Another trick he had learned from his father. Make sure they know their place, but make that place seem as if it's an important one.

When the global was off and back on the bedside table, Joshua peeled off his shirt and walked to the bathroom before returning and crawling beneath the covers. He rolled onto his side, trying to get comfortable. Should he have stressed more urgently the importance of the artifact to Renée? No. Better not to give away its importance.

As his father used to say, when people are told too much, they get curious—and if there was one person Joshua could not afford to have asking questions, it was Renée Palmer.

FIVE

After pulling on a pair of sweats and some gym socks, Waneta poured herself a glass of red wine and turned on the TV. In years past, she would have exercised on an evening such as this, but her pursuit of tenure had sucked away the bulk of her free time and most of her energy. Even so, she did not drink often—alcohol provided too tempting a release—but after today's events at the dig site, she just wanted to relax.

A vampire movie was on. Immediately she reached for the remote. She did not like horror movies, but she paused before changing the channel, attracted by the image on the small screen. Men in old-fashioned suits stood in a bedroom, shouting at each other. In front of them, a flame-haired woman dressed in red lay among the pearly white shimmer of satin sheets. The colors of the image were startling, like a carefully crafted portrait.

Waneta had the sound turned too low to make out many of the words, but she could hear the groans of the woman crying out in pain and the shouts of the doctor saying the woman needed blood.

Syrupy red liquid flowed into the young woman through a yellow tube, reminding Waneta of her mother. Toward the end, she had been given transfusions to keep her going. Once she described the progression of the cancer by saying, "It feels like I have the flu all the time."

Waneta did not want to die by wasting away, the way her

mother had died, the way the woman on the TV seemed to be dying.

After another sip of wine, Waneta turned up the volume and set down the remote. The men were outside now, the doctor scolding the others. He was speaking in a foreign accent and looked familiar, even with his wild white hair and stubbly beard. She was certain she had seen him in other movies but did not know which ones. He admonished the others to believe in things they could not understand, then vanished.

His disappearing act was a movie trick, but it made her think of the old woman at the dig site. She had to be at least sixty-five. Why would an old woman like that be wandering around on the mountain at night? True, it was unseasonably warm with a full moon—doubtless one of the last gorgeous evenings before winter—and many of the people who had grown up in that area felt as much at home in the mountains as most folks did on a city street. Still, it seemed unnatural.

Waneta got up and walked to the kitchen of her small apartment. She missed the quiet of living in a house and hated the way she needed to keep her TV low this time of night. Unless she was sitting right in front of it, she could not hear what was said.

But she had sold the house, her mother's house. She could not live there knowing her mother had died in the bedroom.

Cold air rolled down Waneta's body as she stared into the mostly empty freezer. On the upper shelf sat a frozen entree, one of those low-fat tasteless pasta things, but little else. She would eat later. For now, the wine was enough.

She filled her glass and returned to the living room. On TV, a woman dressed in blue was visiting the sick woman, propping up her pillow and feeling her forehead, sitting with her through the lonely hours.

Waneta could not bear to watch the woman die. She reached for the remote control, but the scene suddenly switched.

The visiting friend sat across from a strange man in a

restaurant. They were talking about his home—mountains and forests and flowers. Beauty. Waneta empathized with the woman. When a loved one is dying, the mind craves escape. And this was a prince, no less. Dressed in a black coat with gold soutache, he had long dark hair that flowed to his shoulders. She wore scarlet, and her ebony locks framed her white face in rivulets.

Again, the imagery was startling, but it was just a movie, a fantasy that had seduced too many of her friends while they were growing up. No Prince Charming ever came along to sweep them away to distant lands. Most often, they married the boy next door, a more compatible match anyway.

Waneta did not have even that. No boy next door, no male coworker, no stranger she met on the street. Not that she needed any romantic distractions in her life—she was too busy for that—but sometimes, on nights like this, watching an old movie after a bad day, she longed to have someone waiting for her when she returned home, a man who cared more about her than he did about tenure, publications, and longevity pay.

Sighing, she turned down the TV, her thoughts returning to the dig site.

The odd old woman who had confronted her would be just the first of many. She dreaded facing the representatives of the Eastern Band of Cherokees. How would she explain the loss of the pottery vessel? The temptation was great to do as Jason suggested and pretend it never happened, but she could not do that—would not, regardless of the professional consequences.

In the end, she was to blame. The students were her responsibility. How could she have failed so miserably? They should have known better—she had made procedures perfectly clear. All had worked at the site this summer, and though they never found anything beyond pieces of pottery, they had recorded each find properly, tagged each new level, made careful notes. What caused them to suddenly abandon all they had been taught?

She had not been paying much attention to the movie. On

the screen, a man, perhaps the boy next door, had slogged through a muddy ravine to a church while the black prince had danced with his scarlet conquest in a room encircled by candles.

Now the woman danced on a veranda with the doctor. She wore an innocent dress of baby blue, its bustle covered by layers of cloth piled up like icing on a wedding cake. Waneta preferred loose fitting jeans, but she had never attracted the attention of a prince, either.

In the next scene, the sick woman pulled the wedding ring off her finger and gave it to Baby Blue. A woman did not give that up unless she was ready to die.

For Waneta's mother, it had not been a wedding ring but a metal lockbox, the old-fashioned kind with a mechanical three-digit combination. The box contained all her important papers. They went through it one afternoon about a month before she died.

Waneta walked to the kitchen. After a moment's hesitation, she emptied the last of the bottle of wine into her glass. She felt a buzz in the back of her brain and knew she should not be drinking on an empty stomach, but she no longer cared. To escape, for just a little while, would be worth a headache in the morning.

She kept seeing the jar at the dig site, exploding again and again. How could Jason have done such a thing? He felt no passion about the site. What did it matter to him if they stopped digging? The pittance she paid from the grant money could not make that much difference. Perhaps the vessel really did slip when she shouted at him.

No. She had seen the look on his face. He had dropped it on purpose. It just made no sense.

When she returned to the living room, Baby Blue was dressed in gray and getting married to the man from the ravine, the boy next door. His hair had turned white but he did not look any older.

Suddenly a grizzled, wrinkled man appeared at the window of the sick woman. She responded to his presence by writhing on the bed, then ripped the necklace from her throat, revealing two puncture wounds.

Waneta groaned and picked up the remote. She had not paid close attention to the movie, but she had enjoyed the images and the bright, contrasting colors. It disappointed her to have all that wonderful imagery ruined by violence and blood. She watched a moment longer, mesmerized as the scene flashed between the sick woman's death at the hands of the beast and the couple taking their solemn vows in the cross-adorned church. Both acts concluded at the same time, and Waneta understood the director's message. One woman had married light. One had married darkness. Real life was seldom so black and white.

The next scene showed the woman in her coffin, looking pasty in an ivory dress, a tight-fitting hat covering her head as if she had lost her hair.

Waneta immediately clicked off the TV.

She had searched for hats with her mother, back when they thought the radiation treatments might make her go bald. Her mother had not lived long enough for that.

Waneta stood up, nervous and edgy in the sudden silence, and pulled the red stone from her jeans pocket.

She held it up, fascinated with the way light passed through it, as if amplified from within. Perhaps it was comprised of carnelian, a red variety of chalcedony. That would make sense. Chalcedony was a form of quartz, a stone used as a charm in several southeastern cultures including the Creeks and the Seminoles.

But why had she kept the crystal with her? Why even bring it inside? She could rationalize that it would be stupid to leave it in her SUV, but no one knew it was there. What were the chances it would be stolen?

This crystal attracted her somehow. It was different, special—but that made no sense.

She was being silly, starting to think like her mother. She frowned and tucked the stone back into her pocket.

Toward the end, her mother had desperately tried to tell her all the Cherokee stories, the ones she had once said were meaningless fairy tales. Waneta humored her for as long as she could, listening to bits and pieces of myths that she had studied complete as a graduate student. She found them no more believable coming from the lips of her mother than she did when she first read them.

It seemed ridiculous to think of Earth as a giant island formed when Water Beetle scooped up a bit of mud from the ocean floor, or to accept that it was suspended at the corners by cords hanging down from the sky. Even more ludicrous was the idea that Grandfather Buzzard had flown over the land when it was new, his wings beating down valleys and tossing up mountains. One story even claimed that Spider first brought fire to the people in the *tusti* bowl attached to her back. While such legends were interesting, how could anyone seriously believe they were true?

Especially her mother.

Waneta drained the last of her wine and stared at her reflection in the patio door. She looked so plain compared to the woman in the movie. Perhaps if she wore scarlet, or garbed herself in baby blue dresses with big bustles . . .

Suddenly she dropped the wine glass. It shattered against the edge of the coffee table, spraying her with bits of glass and tiny droplets of wine.

For a moment, just outside the door, viewed through her own reflection, she had seen movement—and the face of the old woman from the dig site.

"Oh, God, I'm going crazy."

Once before, on a night like this, just after her mother's death, she had seen another face in another window. That time, it had been her mother looking in at her.

Waneta stood, frozen and helpless, waiting for the face to return.

When it did not, she stared at the broken glass strewn

about her feet and scattered across the table. Red wine clung to the shiny fragments like drops of blood from the movie. Her stomach lurched and she felt as if she might throw up.

After several deep breaths, she calmed somewhat. The face, like the drops as blood, was probably a reaction to the movie— just another reason she did not watch horror shows.

Twisting her body, she lifted one of the cushions from the couch, then stepped onto the area she had just cleared and made her way to the coat closet. She retrieved the vacuum cleaner, plugged it in, and sucked clear a path back to the couch. Her steps were unsteady, the wine making her dizzy. She knew she should put on shoes, but instead she just kept cleaning glass from the floor and the furniture.

Every few seconds, she glanced at the window. The old woman's face never returned—Waneta did not expect it to— but she could see it in her mind, the misty brown eyes staring at her.

She knew that face from long before tonight, had memories of it buried deep inside her.

Suddenly she recalled where she had seen it before.

She dropped the vacuum cleaner hose and stumbled to the closet in her bedroom. Standing on a chair, she almost fell twice before she managed to retrieve her mother's lockbox from the top shelf. The floor rocked and the room twisted as she carried her prize back to the living room.

After taking a seat on the cleaned part of the couch, she opened the box and stirred through it, then found what she was looking for.

It was an old black-and-white photo, a web of white crease marks marring its surface. Waneta stared at the high cheek-bones, the wide nose, the deep-set eyes. The person in the photograph was younger than the woman she had seen at the clearing, but they were the same.

Waneta turned over the photograph and studied the faded cursive writing on the back: *Tala Wachacha, 1959.*

Her great-grandmother. The woman in the clearing.

"That's impossible."

This woman had been in her late sixties. If Tala Wachacha were still alive, she would be around ninety. It had been dark, and most fullblood Cherokees in North Carolina were related. The two women looked similar, but it must have been merely coincidence, nothing more.

Waneta put the photograph back into the metal box, but she could not resist taking a peek at the window, half expecting the face to return.

It did not, could not. Her great-grandmother was dead. She had died when Waneta was eight.

Waneta remembered the day she found out. She got off the school bus and came into the house to find her mother waiting for her.

"I've got something to tell you."

The simple words had been said in such a serious way that Waneta knew something terrible had happened.

They sat at the kitchen table, and her mother wiped away a tear. Her voice cracking, she talked about death and funerals and going away for a while.

"I'd take you with me, honey, but you're too young."

Then she asked if Waneta understood.

Waneta nodded, but she had been too young to comprehend the finality of death or why a mother might wish to hide that finality from her daughter. Now she understood both.

Although she could not remember her great-grandmother, sometimes, especially of late, she dreamed of comforting arms around her and knew she was sitting in a woman's lap. In one dream, she clearly recalled holding someone's hand as she walked along a trail covered in pine needles. Birds chirped in the background and a squirrel ran across their path.

"*Saloli*," Waneta said aloud. Squirrel.

How did she know that? Her mother refused to speak Cherokee. Waneta may have learned the word from her great-grandmother, but she had no way to know.

The subject of her great-grandmother had been forbidden

in their house since Waneta could remember. The only time her mother had voluntarily spoken of her was when she went to the funeral. As for Waneta's grandmother, she had died giving birth to Waneta's mother.

Waneta knew even less about her father. She had never met him and did not know his name. When Waneta asked about him, all her mother would say was, "He gave me you. That's all that matters."

Only once did Waneta force her mother to tell her more. She was seventeen, and she and her mother were fighting, the way they seemed to fight about everything then. At the end of the argument, her mother broke down, crying in a way Waneta had never seen her do.

Waneta apologized, and between tears her mother told her she was sorry for getting pregnant, for bringing a baby into the world before she was ready to be a mother. Waneta gently asked about her father again, but even then, all her mother would admit was, "He came from good Indian blood."

Then, in an unexpected fit of rage, she added, "Your great-grandmother got what she wanted. I had the baby—but the mountain can't have you, just as it couldn't have me. We won't waste our lives the way she wasted hers."

Waneta never understood what her mother was talking about, and her mother refused to explain.

Now Waneta would never know. She had no other family. No mention was ever made of any grandfathers or great-grandfathers, and she suspected there never were any, not in the traditional sense anyway.

Looking back on it now, it was easy to say she should have asked more questions regardless of how much they upset her mother, but she had grown up not knowing.

So much she should have done.

She started to close the lockbox, then changed her mind. One by one, she pulled out the papers and set them on the coffee table, sorting them into piles. She came across her mother's social security card, her driver's license, an old savings account book, insurance papers, and a deed.

Waneta had never before gone through the box carefully. After the funeral, she had been too upset to do anything more than retrieve the insurance information. She never worried about the rest, always assuming she would go through it later.

After unfolding the deed, she squinted at it, her eyes not wanting to focus on the fine print. The property was located in Swain County, North Carolina, but she did not recognize the address, and the lot number would make sense only to the county clerk. It had her mother's name on one page, along with official seals and stamps and lots of legal jargon. The date was 1984, the year her great-grandmother died.

Staring at the paper, Waneta remembered a cabin surrounded by thick trees, and an old man on the porch, his long white hair pulled back into a ponytail, a dusty hat covering his head.

Who was she seeing? Looking in this box was like stirring through the memories of a stranger. But they were her memories, frozen moments left over from a little girl she no longer knew.

She put away the deed. It was obviously old and outdated, kept as a memento only. To Waneta's knowledge, her mother never received any tax notices, but even if she kept them hidden while she was alive, Waneta, as official executor, would have received them after her death.

Who owned the property now? Did a cabin still exist there? Perhaps the next time she went to the dig site, she would try to find the address.

Waneta sighed and looked at the patio window again. Only her reflection remained, staring back at her.

Tired, sick, drunk.

She pushed herself to her feet and stepped uneasily across the carpet toward her bedroom, not trusting her hasty vacuuming job but too exhausted and sleepy to finish it tonight.

Waneta staggered through the doorway and collapsed on her bed. She lay on top of the covers, intending to rest just a moment before brushing her teeth and putting on her nightshirt.

The moment was interrupted by the sound of her global.

When she lifted her head, the gray light at her bedroom window and the cotton in her throat told her she had fallen asleep. Groaning at the stiffness in her neck and shoulders, she sat up and looked around, blinking and squinting as she swayed on the bed, trying to focus on what she was doing there.

The global chimed again and she shuffled toward the sound, following it to the living room.

"Ow!"

She had stepped on a piece of glass. Lifting her foot, she found a small but growing red stain on the bottom of her sock. Cursing, she pulled the sock down and examined the wound. A short, shallow cut, but it hurt like hell.

The global continued to chime.

"Screw you!" she yelled. Walking on her heel, her sock still covering her toes, she limped to the bathroom.

The chiming stopped while she was cleaning and bandaging her injury, but it started again as she emerged from the bathroom. Whoever it was had no intention of leaving her alone until she answered.

She stumbled through the living room, this time being more careful of the glass, and followed the chiming to the kitchen. She found the global on the counter and pulled it open.

"Yessss!" she said, drawing out the word.

The beaming face of her department head appeared on the small display. Dr. Robert Messmore, less affectionately known as Dr. Bob, was the last person she wanted to see this morning.

"Ah, there you are."

She rested her elbow on the counter and propped her head on her upturned hand. "What do you want?"

He wrinkled his brow and squinted at her. "Sorry. Did I wake you?"

The clock on the stove said 7:29, but he did not sound apologetic.

Waneta sighed and combed her fingers through her tangled hair. She must look like death warmed over. She felt worse.

Be nice, she reminded herself. "My first class doesn't start for three hours."

"Excellent," he said cheerfully. "I just called to let you know how excited I am about your find and to see if you planned to register it with inventory as soon as you arrived this morning."

She frowned. "What find?"

"Why, the gem, of course. You didn't find anything else of interest yesterday, did you?"

"The gem, right." She cleared her throat. "May I ask how you know about the artifact so soon? It was just uncovered yesterday evening and I haven't had time to tell anyone about it yet."

His face grew stern and fatherly. "Now, now. Don't you worry about that. I just called to check on the stone's registration status. It's university property, you know."

She nodded, but he had already closed the connection. She pushed her global together and lay it on the counter, then leaned against the walls for support as she made her way back to the bedroom.

What was Dr. Bob doing using her personal connection? Like most people, her global was programmed to respond to multiple numbers, each of which could be turned off individually. She disabled her business connection whenever she left the university. No surprise that Dr. Bob had her personal number— it would be in her file—but why use it just to remind her of something she already knew?

Any artifacts found were always university property. Was he insinuating she thought otherwise?

She frowned. Dr. Bob was in for a surprise. Whoever told him about the artifact—Jason was the only possibility she could think of—neglected to fill in all the details. She did not want to be there when he found out this artifact would be headed to the Eastern Band of Cherokees, not the university's McClung Museum.

That was too awful to contemplate so early in the morning. A headache pounded behind her eyes and her stomach threatened to torture her with dry heaves.

She used the bathroom, then sipped half a glass of water. At her bedroom doorway, she paused, considering her options. If she started getting ready now, she could be at the university in plenty of time to register Dr. Bob's pretty stone before her first class. Or she could go back to sleep for a couple of hours and feel halfway human.

Waneta did not even bother to pull off her clothes. She sprawled across the covers, lying on her stomach, and closed her eyes.

When the room quit spinning, she fell asleep.

SIX

As Liam walked past the four-story red brick building, he pulled his jacket open. The sunshine of late morning had stolen the crispness from the air. It would be another warm day.

On the wall to his right, set inside a painted gray oval, three lines of white letters proclaimed "Flat Planet Café." A planet hovered above the letters, and the light gray of an oval shadow highlighted the sign, making it appear three-dimensional while the planet remained stuck in only two.

Liam walked to the end of the building and turned inside. The round red-topped tables of the café were empty. It was too early for the lunch crowd, and Augur stood alone behind the bar, his back to the doorway. The thin black ponytail growing out the back of his shaved head made him unmistakable, even to people who had met him only once, but Liam would have recognized him from the clothes alone: slick black pants and a lavender silk shirt with pink zigzag lines slanting across its surface like lightning bolts.

"We're not open yet," Augur said, then turned around and shook his head. "Oh, no you don't. I have some very important clients stopping by, and I don't need you or the Resistance stomping in here and stealing this week's best chance at increasing my holdings."

"No need to worry about your holdings. This is purely a social call." Liam could not help grinning as Augur's eyebrows went up. "Almost."

Augur nodded and came around the bar. "That's what I thought. Now begone. Beat it. Nobody's home." He flipped his hands at Liam, as if shooing pigeons away from his lunch.

"Relax, Augur. You know, you should take a vacation."

"Yes. Exactly! But every time I try to go anywhere, you or Renée bursts in here and cancels the trip."

"We'd never do that."

"You always do that."

Liam shrugged. "Not this time. I was just on my way to Ford's Theatre to catch the matinee."

"The Irish dancer show? The one with the boy?"

Liam nodded. "You've heard of him. I'm impressed."

"I'd be more impressed if I had tickets, main floor, center stage. I had two of the most fascinating ladies in here last night, both talking about how they'd love to go to the show today. I lost them to a big guy with a hairy mole on his cheek—and a sister who works at the box office."

Augur peered at Liam through yellow-rimmed glasses. "So how are you getting in? Tagging along with Da'an?"

"No. We saw the show yesterday—private performance. That's what I wanted to talk to you about."

"The show? Listen, last night, I would have been happy to hear all about it, especially if it kept Martelle and Lavina here, but I got people coming, remember?"

"The boy injured Da'an."

Augur had already started away, but stopped and glanced back, then continued around the bar until he faced Liam across its shiny red surface.

"How'd the boy manage that? Fall off the stage and land on Da'an's head?"

"No, he danced."

"Danced? How could a little boy hurt a Taelon just by dancing?"

"That's what I want you to find out."

Augur shook a finger at Liam. "No-no-no-no. Any minute now I'm going to make a deal that should turn into enough work to keep me fully occupied for the next several days. I don't have time for any research."

"Come on, Augur. All you need to do is dig up some info on the boy and his mother. Find out where they come from and what they've been doing for the past couple of years. It'll take you five minutes."

"It's already taken me five minutes."

Augur reached down and pulled a bottle of water from one of the bar's coolers. After opening it and throwing the cap in the trash, he added, "I'd offer you something to drink, but you won't be staying that long."

Liam took a seat and leaned on the bar but said nothing. He just sat on the stool, staring at Augur, and waited.

Augur tapped his fingers on the bar and pressed his lips together, then rolled his eyes. Finally, he said, "All right, I admit it. I'm curious. What happened when the boy was dancing? Did laser beams shoot out his feet?"

"No, nothing like that. To tell the truth, I don't have any proof the boy caused the problem, but from the way Da'an's been acting, no other explanation makes sense."

"But Da'an's okay? There's no chance he's going to turn into an Atavus again and crash my place or anything like that, right?"

"No, he's fine now. He had a spell in the theater and collapsed just as the boy finished dancing. I thought at first he'd been shot. He momentarily changed state, but after I got him back to the embassy, he recovered in a couple of hours.

"I wanted to go back and speak with the boy then, but Da'an told me he needed me there in case he had a relapse. I suggested we go to the mother ship, but he refused. Said he didn't want to bare his illness before the Commonality."

Augur took another sip of water. "You know, Liam, maybe you're the one who needs a vacation. A little boy dances, Da'an has a fainting spell, and you're seeing conspiracies everywhere. I'm not hearing anything that makes me think the boy caused the problem. Maybe Da'an really did get sick, the Taelon version of Montezuma's revenge. You two done any traveling lately?"

"You didn't see this kid. You didn't hear the tone in Da'an's voice when he told me to stay at the embassy last night instead of going to the theater to talk with the boy."

"You should know better than that. Nobody can read Taelons. They've got the best poker faces in the galaxy. Just assume the worst and move on."

"Maybe that's what I'm doing."

Augur leaned on his elbow and tapped his chin with one finger. "I see what you mean."

He reached under the bar and pulled up another bottle of water, which he uncapped and shoved toward Liam.

Liam grinned. "I thought I wouldn't be staying long enough for a drink."

"You can take it with you."

Liam laughed and lifted the water to his lips. On the wall to one side of the bar, two columns of painted eyes, every one unique, stared at him. They always made him think of George Orwell's *1984* and then the Taelons, not always in that order. Perhaps that's what they were supposed to do.

Augur removed his glasses and cleaned them with his shirt. "So you think Da'an's holding out on you? You think he knows what caused his problem but won't tell you?"

"I'm not sure, but if my hunch is right, I'm not going to find out much from the boy, either. That's why I need you to get all the information you can. The boy's called Daniel Shaunessy. His mother's name is Triss."

Augur put his glasses back on. "I have a meeting, remember?"

"That's okay. I don't need it this second, just as soon as you can get it, say in a few hours."

"A few hours?" Augur shook his head. "Just once, I'd like to have a project without a deadline. Now that would be bliss."

"Bliss?" Liam's brows went up, his eyes ridiculously wide. "I'm surprised, Augur. You know bliss is bad for you."

Augur sighed, but the corners of his mouth turned up, threatening to smile. "Don't start. You're here asking *me* for a favor, remember?"

"I remember," Liam said. "That's why I'm leaving."

He turned and walked away from the bar. As he reached the exit and pulled open the front door, Augur called out, "You're welcome."

Liam heard muttering behind him. Then the door shut and he stepped quickly out onto the sidewalk. The matinee started in less than an hour. He would need to hurry if he hoped to talk to the boy before the next show began.

SEVEN

Zo'or's fingers traced a gesture of impatience as he stood on the bridge of the mother ship. The sensations from the day before had not returned. He worried they might never return, leaving his base of power barren, impotent, no better off than it had been a day ago, a month, a year.

Around Zo'or, three Volunteers monitored the controls, their faces impassive. One announced an incoming transmission. Zo'or acknowledged the news by stretching forth his hand in a precise arc that moved across his body.

He lifted his chin and stared into a projection of Agent Sandoval's face. "You have news. Has Da'an led you to the root of the disturbance?"

"No," Agent Sandoval said, undertones of respect in his voice. "Da'an has not left the embassy since yesterday evening, when he returned from a performance at Ford's Theatre in Washington, D.C."

The name of the theater sounded familiar, but Zo'or could not remember why. He dismissed the information as insignificant.

"Studying another cultural ritual? Da'an spends too much time in these meaningless pursuits."

Agent Sandoval nodded. His embedded CVI prevented his open censure of any Taelon's actions, but it also compelled him to agree with whatever Zo'or said—a particularly delicious paradox Zo'or never failed to enjoy.

"Da'an attended a private exhibition of traditional Irish dancers."

Zo'or wondered if any of the humans understood that Da'an's fascination with them was that of a scientist studying an unusual genus of indigenous life. True, Da'an defended them more than most Taelons would, but only because he saw their potential as being greater than it was—a misguided notion that should not be mistaken for compassion, an error often made by humans who thought they knew Da'an better than they did.

"You have no new information, then? Why have you disturbed me?"

Agent Sandoval lowered his head, his posture that of a faithful servant. "Da'an fell ill at the end of the performance. According to witnesses from the dancing troupe, he fainted and reverted briefly to his energy state. Major Kincaid ushered him from the theater and returned him to the embassy."

Zo'or's fingers moved in a pattern of excitement. "What time did this occur?"

"The private showing started at six-thirty and lasted about forty-five minutes. Volunteers at the embassy corroborate the shuttle's return about seven-twenty."

"What time were you and I speaking yesterday?"

Zo'or rarely tracked the hours by human reckoning. The length of a day on the Taelon's home world differed from a day on Earth, and Zo'or had never seen the need to tie his mental clock to the rotations of this planet.

"Our conversation started around seven-fifteen, about the same time Da'an became ill and left the theater."

"Excellent."

Zo'or allowed his eyes to half close in pleasure, then opened them and stared hard at Agent Sandoval. "This confirms my suspicions. Da'an is part of this. We must—"

A prickling at the back of Zo'or's mind told him that another communication link demanded his attention.

"Wait," he told Agent Sandoval, then waved his hand, activating the other link.

Sandoval's face froze, his mouth open. His image faded to a mere shadow as a holographic projection of Da'an's head and upper body materialized beside it.

Zo'or acknowledged the incoming transmission with a slight nod, then allowed his fingers to create a pattern of amusement as he adopted a human greeting.

"Da'an. How good to see you. I trust you are in good health."

"The situation is not a joyful one. I see no reason to take pleasure in danger."

"Danger? Of what danger do you speak?"

Da'an's head turned, his eyes focusing on the Volunteers flanking Zo'or. "You know perfectly well. You felt it as well as I."

Zo'or closed his hands and forced them to his sides. "I detected nothing and you are the first to mention this unspoken danger."

"Unlike other members of the Synod, several strands from the web that forms your link to the Commonality pass directly through me. I cannot believe you did not feel echoes of the energy that I sensed yesterday."

Zo'or refused to step into Da'an's trap. "Our palms cannot touch through this communication link. If you have something to tell me, you must speak."

Da'an half closed his eyes and looked to the side, the pace of his movements indicating great irritation. "You may feign ignorance to me, but we shall see how long your nescience lasts. I request that you call an immediate meeting of the Synod. We must discuss the coming and what we plan to do to stop it."

Zo'or's hands came up, his fingers betraying surprise before he could stop them. "What coming?"

Da'an's fingers showed amusement, but to a more refined degree than Zo'or's had been. "Call the meeting of the Synod, and you shall know."

Zo'or glanced at the Volunteers beside him. Their attention remained riveted to the instrument displays, their expressions revealing no trace that they understood the coup Da'an had initiated. Did they understand even half of what took place before their eyes?

Inferior life forms.

"The meeting of the Synod will not happen until I have full information about why it should be called."

"I will not trust you with access to that kind of knowledge until the entire Synod is informed. Too many times you have demonstrated your willingness to abuse power to serve your own objectives."

Power. Another confirmation that the sensations from the day before were real. Zo'or kept his hands rigidly at his sides to conceal his excitement.

"You cannot dictate terms to me. I am leader of the Synod."

Da'an hesitated before he spoke. "As a member, I can call the meeting myself, but to do so would bring your authority into question."

"Do not threaten me. My authority would not be the only position called into question. You would also need to justify your mistrust and your failure to disclose the details of this unspoken danger."

Da'an did not immediately reply and Zo'or pressed his advantage.

"I suggest you reconsider. My support in the Synod remains strong. Yours does not."

"You are making a mistake."

"It is mine to make."

Da'an cocked his head, then tilted it farther, his chin dipping slightly. "For now, your will prevails. We will discuss this again."

"Not at my insistence."

Da'an bowed slightly, and the transmission ended.

Zo'or's fingers moved rapidly for several seconds, then he moved his hand through the air, reactivating the other signal.

The frozen image of Agent Sandoval brightened before it

flickered and reformed to show the Companion Protector, his head staring down at a computer monitor, his fingers pushing keys as he performed some time-filling activity.

Zo'or did not immediately speak but took the next several seconds to gather his thoughts, his excitement barely controlled. His intuition concerning the energy he had felt the day before had been proved correct. Now all he had to do was find the source of the power before Da'an could do so.

Agent Sandoval looked up, then pushed a final key before straightening. His face became rigid but attentive.

Zo'or spoke slowly, his voice revealing nothing. "The sensation I felt yesterday goes beyond Da'an. I expect that the true source of this disturbance will manifest itself in ways your species will not understand. But there will be signs—isolated and unexplained pockets of disruption."

Agent Sandoval looked at him blankly. Despite the man's clever nature, he sometimes seemed as dim as dark matter.

Zo'or spoke plainly. "Tell your people to monitor the news broadcasts. Give special consideration to any story originating in the eastern United States. I will recognize the key when I see it. Report back to me in six hours."

Agent Sandoval nodded and Zo'or terminated the connection. He did not know what the agent would uncover, but he must be ready to take advantage of any new information.

Da'an's threat to call a meeting of the Synod had been unexpected. Such openly aggressive behavior was not characteristic of Da'an's personality. The fact that he had acted in such a fashion indicated that he had plans of his own. But when pressed on the issue, he had backed away. Da'an's actions were plodding and methodical, but without fail they were thought all the way through. If Da'an had capitulated so easily, he must have always intended to do so.

Zo'or closed his eyes and felt the slight tremor of the mother ship beneath his feet, its hum of life coursing through him.

He had defeated Da'an before. He would do so again—and this time, the victory would be complete.

EIGHT

When the paper shuffling started, Waneta was in midsentence, chalk pressed to the board, writing as she spoke. As she finished her thought, the soft thumps of closing books, scuffing feet, and creaking seats joined the paper shuffle. Like all classes at the University of Tennessee, no bell signaled the end of the period, but Waneta had never needed one—or even a watch. Since her first day in a classroom at this university, the noisy restlessness triggered by the room's careful clock-watchers always let her know when time had run out.

She leisurely finished her thoughts, both in writing and orally, then turned to face the young men and women, all of whom looked like racers settling into their starting blocks.

"Remember, we have a test in a week. Also, the homework for this chapter is due next time. See you then."

They bolted, but when the first one opened the door, a dozen students for the next class charged inside, squirting through the exiting mass like a band of hyenas descending on an abandoned kill. They had no need to hurry. This auditorium, the only true classroom in McClung Museum, held more than two hundred students. They could come in at the last moment and still find a seat.

Waneta packed her notes into a file folder, then pulled the crystal from her pocket. It felt warm in the palm of her hand, and she rocked it gently, fascinated with the way it refracted the light, making it appear to glow. She wanted to get it to the lab and examine its properties, but first she needed to take it by inventory and have it registered.

Those thoughts should have sped her along, but her body refused to obey.

The two extra hours of sleep had helped to reduce the effects of her hangover, but she felt far from right. Making matters worse, she had drunk her supper last night, and had overslept this morning, giving her no time to eat.

With the crystal still in hand, she left the auditorium and walked past the hall exhibits to the stairs. As she climbed to the main floor of the building, she swore she could smell freshly baked muffins. Her mouth watered and she paused at the top of the stairs to glance around the museum's lobby. No muffins in sight. Even so, she kept having a vision of herself wresting away food from a surprised student and galloping away in fevered delight.

She smiled at the image, then noticed a small crowd of young people between her and the building's exit. Bright lights turned in her direction and she spotted a TV camera on the shoulder of one of the students.

Perhaps they were here to film one of the new exhibits. She moved left, out of their way, but the group shifted with her, blocking her escape.

She stopped. They could not be here for her. What would they want? They rushed at her then, the lights blinding, the camera zeroing in on her like a rifle scope.

A short brunette shoved a microphone forward. "Dr. Long, I'm Melissa Olson from the university TV news team. We're here to interview you about the crystal you found at the Swain County dig site yesterday evening. Could you tell us, please, how much you think the crystal is worth and whether the proceeds from its sale might be used to upgrade the labs or sponsor students at additional field sites?"

Waneta started to raise her arm to shield her eyes from the light, but the crystal gleamed and sparkled as she brought her hand up. Quickly, she shoved the stone in her pocket and shadowed her eyes with her other arm, the folder of notes hiding her face.

She peered around the folder at the young reporter, whose pretty face was covered with too much makeup. The girl looked familiar, but Waneta could not remember where she had seen her.

"Excuse me, I, uh, wasn't prepared for an interview. What did you say your name was again?"

"Melissa Olson."

Now Waneta remembered. Melissa was Jason's girlfriend. When Waneta saw him again, they would have a long talk about scientific discretion and the proper avenue of announcements for important finds.

The student reporter skillfully changed her angle of attack, the camera and bright lights dutifully following her, then shoved the microphone in Waneta's face again. "Can you tell us why an aboriginal people who cared little for material wealth might keep such a large and valuable gem?"

The ignorance of the question tempted Waneta to set the girl straight, but the cultural attitude of traditional Cherokee people toward material possessions was a topic well beyond the scope of a sound bite. Besides, seeing the eagerness and intensity in the girl's face, Waneta wondered if the question had been carefully crafted just to goad her into a response. Jason had never done all that well in class, but he knew enough to be dangerous when he used his meager mental powers for evil rather than good.

"I'm sorry. I haven't had time to analyze my results. I have no comment at this time."

Waneta again shielded her face with the folder and stepped briskly toward the bright sunshine beyond the doorway. The camera and lights tracked her mercilessly, and the microphone hovered near her face like a pesky fly.

Waneta did her best to ignore all of it. Keeping her eyes focused straight ahead, she doggedly marched toward the exit.

A tone of desperation came into Melissa's voice then. She

fired questions at Waneta, the real ones she had most likely been saving for after she got her victim talking.

"How do you plan to answer allegations you were conducting an illegal dig on government land? Do you believe your Native American heritage gives you the right to break laws the rest of us must follow? How do you respond to the charge that you destroyed artifacts to conceal the true nature of your activities?"

Waneta's step faltered at the last question, anger bubbling inside her. So that's how Jason was going to play it. Claim she had dropped the jar rather than him, or claim he had done it on her instructions.

This interview had gone far enough. Waneta scanned the entrance for some means of escape and spotted a large group of students coming through the double set of doors just ahead of her. She angled sharply toward them. As she intended, the cameraman, who was filming her from in front and to the right, angled with her. He backed right into the group. The collision jarred loose his grip on the camera and it slipped from his fingers. He tried to catch it as it fell but only managed to deflect it.

Melissa let out a squeak as it skittered across the floor. Its case remained intact, but with luck, the insides were temporarily wrecked.

Head down, Waneta burst out of the building. She walked quickly down the sidewalk to Circle Park Drive and turned right, then cut through Student Services, emerging on the other side of the building.

She sneaked around the corner and risked a glance back at McClung Museum. No sign of pursuit. Apparently the camera had broken. A twinge of guilt flashed through her. She had been angry, but she knew better than to take it out on those students. They could hardly be blamed for wanting a story. Still, her problems were bad enough without making them worse through an unsanctioned interview.

Besides the ire and paranoia of the Cherokee Cultural Resources Office, she would also need to deal with Dr. Bob, who would be unhappy no matter how she handled the situation. His phone call from that morning already seemed like a bad dream, but she knew it served merely as a portent for the explosion yet to come.

Sunshine warmed her face as she turned and headed toward her office. The day was unseasonably hot, a last memory of summer before fall regained control. Unlike in the mountains, trees here were just starting to change color. Overhead a bright blue sky lay like a protective blanket and the wisp of a slight breeze ruffled the permed curls of her hair.

A truly gorgeous day. She only wished she could enjoy it.

What would it be like to walk outside and look around, unmarred by the complexities of life? To live for the moment, free of worry about tomorrow or regret for yesterday?

Probably boring as hell, but it sure would be fun to try for a while.

She passed the imposing central structure of the administration building, the Andy Holt Tower, which most people on campus referred to as the Power Tower. Glancing up, it made her think of pyramids, church steeples, and the Washington Monument—tall structures, all meant to impress. People never tired of trying to outdo the grandeur of Mother Nature, but thinking of the mist-covered mountains she saw several times each week, she doubted they would ever come close.

Giving up her work at the site would be hard. While the drive back and forth had been trying at times, especially during the height of the tourist season, she also found it relaxing and sometimes even comforting, as if the misty giants were there to watch over her. A silly thought, but one that nevertheless felt right.

She cut across a faculty/staff parking lot and headed for Neyland Stadium. On its side stood an orange sign, several stories tall. It proudly proclaimed "Vols" below a white UT football helmet with the traditional orange T on its side.

Waneta liked football well enough—she had gone to a few games over the years—but the people around here sometimes forgot it was only a game. They still talked about their last national championship as if it were the culmination of the university's history.

After waiting for a car to pass, she crossed the street and entered the jungle of white pillars that supported thousands of screaming fans on game day. The whir of window air conditioners—a rare sound for this time of year—hummed their greeting as she turned into Stadium Hall and started up the stairs to her office.

She had no idea what possessed some long-gone administrator to put the Department of Anthropology in the football stadium, but if a devastating plague wiped them all out tomorrow, she would love to accompany the future archaeologists who uncovered this site. It would be interesting to see how they interpreted the indestructible plastic of football helmets mixed with aboriginal artifacts and surrounded by a combination of some of the most—and the least—advanced equipment at the university. It would provide a puzzle they would never figure out.

The coolness of the building welcomed her as she made her way to the second floor. If she ignored the whitewashed cinder-block walls, this place reminded her of a spaceship, with its many stairways, gently curving hallways, and steam pipes suspended from the ceiling like power conduits.

Its reality was much less interesting. Heated in the winter by old-fashioned radiators, its floors covered by black vinyl squares, ceilings rising high overhead, the building had probably changed little for decades. At least she had her own office.

As Waneta unlocked her door, Dr. Jill Hoffman came down the hall and stopped to watch. "Are you sure you want to do that?"

Waneta tucked her keys back inside the pocket of her slacks. "Don't worry, my week can't get any worse."

"Don't bet on it."

Jill followed Waneta inside and shut the door. As Waneta took a seat behind her desk, Jill pulled out the room's other chair from under a worktable and turned it to face Waneta before sitting down.

Waneta welcomed these little visits. No matter how busy Dr. Jill Hoffman was, she always made time to say hello. When Waneta first started at UT, it was Jill who made her feel like she wanted to stay. It was also Jill who had taken over her classes when Waneta's mother fell ill. A beautiful person from the inside out, Jill was a rare combination—both an outstanding instructor and an excellent researcher.

"So what's the big emergency?" Jill asked.

"What do you mean?"

Earlier, Waneta had come by her office just long enough to lock her purse in her desk and grab her notes. On the way to class, she had swung by the lab and dropped off the crystal's dusty wrapping, which seemed to be made from deer hide. Apparently Dr. Bob did not care if that was registered—as long as she registered what had been inside it.

She pulled out her global and reconfigured it to accept university calls. Immediately the message light began flashing.

Jill studied her critically, the way she did when students came in with excuses about why they missed an exam. "Dr. Bob's been down here at least three times this morning checking your office. What'd you do? Steal the coffee fund?"

Waneta sighed. "I don't know. He called this morning, all worried about an artifact I found."

"Called you at home?"

Waneta nodded. "I don't know why he's so worried about it. I always—oh, my!"

The global's screen had filled with message headers.

"I can't believe he did this."

"What?" Jill asked.

Waneta paged down. "I have fourteen messages, all from Dr. Bob."

"That figures." Jill laughed. "He never pays attention to office hours—or vacations or sabbaticals, for that matter. Did I ever tell you? I once returned from a seminar to find sixty-two messages from Dr. Bob waiting for me. He quit calling only after he complained to the departmental secretary about my not responding and she set him straight."

Jill stood and started for the door. "I better let you check all those messages."

"You don't have to leave," Waneta said. She could use a friendly face right now. "I'm sure the messages are nothing personal."

Jill paused but did not retake her seat.

Waneta pushed the play button and Dr. Bob's face appeared on the global's small display, the crushed velvet of a red robe hugging his neck and plunging down to reveal a white T-shirt. The top of an easy chair and part of a painting were visible above and behind him. Obviously he had placed this call from his home—and she was shocked at the time stamp: 3:42 A.M.

"Dr. Long," he drawled, "I'm calling now to make sure this message appears at the top of your queue. I understand you've discovered an item of interest to the department. My sources tell me it's a gem of obvious value. You, of course, know the university's policies on discoveries of this magnitude. First thing in the morning, even before you register the item with—"

Waneta pushed the skip button. Dr. Bob continued, still in his robe and easy chair. In his lap he held his wood-handled, black umbrella, the one he always carried with him across campus. He fondled it like a security blanket as he spoke.

"I've considered the matter, and rather than requiring you to jump through the bureaucratic hoops necessary to process the crystal you found, I'd like you to—"

Waneta skipped again.

Dr. Bob now wore a suit. He sat in the black leather chair of his office, the edges of diplomas and award certificates framed on the wall in the background.

"This is Dr. Messmore. I'm in my office. Please come by as soon as you receive this message. I would like to further discuss the ramifications—"

Skip.

"I assume since you have not responded to my other messages, you have some reservations concerning my plan. Please come by and discuss these with me at your earliest convenience. This matter is vital to the department's—"

Waneta punched off the message. "Why can't the man just leave me alone?"

Jill shook her head. "That's not his strong suit."

Waneta pushed her fingers against her forehead. The pain of a sinus headache was starting above her eyes.

Jill held out her hand. "Here. Let me fix it for you."

At first, Waneta thought she was talking about the headache, but then Jill took the global, keyed off the video, and after searching the university database for several seconds, called up a number.

After a moment, a voice came on, which Waneta recognized as the departmental secretary's. "Anthropology. May I help you?"

Even with the video off, Jill buried herself in the part. As she spoke into the global, she rocked her head and rolled her eyes. She looked like a ditsy freshman in her first semester on campus. "Hey, um, is this, uh, Dr. Messmore's office."

"Yes," the secretary said in a guarded voice.

"It is. Great. Can I like, you know, talk to him?"

"Just a moment please."

"What are you doing?" Waneta whispered.

"Getting you parole. Dr. Bob never takes calls from students."

Dr. Bob's cheerful voice came over the connection. "Hello. I'm unavailable at the moment because I'm in a meeting or already engaged in another important call. Please leave a short message and I'll contact you as soon as I can."

While Dr. Bob was speaking, Jill keyed on the video and handed the global to Waneta. When the message finished, Jill motioned with her hands, as if to say, "Go ahead."

Waneta stared at the frozen image of Dr. Bob's smiling face for several seconds, then said in a halting voice, "Dr. Messmore. Sorry I missed you. I was returning your call. I'll try again later."

Waneta punched the off button. "Why'd you do that? Now what am I supposed to do?"

"Go to lunch," Jill said and opened the door, "before Dr. Bob comes looking for you again."

"I better not."

"Why not? You tried to call him back. He wasn't there. Come on. A bunch of us are going down to the Arena. Tag along."

"I can't do that."

"Sure you can. Dr. Bob respects anyone who makes him wait."

"That's easy for you to say. You have tenure."

"That's right," Jill said, smiling. "That makes me wise and all-powerful. Don't forget it."

Waneta closed her global and put it in her purse but still did not move toward the door.

Jill hung her head and sighed, then looked seriously at Waneta. "Listen. I've been here long enough to see department heads come and go, and I doubt Dr. Bob will stick around long. Hell, the last time we spoke, the man spent half his time staring at my chest. People like him do not represent the quality of this university. He's not what we're about. Don't let someone like that control your life, okay?"

Waneta thumbed the crystal in her pocket. Why was Dr. Bob so concerned about this rock? He had never taken any interest in her work before. She thought of the TV crew and wondered what Jason had told the department head. Whatever it was seemed to be part of a master plan to discredit her. Jason had never seemed particularly clever or motivated. Obviously she had underestimated him.

"Come on," Jill urged, "everyone has to eat."

The idea of food set Waneta's stomach rumbling. "I have a class at one twenty-five."

"So take your materials with you. From lunch, you can go

straight to class—another reason not to be in your office when Dr. Bob comes around."

Waneta nodded feebly and rose to her feet.

Jill opened the door and stepped into the hallway. After glancing in both directions, she said, "Coast clear."

In the hallway, Waneta checked to make sure that her door was locked, then followed Jill in the wrong direction. They were headed away from the Arena, but also away from the departmental office. Once out of the building, they could double back, successfully avoiding Dr. Bob.

"Tell me, Jill," Waneta said. "Why are you always watching out for me?"

Jill peeked over her shoulder and smiled. "Because sometimes you forget to watch out for yourself."

NINE

When Liam arrived at Ford's Theatre, a long line of people already snaked along the sidewalk, slowly working their way inside. Liam used his Protector ID to bypass the line and work his way through security until he was backstage. Wandering down the hallway, he glanced at doors and tried to figure out where he could find Daniel Shaunessy. Male and female dancers rushed by, paying him no heed, but the boy was nowhere to be seen. Finally he stopped a young woman and asked who was in charge of the show.

She pointed to a short, red-faced man with bushy sideburns who stood in a corner between two taller men in costume. He was shaking his fist and glaring up at them.

"That's McGilley, the stage manager." She rolled her eyes. "He thinks he's in charge."

Liam approached the corner.

"If you miss your marks by that much next time," McGilley said in a sharp Irish accent, "you'll be dancing for tourists outside a pub in Dublin."

The two men walked away without looking back. McGilley shook a fist at them and called out, "I'm not talking to myself, lads, I mean it!"

He started to storm away in the direction opposite where the dancers had gone, but Liam stopped him with a hand on his shoulder. "Excuse me, I need to speak with Daniel Shaunessy and his mother. I believe her name is Triss."

McGilley looked down at the hand. "You and everybody else. Bit of bad luck for you, then. They're not available."

He pushed his way past, but Liam grabbed his arm. The man spun, as if he intended to punch Liam, but stopped short, nostrils flaring like an old bull's.

"Are you deaf, then? I said you can't speak to them. Now leave before I have security put you out on your ear."

Liam showed him the Protector ID. "This is important. I can shut your show down and we can all go to the mother ship to talk about this—or you can tell me where to find Daniel now."

"Oh, for love of the Lady, I know whose lapdog you are. You don't have to go stomping about all high and mighty now, do you?"

Liam remained unmoved. "Daniel?"

"Danny and Triss Shaunessy left last night after the show. You can't talk to them, because they're not here. Now let me alone. I've got a show to run."

The man started away, but Liam stopped him again.

"I need to know why they've left and where they've gone. Also, I need any background information you have on them."

McGilley tugged at his sideburns with one hand. "I've answered all these questions already, and once is enough. Can't you just ring up your friend and get his report?"

Liam kept a firm hold on the man's arm. "What friend? What are you talking about?"

"The other one of you Protectors, the one who takes care of that top blue beastie up in the sky."

"Agent Sandoval?"

"That's his name, right enough. Are you telling me you've been walking in his footsteps and never knew it?" The manager shook his head and grunted. "Ruddy fools. And I thought *I* ran a confused operation."

"When did you speak with him? What questions did he ask?"

"I don't have time for this," the manager said irritably and tried to pull away again.

"Make time," Liam said.

" 'Make time,' the man says. What do I look like? A bloody fairy?"

When Liam did not release him, the man sighed. "Five minutes. Here, step into my office."

Liam let him go and followed him through a narrow door that led to what looked like a closet. A small suitcase filled with an odd variety of papers, cards, and glossy photos stood open on a low desk. The man took a seat on the room's only furniture, a short stool, and folded his arms as he stared up at Liam.

"I'll tell you all I know," the man said, "so listen up. I'm getting tired of this tale."

Looking down at him, Liam thought the earlier comment about fairies was close to the mark. All McGilley needed to pass as a leprechaun was a pipe and a pot of gold.

The manager started his explanation slowly, his accent growing stronger as he spoke.

"Danny and his mum left an hour after we finished the show for that blue beastie man of yours. He didn't die, then? Can't win them all, I suppose."

"Da'an's fine. What about Daniel and his mother?"

"Family trouble, they said. Sick aunt, they said. Had to take the portal back to Ireland right away. No chance of staying for today's show. Without so much as a by-your-leave, they pack up and head out. Do you have any idea how many people in that audience have come to see the boy? I'll be lucky if I don't have a full revolt on my hands by the end of the show."

"Where did they go?"

"Not a word. It's bad enough Danny already makes more than the other dancers, but to leave with no notice? 'Twould be different if his mum's sister were ill, but if I'm believing that, I've lost what little sense God gave me."

"Why do you say that?"

"I was in Danny's dressing room before his first number and saw nary a sign he and his mum were going anywhere. Yet an hour after the finale, she and Danny were on their way out the door with their flimsy excuses and their so-sorrys. But Triss Shaunessy never carried a global—thought they were bad luck—and this theater's only phone is in the manager's office. No messenger showed up backstage, no friend came to tell her, so how did she know her sister had taken ill? Explain that to me, Mr. Protector."

Liam ignored the request. "Do you know where they went?"

McGilley was no longer looking at Liam and seemed to be talking to himself. "I can tell you. Not a one of us wanted to do this show. We were promised holiday, we were. Two days. On the company account, no less. I must be daft to believe such nonsense."

"McGilley!" Liam said, exasperated. "Where did the boy and his mother go?"

The manager looked at him blankly. "How am I to know? They didn't say. You think they take me into their confidence?"

Liam shook his head.

McGilley continued on. "To speak God's own truth, I'd normally fire anyone who left me hanging before a show the way they did, but they're the biggest draw I have. Danny may be dense as a dead sheep, what with his staring off and mumbling to himself the way he does, but he's still the best dancer I've ever seen."

"Mumbling?"

McGilley lowered his voice. "Worse than ever, just before he and his mum left. Could be she arranged the whole thing to protect her little boy. She'd do anything for that tot. Anything."

Anger flashed in McGilley's eyes and he jumped to his feet. "As if you don't know all this already! Your blasted blue friends are to blame. They're the ones who scrambled the wee lad's brain."

Liam looked down at the shorter man. The stage manager might not respond well to direct questions, but over a pint or two, he would probably tell Liam anything. "What are you talking about?"

"I'm not completely daft. Whatever growth program they've got him on's going to put him over eight feet tall before he's sixteen. And if your Taelon overlords are trying to hide what they've done, I recommend they get rid of those eyes. How can they fool anyone when the lad's eyes glow like a banshee's?"

"I thought they were contacts."

"As did I. Adds to the mystique—wish I'd thought of it— but the first time Danny showed up in my office, his eyes all aglow, I told his mother to take the ruddy things out. That's fine for the audience, but I don't need to stare at them. Said she couldn't do it. Said it's just the way his eyes go. I don't know if she's telling the truth, but if not, I've never seen Danny when he had them out."

"You also mentioned how fast the boy grows. What did you mean?"

"I know how quickly lads grow—got six children of my own—and Danny hasn't been around long enough to change as much as he has. When they showed up at my door, his mother claimed he was five, but by God's own grace, I swear he looked more like three or four. He's six now, celebrated his birthday when we were doing shows in New York, but he looks more like seven. No lad grows that fast—it's not natural."

Liam thought of his own accelerated childhood. "How long have you known the mother and child?"

"Not long. They came in off the street about five months ago, just before we headed across the pond. Miss Shaunessy said she wanted an audition. I told her we had every spot filled, promised her she could come to open tryouts the next spring. I also said to forget about the boy—we don't do children—but then she produced a note from the owners."

"Owners?"

"Not that it would have mattered. I won't be cluttering my show with anyone, regardless of how high their friends fly, but then that lad started dancing."

For a moment, McGilley's eyes glazed over and he stared

off at nothing, a small smile on his face. Then he suddenly scowled and shook his finger at Liam. "You know how much trouble it caused to add the boy to the show? Lead dancer walked off for two days."

"Did Triss or Daniel ever talk about where they were originally from, or where they lived just before they joined the show?"

"Miss Shaunessy gave me the name of a dancer in Dublin— said he taught Danny all he could—but I'd never heard of him, and I've heard of anyone who's anybody. So I checked. There's no man in Dublin by the name she gave—never was—and not a soul there who's ever heard of Miss Shaunessy or her boy. As far as I can tell, both of them dropped out of the sky and landed on my doorstep."

Liam had heard enough to know he was on the right trail. Sandoval had been here. The boy was unnatural. The Taelons had tried before to crossbreed humans and Taelons, but even if Daniel were part Taelon, that did not explain his attack on Da'an.

"I only have a couple more questions," Liam said. "First, was Triss on stage the other night? If you told me which dancer she was, I might remember her."

That was not exactly true. Thanks to his Kimeran heritage, Liam remembered every dancer, just as he remembered every face he ever saw, every fact he ever uncovered, every snippet of conversation he ever heard. But as he had learned, knowing the facts was not the same as making sense of them.

McGilley answered his question with a guffaw. "Hah! That left-footed stork? What makes you think she's one of the dancers?"

"She's listed in the program as a dancer."

"What? Ah, yes. Well, those were just terms, you see, for signing her son. We agreed she could fill in, if the need arose. Not that she'd ever get on stage, mind you. By God's good graces, I'd get out and hop around before I let that woman in front of an audience. Not that it's a problem here. The stage in this theater's so small, we had to hold back a third of our dancers as it is. Ruins the final number, I say. What's the use in having an impressive line of dancers if not all of them can fit up there at once? Makes us look like a gypsy road show. I've a mind to speak with whoever scheduled us for this stage and give him—"

"One last question," Liam interrupted. "You said this trip was supposed to be time off, but then these two shows were added at the last minute."

"Right you are. Two weeks. That's all they gave us. I'm surprised they managed to sell all the tickets in time. Speaks grandly for the show's popularity, I'd say."

"What I want to know is, why? If it caused so many problems, why add the shows to the schedule?"

"I'm not privy to the whims of the owners. I'm just a lowly stage manager, doing as I'm told and running the show as best I can—which you're keeping me from doing."

McGilley looked down at his watch, then hopped off the stool. "Your five minutes are more than up. I've got to get back to work."

"Who are the owners? Give me their names and I'll bother them with my questions."

McGilley turned on him, his eyes blazing. "Blast you! You don't know when to give it up, do you? Leave me in peace."

Liam stepped in front of him, blocking his exit. "The owners."

"Be a sport. I've answered enough questions; I'll not be answering another. Now let me run my show."

McGilley pushed his way past. This time Liam let him go.

By the time Liam stepped back into the hallway, McGilley was already shouting at one of the dancers. "No, man, you can't wear that! We switched opening numbers at this morning's meeting. Don't just stand there. Get changed! We've got less than ten minutes to curtain."

As Liam started away, McGilley called to him from across the room. "If you find Danny, bring him back, will you? We've sixteen more cities to do, all of which have promotions featuring the lad."

Liam smiled. "I'll see what I can do."

McGilley was already rushing off down the hallway.

As Liam climbed the stairs and left the theater, he turned over everything he had heard, but little of it made sense. All he knew for certain was that he was on the right track. To figure out the rest, he needed to find the boy.

But first, he would talk with Da'an.

TEN

Robert Messmore, Ph.D., sat in his office, the door closed. Around him stood antique oak furniture from the nineteenth century and walls lined with shelves of leather-bound books, none of which he had read. Plush carpet covered the floor, protected by a large plastic mat that allowed his high-back executive chair to roll freely behind his huge desk. His umbrella hung on the corner of the desk, within easy reach, and the inspiring oratorio of Handel's *Messiah* masked the sounds of the faculty and students beyond his sanctuary, allowing him to concentrate on the image displayed on his computer monitor.

Dr. Waneta Long, caught in the lights from a TV camera, stood frozen, her arm raised, her right hand clearly holding a red crystal, the one the call he received in the middle of the night said she had found.

How did the donors of the grant find out about it before he did? Perhaps that conniving snitch Jason was double-dipping, but that seemed unlikely. Although an ambitious boy, he was not overly bright and lacked organization. He had not called with news of the crystal's discovery until this morning, long after Dr. Messmore had been briefed in full by the donors of the grant.

Much more curious was how the donors had known what the stone would look like even before it was found.

Dr. Messmore opened a drawer and retrieved the replica of the crystal they had given him weeks before. This stone would replace the original in the university museum, while the crystal Dr. Long had now would go to the dig's sponsors.

He glanced at the screen, then back at the fake crystal, which he turned over and over in his palm. Whatever ancient document had described the stone had done so in some detail, but not with complete accuracy. The fake was larger than the original and in comparison, seemed lusterless and plain. Side by side, no one would mistake one for the other, but the copy was good enough to pass casual examination.

All he would need to do is switch the crystals before Dr. Long started her analysis. Even if that failed, he had already set his backup plan in motion. One way or the other, he would get the crystal and then his money.

Not that he would keep the funds for himself. They would go to the university in the form of an anonymous grant. True, he would shave off a percentage. Carrying charges, as he liked to think of them, which would go to purchase furniture for his office, or would be used to pay his way to professional seminars. He did not steal. When he profited, so did the university.

In only his second year at this position, he had already brought more funds into the department than his two predecessors combined. Department heads were not normally thought of as fund-raisers. His success had attracted the attention of both the dean of arts and sciences and the provost, increasing his prestige and political power—and providing fuel for his résumé. After a couple of years, he would move on, as he always did, perhaps to dean of his own college at another university, but even then, his salary would lag ridiculously far behind what he could make in private industry. If society properly recognized his contributions to higher education, he would not have gone down this road of compromise.

The university, as a recognized institution of higher learning, would not sell the stone but instead would place it in a museum. The fake would serve just as well for that purpose. The donors of the grant, who cared most about the crystal's authenticity, would get exactly what they wanted. For himself, he would profit from his "carrying charges" and, eventually, from his good record for bringing grants and endowment funds into the department.

But before anything could happen, he needed to get the stone from the woman whose image was on his computer screen.

Dr. Long had not returned his calls, which indicated to him that she might suspect the crystal's true worth. Supporting that hypothesis was the fact that she had kept the stone with her and had not yet registered it as university property.

Not that it would do her any good. He had stacked the deck against her by hand-picking the graduate students for her project. One of them, at least, had already delivered beautifully. The others would bend readily enough to his will. He would see to it that their personal costs were too high if they failed, just as he would see to it that Dr. Long was discredited and her employment terminated by the university if she showed any-thing more than token resistance.

That would be messy and time-consuming. He much pre-ferred to settle this matter while causing as few waves as possi-ble. He was certain she would want the same.

Yet she had not called.

She was a simple professor, not even tenured. He should easily be able to outguess her plans, but without information on how much she knew, the problem was proving more difficult than he would have expected.

He liked the challenge, though. Most of his duties made him feel like a cross between an arbitrator and a bookkeeper. Finally he had the chance to exercise his mental prowess.

Even so, he found the situation slightly depressing. For many years, during his time as a struggling professor, just find-ing an ancient relic would have made his blood run wild and his imagination soar, but he had lost the ability to derive satisfac-tion from discovering bits and pieces of the past. His pleasure now came from money and the power it brought him, but sometimes, he missed his old innocence the way a person misses his first love late at night when the house is quiet and the moon is full and sweet.

His desktop global chimed. He put the replica of the crystal back in his drawer and answered the call in his best business voice. "Dr. Messmore."

He recognized the face that appeared on the display. She wore dark glasses and her blond hair was tucked beneath a short brunette wig, but he could have identified her from the voice alone. He had understood who she was even while they were negotiating the terms of the original grant last spring.

Her words were marked with the rhythmic vibrations of a helicopter motor, and her image wobbled in the display. "How lovely to see you, Doctor. I assume you have the crystal in your possession."

"No, not yet, but I should have it before the end of the day."

"You'd better. Our agreement is nonnegotiable."

"There's always room for negotiation," he said slyly. A stony look crossed her face and he quickly added, "But that's not the problem. We may have some unforeseen difficulties with the archaeologist who found the stone, Dr. Waneta Long."

"Does she have the crystal now?"

"Yes, I believe so. A student news team photographed her with it less than two hours ago. I have the video."

Dr. Messmore instructed his computer to send a copy of the news report using his global's active communication link. He waited while Renée switched away a moment, then switched back.

"The woman is Dr. Long?"

"Yes. So far, she's refused to turn over the crystal. I'm afraid she may know the true value of the stone. If so, we'll need to supply the proper incentive to bring her around to our way of thinking."

Dr. Messmore raised his hand to where it could be seen by the global's camera, then rubbed his thumb against his middle and index fingers.

The woman's voice remained cool and unruffled. "I'm afraid that's impossible. The spending on this project has already exceeded expectations. We have a budget to consider."

He cocked his head and raised his eyebrows. "Frankly, Ms. Palmer, I find it hard to believe a few thousand dollars has any meaning to a company as large as Doors International."

To her credit, Renée Palmer did not even blink. "There must be some mistake. I represent the Aboriginal Research and Protection Society."

He noticed that she was wearing a tight-fitting sweater and wished he could expand the angle of the global's picture. Smiling, he said, "Ms. Palmer, I'm surprised by your modesty. Before his death, Jonathan Doors announced your promotion to billions of people on live TV. I'm not the only one who would recognize you. Perhaps I have a keener eye for faces than most, but I must admit, it was your assets I admired most."

"Let me tell you a secret."

She leaned close to the global's camera, her face filling his display. With a suggestive grin, she closed her eyes slowly, seductively, opening them again in a flutter of long eyelashes. Then her chin suddenly lowered and her eyes hardened, her stare penetrating and unsettling. "If you don't get us that crystal by tonight, you'll wish you had never seen my face—or my assets."

She pulled back and looked away. "Call me as soon as you have the crystal in your possession."

The connection terminated and the display went black.

Dr. Messmore leaned back in his chair and adjusted his tie. That could have gone better.

He should have known that a man of his meager means could never impress a woman like Renée Palmer. Seats at her private table surely required a stake much higher than what he could afford.

She may have won this battle, but when he controlled the crystal, she would treat him with a great deal more respect. He would see to that. She would beg him for the crystal before he surrendered it to her.

That was when he realized his mistake. He had transmitted an image of Dr. Long and had verified that she had the crystal. What would keep Renée Palmer from dealing with Dr. Long directly and cutting him completely out of the loop? Surely other forgeries of the stone existed, and once the exchange was made, he would have no way to prove that the original had been lost.

Dr. Long would undoubtedly keep the money. He would lose his carrying charges and the university would lose a valuable grant. Not everyone was as scrupulous as he was.

He picked up his umbrella and headed for the door. The time had come to pay yet another visit to Dr. Long's office. This time he would not be so concerned with protocol and procedure.

ELEVEN

Zo'or was on the bridge when he was told of his parent's arrival.

For most of his race's history, the news of a parent's visit would have brought joy. Taelon offspring were not nurtured as helpless infants for years the way human children were, and as such, Taelon parents did not develop the ridiculous zeal to protect and love their children the way humans did. Nevertheless, the relationship between Taelon parent and child had long been important. Besides its intellectual rewards, the bond created had been treasured as a way to narrow the gap between Taelon generations. It had been hoped that eventually only a linked and unified force of will would remain.

Zo'or rejected such notions as outdated and even harmful. The idea that each generation should respect and emulate those who had come before, striving to merge ever closer to a single mind, appalled him. It was this constant drive toward oneness that had ruined his species, this desire for harmony above all other considerations that had made them weak against their enemies. They had intentionally forgotten how to fight, had buried their survival instinct so deeply inside themselves that they could no longer draw it forth when needed.

This much he had learned from watching humans interact with their teenage children: Rebellion in an offspring was good, even necessary, if a species was to grow and thrive.

So Zo'or remained on the bridge. Da'an could come to him.

But Da'an did not come. Instead he sent a Volunteer with a

request for a private meeting. Da'an had gone to Zo'or's quarters and wished to speak with him there.

Zo'or thought of using the intercom to tell Da'an he would not come, but if he did, Da'an might leave—and Zo'or wanted desperately to speak with him. Instead, Zo'or decided on a counteroffer.

"Tell Da'an to meet me in Foundation Room One," he told the Volunteer. "If Da'an has news of an official nature, that is where it should be discussed."

Zo'or watched the Volunteer depart, then walked leisurely through the mother ship, feeling pleased with his small victory.

In truth, he would have rather met in his personal quarters, as Da'an requested. The foundation rooms were preparatory areas Taelons used to ready themselves for an appearance before the Synod. As such, they were located directly next to the Synod Council Chamber—not the place Zo'or wanted to be at this moment but certainly as far away in purpose from Da'an's request as could be had on the mother ship while still allowing a private meeting.

If Da'an sought comfort in the familiarity of personal quarters, this choice of meeting space should put him ill at ease.

When Zo'or entered the Foundation Room, Da'an was already there.

"I see you received my message. I am gratified that you responded so quickly."

"What message?" Da'an asked. "I merely assumed—"

Just then the Volunteer Zo'or had sent to find Da'an entered the room.

"I apologize," she stammered. "Your quarters were empty when I arrived. The computer indicated, that is"—she looked at Da'an, then back at Zo'or—"I came here to deliver your message."

Before he could stop himself, Zo'or slowly turned his head to the side and half closed his eyes. The motions would be meaningless to the human, but Da'an would recognize them as signs of extreme irritation.

Zo'or spoke to the human. "Your services are no longer needed. You may leave."

To Da'an's credit, his gentle hand gestures revealed no trace of conquest. "I ask that you call a meeting of the Synod."

Zo'or forced his body posture to remain neutral and his hands to be still. "Your request is repetitious and inefficient. The matter has been discussed. My decision has been made."

Da'an angled toward him in slow, precise steps. "Perhaps you would feel differently if you understood the danger involved."

"You have decided to reveal the nature of the threat?"

"I have decided to give you the knowledge you need to take the proper action."

Zo'or nodded once, then stepped forward and offered his palm.

Da'an responded by lifting his hand and bringing his palm forward until it almost touched Zo'or's.

They stared at each other, each silently acknowledging the increased awareness they were about to allow, then brought their hands together, palm to palm.

The touch, as always, was both joyous and painful. Their backs slightly arched, Zo'or and Da'an instinctively closed their eyes to reduce the clutter of external stimuli. If others had been in the room, they would have seen a flash as the palms touched, then rainbow lines of energy dancing over the skin before the Taelons separated.

For Zo'or and Da'an, time inside the link passed much more slowly. Both would be weary by the time they severed the connection.

The first impression Zo'or received from Da'an was great pain—the blinding hot, intense agony of a Taelon life force being overloaded. Battle raged around him, not in human or Jaridian terms, but in the violently Taelon ebb and flow of energy.

Zo'or recoiled, but beyond the pain, he felt power. He concentrated on it, bringing it to him, caressing it in all its magnificent glory. He had never known such power, but in its essence, he recognized the flavor he had first tasted the day before.

He wanted that power, hungered for it in a way he did not fully understand. The lust to take it for his own brought him deeper into Da'an's mind—and he struck cold. Bitter, tasteless ice that cradled him in a suffocating embrace.

Zo'or's body locked rigidly, the Taelon equivalent of a human's terrified shudder.

The link terminated abruptly, the emotional echoes bubbling and churning around him as the main thrust of the sharing faded. In those few seconds, before the impressions from the link dissipated completely, Zo'or glimpsed Da'an's true depth, towering pillars of knowledge gained through a life lived decades, centuries, millennia longer than his own. Only in moments like this did Zo'or's confidence falter. Perhaps his wisdom had not exceeded his parent's.

But the subtle impressions were short-lived. The only lasting knowledge Zo'or obtained from the link was an intimate familiarity with the unnamed, unseen power that had pervaded every tendril of their connection.

Intellectually, Zo'or knew he should be frightened by the potential power he had felt, just as Da'an had said he was frightened. Instead, he found it enticing, alluring to him in a way he could not resist, did not want to resist.

Da'an studied him. "Now you know all you need to understand. You will call a meeting of the Synod."

He did not phrase the words as a question—an obvious offense.

"I shall not."

"Then I will do so."

Da'an turned to go.

Zo'or took a step after him, his hand outstretched. Stopping, he brought the hand back toward his chest, his fingers moving with the slow rhythm of determination.

"I use my authority as Synod leader to block your action."

Da'an turned and stared. "On what grounds?"

"I have already stated them. You must tell me all you know about this mysterious power and the danger it represents to our species. Until you do so, no meeting will be called."

"A call for a meeting by a Synod member has not been blocked in this way for more than fourteen hundred years."

"It is still within my authority to do so."

"That is true, but I recommend against your taking this action. It is ill-advised."

"It is done."

Zo'or waited for the arguments that he knew must come. Da'an would not accept defeat so easily.

But he did.

"As you wish. You will come to regret this decision. When you do, remember it was I who twice asked for the meeting to be called, and it was you who twice denied it."

Da'an left the room.

Zo'or watched him go, his fingers tracing out a pattern of puzzlement.

He had felt the power and knew that Da'an's warning was real, but he also knew that he must have the power for himself. If he brought in the Synod, he would lose control. While his political power was great, it was far from absolute, and he knew how his fellow Taelons reacted to danger—by boring and fruitless meditation. He alone was unafraid to take action.

And with power of the magnitude he had felt, instant action would be required.

First, he must identify its source, but that would have to wait. The link had fatigued him, and the peripheral thoughts in Da'an's mind had troubled his peace and disturbed his confidence.

For a few hours, he would rest. Then he would contact Agent Sandoval.

TWELVE

By the time Waneta Long returned to her office around 2:40, she had almost forgotten about Dr. Bob.

Lunch had been interesting. Besides Jill, three other professors from the department had been there, just catching up on what everyone was doing. She told them about the artifacts and about Jason dropping the pottery jar. All of them were supportive, saying she could do only so much; at some point students had to become responsible for their own actions.

Waneta did not completely agree with them—and she did not show them the crystal. Perhaps she was just reacting to Dr. Bob's zeal, but she found herself being overly protective, carrying the stone around in her pocket like some secret promise ring.

After lunch, she taught her second, and last, class of the day: Anthropology 311, Southeastern Indians. While this class covered many tribes of the Southeast, including Seminole, Choctaw, Creek, and Shawnee, its emphasis was on Cherokees—partly because UT lay so close to so many Cherokee sites, but also because Cherokees were in many ways unique.

While Waneta had never considered herself a Cherokee as much as an American, she did take pride in the fact that Cherokees developed their own written language, wrote their own constitution, and started their own national press, all before 1830. As far as she knew, they were the only people in history to employ an alphabet developed by just one person.

George Gist, better known as Sequoyah, never learned to read or write—until he developed his own syllabary. It took him twelve years, during which time he faced incredible ridicule, but when he was done, he gave a nation the ability to communicate in a new and powerful way. He proved that one person could make a difference.

Even Waneta, who did not speak any Cherokee, could read the language. That's because Sequoyah named each of the eighty-five symbols in his alphabet after the sound it made. To read, one only needed to say the names of the letters. In English, this would be like writing *effigy* as *feg* or *icy* as *ic*.

Of course Waneta's students were never quite as fascinated with this information as she was. Waneta herself thought of it only as a mental exercise. Cherokees had always numbered in the thousands, and most of them now did not speak their native tongue. Why learn a language so few people knew?

If she had wanted to do that, she would have become a sociologist rather than an archaeologist. What intrigued her most was what she planned to do today: use an object from the past to reveal a culture and a society that no longer existed. To do that, she needed to get the crystal into the lab—the sooner the better. The moment the paperwork went through, she would lose the stone, probably to the Eastern Band of Cherokees. Until then, she wanted to learn all she could about it.

First, she needed to register it, which she would do as soon as she dropped off her class notes.

Waneta pulled out her keys and started to unlock her office, but stopped, her hand still several inches from the knob.

The door was cracked open.

She paused, trying to remember if she had closed and locked it.

Yes, she had double-checked it before she left with Jill. She inched forward, leaned close to the door, and heard the sound of a drawer being pulled out.

Thinking back on it later, Waneta realized that she probably should have gone to the main office and called campus security, but at that moment, standing outside her door, she felt no fear, only anger.

Lots of possibilities flashed through her head. Perhaps the janitor was just being snoopy or looking for candy, or maybe a student had broken in hoping to find answers to next week's test. The most likely person never occurred to her—until she burst into the room and saw the wood-handled, black umbrella hanging from the front corner of her desk.

Dr. Bob stood up at the squeak of the opening door. He had been sitting in her chair, a bundle of papers in his hand. The notebooks and in/out boxes from her desk had been moved to her worktable and the file folders from her bottom drawer were stacked across the desk in neat piles.

Waneta stormed forward, one hand crushing her class notes to her chest, the other hand balled into a fist, her arm rigid and held tight to her side.

"What the hell are you doing in my office? Get away from my desk! Leave my things alone!"

Dr. Bob put down her papers and picked up his umbrella. "This is not your office and this is not your desk. Both belong to the university, and if I am trying to locate missing, possibly stolen, property, I am allowed to enter these premises and conduct a thorough search without your permission. Why do you think I have a master key to all the offices?"

Waneta stepped forward, her whole body shaking. "Not for this. Not to invade my privacy."

"If I were you," Dr. Bob said, pointing his umbrella at her like a gun, "I would take a more respectful tone. Your problems are great enough without complicating them further."

"I've done nothing wrong," Waneta protested, but that was not exactly true.

Contrary to the reassurances of her colleagues, she was responsible for the actions of her grad students at the dig site. Once she identified the jar as an artifact from the Mississippian rather than the Woodland period, all activity at the site should have been stopped. Yet the jar was moved and broken, its contents disturbed, its remains carried away in pieces.

Dr. Bob raised an eyebrow. "Nothing wrong? On the contrary, several incidents and breaches of procedure have been brought to my attention. Your position at this university is in jeopardy. I suggest that first, you get hold of yourself, and second, you start cooperating fully."

Waneta backed away from the desk. What had Jason told this man? "Let me explain. One of the graduate students, without my permission, picked up the artifact and accidentally dropped it. Once its contents were disturbed, I thought it best to remove them from the site."

Dr. Bob suddenly smiled, the expression more unnerving than anything else he had done. "Of course you did. There's no need to go into any of that. I want you to know that I understand—and I'm here to help."

He came around the desk, the tip of his umbrella clicking against the vinyl floor like a cane. Waneta stepped toward the door, and the edges of the stone in her pocket pressed against her thigh.

"From what I understand," Dr. Bob said, "the crystal was contained in a Cherokee jar. You know what that means. You know the delays that could be involved. Even if you are eventually allowed to continue at this dig site, you won't have time to publish the results of your research. That alone could prevent you from gaining tenure at this institution."

Dr. Bob's voice took on the smooth silkiness of a diamond jeweler. "Of course, I have some influence. If I insisted that you be given another year to complete your tenure track, that might make all the difference in the world."

His tone and manner frightened her. "What do you want?"

"The crystal you found. Give it to me, and I'll take care of the paperwork. I'll make sure no one misunderstands what happened at the dig site."

He raised his umbrella and held it like a club as he closed on her. His eyes were bright, his gaze unblinking.

Waneta backed out of her office and into the hallway. Dr. Bob followed.

None of this made sense. The stone was just another artifact. They had hundreds in the museum and thousands more in storage. Granted, this was a crystal, an unpolished gem, but certainly no more valuable than many other items they had. Why did Dr. Bob want it so desperately?

Waneta almost never lied, but the man's eagerness unsettled her. Carefully, she misled him with the truth. "The object was wrapped in what I believe to be deerskin. I already dropped it off at the lab, but you can stop by and take a look at it if you want."

Dr. Bob halted, his eyes wide, his face suddenly pale. "The lab? You were supposed to register it first."

The crystal in Waneta's pocket seemed warmer now, as if it knew Dr. Bob wanted it and did not like her keeping it from him. "The lab will register it."

"But they were told to watch for—I was to be notified when—damn!" Dr. Bob shoved her aside as he rushed by. "Out of my way!"

He started off in the direction of the lab, but Dr. Janson, who was coming down the hall, stopped him. Dr. Bob said something and tried to move around him, but Dr. Janson waltzed in front of him again, blocking his path.

Waneta scanned her office. She would put her things away later. Right now she needed to get out of here before Dr. Bob discovered that the crystal was not in the lab and came back looking for it.

She closed and locked her door, then headed in the opposite direction from the way Dr. Bob had gone.

If she disappeared for three or four hours, she could come back tonight and do her research. Dr. Bob never worked evenings. Then, in the morning, she could surrender the crystal with no real harm done.

As she trotted down the steps, the stone in her pocket burned, as if on fire.

THIRTEEN

Renée Palmer paced in front of her office window at Doors International. She had spent the afternoon trying to bury herself in the normal administrative details of her position as a major division head at the world's largest company, but all she could think about was the sleazy comment made by Dr. Robert Messmore.

Assets, indeed.

She smoothed her skirt against her thighs and pressed a hand against her stomach. Soft. Perhaps she should have found Dr. Messmore's comment flattering. Between her normal duties and her activities with the Resistance, she no longer had the opportunity to exercise as much as she once did. There had been a time when she could have kept up with anyone. These days, she tried to ignore the fine lines at the corners of her eyes while putting on her makeup, and only on her bravest mornings did she risk a glance in the mirror when she stepped out of the shower.

Regardless, she had yet to slip so far she needed the crass compliment of some two-bit department head from Hillbilly U.

She still had some effect on men. Their eyes turned when she walked past and most people agreed she remained strikingly beautiful. Those same people would say her personal standards were simply too high, but she had always strived for perfection, and it irritated her that her body had fallen behind.

But it was not Dr. Messmore's manners that concerned her at the moment.

When she called earlier, he did not have the crystal. Now, four hours later, he still did not have it—or if he did, he had decided not to let her know.

That possibility must be considered. While useful to Doors International, any department head willing to steal artifacts from his university could not be trusted. It would not surprise her to discover that he had plans to double-cross her as well.

He would find that harder to accomplish.

Renée picked up the global from her desk and pulled it open. "Access personal database, encryption code M-A-I-L-R-U-G-U-A-6-9. Cross reference tag freedom with Knoxville, Tennessee, geocode range . . . two hundred miles."

The global returned several pages of results. Most of the names belonged to Resistance members. Others belonged to people who had said or done something against the Taelons, thereby making themselves potential recruits to the Underground movement but who remained too great a risk to bring fully into the fold.

If Liam knew she had this list, he would be unreasonably angry, but she had never been one to tell Liam everything. He thought it was too dangerous for one person to have access to so many Resistance members, unless, of course, that person was him. Renée had never bought into that. While she trusted Liam more than anyone else, she had learned through experience not to trust anyone completely.

Still, Liam had a point about the security risk of having so many names in one place, which was why she encrypted the names at the highest level possible on a global. In addition to a password, the file could not be accessed without proper voice ID. Still, she had defeated such measures herself. That was why her global contained a special chip that modified its standard access routines. If anyone attempted to circumvent the security surrounding the data, all the names would be wiped from the device.

As she paged down, she decided it would take too long to

look at every name. "Filter and rank by experience: military, security, police, FBI, CIA."

Most of the names disappeared. Of those left, one caught her eye.

"Gil Ledford," she said.

The global dialed his number. When Gil answered, he wrinkled his brow and stared at her for several seconds before giving her a tentative, "Ya."

Perhaps he did not remember her. They had met in the earliest days of the Resistance, before Renée had buffered herself completely against contact with all but the most senior Resistance leaders.

She remembered him, though, especially his long black hair. Tied in a ponytail now, he had worn it loose when she first met him. Like some long lost Sampson, that night he stared at her with fierce brown eyes, his powerful brow and above-average height adding to his projection of power. She recalled thinking that he looked as if he could handle anything—or anyone.

"We met at Jennifer's party."

"Of course we did."

That was not the proper code response. She hesitated, trying to decide what to do.

He looked tired, beaten. Perhaps the troubles of the world had caught up to him, robbing him of his interest in the Resistance. It happened often, yet another reason the Resistance had become so fragmented and unreliable.

"Perhaps I dialed the wrong number," she said.

He sighed and looked down. When he lifted his chin, he said, "No, Renée. You don't make mistakes. What is it you want?"

"A favor."

"I'm not in the favor business anymore."

She should cut the connection, but something about Gil's eyes kept her talking. She did not want to ask the question, but found herself doing so anyway. "How's Shumana?"

Gil flinched, as if struck. He closed his eyes and his jaw tightened. After several deep breaths, his face calmed into an emotionless mask and he looked at the global again. "She's dead, like the others. They're all dead. Besides me, not one person from our cell survived the crackdown."

Renée did not need to ask which crackdown. Hundreds of Resistance members had died or mysteriously disappeared during President Thompson's brief enforcement of martial law after the last election. Maybe Gil was no longer an official member of the Resistance, but he would never betray them.

"I'm sorry." Renée shook her head. She had said those words too many times to too many people.

Gil's expression remained rigid. "You didn't call after all these years just to see how I was doing. What do you want? And how much are you willing to pay?"

"Pay?"

"Pay. I don't have Doors International taking care of my bills."

Renée paused to consider. What she had told Dr. Messmore had a grain of truth. This project did have a budget. She was within that budget, but she always liked to come in comfortably beneath her initial estimates. This time, that might not be possible.

"You may have to do nothing—beyond a little observation. You're not the primary contact."

"How much?"

"Five thousand."

"Agreed."

Renée felt a twinge of disappointment. She had offered him too much. While she felt sympathetic toward Gil because he belonged to the Resistance, the amount she paid for his services reflected directly on her business skills, and if Gil accepted this task without knowing what it was, he was more desperate for funds than she had guessed.

Renée pushed a button on her global. "I'm transmitting the data now."

She watched Gil's eyes and knew he was no longer looking at her. Still, he would hear her voice. "The primary contact is Dr. Robert Messmore. By tonight, he should have what we believe to be a Taelon artifact. If he fails to deliver it to the Resistance, you will need to convince him to surrender it to you. If he does not have it, get it directly from the person who discovered it: Dr. Waneta Long."

Gil jerked his head up. "Who?"

"Waneta Long," Renée repeated. "You have video of her as well as the official photo of Dr. Messmore from the university's Web site."

Gil's brow wrinkled again. He was pulling up the data, watching the video.

When he spoke, he sounded angry. "Where did you get this? When did this interview take place?"

Renée frowned, suddenly unsure of how to proceed. "This afternoon."

His eyes refocused, probably looking at the video again. Renée started to ask what his connection was to Dr. Long when Gil suddenly flinched.

"*Uluhsati*," he whispered, then looked away from the global. His face showed fear, as if he had just seen something terrible across the room. "*Uktena.*"

Renée did not recognize the words, but from the expression on Gil's face, she worried that Dr. Long might be a Taelon informer. If so, the Taelons would also be after the crystal, if they did not have it already.

"Gil, this artifact is important to the Resistance. I need you to be professional."

"The time has finally come," he said, still looking away. Then his face hardened, the emotionless mask back in place as he stared into his global. "Of course. I'll do what needs to be done."

The way he said it made her shiver. Quickly she added, "The rendezvous time and coordinates are contained with the other data. If you miss the first drop-off, someone will return every ninety minutes. But Gil, make sure you show up on time."

"I understand."

Staring at that expressionless yet powerful face, Renée suddenly wished she could cancel the assignment, call Gil off. But if he planned to compromise the objective, it was too late now to stop him. He already had the data.

Only after she ended the connection did she realize that she might have misread Gil completely. Years had passed since they had known each other, and it had seemed so unimportant at the time, she had forgotten.

Gil was Native American. She did not know what tribe, but he and another Resistance member got into an argument one night about the Taelon occupation—how it resembled or failed to resemble the conquest of America by Europeans.

She could no longer recall the details, but at the time, it had been clear that Gil viewed Taelons and whites in much the same way.

And the Taelon artifact had been found at a Native American dig site.

She set her global to emergency contact. For the next two hours, it automatically redialed Gil's global every five minutes while she tried vainly to concentrate on her work. Gil's global never answered.

If Dr. Messmore delivered the stone, nothing else would matter—but Renée Palmer had never been one to leave things to chance.

After discontinuing the global's automatic redial, she gathered her purse and her global, then headed to the parking garage and slid into her black Porsche 911. She would swing by her place to retrieve a few things, then hop on I-66 and cruise over to I-81. From there, she would let her onboard computer guide her to Knoxville, Tennessee, and get her to the university.

If she used a portal instead of her car, she could be there in a half hour, but that would leave a record of her travel in the

Portal Authority computer. If this deal blew up, she wanted no trace of evidence she had ever been involved.

To get there in time to be of any use, though, she would need to ignore the speed limits—but that was one reason she owned a Porsche.

FOURTEEN

The Volunteers escorted the last of Da'an's official visitors from the Companions' North American embassy, leaving Da'an and Liam alone.

The afternoon had been busy, with the entire day's schedule of meetings squeezed into the last few hours of the afternoon and running over into the evening. Liam had suggested that the appointments be rescheduled, but Da'an had refused. In fairness, the Taelon had performed his official functions well enough and, from all obvious indications, had recovered completely from the episode at the theater the day before. Liam alone knew Da'an well enough to recognize the subtle differences: a somewhat greater tilt of the head, eyelids open less wide than usual, and a more expansive use of hand gestures.

Da'an, his fingers curling gracefully, glanced sideways in Liam's direction. "Your continued observation is no longer warranted. As I have stated, the feelings of illness have passed. I did not mean to cause so much concern. I have even heeded your suggestion and canceled my appointments for the next three days. If I use this time to relax and meditate, I will soon be fully functional again."

With the rest of the people gone, the odor of the embassy walls and the scent of the Taelon grew more pronounced. To Liam, this building had always smelled like a nursery, and Da'an, like a newborn—although that was hardly the case.

Da'an had been traveling among the stars when Liam's human ancestors were still trying to figure out the benefits of plumbing.

The smell of the Taelon grew stronger as Liam quit stalking the room's edges and walked to its center. Since this morning's excursion to the theater, he had been waiting to discuss matters with Da'an.

He stopped several feet away. "If you told me what happened, I might have a better chance to find out who did this to you."

Da'an stared off at nothing, his eyes half closed. "We have already discussed yesterday's unfortunate mishap. I told you my illness was caused by a disturbance in the Commonality. That disturbance subsided before I could pinpoint its exact location or determine the nature of its source."

"That's it?"

Da'an's fingers weaved an intricate pattern in the air. "What else do you want to know?"

"I want to know everything," Liam said. "I want to know what kind of disturbance could force you to revert to your energy state. I want to know why a little boy can dance as well as an adult and why his eyes make me wonder if his father was human. I want to know whom you're protecting and what their reasons were for trying to harm you."

"I am protecting no one."

Liam sighed, the outrush of his breath unnaturally loud in the stillness of the room. This place could be so quiet, yet so noisy; working here had taught him the true sound of silence. Taelons, by nature, were extremely quiet beings, and while the virtual glass and the walls of the embassy made no detectible noise, this room always made Liam feel as if a cacophony of hums, buzzes, and rattles was going on just beyond his range of hearing. He once thought he was the only one who noticed it, but Augur, Renée, and others had spoken of experiencing the same sensation.

Liam stuffed his hands in the pockets of his jacket and

stared at Da'an, who had yet to meet his gaze. "Perhaps you're not protecting someone—but you know more than you're telling."

"A safe statement, since everyone knows more than he could ever possibly tell. But you must believe me: When it comes to what happened yesterday, I cannot explain more than I have."

"Can't explain? Or won't?"

Da'an's hand movements stopped, and he cocked his head to stare off at nothing. Liam had never grown used to this lack of eye contact. For the most part, Da'an looked at people only when he was about to insult them.

Da'an spoke slowly, precisely. "Your concern in this matter seems excessive. Perhaps you are the one who knows more than he has chosen to reveal. Tell me, Liam. Where did you go this morning?"

"I went to the theater to talk to Daniel Shaunessy."

Da'an looked directly at Liam for the first time. "What did you discover?"

"The stage manager was not happy to see yet another Companion Protector. Turns out, Agent Sandoval was there a couple of hours before I was."

"Agent Sandoval?"

For the first time since they started this discussion, Liam felt that he had said something unexpected. "That's right. He was checking up on Daniel, just like I was."

Da'an remained completely motionless for several seconds, then started moving his fingers again, more quickly than before.

Liam noticed the change. "Seems strange that Sandoval would show up to speak to the same boy I wanted to see. It seems doubly strange that the boy would have disappeared immediately after yesterday's performance. Quite a coincidence that you have a fainting spell of some kind while he's dancing, then only hours later, he and his mother decide to return home, because his aunt is ill."

Da'an looked straight at Liam again, his hands temporarily motionless. "Humans are not immortal."

Liam shivered, partly from the lack of emotion in Da'an's voice and partly because the temperature in the embassy seemed especially cold tonight. Taelons always kept their living spaces below human norms, one reason Liam and other Protectors so often wore jackets.

"I suppose it's possible the boy's aunt came down sick, but the stage manager said no message came and the boy's mother never carried a global. That seems a bit strange, doesn't it?"

Da'an did not answer, and for the first time, Liam realized that Zo'or might not be involved in this incident at all. But if not, why had Agent Sandoval been at the theater?

Liam studied Da'an, trying to figure out what might be going on in that Taelon brain. "The boy and his mother left no word with the stage manager about where they were going, no address where he could contact them. Tell me. Where did they go?"

"I am the North American Companion. That does not mean I track the movements of every human being on this continent."

Liam walked to the window and gazed out at downtown D.C. To his left stood the Lincoln Memorial. To his right, beyond the end of the reflecting pool, rose the Washington Monument, high and majestic, like a white headstone for a watery grave. Liam worked within sight of both but had never taken the time to visit either.

From behind, he heard the distinctive sound of Da'an's shuffling feet. When Liam turned, the Taelon was already halfway up the ramp leading out of the room.

Liam called out, "I'm eventually going to figure out what happened between you and the boy. You might as well tell me now."

Da'an stopped, his head cocked as he answered. "Do not worry about the boy, Liam. He did not cause my illness."

"I wish I could believe you."

Da'an twisted his head and glared over his shoulder. His fingers gestured violently, then settled into an intricate and somewhat accelerated dance. "I have not lied to you, Liam. I cannot tell you what I do not know."

Liam stared back at Da'an, studying the appearance of the Taelon's deep gray, emotionless eyes, eyes Liam had once thought held compassion for the human race. Now they just looked worn and cold, like old snow. "If you're canceling your appointments for the next several days, I'm going to take some time off, too—if that's all right."

Da'an turned away and took several steps up the ramp, then stopped. "When you leave, do not take the shuttle. I may have need of it."

"Where are you going?"

Fingers on both of Da'an's hands shifted in a wild pattern. "It is a Taelon shuttle. That is all you need know."

Liam forced a tight-lipped grin. "Whatever you say, boss."

But Da'an had already topped the ramp and exited the room.

FIFTEEN

Twenty-four hours had passed since Zo'or first felt the power in his mind. Twenty-four hours since he had seen the face of a human woman and the eyes of a human boy, distorted and multiplied in a red montage of juxtaposed images.

Then nothing.

With each passing hour, he became more convinced that he had somehow missed his opportunity. That possibility ate at his mind, swirling and whirling in a storm of self-doubt and envy. Since his first taste of the power, he knew he needed it for his own. Then Da'an had revealed its full flavor to him, and the desire to feel it coursing through his being had dominated his every thought.

Agent Sandoval, whose complete devotion to the Taelons had always been questionable, had come up with nothing— nothing! Every time Zo'or contacted his Protector, he received the same inadequate excuse.

"I've had my best research assistant on it all afternoon. She's still reviewing and sorting the data."

When twenty-four hours had passed, Zo'or could stand it no more. "Bring her to me."

Now, as Agent Sandoval and his "best research assistant" stepped out of the portal onto the mother ship, Zo'or felt animalistic frenzy. If he could have kept some measure of objectivity, he might have enjoyed the sensation, but the desire to obtain the power overrode all other concerns.

He must have it. He must. Now.

Agent Sandoval stepped forward. "Zo'or, this is Laura Heward."

Zo'or bowed his head and blinked slowly. "Follow me, Laura Heward."

As Zo'or escorted them to the bridge, he studied Agent Sandoval's research assistant. Human. Female. Previously unknown to him. In her hand, she carried a Taelon/human data module. How many times had she provided information to Agent Sandoval, which he had passed on without giving her the credit she deserved? Many times—or he would have no reason to praise her now that she had taken center stage.

When they reached the bridge, Zo'or took his seat at the central Taelon control station. He glanced once at the Volunteers around him, but the bridge crew for the Taelon mother ship had their CVIs set to the highest level of control. This made them little more than drones, unable to function in normal human society, but it also made them safe. They could witness anything and their loyalty would remain beyond question.

"What have you discovered?"

Zo'or had asked the question to the female, but Agent Sandoval answered. "The results are incomplete. As I told you, Zo'or, we need more time—"

"Have you personally reviewed the data?"

Agent Sandoval shifted uneasily and clasped his hands before him, an instinctive gesture of defensive submission. "I apologize, but you did not provide enough time for me to review—"

"Do you know what she knows?"

Agent Sandoval raised his eyebrows, then shrugged. "No, she is the only agent who reviewed all the data."

"Then be still. I have no need for your babbling commentary."

Zo'or stepped close to the human female, who stood at rigid attention. She did not smirk or make any other expression that would suggest she had enjoyed seeing her boss receive his comeuppance. Little wonder Agent Sandoval praised her. Such devotion without the use of some kind of external control was rare.

"What have you discovered?" Zo'or asked again.

The woman answered in a soft but firm voice—easy to hear over the hum of the ship. "About a dozen major news stories concerning the eastern United States have broken in just the past day. All are political or economic in nature and appear to be normal and expected, the kind of stories that always appear on the evening news. To examine more minor items, I had a dozen other research assistants queuing up news clips on a continual basis throughout the afternoon. In all, I've personally reviewed hundreds of stories that fit your broadest requirements—but to provide any results, I need more information."

Unlike Agent Sandoval, this woman gave credit to those who helped her, an unwise move unless she planned to transfer blame to them for her failure, a possibility she had already eliminated.

"What kind of information?"

"Anything that will narrow down the results. Subject, people, geographic region . . ."

Zo'or's fingers moved in a pattern of mild irritation. "If I knew that, I would not need you."

"I'm not looking for much here. Just something to point me in the right direction."

Zo'or glared at her, but she met his gaze and did not look away. This woman would not be intimidated, a poor decision for a human in his presence.

After several seconds, he lifted his chin slightly and half closed his eyes. His initial encounter with the power had served as a divine revelation, personal to the point of pain. He did not want to reveal a single shred of that experience to anyone, but he saw no other choice.

"There was a boy."

"What boy?"

The woman's short interrogative style grated against

Zo'or's sensibilities. "I cannot say. I saw his eyes only. Special. Unnatural."

"Unnatural in what way?"

Zo'or's fingers danced a slow rhythm. "Green, full of energy. They were Taelon eyes—but the boy was human."

The woman frowned and her brow wrinkled. Her gaze focused on the floor for several seconds, then she shook her head. "None of the pictures or videos I reviewed contained anyone with eyes similar to what you described."

Zo'or started to ask if she was certain, but he eyed the CVI on her throat and knew he had no need.

Agent Sandoval stepped forward. "If you will excuse my babbling commentary, I may know who the boy is."

Zo'or's fingers stopped momentarily. "Speak, Agent Sandoval. I am listening."

"I never met him, but some of the people I interviewed from the dancing troupe described the star of their show, a young boy, as having unusual eyes—bright green, which seemed to glow. This boy was the one dancing when Da'an fell ill. He and his mother left the show on a family emergency shortly after that performance."

Zo'or tilted his head slightly as he considered this possibility.

Laura Heward spoke brusquely. "So that's it? I spent most of a day reviewing national and local news from half the country, and I wasn't even needed?"

Zo'or curled his fingers in amusement. He was half tempted to let her go back to Earth believing that, but he still had use for her.

"Perhaps you can tell me about the woman."

"What woman? What did she look like? Give me exact details."

The volley of questions came out quick and clipped, lacking all respect. Laura Heward was becoming tiresome. If Zo'or did not need her services, he would show her the folly of her provocations.

For now, he restrained his temper.

The woman associated with the power remained clear in Zo'or's mind, but he had never needed to describe anyone before—Taelons did not identify other Taelons by anything so crude as sight. How did humans do it? He did not know. Agent Sandoval and other Protectors always supplied photographs for any humans of interest, just as he supplied visual data to them.

He tried to delineate the image he had seen but did not know where to begin. "She had . . . a human face. And hair. Dark hair."

"Good. What else?"

"I would estimate her age at approximately thirty Earth-years old."

"Wonderful." Laura Heward sounded absurdly pleased by this simple detail.

Zo'or did not pay much attention to humans, but compared to Taelons, they aged in a ridiculously obvious way. Anyone could tell their approximate age just by looking for telltale signs. Elongation of the face as they transformed from child to adult. Lengthening and rounding of the nose. Eventually creases around the eyes and hardening and drying of the hands. Brown blemishes and severe wrinkling of the skin as they progressed to their final years.

"What about her face? What did it look like?"

Zo'or did not like the question. To him, most humans looked similar. He identified them more from the distinctive patterns of electromagnetic radiation surrounding their bodies than he did their facial features.

"That is all," he said.

"Surely she had other features you can remember. Perhaps—"

"Enough! I do not have time for this."

The woman's voice remained calm but unyielding. "You must make time. I've reviewed dozens of stories that involved a dark-haired woman, as either reporter or subject. In a few dozen more, a woman fitting that description was involved, but not as the main focus. To pinpoint the story, I need a better description. Surely you can tell me something more about her face. For example, did she wear glasses like me?"

Zo'or looked at the research assistant again and noticed her glasses. He had absorbed that detail about her, just as he absorbed everything he ever saw or did, but he had paid it no heed.

He thought back about the woman he had seen just before the power dissipated. "No glasses."

"Good! Now we're making progress."

She smiled, a disgusting dental display Zo'or had never appreciated. That was one of the reasons he valued Agent Sandoval. The man rarely showed his teeth.

"What about her eyes? What color were they?"

"Brown."

"Excellent. And the shape of her face. Would you say it was more oval-shaped, or more heart-shaped?"

"Neither. Her face looked like a typical human face. No geometric figures were involved."

"It doesn't need to be an exact match, just something I can use to build a picture of the woman in my mind."

That concept Zo'or understood. If the research assistant were Taelon, they could join palms and he could share the memory of the face with her directly the way Da'an had shared his experience of the power. Words could be so inefficient.

"I can supply nothing more."

"You must."

"No. I must do nothing whatsoever," Zo'or said. "It is you who serves me."

The woman sighed. "I'm not a mind reader. To zero in on the exact story you seek, I need additional information. Your only other option is to review every news story I have, a waste of both my time and yours."

Zo'or looked at her keenly. Of course. That was the simple answer.

Memories of the power tingled through him, agitating his mind. He could not wait any longer. He must act.

"You have made an excellent suggestion, Laura Heward. The most direct solution is always the best. Would you agree?"

She frowned and pushed up her glasses. "Yes, but I thought you did not have much time. Surely going through a few questions about this woman you seek would be more efficient than your watching hours and hours of video clips and absorbing the information from hundreds of print articles."

"Why would I do that when you have already done it for me?"

"Exactly!"

"Exactly."

Zo'or pressed a button on the main control console. Immediately the human female's face contorted in pain and her skin glowed softly as her Cyber-Viral Implant translated the biological data from her neural pathways into a form compatible with Taelon physiology. The results were then transmitted through the main console to Zo'or, whose skin flashed with the soft rainbow lines of his energy state.

Zo'or consumed the information, absorbing every memory the woman had, drinking in her experiences in a bawdy display of self-indulgent pleasure.

For the most part, the woman had lived a tediously boring life. There had been relationships with other humans, emotional gibberish with family and friends, confused mosaics from her juvenile years and her days as a carefree child—all of it inconsequential and unattractive. What Zo'or found interesting was her organized approach to adult life. Relatively uncluttered by romantic interests and focused on a tight set of successively accomplished goals, she had a remarkably organized mind for the female of this species, but she also enjoyed the benefit of being able to manage all the different elements of her life easily, almost effortlessly—a skill Zo'or had never seen in a human male.

Zo'or closed his eyes and concentrated on the woman's

memories from the past few hours. She had reviewed as much information as she claimed, and it took Zo'or's mind several long seconds to digest all she had seen and done. He would fully savor several especially interesting tidbits of information later, including her first impressions from meeting him in person, but for now, all he cared about were memories of the woman—which he found.

Agent Sandoval squatted beside the research assistant, who had collapsed, and pressed his fingers against the carotid artery in her throat. "She's unconscious. What did you do to her?"

"It was her suggestion," Zo'or said casually. "I needed her memories, so I took them."

Sandoval swallowed, his gaze locked on the woman. "Will she die?"

"Her life can be saved. With time and a serious investment of resources, she can even be retrained. But why bother?"

"She's my best research assistant."

"Not anymore. You will need to replace her. Phase IV implants allow a full transfer from human to Taelon, but the process has some serious side effects."

"Serious side effects?" Sandoval rose to his feet, and his voice grew high-pitched. "What have you done?"

"The process of assimilation destroys the neural pathways. She has no memories left."

Agent Sandoval bent low again and cradled the woman's head in his hands. "She was a faithful Volunteer. She obeyed orders diligently. She did all she could to help the Taelons— and you destroyed her!"

Zo'or felt no pity for the woman. She had been arrogant and disrespectful. "A necessary trade-off for the information her mind contained."

"Necessary? You could have just answered her questions. She would have found what you were looking for. You had no right to do this. We are not machines that you can just turn off or wipe clean whenever you feel the whim."

Agent Sandoval was overly concerned about the female.

Perhaps she was more to him than an assistant. "You are correct. Machines are harder to replace."

Agent Sandoval lifted his head slowly. "Even for you, Zo'or, that comment is beneath contempt."

"I suggest you remember your place."

Agent Sandoval released the woman and stood up. "I remember my place. I have no choice."

Zo'or scrutinized his Companion Protector. The man's hands shook slightly, but his eyes were fixed straight ahead and unblinking.

The CVI was under stress but holding fine. Good. While Agent Sandoval could be replaced, Zo'or had no time to do so now. He also had no time for the man to be distracted by excessive stress and grief.

"Would you give your life for me?" Zo'or asked.

Agent Sandoval's eyes remained hard. "My CVI would force me to do so."

"Exactly. As a Volunteer, you have volunteered your life in service of the Taelon race. That is all your research assistant has done—given her life so that the Taelon race may survive."

"How has she done that? What is so important that it requires the sacrifice of one of my best people?"

"Power." Even the word rang sweet. "What I seek goes well beyond anything I have ever experienced. It is the power to defeat the Jaridians. It is the means to rule Earth as it should be ruled."

His words were not exactly true. The power he had felt was greater than any he had felt before, but alone it would not be enough to defeat the Jaridians. It would, however, give him enough political influence to take total control of the Synod and then total control of Earth. Once freed of all shackles on his authority, he would be able to defeat the Jaridians the way they must be defeated, with humanity's full, albeit involuntary, cooperation.

"I still don't understand. How can the sacrifice of one human do that?"

"Because she provided me the information I need. Observe."

Zo'or retrieved the data module from the clenched hand of the fallen research assistant, then placed it in the control panel. Standing up straight, he waved his hand.

Words appeared in the air, identifying the video segment they were about to see, followed by the image of a dark-haired woman with brown eyes.

She wore the look of a trapped animal as the image enlarged, the camera closing in on her face, the same face Zo'or had seen in his mind when he felt the power.

For one brief moment, the approaching lights were reflected in her eyes, then she raised her arm to shield them.

Zo'or twisted his hand, freezing the image. There, in her upraised fist, sparkling crimson like a fresh drop of blood, were the edges of what appeared to be a stone. The picture was low quality and blurry. Zo'or moved his fingers, his mind manipulating the controls. The image sharpened somewhat, but he still did not recognize the object in her hand.

"What is it?" Agent Sandoval asked.

"I believe it is the source of the energy I sensed."

Zo'or considered what he had experienced the day before. The power had been tinged with emotion. Not raw, physical force then—but a life of some kind.

From the research assistant's memories, Zo'or knew the woman's name. He also knew every word said during the interview.

"This is Dr. Long. She is an instructor at the University of Tennessee. The crystal in her hand she allegedly found yesterday evening at a dig site in Swain County"—Zo'or shifted through his newly acquired memories—"North Carolina."

Zo'or pulled the data module from the control panel and handed it to Agent Sandoval. The man's CVI would allow him to remember everything he had just seen and heard, but Zo'or's attempt to explain how a person looked to the research assistant had made it clear that a picture truly was worth a thousand words—or a billion, billion memories.

"Find this Dr. Long," Zo'or said. "Bring her here—and make sure she has the crystal with her."

Agent Sandoval nodded, then turned to go.

Zo'or stopped him with a question. "Do you want the woman?" He gestured at the unconscious body on the floor.

Agent Sandoval looked at the fallen form and shook his head. "No. Do with her as you will. She is no longer of any use to anyone."

"She is of use to us." Zo'or motioned to two of the Volunteers. "Bring this woman to the fields."

The human female had no useful higher memory functions left, but she could be fed, as a human infant is fed, and kryss collected from her stomach.

Kryss allowed Taelons to exist on Earth, and since they had moved the fields of humans used to produce kryss from their home countries to a secret base on the moon, recruiting additional humans had proved more difficult.

Such secrecy should not be necessary. Once Zo'or had the crystal, it would not be. He thought of what the power would do for him, and in his excitement, radiating lines of energy crawled across his skin.

"Stop at nothing, Agent Sandoval," Zo'or said, reassuming his normal human facade. "No task I have ever given you is as important as this one."

Agent Sandoval watched the Volunteers pick up his ex-assistant, still unconscious, and place her on a gurney. As they wheeled her away, he said, "I understand perfectly."

Zo'or waited until Agent Sandoval was gone, then returned to his quarters to rest and meditate.

He thought he understood now why he had seen the woman when he first felt the power—she had been present when the power awoke. But what about the boy? He seemed to have no connection at all, beyond the obvious one that he was dancing when Da'an first detected the power.

An accident? Unlikely.

Zo'or searched the assistant's memories and found one of a printed article relating to the show, complete with pictures. Several of the media shots showed the boy, but in all of them, his eyes were closed, his body held in an artistic pose.

Sometimes Zo'or wished that the mental transfer equipment worked on other Taelons. If so, he would have used it on Da'an long ago.

The boy was obviously connected to the power somehow. Besides coincidence, a few facts pointed in that direction: Zo'or had perceived no impressions of the other dancers, and with the boy, he had seen only his eyes, special eyes, Taelon eyes.

Even so, Zo'or suspected that his certainty came from more than logic. Da'an had linked with him, intending to reveal only the magnitude of the power involved, but while no Taelon would open himself up completely in a link—that way lay madness—neither could he precisely control what was revealed.

Many times, after sharing a link, related information could be guessed with a higher degree of accuracy than what could be explained by chance, what Taelons called the shadow effect. Sometimes Taelons purposefully tried to hide or distort this information in the link, but few could.

Zo'or did not know what part the boy played, but he certainly had a role. For now, though, the woman—and the crystal—were more important.

Soon, he would have both.

SIXTEEN

Waneta was alone in the lab.

After evading Dr. Bob outside her office, she should have walked straight to the dean's office and filed a complaint about Dr. Bob or started the steps necessary to have Jason expelled from the department, but she was tired and still suffering the aftershocks of her hangover. Instead, she had gone home. Too exhausted to clean up her apartment from the night before, she skipped supper and took a nap, then returned to the university around seven-thirty with plans to take a break around ten and order pizza. Her global, attached to the belt of her jeans, remained off, and rather than stopping by her office as she usually did, she avoided that mess and went straight to the lab to begin her analysis.

Her time was limited. In the morning, she would have to surrender the stone to Dr. Bob as well as provide an explanation for misleading him. That meant she had only tonight to learn all she ever would about the crystal. Instead of completing her analysis, though, she had spent most of the thirty minutes since her arrival bent over the Taelon mass analyzer, trying to figure out what was wrong with the device.

The Taelon mass analyzer, dubbed TMA for short, consisted of little more than a clear tube sitting on an equipment base complete with an external display, computer port, and power module. It had no visible adjustment knobs, no configuration or setup screen, no way to tinker with its internal mechanisms in any way.

Last fiscal year, when the department received a grant to purchase the TMA, Waneta and the rest of the anthropology faculty had been thrilled. Before they obtained this new equipment, determining an artifact's age required burning a small sample of the object in their carbon-dating lab—that is, if a small sample could be taken from the piece without ruining it. Similarly, if they wanted to know the chemical composition of an artifact, they usually sent off a sample for AMS analysis. The samples went to Zurich, one of the few places with an accelerated mass spectrometer, and they were forced to wait weeks or even months for the results.

With the TMA, none of that was necessary. They simply placed the artifact to be analyzed inside the device, pushed a button, and almost instantly it returned a wealth of information—all with no apparent harm to the artifact.

But this time, Waneta could not get the machine to give her what she wanted.

Ultrasound and X rays revealed the crystal as nothing more than a colorless blob, radioactivity readings were minor but confusing, and the composition results were incomplete.

She had been told that the TMA performed its analysis by destroying individual molecules of the artifact, then measuring the elements they released. In the past, the device had performed so well that she never cared about the functional details. Now she wished she knew more about how the machine actually worked.

Waneta replaced the crystal with a small piece of granite, which the machine identified correctly as being comprised of potassium, aluminum, silicon, and oxygen, along with trace amounts of iron and lithium.

When she placed the crystal back in the device, however, the machine again returned a long list of elements, few of which made sense.

Before she started the analysis, she assumed the stone was comprised of crudely polished carnelian. Indeed, the crystal contained large quantities of silicon and oxygen, as well as aluminum and carbon in trace amounts. But according to the readout, the crystal also contained iron and calcium. Strangest of all were three elements the machine refused to identify.

The TMA did not report the elements as unknown but rather as undiscovered, as if the stupid machine knew what they were but refused to tell her.

Waneta picked up the crystal. It felt warm in her hand, perfectly reflecting her own body heat. This was not carnelian or any other known gem. In truth, the results indicated something much more complex.

Most gems were comprised of two to four elements. Some, like flawless diamonds, were pure carbon. This stone had the properties of—what? Rarely were inorganic substances naturally formed with so complex a structure.

She lifted the crystal above her head and watched the light form reflections and patterns inside the stone. Beautiful. It was easy to see why the ancient Cherokees had kept it, but why wrap it in deerskin and put it in a pottery bowl?

To hide it?

Perhaps.

To protect its powers?

More likely. For hundreds of years, Cherokees had wrapped quartz charms inside deerskin, but this crystal was no normal charm.

Waneta paced around the small lab. She often worked on campus at night. Usually it did not bother her, but tonight the quiet stillness of the empty lab made her uneasy and nervous. She walked repeatedly to the window and looked out through the slats of the venetian blind. The ugly concrete parking structure next to the stadium dominated the scenery. All its levels were nearly empty—few students parked there at night—and no cars at all were visible on the top level, the roof. Full night had fallen, and beyond the garage the lights of Knoxville shined from across the river. All in all, a poor view—not like the mountains at night, where the sky seemed endless and the stars beyond number.

She returned to the TMA and placed the crystal back inside the tube. Running her finger down the screen, she reexamined the list of elements. The crystal contained carbon. That meant she could use the ratio between carbon isotopes to determine its age, but this silly machine claimed that the crystal's proportion of carbon 14 to carbon 12 was at the same level as what she would find in any animal or plant alive today.

That did not mean the crystal was alive, but if this crazy Taelon contraption was correct, the crystal had been formed recently, certainly within the past twenty-five to fifty years.

That was long after the Mississippian period had ended. It was even long after the Trail of Tears in 1838, when most historic Cherokees were driven from their homeland to live in Oklahoma.

So was the stone man-made?

Waneta did not understand how that could be. She removed the crystal from the TMA and replaced it with a piece of the pottery jar. Comprised of silicon, oxygen, hydrogen, and other trace elements, including carbon, the machine dated the material at around A.D. 750.

That was older than she would have guessed, especially considering the artwork she had seen when the pottery jar was intact, but it was not unreasonable.

So someone had placed a new, possibly man-made crystal into an exceptionally old pottery jar and hidden it in a cave?

Why?

Waneta examined the wrapping material that had surrounded the crystal. From its size and where it was found, she believed it to be deerskin. Although mostly gray from dust, spots marred its surface, as if it had once been decorated with pigments that had darkened and smeared.

But how old was it?

Normally an animal hide buried in the ground would deteriorate within a year or two, but only if it were exposed to moisture. If it was stored in a jar on the shelf of a dry cave, for example, it could last for many, many years.

The Taelon mass analyzer took much longer than usual to complete its analysis of the hide, but finally it reported that Waneta's suspicion was correct—the hide belonged to a deer that had been slain from thirty-five to sixty years ago—but it also identified the results as divergent.

Waneta worked through the various functions of the TMA, gradually digging out details about the hide.

After several minutes, she discovered that materials of many different ages existed within the tube, all from twenty-five to sixty years old. She reset the machine, switching it from identifying individual elements to identifying as many of the materials present as possible, then watched in amazement as several kinds of animal blood registered on the display: rabbit, squirrel, mouse, deer, even bear.

Blood. Animal blood had been smeared on the stone before it had been wrapped in the deerskin.

The *Uktena*.

In Cherokee mythology, the *Uktena* was a giant serpent with a magical crystal in its forehead. A warrior killed the *Uktena*, then used the crystal from its head for conjuring. To keep the crystal under control, he had periodically rubbed it with blood.

Waneta held up the stone and watched the subtle change of color as she turned it over in her hand.

Could this be the fabled crystal from the mythological *Uktena*? The idea seemed plausible; an *Uktena* had been incised on the outside of the vessel Jason destroyed. But if this were the *Uktena*, it meant that someone, perhaps as recently as when Waneta was a child, had kept it in that cave, practicing the rituals necessary to control it.

She did not want to believe that. It would mean that someone from the modern world had gone out and killed small animals, then offered their blood to an inanimate stone—a cruelty that unfortunately did not seem far-fetched at all.

People believed a lot of crazy things. They bought lottery tickets, thinking they had a chance to win. They even watched professional wrestling on TV and thought it was real.

But if this was the crystal of the *Uktena*—what an incredible find! The Eastern Band of Cherokees would be so pleased by her discovery that they might even forgive her the transgression of digging at what they would certainly claim was a religious site.

Waneta heard the metallic click of a key being pushed into a lock and the squeak of a door opening, but her concentration was so focused on the crystal that the noises did not fully register. Only when footsteps crossed the room did the sounds finally penetrate her brain.

She jumped, spinning toward the door with a small cry of alarm.

Dr. Bob stopped, his umbrella in his right hand. "A little edgy tonight? I'm not surprised. I'd be nervous, too, if I'd sabotaged a dig site, stolen an artifact belonging to the university, and lied to my department head."

Waneta's excitement at discovering the possible history of the crystal evaporated. "What are you doing here?"

"A better question is, what are *you* doing here? This afternoon, you told me you dropped off the crystal at the lab. I checked. The only item they had from you was a dusty old animal hide, which I see there inside our expensive TMA."

Waneta tried to keep her voice calm as she spoke. "That's right. I said the crystal was wrapped in deerskin, and that I dropped it off at the lab—meaning the deerskin."

He eyed her coldly. "If you think that little twist of words makes any difference, you are incorrect. You blatantly deceived me."

"I didn't mean to cause any problems," she said carefully, "but I have fantastic news. The stone we found at the dig site might be the *Uktena*. If so, we've located a crystal that's been part of Cherokee legend for centuries."

"You've already started examining the crystal?" He sounded alarmed and angry.

"Yes, and everything looks extremely promising. I'm still in the middle of my analysis, but I'd be happy to summarize my findings from tonight and drop a copy by your office in the morning."

The lines around his mouth deepened. His eyes, staring hard, never blinked. Drawing himself up straight, he spoke in his best authoritative voice. "I have no intention of allowing you to remain at this university, let alone finish your *analysis*. You are immediately suspended, pending the results of an ad hoc committee that will consider your inappropriate behavior and recommend further action."

Waneta felt as if someone had punched her in the stomach. She had to fight for breath before she could speak. "On what grounds?"

"You know the reasons. Now hand over the crystal and surrender your university keys. If you refuse, I'll be forced to call university security and have you escorted off the premises."

He put out his hand and stepped toward her.

"No!"

She backed away, clutching the stone tightly. There must be some misunderstanding. Could he do this? She desperately tried to remember the rules and regulations from the faculty handbook, but the stone felt hot, distracting her, burning her palm.

Suddenly Dr. Bob stopped and pointed his umbrella at her. "My God, it's glowing!"

She looked down. The stone radiated between her fingers, sending out shafts of bright red.

"I think it's just a trick of the light," she said feebly, but even she did not believe it.

With each passing second, the crystal grew brighter—and warmer.

He smiled then, the light of the stone painting his cheeks in crimson. "Exquisite. I'm sure they'll be pleased."

"Who will be pleased? What are you talking about?"

Dr. Bob stepped forward at a deliberate pace and reached for the stone. "I must have it."

Waneta moved, putting the lab table between herself and her department head. He continued forward, his eyes focused on the crystal, its red light reflected in his dark eyes.

Only when he bumped into the table did he stop. He looked down and frowned, as if trying to figure out how the table had jumped in front of him.

Was he drunk? No. He blinked several times, shook his head slightly, and when he lifted his chin and looked at her, his eyes were clear. He seemed alert and under control, although still angry.

"I do not have time for this," he said and touched something inside his pocket. "I have an important meeting scheduled for tonight, and I'm already late. Come, give me the crystal."

Beckoning to her, he rounded the table. His steps were quick at first, but as his gaze drifted back down to the crystal, he stumbled and slowed until he was shuffling after her like an undead mummy from some old movie.

Waneta danced away. She considered running for the door, but that would simply substantiate the accusations against her. If she surrendered the crystal now, she could claim that the mixup from earlier in the day had been a simple misunderstanding. No ad hoc committee would fault her overmuch for not following procedure to Dr. Bob's exact standard. The claims of Jason and the other students would not be so easy to dismiss, but they were hardly insurmountable.

As she stopped, uncertain what to do, a dull roar rumbled menacingly over the building. Beakers rattled on the shelves and slow vibrations came through the floor and into her shoes, tickling the bottom of her feet.

At first, Waneta thought a jet was flying low over the city— a very rare sound in this age of portals—but then she recognized it as the deeper, more throaty bellow of a Taelon shuttle.

Dr. Bob lifted his face toward the ceiling, his eyes wide. He rushed to the window and pulled open the blinds as the bright lights of the shuttle descended slowly just outside the building.

The ship settled onto the top level of the parking garage, only a few hundred feet away.

"My God! They're after the stone!" He looked about him, as if searching desperately for help. "They can't be allowed to take it. I've got to stop them."

He ran from the room, leaving Waneta alone and confused. She walked to the window. Blinking against the bright lights trained on the building, she squinted at the shuttle across the small open space that separated Stadium Hall from the garage.

The shuttle had landed neatly between the tall light poles on the top level of the garage. Their illumination seemed insignificant next to the brilliance of the Taelon craft.

Two black-clad men in body armor and helmets, each carrying a long metal cylinder, hopped from the shuttle's side and ran several steps away. They stood up their cylinders about three steps apart, then ran to hide behind the barrier that circled the roof, taking up positions about ten yards apart. After a moment, they popped back up, their weapons resting on the white metal railing of the low wall. Their guns were trained at the building in Waneta's direction.

Waneta backed out of the light but continued to watch, fascinated as the cylinders behind the two men unfolded, rising up until they stood as circular objects about seven feet high. The devices flickered, flaring up repeatedly as more men portaled in carrying guns and wearing riot gear.

Volunteers.

Waneta shook her head, confused as more and more men poured from the flashing circle. Why would Volunteers be storming the university?

They split into teams of four and sprinted for the columns of the concrete roof that protected the stairs. One ran through a pool of overhead light and she saw his face: young, determined, with no hint of emotion or understanding.

She looked down at the crystal in her hand. It no longer glowed, and she tucked it safely into her pocket.

Could Dr. Bob be right? Had they come for the stone?

That seemed unlikely. They had no way to know it even existed. Besides, what would they want with an ancient Cherokee artifact?

A man in a business suit, flanked by several Volunteers, stepped from the shuttle and, bending low, ran to the wall. She saw him for only a few seconds but thought she recognized him from the Eli Hanson talk show. About a year ago, the show had featured an interview with the Taelon leader, Zo'or, but before they started that interview, they spoke to this man, Zo'or's Companion Protector. She could not recall his name, but if he was here . . .

Waneta thought back over the legend of the *Uktena*. Unlike the Aztecs and many other cultures, including ancient Christianity, the Cherokees did not normally sacrifice animals—or humans—to a greater power. That was one of the reasons the *Uktena* was unique in Cherokee mythology, but not the only reason.

The legend also talked of what would happen if the crystal were not given blood at the proper time: It would come out from its cave at night, like a blazing star, and fly through the air in search of the conjurer who owned it.

In all the Cherokee legends Waneta knew, if flight was mentioned, it involved an animal. For example, Cherokee witches could fly by turning themselves into owls or crows or even flying squirrels, but they did not fly around the mountains at night, and they certainly were never brightly lit and glowing.

Ancient Cherokees had not had electric lights. Their illumination at night came mostly from the moon, or the glowing bodies of gently moving lightning bugs. What little light the Cherokees made themselves came in the dancing form of flickering firelight. She doubted they could imagine anything as bright as a blazing star come to Earth, unless they had seen something that could only be described that way—such as the brightly glowing form of a shuttle.

Waneta considered the possibility. If true, it meant that the artifact was Taelon. The more she thought about it, the more sense it made.

But why the guns? Why so many men? Why not simply ask for the stone?

Just as she would have surrendered the crystal to the Eastern Band of Cherokees, she would have voluntarily given it to the Taelons.

Waneta flinched as the door burst open and a man in fatigues and army boots darted into the room. She thought he must be one of the soldiers—the Volunteers—but the difference in his clothing and his manner convinced her otherwise. He checked the hallway behind him, shut the door, then ran to her, staying low and avoiding the window.

"Get down!" he ordered, his voice suppressed but harsh.

When she did not move, he grabbed her wrist and pulled her to the floor with a sharp tug.

"Ow! What are you doing?"

"We've got to get out of here! Do you have the *Uluhsati*?"

"The what?"

"The stone! The one you took from the sanctuary? Do you have it with you?"

"Yes. It's in my pocket, but I don't—"

He hauled her to her feet and started to pull her roughly toward the door.

Waneta twisted her arm free and backed away, ending up beside the window again. "What are you doing? I'm not going anywhere. I've done nothing wrong."

The man shuffled toward her but stayed near the wall. "Listen," he said, looking into her eyes, "I don't have time to explain. Come with me, or you'll be dead within minutes."

She could see him better now. His long black hair was tied in a ponytail and tucked inside his collar. Camouflage paint on his face blurred his features, but she could tell he had high cheekbones and a short, wide nose. He looked distinctly Cherokee.

"I don't even know your name," she said.

He frowned. "I'm Gil. Gil Ledford."

She shrugged. His tone and mood became more formal, more distant. "Professor, please trust me. I'm here to help you."

She glanced down. A military gun and holster hung from his belt and a large knife protruded from a sheath strapped to his calf.

His head twisted toward the door, as if heeding a sound beyond Waneta's hearing. The look in his dark eyes changed, narrowing, reminding her of a wolf.

When he spoke, his voice lacked all emotion. "We're out of time. I need a decision. Now."

Waneta hesitated. She wanted a chance to think, to understand what was going on. Why should she run? She had no reason to fear the Taelons. While she had heard rumors about the Taelons, she assumed the rumors were merely stories spawned from ignorance and fear, like the ancient and silly superstitions her mother had come to believe before she died.

None of them were real.

Shouting came from outside the window. Waneta recognized Dr. Bob's voice but could not understand what he was saying. More voices joined the commotion, several rising in pitch—then Dr. Bob's voice again, excited, pleading—just before several loud percussions shook the window.

Waneta flinched at the blasts, then cringed as someone cried out in pain. She could not make out any words, just a mournful wail mixed with groans.

The Volunteers on the roof of the parking garage had their weapons pointed down toward the front of Stadium Hall. She raised her head, her eyes following their aim, and spotted Dr. Bob. He was on his knees, clutching his shoulder. Several more shots went off as the Volunteers opened fire with what she now saw were energy weapons.

Several blasts hit Dr. Bob in the chest, lighting up the front of his business suit in flashes of sparks and smoke.

She screamed and the Volunteers turned their weapons in

her direction. Just before they opened fire, Gil's arm circled her waist and jerked her to the floor. Explosions echoed around her as shots shattered the window and sprayed the room with broken glass.

Gil pulled her up, his hands tightly squeezing hers. "They're coming for you next."

Waneta was shaking, her shoulders trembling. She tried to control the reaction, but could not hold still. Dr. Bob had just died. She had seen him die, had seen his chest explode.

Dr. Robert Messmore. Calling him Dr. Bob now that he was dead seemed ridiculously petty and disrespectful.

She turned on the global attached to her belt and considered calling the police, but would they even come? Suddenly the silly rumors about the Taelons seemed all too real. That idea frightened her more than anything else that had happened. She had dismissed those rumors as easily as she had her mother's stories. To find out that the rumors might be true made her wonder about the stories, especially if the stone was Taelon.

Still trembling, she reached for the crystal in her pocket. While its surface remained warm to the touch, the stone was no longer hot. What had happened to trigger its earlier reaction? Anything might have activated it—a mental pattern, a physical presence . . . she had no idea how Taelon technology worked but wondered if the crystal's glowing meant it had sent out some kind of homing beacon allowing the Volunteers to locate it.

Gil's voice came again, low, under control. "Professor, please."

She looked at his face and saw kindness, but also cruelty. Would going with him be running away from danger—or toward it?

Angry shouts came from outside the window. Those men were coming to kill her—she knew it—whereas Gil could have killed her at any time and taken the stone. Instead, he had offered to help.

She nodded and pushed herself to her feet.

Staying low, Gil pulled her to the door of the lab. He hesitated for a moment, listening, then dragged her along the hallway to the far staircase. Still holding her hand, he led her down the steps, then shoved her around the corner on the first floor and pushed her flat against the wall, his body pressing hard against hers.

The cold of the wall's surface seeped through her shirt and chilled her back. "What—?"

His hand clamped tightly over her mouth and she felt his warm breath against her cheek. She squirmed, and his other hand tightened around her upper arm.

"Quiet!" he hissed.

Footsteps slapped against the stairs, then paused. Two footfalls continued up, but from the way Gil's body stiffened, she knew more men were waiting just steps away, perhaps communicating with hand signals before they struck.

Gil released her arm. Graceful as a ballet dancer, he lifted his knee and reached down to his ankle to retrieve the knife from the sheath on his leg. The long blade gleamed in the lights of the hall.

He spared a glance toward her. A look of hardness had settled in his eyes. His jaw was set and his brow low and menacing, but behind the cold edge, she noticed a hint of warmth, a deeply buried lining of compassion. He glanced away and swallowed, as if remembering another time and another place. He twirled the knife halfway around in his fingers and grabbed it again. His thumb pressed against the hilt, and a short needle popped out, a drop of liquid on its tip.

The hardness in his eyes returned as he rolled away from her and pressed his back against the wall.

Waneta could barely stand the tension of those next moments. She wanted to scream, to run, but instead she remained motionless, silent, a statue in a hall.

The end of a gun barrel poked around the corner before its owner pulled it back out of sight.

Gil's body tensed, like a cat about to spring.

What was he going to do? These people had energy weapons. All he had was a knife, which was turned the wrong way.

She could not allow him to get killed for her sake and reached for his shoulder—but it was too late.

A single pair of footsteps rushed forward.

Gil reacted by moving faster and more precisely than Waneta thought any human could.

Leading with his head and the hilt of the knife, he spun past the corner. After a lightning quick jab of the knife into the first Volunteer, he helicoptered flat against the floor and tripped the other Volunteer. The man's energy weapon clattered across the slick vinyl tiles as he sprawled on the floor.

Gil's momentum carried him into a rotating slide that brought him on top of the fallen Volunteer. Pressing his knee into the man's back, he jabbed the knife's hilt against the back of the man's neck.

The soldier pressed his hands against the floor and started to rise, then wavered and collapsed, his face shield striking the floor with a soft thunk.

Behind Gil, the other Volunteer was falling into the hall like a cut tree, one hand on his throat.

Waneta wanted to shout a warning, but Gil was already on the move. Kicking his legs underneath the falling body, he caught its full weight against his chest. Pointing his toes, he kept the man's rifle from hitting the floor by trapping it with his ankles.

Except for the clatter of that first energy weapon, Gil had silently disposed of both men in less than five seconds.

Waneta was shaking again, but Gil seemed unaffected. He pulled himself from beneath the man he had caught, then dragged the limp body around the corner and pushed it into an empty room.

Had he killed both men? What had been on the needle from his knife?

As the second Volunteer was pulled past, Waneta saw with relief that the man's chest was moving. The Volunteers were alive.

Gil placed one of the energy weapons with the fallen men, then retrieved the other and started down the hallway. "Come on!"

Waneta remained with her back against the wall, still shaking. She could not do this. She was a professor, not some kamikaze ninja. These people had guns, and they planned to use them.

Gil returned and stopped in front of her. She expected him to demand that she grow up and quit acting like a frightened child. Instead, he gently touched her cheek with the back of his hand. Surprisingly, his skin was smooth, reminding her of the softness she had seen in his eyes just before he flipped his knife around. This man could kill but had chosen not to.

"There will be more."

His words were simple but effective.

She quit shaking and followed Gil down the hall but could not keep her mind off Dr. Messmore, lying on the cold concrete outside the building. Except for her mother, who had lost her life one breath at a time over a period of months, she had never seen anyone die. For someone whose research fed on death, she found it ironic that her entire professional life had been based on theory.

It was one thing to examine a long-buried skull and coldly report that the owner had suffered a severe blow to the head by a blunt object. It was quite another to witness the sights and sounds of a violent end.

In a daze, she trailed after Gil. Later, she remembered those few minutes as a haphazard collection of halls and corners and steps, all leading to more of the same.

They ended up in a room she did not recognize. Above their heads, the concrete tiers of the stadium formed inverse stairs across the ceiling. It reminded her of an old movie her mother sometimes watched called *The Poseidon Adventure*. If the stadium turned upside down, they could come here and climb to the next level.

The thought was ludicrous and she fought a giggle. Perhaps she had gone into shock.

"Get ready," Gil told her, and raised the energy rifle to his left shoulder.

She started to ask, "For what?" but Gil distracted her by pulling a small, square box from his pocket. It had a single large button and a metal switch, which he flicked with his thumb. He lifted the box to his mouth, then pulled it away, the end of a telescoping antenna between his teeth.

When he saw her looking at him, he said, "Get in the corner. Shield your eyes."

She backed into the corner but continued to stare as he placed the index finger of his left hand against the trigger of the rifle and the thumb of his other hand atop the button on the box.

"Now!"

Waneta closed her eyes just as Gil pushed the button and pulled the trigger.

The low, whistling pop of the energy rifle was deafening in the small room, but as it died away, the echoes of low, distant thunder shook the walls.

Gil had triggered an explosion somewhere else in the building. No one could have heard the discharge from the energy weapon, which had carved a ragged hole in the concrete, revealing the stadium beyond.

Obviously Gil had come prepared. How was that possible? "Who are you?" she asked.

His answer was cut off by another explosion that almost shook Waneta from her feet.

"What are you trying to do? Blow up the whole stadium?"

"If necessary."

Gil pushed his way through the hole in the concrete, twisting his body around the glowing ends of mangled rebar that dangled like snakes across the opening.

He put his hand back through the hole and gestured for Waneta to join him.

She hesitated.

Beyond Gil, she could see the seats of the stadium. Like Alice gazing into the rabbit hole, she had a decision to make. If she stepped through into Wonderland, her life would change forever.

She could stay here. Maybe she could surrender the stone to the Taelons. What did the authorities have against her? Breaking a few university regulations? Being kidnapped at knifepoint by a man she did not know?

Her fingers touched the stone in her pocket. It was hard to believe that this little rock had caused so many problems.

The rumbling boom of another explosion shook the building. She smelled smoke. Would any of Stadium Hall be left by morning?

Distant shouts and screams reached her. The sounds reminded her of Dr. Messmore. She saw him again on his knees as black-clad Volunteers gunned him to silence.

They had killed him without hesitation. They had tried to kill her—and would go on trying.

Gil had not spoken, as if he recognized the importance of this decision. He simply stretched out his hand a bit farther, making it easier to grasp.

She took it.

The feel of his warm, smooth fingers sent a tingle up her arm.

Carefully she crawled through the hole, then followed Gil as he ran down the rows of the stadium toward a distant exit.

SEVENTEEN

What have you got?" Liam asked as he walked through the entrance to Augur's underground lair.

Augur, wearing a dark blue turtleneck with white guernsey-cow splotches, looked up from one of the computer screens. "What? No hello? No chitchat?"

Liam walked to the espresso machine, removed one of the coffee baskets, and dumped the used grounds into the trash. "Don't you ever clean this thing?"

"I've been busy, remember?"

"Yes, but have you been productive?"

Irritation crept into Augur's voice. "More than you."

After twisting a quadruple amount of fresh coffee into the basket, Liam reattached it to the machine, then hit the button to start the brewing process. When the hissing stopped, he divided the coffee into two cups and carried them across the room.

"Sorry. I'm just frustrated." Liam handed one of the cups to Augur. "The boy and his mother left town yesterday afternoon. Nobody knows where they went."

Augur did not ask which boy. "I'm not surprised. Those two have a habit of disappearing. What about Da'an?"

Liam shook his head. "He claims the boy had nothing to do with what happened yesterday, but I'm sure he's hiding something."

"You may be right. That kid has his father's eyes—and from what I've discovered, it doesn't look like his father's human."

Augur set his coffee down beside his keyboard and started tapping out commands.

Liam settled onto a stool next to Augur. Already his frustration was draining away. He had always felt at home here, even more so than in his own apartment. It was the only spot in the world where he felt truly safe, truly accepted.

Not that this place would look like much to an outsider. Except for the loft and the bathroom, the whole living area consisted of one big room hewn out of the surrounding rock. On one side of the cavern, a couch and some chairs huddled around an oval coffee table the way one might see a living room set on display in a furniture showroom. On the other side, Augur's lab equipment sprang up from the floor in no discernable pattern, allowing Augur to move from machine to machine the way a bee flits between flowers.

"First things first," Augur said. "I backtracked the boy and his mother to a little town called Kilnunry, in Ireland."

A map of Ireland, its major cities and rivers marked, appeared on one of the computer screens. As Augur spoke, the map enlarged, the point of view closing in on Limerick and Clare counties in the southwestern hill country. Its focus tightened on the area surrounding the Shannon River, then finally zeroed in on the town of Kilnunry.

Augur tapped the screen with his finger. "Seems the mother, Triss, was born and raised here. It's where she gave birth to a bouncing baby boy, which is where the weirdness comes in."

The map on the monitor was replaced by a picture of a newborn baby with a full head of bright red hair.

"I found this picture in the hospital's records. Daniel Shaunessy when he was just two days old."

"Cute baby."

"Yes," Augur agreed, "but not for long."

Slowly, the image changed. The head and nose lengthened. The hair gradually thickened and the baby fat dropped away.

Augur spoke while the morphing took place. "According to official records, Triss Shaunessy has exactly one child, a baby boy named Daniel, who was born just over a year ago."

"A year? You sure?"

Augur rolled his eyes.

"Right," Liam said. "Is it possible that the boy with her now is an imposter? Somebody else's child posing as hers?"

"I asked myself the same question, so I decided to do a little magic. I took the picture of Daniel Shaunessy and had the computer age it. I don't know about you, but I'd say we got a match."

The picture on the monitor stopped changing. It showed a boy, aged seven years, the same boy Liam had seen at the theater the day before—except for the eyes. The imaging process had failed to capture their energy or their determination.

Liam sipped his coffee, then set the cup down next to the monitor. "This confirms what the stage manager at the theater told me. He said Daniel had been with the dancing troupe only about three months but looked as if he had aged two to three years. Do you have anything else on the boy?"

"Isn't that enough?" Before Liam could respond, Augur said, "No, I don't have anything more on the boy. No records of immunizations, no school information, no more pictures—nothing. The mother's even worse. For her, I have no pictures at all, not even a passport photo, which means she and the boy are traveling on fake papers. I have her last known address in Kilnunry but not much else. Once she finished school, it's like she vanished off the planet until Daniel was born."

"Are you saying she lived for a while on the mother ship?"

"No. I'm not saying anything, except that I wasted most of a day on this instead of working for my client, and I don't know much more now than I did when I started. This woman's almost as secretive as I am."

"Even if we ignore the eyes," Liam said, thinking out loud, "we know that Daniel's growing too fast to be completely human. That means the Taelons are probably involved. It also means there's a good chance Da'an knows exactly what's going on."

"He might," Augur agreed and stood up, "but I guarantee he's not going to tell you."

"That's why I need to go there myself."

"Go where? Ireland?"

"Sure. To Kilnunry. I haven't been home for a while."

"Since when do you consider Kilnunry home?"

"All Ireland's home."

"Yes, and it's all four in the morning over there."

"It won't be by the time I arrive." Liam closed his eyes momentarily, seeing again the map of Ireland that had been on the computer monitor. "I can take the portal to Cork, but from there I'll need to drive to Kilnunry. Da'an told me not to take the shuttle anywhere for the next couple of days."

"Why?"

Liam did his best impersonation of Da'an. "It is a Taelon shuttle. That is all you need know."

Augur shook his head. "Da'an's up to something, and I've got a feeling our boy here's part of it."

Liam grinned. "Our boy?"

"Hey, you got me started on this."

"Yes, and now I'm getting you out of it."

Liam retrieved his cup and set it beside the espresso machine, then cruised over and snatched some grapes and a piece of cheese from the plate on the coffee table.

"Supper," Liam explained.

Augur frowned. "You come in here, you drink my coffee, you eat my food—now you'll get yourself in trouble, then expect me to get you out of it." He tapped a finger to his chin. "Now, let's see. What is it you're paying me again?"

"Whatever it is, I'll double it."

Augur followed Liam toward the door. "Nothing. You're paying me nothing, so don't get in any trouble you can't get out of by yourself. I've got work to do."

"Don't worry," Liam said around a mouthful of cheese. "Go back to increasing your income."

"I will." Augur returned to the computer monitor, but when Liam reached the door, he added, "Be careful."

Liam grinned. "I always am."

He finished the rest of the cheese and the grapes on his way to the portal station.

EIGHTEEN

The bleached-blond reporter stared into the camera with mock intensity. In the background, beyond a crisscross of sooty white superstructure, smoke poured from the windows of a five-story building. Firefighters in heavy slickers and traditional hats directed streams of water from two hoses into one of the windows.

"At eight forty-five P.M.," the reporter began, "multiple explosions rocked Neyland Stadium on the University of Tennessee campus. The blasts were centered in the building you see behind me, aptly named Stadium Hall, which sits below the upper bleachers on the south side of the stadium. So far, at least one death has been reported, but no name has been released."

The picture changed to a glassy-eyed girl, probably nineteen or twenty. She stared into the darkness, the flicker of reflected flames on her face.

The blond reporter shoved a microphone toward her. "What were your thoughts when you first heard the explosions?"

The girl continued to stare into the night until the reporter brought the microphone just under nose, then she jerked her head with a slight start and looked straight into the camera.

"My friend Alicia and I—we were coming back from our test when we heard this loud boom."

The girl had a strong southern accent. She drew out the word *boom* until she sounded like a cow.

"That noise was louder than anything I've ever heard. I didn't know what was going on. Then it did it again—and again—and we saw smoke coming out over on the other end of the stadium. That's when we called the police." She said police as if it were two words: *poe-leece*.

The screen switched back to the blond reporter, still holding the microphone. Even though the night was warm, she had on a heavy dark coat, which went well with her red blouse. Its cowl collar gave her neck a more slender look, and a tasteful silver necklace glittered in the bright camera lights.

"Authorities have refused to speculate on the source of the multiple blasts heard by witnesses in the area, but several sources agree the most likely cause was a rupture to a gas pipeline running under the stadium."

Right. And those sources were the cameraman and the producer.

Renée turned away from the TV. She was not familiar with the UT campus, but she assumed they had a local steam plant that supplied both hot water and heat to university buildings. If so, it was unlikely that any natural gas pipelines were anywhere near the stadium.

Not that it mattered. The explosions were no accident—of that much, she was certain—but why would Gil blow up the place? And where were Dr. Long and Dr. Messmore? Had they died in the blast?

If Gil killed either one of those people, she would never forgive herself. Again, she wished she had not hired him to retrieve the crystal. The way he reacted when she told him about the stone, it was impossible to say what he might have done.

Even so, she smelled the Taelons in all of this. Where was Ronny this evening? She doubted he was sitting up in the mother ship, oppressing the usual masses.

Renée fanned the cigarette smoke away from her face. She had taken a booth as far from everyone as she could, but even so, the fumes were giving her a headache.

This bar had been a popular Underground hangout in the

early days, just as the Flat Planet Café had later become, but it was much seedier than she remembered. They considered it customer service if they gave someone a drink in a clean glass. When she asked for some wine, the bartender pointed out, "You're in luck, honey. We have both kinds tonight: red and white."

Her global chimed and she dug it out of her small purse. Perhaps Gil was finally calling.

"Oh, it's you," she said when she saw Joshua Doors' face on the small display.

"I expect a better greeting than that from my number one employee."

"Sorry. I was hoping to hear from Dr. Messmore."

She had not told Joshua about Gil, did not want to tell him.

"You have the crystal, don't you?"

"No."

"Christ, Renée. We don't have time for delays on this."

She ignored that comment. Joshua said that about every deadline on every project, then often sat on the results for weeks before sending them on to the next phase.

"I'm working on it," she said, "but there's been . . . an accident on campus, in the building where Dr. Messmore works. Apparently there was a series of explosions and a large fire."

"Is Dr. Messmore all right?"

Renée ground her teeth before she answered. "I don't know. As I said before, I was hoping you were Dr. Messmore. He might try to call at any moment."

Sometimes she missed the old-style telephones from when she was a teenager. In those days, if she wanted to quit talking to someone, she simply claimed she was expecting an important call. Globals—and old telephones with call waiting—had ruined that.

Joshua scowled. "What do you plan to do about this? I want Dr. Messmore found immediately."

"Just a moment," Renée said and put Joshua on hold.

The reporter had come back on the TV and was making an

introduction. Beside her stood a Volunteer commander, strongly handsome, his helmet tucked neatly under his arm.

Renée gave the television a slight nod. Just as she suspected, the Taelons were involved. That meant Zo'or and Ronny were in on it, too.

When the reporter quit babbling, the man looked into the camera. He had a kind face, compassionate yet serious, like a Mountie from an old movie. Renée guessed he had never seen combat. Most likely, his only job was doing what he was about to do now: lie to the press.

"Earlier this evening, a squad of Volunteers attempted to arrest a suspected member of the Resistance outside Stadium Hall. When the suspect opened fire with an energy weapon, the Volunteers returned fire, neutralizing the threat. No Volunteers were injured, but the suspect was mortally wounded in the exchange."

Although the commander spoke with variety and emphasis in his voice, his practiced delivery failed to hide the fact that his lines were memorized.

"At this time, I have been authorized to release the suspect's name: Dr. Robert Messmore."

Renée gasped and put a hand over her mouth. Ronny had ordered Dr. Messmore killed. Why? Had the department head recognized that the crystal was Taelon and tried to sell it to the highest bidder? If so, he would forever regret that decision.

The reporter pulled back the microphone just long enough to ask her question. "Besides being a member of the Resistance, can you tell us what crime Dr. Messmore committed?"

Good. The reporter recognized that people were not shot just for being in the Resistance.

The image zoomed onto the face of the commander. "I can't comment about ongoing investigations, but we believe that Dr. Messmore was the leader of an Underground cell in this area. Our surveillance indicated he was using university facilities to manufacture a highly dangerous explosive and was planning an attack on a Taelon. It remains unclear whether the damage to the stadium was intentional or a by-product of Dr. Messmore's ineptitude."

So much for not commenting about an ongoing investigation.

The reporter started to ask another question, but the commander cut her off.

"That is all," he said, dismissing her as if she were under his command. He pivoted precisely and strutted off camera.

Go after him, Renée silently urged the woman. Push him for details.

Instead, the reporter faced the camera and started her wrap-up. "There, you have it, Jim. This has been . . ."

Renée shook her head, then reactivated her global. "Sorry to cut you off, but the local news just reported that a group of Volunteers shot and killed Dr. Messmore earlier this evening. They're claiming he was a member of the Resistance."

"Was he?"

"Of course not."

"You should have moved more quickly, Renée. That's why I called last night, so this wouldn't happen."

Already he was trying to assign blame. "I couldn't move more quickly," Renée said, glaring into the global. "I left specific instructions for him to contact me as soon as he obtained the stone. I never heard from him, so either he failed to get it, or he was holding out on us."

"How likely is that?"

"That he was holding out on us? I'd say fifty-fifty. That's why I brought in help."

"What do you mean? I never approved anyone else's involvement on this project."

"He was from outside the organization."

"That's supposed to make me feel better about it?"

"I needed help, Joshua. Dr. Messmore was making noises. He wanted to be difficult, possibly ransom the stone to the highest bidder. I couldn't allow that, but I was too far away to get here in time."

Joshua nodded. "Of course. Sorry. I trust your judgment completely. You know that. Whom did you get?"

"An ex-member of the Resistance."

"What? Are you nuts? It's hard enough keeping the current members from pulling stupid stunts without grabbing someone who quit. What makes you think you can trust this guy?"

"He hates the Taelons. He'll do anything to see them leave the planet."

That had once been true for Gil, but Renée did not know him anymore. She couldn't tell Joshua that, especially not now.

"Where is he?"

Renée sighed and looked away from the global. An unshaven slob at the bar was staring at her. In your dreams, she thought, and turned back to the display.

"I don't know where he is, Joshua. He was supposed to meet me here. Perhaps he was taken prisoner by the Taelons. That's why I want to bring Liam in on this."

"Liam? No."

"We don't have much choice. We need to find out whether this guy was taken to the mother ship. Liam's the only one who can do that for us."

"Absolutely not, Renée. I won't have Liam involved in any way. Don't even talk to him. Don't worry, I'll find out if this guy is being held on the mother ship."

"How will you do that?"

"Leave that to me. Just tell me his name."

Renée glanced at the bar. The man was still leering at her. She crossed her legs, squeezing her thighs together, and wished she had worn jeans instead of a skirt.

"The man's name is Gil Ledford, but I don't understand why you won't let me bring Liam in on this."

"You've already jeopardized this operation by opening it up to someone from the outside. It's imperative we keep the rest of it in-house."

"Why? We can trust Liam."

Joshua said nothing. She hated it when he did this. She

would have much rather discussed the point—at least been able to make her case before he refused her request.

She tried again. "If we're going to keep this operation entirely in-house, I think it's time you told me more about this crystal. What is it? And why have we gone to such lengths to obtain it?"

Joshua still said nothing.

"If you expect me to do my job effectively, I need to know what's going on."

Anger flared in Joshua's voice. "You understand security better than anyone. You know how important it is to restrict information to a need-to-know basis."

"I need to know."

"No, you don't. What you need is to find that crystal and return it to D.C. as soon as possible. This operation is already behind schedule. I don't intend to have it slip any farther."

"Whatever you say."

"That's right, Renée. Whatever *I* say. Don't forget. You may have worked for my father, but now you work for me. Either you do as you're told, or you'll force me to make some adjustments. Is that clear?"

Renée looked away from the global. The cigarette smoke seemed to be getting thicker. As soon as this conversation was over, she would go find some place where she could breathe. She had waited for Gil long enough. He was not going to show, which meant she needed to figure out where he might have gone.

"I asked you a question," Joshua said.

Renée nodded. "Yes, Joshua, you're in charge."

Saying the words made her feel like a slave. She hated working for someone with an inferiority complex, especially now that Jonathan Doors was dead, which meant that Joshua would never get the affirmation he needed.

Joshua smiled kindly at her. "You know I don't like reminding you of that any more than you like hearing it. It's just that sometimes you forget you don't have all the facts. Believe me, there are reasons for what I do. I don't want anybody working on this project whom I can't trust completely—and Renée, I trust you."

She nodded and closed the global.

"Like hell you do," she said softly and got up to leave.

The man at the bar caught her by the wrist as she passed. She thought about driving her palm into his face. It would be fun breaking his nose, but she could not afford trouble now.

"Hey, honey," he said, "how about a drink?"

She leaned close to his ear and whispered, "Just so you know, I used to be a man."

When she pulled away, she asked in a husky voice, "So, you still want to buy me that drink?"

He stared at her, his gaze traveling down her body to her feet, then back up until it focused on her crotch.

She gave him her best smile. "No. I didn't think so."

As she walked out of the bar, she made sure to put an extra sway in her hips, certain he would be staring at her ass.

For once, she enjoyed it.

NINETEEN

Zo'or still tingled with the power. He had felt it again—as briefly as before—disagreeable, yet distinctly pleasurable in a way he did not want to admit. It had already become familiar, expected, and he longed for it terribly when it was gone.

He must have it.

That was the only thought that stayed in his mind. Even when Agent Sandoval contacted him with news that the crystal was missing and the human archaeologist had escaped, all he felt was rage.

The power. She had taken the power.

He blindly approved Agent Sandoval's actions, an extremely dangerous precedent, but what had been planned as a simple detainment had become a nightmare. Although he had listened to Agent Sandoval's report, he could not concentrate on what he heard, could not apply basic problem-solving skills to the situation. After the conversation, he had retired to his private chambers. He needed time to meditate, to recover from the powerful sensations he had felt, but the duties of state would not let him be.

A tickle at the back of his mind alerted him to a top priority message coming in from the planet below. Da'an wanted to speak with him.

He could refuse the communication request, but that would likely bring Da'an to the mother ship again. He could not risk that, not now, not when he was so close. If Agent Sandoval located the woman again—or if Zo'or felt the power reawaken—he might need to act at once, and he could not have Da'an around asking him questions.

Zo'or walked to the communication console and waved his arm to activate the signal.

When the image of Da'an materialized, the North American Companion was moving his hands in a gesture of outrage. "I see that your connection to the Commonality remains intact. From your most recent actions, I feared you had become an Atavus and were lost to us forever."

Zo'or's fingers twitched nervously and he did his best to quiet them. "I do not know the meaning of your comment. You have interrupted my meditation. Why?"

"It is you who have interrupted me. News agencies around the world are demanding to know why a group of Volunteers attacked and killed a man at the University of Tennessee."

"The death of a human does not concern me."

"The death of a single human may not, but the death of the planet will. You have interfered with my ability to warn our race. You have tried to confront the creature yourself. You are acting irresponsibly and selfishly—in all ways violating the purpose and the power of the Commonality."

Zo'or made the sign for deep curiosity. "Creature?"

He had detected sentience in the power but did not want Da'an to know how much he understood. At the same time, he hoped his parent would reveal more.

"Your veil of ignorance cannot hide your actions. This time, you have reached beyond your grasp. How fortunate that you did not encounter the power as you wished. You would not have survived."

Zo'or could not control the tone of his voice, which rose in anger. "Your words are controlled by your fear, the same fear that has always blinded you to the potential of possibilities. You are like the others: petrified by risk, by your unwillingness to act without knowledge of the outcome."

"It is our caution that has protected our race for millions of years."

"It is our caution that will destroy us."

Zo'or and Da'an glared at each other, each certain he was correct, neither willing to consider the points the other wanted to make. Zo'or knew this but could not change the way he felt.

At last, Da'an spoke. "The Synod must know of the danger. You will no longer prevent me from communicating with them."

"That matter is already settled. A meeting of the Synod will not be called until you disclose all you know about the power. I have made my decision."

"The time has come for you to reconsider."

Zo'or peered keenly at the holographic image. Da'an appeared calm, and his fingers moved with the gentle motions of determined insistence. The time Zo'or had been expecting had come. Da'an would not back away from this challenge.

Raising his hands, Zo'or mimicked Da'an's gestures. "I will use my powers as Synod leader to block your call for a meeting."

"That will be difficult since I will not call the meeting. You will."

Zo'or's hands went still. "Explain yourself."

"The Synod will never stand for your actions. Twice you denied my petition for a meeting, perhaps extending your powers beyond what you have been granted—but now you have removed all room for doubt. You ordered the execution of an innocent human. Your Volunteers set fire to a public building."

"No. We had no part in that."

"Given your other actions, I doubt the Synod will believe you."

"They are a bunch of closed-minded antiques who are linked so tightly to the past they cannot see the future. I should be given autonomous authority over this planet, because I alone am unafraid to act. Instead, we tread lightly around the humans, squandering the resources available to us and wasting time. The Jaridians will be here soon. I, for one, am tired of fleeing before them."

Zo'or's fingers danced in frustrated rage. Da'an's hands dropped quietly to his sides.

"Call a meeting of the Synod."

Zo'or struggled to concentrate. The power. He must have the power. He would have it—and when he did, his will would prevail in all matters.

"If the meeting is called," he said, forcing his fingers to mock a sense of calm, "you will be forced to explain your actions. You will need to state why you kept information vital to the safety of our race from the leader of the Synod."

"I am prepared to do so. Are you prepared to justify your attack on the humans and your repeated refusals of my earlier calls for a meeting? If so, I would suffer some, but your loss of political prestige would be irrecoverable. Either way, we will have a meeting of the Synod and all will be revealed. What do you wish to do?"

Zo'or could no longer control his hands, and they gestured in violent rage. In increments, he managed to lessen their activity, working them into slower and slower movements until they signaled nothing beyond confident authority.

"I will call the meeting."

Da'an drew the elegant figure for contentment. "That is all I have asked."

TWENTY

As Gil's old Buick wound its way down the mountain toward Cherokee, North Carolina, Waneta looked out at the night and tried to gauge whether she would survive if she opened the door and threw herself out.

"Please let me go. I swear I won't tell anyone you were at the university. For all anyone needs to know, I escaped by myself."

She had asked Gil to be let off at her apartment after they left the university in his car. Gil refused, claiming that the Volunteers would be there waiting for her. She then tried to convince him to take her by a friend's house in Oak City, and later, begged him to drop her off at a motel as they passed through Pigeon Forge.

If she had known he would refuse the motel request, she might have jumped out at one of the stoplights and tried to lose herself among the escapees from Dollywood. She doubted he could have hit her with his knife at more than a few paces, and he had left the energy rifle tucked under a seat at Neyland Stadium—not a good thing for a rabid Vols fan to find just before the big Florida game.

Unfortunately, he still had his pistol. Tucked in a holster at his left hip, it remained within easy reach.

"You have no reason to fear me," Gil said. "I'm on your side."

He spoke the words with such sincerity, such absolute con-

viction, that Waneta wanted to believe they were true, but
although he had said little on their ninety-minute drive over
the mountains, she knew he was capable of killing. It showed in
everything he did, standing out in stark contrast to the tender-
ness in his eyes when he looked at her. She did not understand
him, and that frightened her most of all.

Gil pulled a pack of cigarettes from the breast pocket of his
fatigues and shook one loose with a practiced hand. Pinching
the cigarette between his lips, he pulled it free and lit it in one
fluid motion.

"I wish you wouldn't smoke," she said.

"You and everybody else. I get so sick and tired of all the
damned do-gooders trying to take away what is rightfully mine.
Tobacco is holy. For as long as anyone can remember, we have
used it in almost every ceremony, from war plans to peace
councils, for confirming trade or establishing a good hunt, for
driving off evil spirits and healing our sick or injured."

He looked at her coldly. "Don't tell me not to smoke.
Tobacco is sacred."

"Yes," she agreed in her best professorial voice, "tobacco
has always been sacred for the Cherokees. But they smoked the
old, wild tobacco, not the stuff Philip Morris puts out. Also,
they smoked it in pipes or threw it directly on their fires, never
rolled it into cigarettes and cigars or chewed it directly—those
habits they learned from the early Europeans. Most of all, they
never smoked tobacco for pleasure alone, which they considered sacrilege. So tell me. What sacred ceremony are you conducting now?"

Gil's mouth dropped open. After staring a moment, he
closed it, then looked at the cigarette as if he had never seen it
before. Carefully, he crushed it out in the ashtray.

His gaze returned to the road, his face unreadable. "She said
you would remind me of the old ways. I never believed her."

"Never believed who?"

"You will see her again soon enough."

Waneta shook her head. Whom was he talking about?

But she did not want to think about that now. Instead, she dreamed of food. She had not eaten since her lunch with Jill, and even then, all she had was a salad. Not that she had wanted a salad, but whenever she went out with other women, she always felt embarrassed about getting a lot to eat, especially when so many of them, all heavier than her, were counting calories. Now she wished she had ignored the peer pressure and scarfed down a greasy hamburger topped with lots of onions along with a large side of french fries.

Suddenly her global rang, the sound shrill and unexpected.

Waneta pulled it from her belt and opened it. She was surprised to see the Companion Protector, the one who had been on top of the parking garage earlier that evening.

"Dr. Long, my name is Agent Sandoval. I'm calling to inform you that earlier this evening a burglary occurred in your office at the university. Also, there's been—"

Waneta let out a cry of alarm as Gil ripped the global from her hands and thrust it out the driver's side window. She caught a few words such as "fire" and "explosions" as Gil lifted the machine up high, then slammed it down into the middle of the highway.

The global burst apart with a loud pop. Waneta looked out the back window. Bits and pieces of the shattered machine rolled and scattered along the roadway.

"What the hell are you doing? That was my global, you idiot!"

Gil's voice remained completely calm as he rolled the window back up. "All the newer globals have a built-in GPS that can be triggered by the authorities as soon as you answer a call. You just told the Taelons exactly where we are."

"So? Didn't you hear him? He was calling to tell me my office had been broken into. Maybe he doesn't even know I was at the university tonight. I think all he wants is the crystal. If I gave it to him—"

"You'd be dead."

"How can you say that? Maybe tonight was just some big

mixup. Dr. Messmore kept talking about how *they* would be pleased and how *they* were expecting him. Perhaps he was selling the stone to some black market dealing in Taelon artifacts. Maybe the Volunteers came to the university to break up that smuggling ring and Agent Sandoval was contacting me because he was the one who discovered my office in shambles."

"Agent Sandoval doesn't call anyone to be nice. If he contacts you, he has his own reasons, none of them good. He works for the Taelons, and the Taelons are interested in only one thing: themselves. They're the lowest form of life in the universe."

At UT, political correctness was a way of life. It had been a long time since Waneta had been around anyone who expressed ideas like Gil's in such an open manner.

"That's a very racist thing to say. Not all Taelons are bad just like not all Cherokees kidnap archaeology professors in the middle of the night."

"Kidnap? Is that what you think I've done?"

"Isn't it?"

"No!" He sounded indignant.

"Then why won't you let me go? Why not let me off somewhere?"

He wrinkled his brow and tilted his head, as if fighting an internal battle. "I have to bring you to the mountain. You won't be safe anywhere else."

She resisted the urge to ask which mountain. "Why? What's so special about the place you're bringing me?"

He focused on her, and for the briefest instant, all the road noise seemed to fade away. "Because if you leave there, you will die."

She shivered and folded her arms across her chest. "I don't know why you'd say that."

His eyes were watching the road again. "Because you're naive, Professor. You don't even recognize the danger. The Taelons will stop at nothing to dominate this planet. They've killed thousands of people and made thousands more into mindless slaves. You think those Volunteers from earlier tonight cared whether you lived or died? You think they cared that they gunned down that boss of yours?"

She thought of the face she had seen as it passed beneath the lights of the parking garage. It revealed no intelligence, no emotion. Then she thought of Dr. Messmore, his chest grilled like hamburger. She shuddered. That could have been her. If Gil had not pulled her away from the window when he did . . .

He took a deep breath, then laid a soft hand against hers. "If they find you, they will kill you."

"You don't know that. You can't."

He shook his head. "I can know that. I do. They will take you to the mother ship for questioning, and no one will ever see you again."

"No, you're wrong." She pulled her hand away. "How can you know what they'll do? What makes you so god-awful smart?"

"Because I've seen people die on orders from the Taelons. People I cared about, people who deserved better."

He shut his eyes tightly, and the softest of groans escaped his lips. When he looked at the road again, the hint of a tear formed along the corner of his right eye. "I'm not going to lose you, too."

You can't lose what you don't have. Waneta almost said the words aloud but was glad she kept them to herself. They seemed overly cruel and heartless next to the pain on his face.

Gil turned off Highway 441 and onto the Blue Ridge Parkway. Waneta felt for the stone in her pocket. It was still there, still slightly warm.

"You're taking me back to the dig," she said. "Why? I thought we were going to Cherokee."

"Dig?" Gil scowled, then raised his eyebrows and nodded. "Oh, right. The sanctuary. I'm not taking you there—that's your destiny, not mine. I'm taking you to my great-grandfather's cabin. No one's lived in it for years. We'll be safe there—until *Uluhsati* decides otherwise."

Waneta nodded, but as the car started its climb up Rattlesnake Mountain, she studied the quickly passing trees. She could not jump out, not yet, but she needed to get away from this man. He acted like he knew her. Even creepier, he called the crystal *Uluhsati* and talked about it as if it were alive. Her mother had told her stories of old-fashioned Cherokees who were this nutty, but Waneta had never before met one.

"What part do you play in all this?" she asked. The twisting roads were making her nauseous. "Why should I trust you? Maybe you're no better than the Taelons."

"I'm the *only* one you can trust. Unlike everyone else, all I care about is taking care of you."

"Why? Who am I to you?"

The pain came into Gil's eyes again, but he did not answer.

Waneta tried a different approach. "Who told you I was at the university? How did you know where to find me?"

She expected him to say the God of Thunder, what many Cherokees called the Red Man, or perhaps his sons, the Thunder boys.

He spoke hesitantly. "I have . . . a friend in the Resistance."

"You're doing this for the Resistance?"

Waneta was surprised at the anger in her voice. If the Taelons were interested in the crystal, it only made sense that the Resistance would be, too, but she assumed Gil had rescued her on his own initiative. To find out he was under orders bothered her a great deal, though she could not say why.

"No," Gil said. "I was supposed to find *Uluhsati* and deliver it to a woman named Renée Palmer, an executive at Doors International. She also works in the Resistance."

Waneta nodded. She had seen the woman on TV.

Gil's voice grew angry. "Giving it to the whites is no better than giving it to the Taelons. None of them understand the danger."

"And you do?"

"No." He grinned. "You do."

As Waneta struggled to make sense of what he said, he

killed the car lights, then turned off the Blue Ridge Parkway and onto the road leading to the dig site.

"Why are we going this way?" she asked. "I thought we were headed to some cabin."

"We are."

"But it can't be this way. This is all government land."

"It's Cherokee land," he said sternly. "It's always been Cherokee land. It always will be."

Waneta raised her hands and rolled her eyes but decided saying more was not worth the argument.

The full moon provided enough light to drive, but the road was rough and the car slowed to a crawl. She felt for the door handle but could not bring herself to jump out. In the city, she might have had a chance, but here she was miles from any town, surrounded by dark trees and unknown terrain. She hated to admit it, but being alone in the mountains at night scared her as much as being alone with Gil.

Still, this would be her best chance. If only she could force herself to pull the handle.

Suddenly Gil stopped the car and shut off the motor.

"A few friends and my cousins use the cabin when they come up here to hunt, but it's not safe for anyone to know you're here—not even them."

He opened the door and got out. "Stay here. I'll check the cabin and be right back."

The keys were still in the ignition. Waneta knew some people who took their keys out of the car when they pumped gas. Others never took them out, daring thieves to help them collect the insurance money.

Considering how old this car was, it seemed likely Gil was one of the latter. Perhaps he would forget out of habit.

He shut the door with a soft click, then labored a few steps up the road and veered left into the trees. Even after he disappeared, she waited. This had to be some kind of trap. Why would he drag her all the way here, then set her free just as they reached their destination?

She did not wait around to figure it out. After scooting across the seat, she took one last glance around for Gil, then started the car and pulled the gearshift into reverse. Twisting in the seat, she stared back over her shoulder. Though the head-lights were off, the backup lights came on. The silver and brown of the gravel road showed up well against the dark shadows that marked the edges of the trees.

The transmission whined as the car picked up speed. She bounced around in the seat, fighting to keep hold of the steering wheel. As narrow as this road was, she would not be able to turn around until she reached the Blue Ridge Parkway.

Suddenly someone stepped from the trees and onto the road, blocking her path. Waneta hit the brakes, the tires scraping against gravel. It was the old woman from the dig site, the one she thought she had seen in her patio window last night—her great-grandmother.

No, that was not right. This was just an old woman who resembled her great-grandmother.

Waneta glanced in the mirror again, but the figure was gone. She turned around, then jumped as the woman stepped close to her driver's side window.

Waneta almost drove away then, but she had to see, she had to know. She rolled down the window and peered out.

The dashboard lights cast a strange illumination across the old woman's weathered face. "You can no longer run from your destiny, young one."

"Excuse me?"

The woman looked remarkably like the picture of Waneta's great-grandmother. The two must have been related, perhaps cousins, or half sisters. Waneta knew so little about her family.

"You must trust young Gil," the old woman continued. "He means you no harm. He is willing to give his life for yours."

Gil had mentioned his great-grandfather—could this be his grandmother? In the old days, many family members settled within walking distance of each other. But even if the old woman lived in close proximity to the cabin, Waneta found it odd that Gil had taken her into his confidence, especially since he was being so careful about his friends and other family.

Waneta pulled the knob for the car's headlights. Their glow bathed the road in light. If Gil came running toward the car, she wanted to see him while he was still far enough away for her to escape.

"I'm sure Gil means well, but I can't stay out here in the woods. I have classes to teach. I have responsibilities."

Even as Waneta said the words, she wondered if they were true. She thought of Dr. Bob and of the Volunteers in black charging out the portal.

"If you leave now, you will die."

The phrase was so close to what Gil had said, Waneta started.

"Wh-what?"

"This is your home, *Sgilisi*. You belong to this mountain."

"No, don't say that."

Waneta swallowed and shook her head, then pulled away from the window. *You belong to this mountain.* How could this old woman keep repeating what other people had said? Her mother had used almost exactly the same words shortly before she died.

Thinking back with the clarity of hindsight, that time seemed so strange. Through the many long months of her illness, Waneta's mother had grown physically worse day by day, but in an odd juxtaposition, her mental health had sharpened considerably. She recalled the tiniest details of what the doctors told her, remembered to take every pill, and was ready for every appointment before it was time to leave. But even as her memory grew more acute, her sanity faded in and out. More than just taking a sudden interest in the fantasy stories of her youth, she also started talking to other people when no one else was in the room. She saw snakes everywhere and talked incessantly of the mountains.

But of all the hours and all the days Waneta spent by her mother's side, one afternoon stood out above the others.

It had happened near the end, the last time her mother was in the hospital.

The sterilized white walls seemed to descend on Waneta again, and she saw her mother's water cup, the straw bent, the condensation collecting around its base and pooling on the adjustable bedside table.

Waneta had gone days with little sleep, and sitting in the chair beside the bed, she thought she heard Death as he walked the halls. He lingered at her mother's doorway a long time before deciding to move on.

Her mother woke slowly, like a cold sunrise on a winter's day. Her eyes opened first, but just stared at nothing for a long time, as if her mind were still walking about separately and had not yet returned from its journey. When she finally did focus on Waneta, her face changed, the struggle of life coming into her features, the skin stretching even more tightly across the bones of her face.

Her hand, so thin and frail, reached out, but Waneta hesitated to take it, afraid the fingers would break at the slightest touch.

"I was wrong," her mother said. The weariness was so heavy in her voice that her words seemed to come across a great distance. "I should have never taken you away."

Waneta tried to speak, but knew if she did, she would cry.

"You belong to the mountain," her mother said. "I thought I could save you if I took you away, but I was wrong. You will take your place as I did not."

Her mother's head lolled to the side and her eyelids closed. Waneta stood up in alarm, then saw her mother's chest slowly rise and fall. Only sleeping. It would be the first of many false alarms that were nothing like the real end, the one that came inexorably yet suddenly all the same.

She never discussed that conversation with anyone, not

even her mother, but the certainty in her mother's voice then was the same certainty that rang in the old woman's voice now.

Waneta turned back to the window, but the woman was gone. Had she ever really been there?

Waneta swallowed, but her mouth remained dry. She felt dizzy and knew she would never make it down the mountain's twisty roads at night. It had been a long day. Perhaps she was imagining things, just as she had last night, as she had shortly after her mother died.

She always assumed that her mother's sudden longing for the old days was nothing more than her natural fear of death. When her mother started telling the old tales, they seemed unimportant at first, a stupid waste of time. But as the end drew near, her mother derived a quiet strength from the stories that went beyond logical understanding. She spoke of the Ghost Country and how she would soon go to the West, to the Darkening Land.

It was her way of coping, just as Waneta's imagined sightings of her great-grandmother were her way of coping now.

Waneta took her foot off the brake and drove back to the spot where Gil had left her. Immediately he trotted out of the trees and into the headlights. She put the car in Park and slid over to the passenger seat.

When he was inside with the door closed and they were once again creeping slowly up the road, she asked, "Why did you leave your keys in the car?"

"To see if it was true."

"To see if what was true?"

Gil smiled. He had a nice smile. His teeth were somewhat stained from smoking, but they were straight, and when he grinned at her, as he did now, it lit up his whole face, complete with tiny crinkles around the eyes. She had not bothered to notice before, but he looked only four or five years older than she did, although in many ways he seemed both much older and much younger.

Gil asked, "Did you see her?"

So it was his grandmother. "Yes, I saw her."

He let out a whoop and pumped his fist. "All right!"

"What the hell are you so happy about?"

"It's not easy when you think you're crazy."

She started to agree that he was crazy, but as if to beat her to the point, he turned the car sharply off the road and plunged it down into an overhang of tree branches. The muffler scraped against the gravel, and branches clawed over the windshield and across the roof like fingers trying to hold them back. Then the car emerged onto a parallel set of steep, narrow trails separated by tall grass. Tree branches scratched against the doors as Gil slowly worked the vehicle forward.

Waneta glanced over her shoulder but all she saw was a wall of leaves—nature's version of the Bat Cave. She had driven to the dig site several times a week for months and had never even guessed that this narrow lane was here.

She frowned at Gil. He had a bad habit of not finishing his conversations. "What did you mean before? What does my seeing an old woman have to do with your sanity?"

Gil grinned again. "You know who she was?"

The words caught in Waneta's throat, but she forced them out. "She was just an old woman, the same one I saw at the dig site last night, the one who must live around here."

He laughed. "Nobody's lived up here steady in a couple dozen years, and I guarantee you, no Cherokee who's been around here all her life would ever go wandering around Rattlesnake Mountain at night."

"But I saw her."

"Ya." He nodded, still grinning like a madman. "You saw her. Not me. Who's the crazy one now?"

"It seems pretty clear that you are."

The trails twisted sharply, and as the headlights swung around the bend, they revealed a tiny clearing, barely larger than the car, and on the other side, an old cabin.

Waneta gasped. "My God. I know this place."

Looking at the rundown shack, she could feel the warmth

of the sun on her face, could smell the trees. An old man sat on the porch, smiling at her, holding forth a tiny stone statue he had carved from a smooth river rock.

Gil stopped the car and stepped out into the empty night.

Waneta jumped out and followed him back to the trunk. Suddenly light-headed, she put one hand to her forehead and rested the other hand on the car for stability. "What is this place? Why do I remember it?"

"We used to play here."

"What do you mean, 'we'?"

She turned and looked. There should be a trail there, curving up the mountain toward the other cabin. The path was gone now, but she could hear a person's approaching footsteps and an old woman's voice calling to her. In her mind, she sprang to her feet, a little girl's legs beneath her as she ran.

Waneta leaned back against the side of the car. Everywhere she looked, she saw afterimages, visions of what had once been.

She spun toward Gil, who had pulled a suitcase and some plastic bags from the trunk.

"Who was that old woman? No riddles. Just tell me."

Gil looked at her, his expression deadly serious. "You know who it was, Walelu. You always have."

Walelu? Walelu! She knew that word: Cherokee for Little Hummingbird. Waneta put her hands to her lips. "Oh, God."

Tears came to her eyes. Her voice cracked as she spoke. "I haven't heard that name, since I was—I was—"

"Five, probably. Your mother never liked it."

Gil set an ice chest on the ground and closed the trunk, then walked to the side of the car and opened the door. He put his knee on the seat and opened the glove compartment.

"Who are you?" Waneta asked.

He stood up, his hand on the top of the car door. "I thought you would remember when I said my name, but I suppose it's understandable—you were younger than me. We used to play together a lot up here, but after you started kindergarten, you moved to town and I never saw you again. Until I received the call earlier today, I wasn't sure I ever would."

Taking her hands in his, he nodded, then drew himself up straight. *"Siyo, Walelu. Giliaduh daquado-uh."*

"What? I don't understand. I don't speak—"

She stopped. The words were tumbling inside her head, as if she knew their meanings but could not hold them still long enough to see.

He tapped his chest. "Giliaduh."

"Puppy," she said, and saw a black-haired boy—strong, tall, handsome—but she could not make out his face.

Memories flooded over her then: the taste of cornmeal mush, the sight of a glittering fish pulled from a stream, the feel of small rocks and twigs digging into her hands and knees as she crawled up a rocky ledge to see a black bear passing by far below. She could still hear the bear grunting as it moved into the trees, could still feel the little boy press his finger to her lips until the bear was gone.

She swayed uneasily. Giliaduh. Gil. "I remember."

That meant the woman— The face, the voice.

Impossible. This was not happening, could not happen. Had she gone insane? Was any of this real?

An old woman called out to her and she pulled away from Gil. Her head light, she stumbled toward the cabin. Before she reached the broken wooden porch, her great-grandmother stepped out of the trees where the trail to the other cabin had been. Only this time—this time—

Waneta's legs gave way and she pitched forward into blackness.

TWENTY-ONE

Agent Ronald Sandoval arrived at the apartment shortly after 11:30 P.M. The two Volunteers stationed in front of the door came to attention, then parted, allowing him to pass.

He paid them little attention as he went inside and closed the door. His mind was already focused on the task before him: examining the personal residence of Dr. Waneta Long.

Although she was listed as a single female, Dr. Long had no knickknacks on her shelves, no plants sitting on the TV or hanging near the patio door, no crocheted afghan folded across the back of the couch. The framed landscapes on the walls revealed no gender biases. Every clue he saw remained androgynous.

Apparently as ambivalent about her race as she was her gender, the good doctor listed herself in some databases as white, in others as Native American. Although she had been officially enrolled as a member of the Eastern Band of Chero-kees shortly after her birth, she refused to associate with them. Hostility or apathy toward her ethnic heritage? Perhaps a little of both.

On the coffee table were piles of papers. He did not touch them but saw a driver's license for an older woman, perhaps Dr. Long's mother. According to the files, she had been deceased for years, claimed by breast cancer only months before the Taelons' arrival—a fact he had already used.

Next to the papers sat an open metal lockbox. Inside, he spied an old document that appeared to have been clumsily—

and recently—refolded. He did not pick it up. Fingerprints were difficult enough to lift off paper without forcing the lab to screen for his.

As he circled the table, glass cracked under his shoes. He bent low to examine the carpet and found the broken stem from a wineglass. Scattered across the floor were other shattered fragments, some stained with tiny drops of red. He touched one of the drops—sticky—then pressed the finger to his lips. Wine.

A narrow path had been cleared through the broken shards. The nearby vacuum cleaner explained that easily enough, but why start to pick up the glass, then stop before the job was finished? And what had made her spill the wine in the first place? A careless mistake prompted by too much haste? A surprise? A struggle? Perhaps she had started to clean but was told she had no time.

Someone had been here with her, perhaps the same person who had interfered when she answered her global earlier this evening. The lab had already enhanced and delivered stop-action video from that call. It revealed a pair of legs in army fatigues, probably male, probably belonging to the person who had attacked his men on campus and let them live.

An amateur's mistake, that. Whoever it was should have killed them. Professionals did not leave eyewitnesses alive. Unfortunately only one of his men had seen anything, and then just a blur before being injected with an ultrafast sedative, military quality. That meant Resistance connections.

Whatever the truth, the state of this room indicated that Dr. Long had been in a hurry when she left. Had she known that the Volunteers were coming? Impossible. Even if someone had wanted to break security, there had been no time. Besides, she had later answered her global. That implied she did not understand the gravity of her situation, a mistake her fatigue-clad compatriot had been in a hurry to correct.

The door opened and a young woman accompanied by two Volunteers entered the small living room. The woman, Agent

Sandoval's new top research assistant, was packing a twin-lensed holographic video recorder. Following her came two lab technicians carrying a trunk. It contained chemicals, timers, and other evidence they would leave for the local authorities to find, plus it would allow them to conceal whatever they chose to take with them.

Agent Sandoval spoke quickly. "I want recordings made of everything, including interiors."

"Do you want the inside of the refrigerator?" the assistant asked.

Agent Sandoval put his hands behind his back and rose on his toes, then settled down before answering. "I do not expect you to rip out the walls, but if you find a door that can be opened, I better be able to see what's behind it."

"Yes, sir."

It would take time for her to learn his habits and anticipate his needs. After a couple of months, she would either master the idiosyncrasies of his personality or she would be taken care of in a way that assured she would never come back to haunt him. He had no time for incompetents.

His tone sharpened. "Start in this room. I want these papers treated for fingerprints, then removed and analyzed. If they contain anything of importance, I want to know it as soon as possible."

After a glance at the table, she opened her mouth as if to ask a question, then closed it.

Good. She was learning—only she'd better not guess wrong. The only thing worse than asking questions was assuming incorrectly.

Already he missed Laura Heward, for more reasons than one. Zo'or had no right to drain her mind the way he had done. As good as dead, she marked yet another life taken by the Taelons. They had claimed so many, although not as many as he had killed in his efforts to defeat them.

Unlike the Resistance, he understood that the goal was

mightier than the methods used to reach it. Members of the Underground, in order to avoid compromising their integrity, planned their token conquests in committee meetings, then settled for half measures and partial victories. Agent Sandoval had no interest in such incomplete acts. When the right time came, his triumph over the Taelons would be absolute, the danger forever eliminated.

But the time had not yet come. He must be patient until each piece was in place. Until then, he would measure his progress in small opportunities carefully realized.

A commotion sounded outside the door: a man's stern voice, low, indecipherable, followed by a woman's high-pitched complaint. "Get out of my way! He asked to see me."

The door opened and one of the Volunteer guards stepped inside.

"Sorry to interrupt, sir. We have a woman who claims—"

"Yes. Show her in."

A female reporter pushed past the guard. After giving him a final glare, she hitched up the shoulder strap of the portable playback unit.

She smiled at Agent Sandoval as she approached. "I think you'll be pleased. I made every effort to stay within the guidelines you set."

Agent Sandoval nodded to the woman and led her into the kitchen. "I'm glad you understand the importance of our investigation.

He purposely did not use the woman's name. She had been chosen because she seemed the most eager and gullible. His only concern was that she deliver what was needed.

"I have to warn you," she said brightly, "this hasn't been edited yet. Also, since you asked me not to release it until tomorrow morning, I predated everything, so people won't get confused when I say 'this evening' but mean 'yesterday evening' for them. Isn't that great?"

Agent Sandoval raised his hand dismissively and nodded. If

she had waited a few more minutes to record her report, it would have been a new day and there would have been no need to strain her meager mental capacities.

She placed the portable video player on the kitchen counter and started the playback.

It showed the reporter standing in front of this apartment building, the wind blowing her hair, a street lamp glowing over her right shoulder.

"Early yesterday evening, a suspected terrorist, Dr. Robert Messmore, was fatally wounded in a gunfight with members of a special Taelon investigative team. Afterward, explosions destroyed a large section of Neyland Stadium, explosions originally attributed to Dr. Messmore. Now it appears that Dr. Messmore was not acting alone."

In the video, the reporter paused.

The live version standing beside Agent Sandoval said, "The cameraman's out now taking shots of the building's exterior. We'll probably do this next bit mostly as a voice-over, which will be remixed at the studio."

The recorded version nodded, as if watching a countdown, then began again. "Inside this benign-looking building is the apartment of Dr. Waneta Long, an anthropology instructor at the University of Tennessee. According to information just released, authorities now believe that last night's explosions, which caused more than five million dollars in damage, were set off by Dr. Long."

Agent Sandoval's assistant walked into the kitchen, slowly panning her camera around the room. If she did her job correctly, he would be able to create a three-dimensional computer model of this apartment, complete with every object it contained.

The video continued. "New evidence found inside the apartment has linked Dr. Long to Dr. Messmore romantically. Apparently their professional relationship blossomed into something more personal early last year, shortly after Dr. Messmore assumed his new position as head of the Department of Anthropology. Additionally, a manifesto was found inside the apartment, which outlines the couple's intentions toward the Taelons. The text of that manifesto will be released as soon as authorities have completed their initial examination."

The assistant paused in her taping to stare at the portable player, then at Agent Sandoval. He had not yet told her she needed to complete the excerpts from the manifesto by early tomorrow morning. She would find out soon enough that working for him often meant going without sleep.

On the video, the reporter's voice took on a grave tone. "Dr. Waneta Long is Native American with black hair and brown eyes. Thirty-three years old, she is five foot five inches tall and weighs one hundred twenty-five pounds.

"If you see someone you suspect might be Dr. Long, do not approach her yourself. She is considered armed and dangerous. Instead, please call the number that appears on your screen."

His new assistant peered over his shoulder at the portable player, an annoying habit that would not happen again.

"That's it," the reporter said and shut off the player. "The people at the news desk will do their own intros to the piece, but they won't use any information that isn't already available. So, what do you think?"

"That'll be fine."

"I can run it, then?"

"Of course."

Agent Sandoval watched with amusement as a huge smile broke over the reporter's face, her tongue darting out a moment between bright white teeth.

She straightened, doing her best to hide her excitement. "Thank you, Agent Sandoval. Thank you so much. If you ever need anything, just call."

He nodded at her until her back was turned, then grinned as she left the apartment.

Reporters were so easily manipulated. They would do anything to be first on a story, even if the story was untrue. All they needed was a little special handling, the right words. In this case, he had traded exclusive rights to their information for the privilege of reviewing her story before it aired. Not that he expected her to come up with anything he had not given her. By providing easy access to more information than anyone else had, he had taken away both her time and inclination to dig for the real story. Best of all, because she already had more data than anyone else had been able to uncover, they would all clamor for the rights to use and expand on what she had already done.

In today's sound-bite-driven world, where old news is no news, the truth took a distant second place to turning in the story on time.

Just in case, the building's tenants would be primed to deliver useful sound bites. He would send around a team of Volunteers early tomorrow, asking questions about Dr. Waneta Long, the type of questions that always stirred the imagination of at least a few neighbors. The best part was that the media would not rest until they ferreted out only those people who substantiated the story they already had on tape.

Agent Sandoval's grin faded as he watched his assistant. She had gone back to taping. "Don't ever invade my space again."

She looked up, a confused expression on her face. "I don't understand."

"When I was reviewing the video, you came and looked over my shoulder. Don't ever do that again."

"I'm sorry. I won't."

He nodded. "As I'm sure you heard, we plan to release excerpts of the manifesto tomorrow. I've already given you the parameters I'm looking for. Do you understand them?"

"Yes."

"Good. I want the excerpts delivered at the same time as the altered video."

She started to speak, stopped, then said, "Isn't that schedule a bit ambitious?"

He sighed. "Being good at this position means knowing what you can delegate and what you must do yourself."

"But you haven't given me authority to supervise—"

"If you wait to do something until someone gives you the authority, you will never get any authority at all. Produce results and the power will de facto become yours. The trick, of course, is making sure your ambition never leads you out of my shadow. If that ever happens, your time on this planet is over. Is that clear?"

"Yes, sir."

"Very well. Finish your recording as quickly as possible. You have a great deal of work to finish by morning."

He watched with amusement as she went back to pointing the camera at the kitchen walls. In one ear, out the other. If she had listened to a single word he had said, she would have someone else doing this menial task, which she would review later for completeness.

So many things in life seemed so simple, yet people of lesser ability never understood them as easily as he did.

Agent Sandoval wandered into the bedroom and closed the door. The bed was unmade and clothes littered the floor. No one could accuse this woman of being a great housekeeper.

He removed his global and contacted the mother ship.

Zo'or answered personally. "Your report is late."

Agent Sandoval's tone was sharp. "I'm breaking in a new assistant. That takes extra time."

Zo'or displayed no reaction to the words but changed topics. "I have called an emergency meeting of the Synod. Once we meet, I will obtain more information about the crystal, but I will be unavailable for an indeterminate amount of time. What steps have you taken to find the stone?"

"I managed to contact Dr. Long on her global, but our communication link was abruptly terminated. Fortunately, we had time to trace the link to latitude 35.51 degrees, longitude 83.3 degrees—just outside the town of Cherokee, North Carolina. I plan to concentrate our initial search efforts there."

Zo'or's fingers moved through their typical annoying motions and his gaze focused offscreen as he spoke. "I have not felt the power since your assault on the university. The stone must be recovered at all costs and the time to do so has grown much shorter. Make every effort, Agent Sandoval."

"Of course." The signal ended and Agent Sandoval re-attached the global to the back of his belt.

During the past day and a half, Zo'or had become increasingly distracted. The gem was having some effect on him even if he did not believe so. That was promising, at least.

It had now become a race to find Dr. Long. If Zo'or found her before he did, she would be brought to the mother ship and her mind drained, just as Laura Heward's had been drained. That, he could not allow.

After a glance at the closed bedroom door, he removed the stone from his pocket. A red, unpolished gem, about the size of an overgrown walnut, he had taken it off what was left of Dr. Messmore.

The Volunteers had made a mistake killing the department head—several people were working overtime to correct that blunder—but finding the stone in Dr. Messmore's pocket made it easy to forgive their error.

Part of the reason he had delayed in contacting Zo'or was fear the Taelon would somehow be able to detect that he had the gem, but whatever had triggered the power the day before on the mother ship was apparently no longer at work. The stone seemed nothing more than a worthless rock. That was why he needed Dr. Long.

Regrettably, she had seen Dr. Messmore die. Of that, he was certain. So why had she answered the global? None of it made sense, but he would find out the answers. That's why he was here.

Unfortunately, he could not stay to see the work through to completion. Instead he would be forced to rely on his assistant to find the clues needed to track down Waneta Long. He only wished he could feel comfortable with that situation.

Agent Sandoval walked out the building's front door, barely paying attention to the Volunteer who reported to him. At this level of control, they were all the same—almost mindless in their devotion to the Taelons, acting on protocols and training alone with no initiative and no surprises. He refused to accept what the Taelons had done to this world, but some of their methods proved useful.

"Commander, prepare your troops for transport. We have a fugitive to catch."

"Yes, sir." The commander saluted and strode off purpose-fully.

The Volunteers would need to be fully briefed before he unleashed them on the tiny town of Cherokee and the surrounding area. He wanted Dr. Long taken alive. If anyone could help him unleash the stone's power against the Taelons, it would be her.

TWENTY-TWO

Liam weaved along the cobbled street of the picture-postcard town of Kilnunry near the Shannon River. As Da'an had instructed, he had left the Taelon shuttle in D.C. Instead, he had taken the portal to Ireland, then used a car to get to the small tourist town, arriving shortly after dawn. Local laws prohibited cars in the town center, so he walked to the address Augur had given him for Daniel Shaunessy and his mother.

Small, cheerfully painted cottages stood shoulder to shoulder along the narrow, deserted street. Beneath the cottage windows hung brightly contrasting flower boxes. Most were empty, but a few still held the dried skeletons of last summer's bloom. In front of the houses, tiny, carefully groomed patches of grass hid behind wooden fences like shy children.

As Liam walked through the silent town—few people were up at this hour—he wondered how much of the town was real and how much had been created for the satisfaction of tourists who had grown up watching old movies and cartoon leprechauns.

Not that it mattered. The tourists who visited this place did not come to see the real Ireland—they came to see the town where a Taelon had lived.

Liam had never even heard the story until he picked up the brochure for Kilnunry in the portal terminal. According to the slick-paper write-up, Da'an had stayed in this town for several weeks shortly after the Taelons arrived on Earth. That was before Liam had been born. Of course, that meant Daniel Shaunessy had not yet been born, either, but the fact that he had been born here—the town where Da'an lived, the place the brochure called "first 'home' of the Taelons"—was no coincidence.

Beyond that, though, Liam was not sure what Daniel's birth in this town meant. Certainly the boy and the Taelon were somehow linked, but Da'an had said the boy did not cause his illness, and while Da'an stretched the truth in every direction possible, he did not lie.

For Liam, the key word in Da'an's statement was *cause*. The boy may not have caused his illness, but he may have been the conduit for what did, the way Irish-born Mary Mallon was not the cause of the typhoid fever she carried from place to place, but rather served it up to more than fifty people, many of whom died from the disease.

Liam stopped at the gate of a large whitewashed house with a traditional thatched roof. An ornate iron number 6, painted black, hung beside a wide oak door. He hesitated for several long moments, not wanting to disturb the building's occupants who might be sleeping but afraid that each passing second might be important to resolving the mystery of the boy.

Liam opened the gate, crossed to the front step, and knocked. After several seconds, a small wicket door at about eye level opened to reveal a woman behind a protective mesh of iron grating.

She peered down at him. Either she was Amazonian, or she was standing on a stool. A strange blue hat, similar to a nun's habit but hard to see through the grating, covered her head.

"How may we help you?" the woman asked in a pleasant lilting voice.

"I'm looking for Triss Shaunessy."

The woman frowned and wrinkled her brow. "Gone. Months ago. I must be asking, are you family?"

"No. I just wanted to ask her a few questions."

"We're sorry," the woman said. "We cannot be of any help today."

She started to close the wicket, but Liam held up his data card. "Please. It's a matter of world importance. I need only a couple minutes of your time."

The woman's eyes widened and the corners of her mouth turned up. "You're a Protector, then?"

Liam nodded.

The woman let out a squeal and hopped down from the small window with a clatter of shoes on stone. The door swung open and the woman, at least a foot shorter than Liam, waved him forward enthusiastically.

"Come in, come in. We're honored by your presence. What questions may we answer?"

Liam stepped inside a small, sparsely furnished parlor and looked around. They were alone. He studied the woman more closely. She was dressed all in blue, and the long sleeves of her garment were slitted on the outside—connected at the shoulder and again just below the elbow. Her hat, small and close-fitting, sported twin crescents set across the back crown of her head. He had seen a similar outfit before, on Sister Margaret and the other cloister members who had participated in the energy sharing ceremony with Da'an and Zo'or last summer. After Sister Margaret, the head of that cloister, killed one of its members, Liam had problems trusting anyone who belonged to this new religion.

Hesitantly he asked, "Was Triss a member of your organization?"

The excitement on the woman's face faded. "Yes, before she was lost to us forever. You see, up until her son was born, Sister Triss served the cloister."

"Her son—Daniel?"

The woman fidgeted. "Yes, that was the name she gave the child."

The woman was nervous, and nervous people provided less

information. Liam smiled and relaxed his arms by his sides. "By the way, my name is Liam Kincaid. I serve Da'an."

The woman brightened again. "Yes, yes, we should have recognized you, but you're much taller in person. We've so wanted to meet you, but you've always been too busy to come before."

Liam frowned. What was this woman talking about?

"My name is Sister Kathrynne. So tell me, Liam, why did you not take the portal? It's a mighty long drive, all the way from the public terminal."

"The portal?"

"Oh, my, of course you would not be doing that. I'm sure you'd rather see the beautiful green hills of your homeland than just pop in and out. Such chances must not come as often as you'd like. So which part of Ireland is your family originally from?"

Liam started to answer, then stopped.

Apparently Sister Kathrynne mistook his confusion for a look of offense. "Oh, please forgive me. I was not meaning to ask so many personal questions, but whenever Da'an visits, it's a momentous occasion for all of us. We will be honored, as always, to share energy with him. That's why I transferred to this cloister, because it's one of the few that Da'an regularly visits. The other sisters will be so excited."

"I'm sorry. You said he often visits?"

"Oh, my, I did. Forgive me." She straightened and gave him a wink, then recited in monotone, "Da'an stayed here once years ago. We sisters of the cloister patiently await his return. At least that's what we tell the tourists." She giggled at this, then added, "How about a nice cup of tea? I have hot water in the kettle."

"No, thank you."

Liam scratched his head but forced himself not to ask any more questions. Instead, he thought over what she had said, then tried getting the information he had come for.

"I'm here because Da'an fell ill. Daniel was performing for him at the time, and I thought there might be a connection."

She gasped. "I always knew that boy would come to ruin. Sister Triss should have known better. Not that we're forbidden to have male children, but we all understand the consequences if we do. She should have accepted that and left as soon as the child was born."

"When was that?"

"Oh, I'm not sure I remember the exact date. Our journey is a long one and we do not measure it day by day."

"I'm just curious how old he is. Exact dates are not important."

Sister Kathrynne hesitated, then smiled briefly before walking across the room and looking out a small window. "The child came to us last fall, about this time of year. The leaves had started to turn but had yet to fall off the trees. I'm afraid I can't be more exact than that."

The woman crossed her arms and continued to look out the window. "He forced the sharing, didn't he?"

"Forced the sharing?"

"The boy. Yes. If you saw it, it would be obvious enough. The person who forces the sharing must transform to an energy state. If the other person does not wish to participate, he does not take on the image of spiritual bonding. Outside of being unable to move, his outward appearance changes not a whit—but it's quite distasteful. Still, I'm surprised the boy could pull it off.

"Why?" Liam was already thinking about Da'an, hovering toward his energy state, and Daniel, frozen on the stage, waiting for applause that would never come.

"We can share energy with the Taelons, but we are not Taelons—not yet. I knew the boy was stronger than any of us, but I never dreamed he could overcome Da'an. I still can't believe it. No wonder we could not contain him."

Kathrynne spoke in a soft voice. "Is Da'an all right? Tell us Da'an is well or we'll be killing ourselves, I swear."

Liam raised his hands, then pushed them down gently. "He's fine. The whole episode lasted only a few minutes."

"Yes, of course. A Taelon's energy is well refined."

She lifted her head to look at him. Tears glistened on her cheeks. "You must understand, we would not have kept the boy, but children are vital to our progress. We need a second generation to carry on what we have started, and we knew only weeks after he was born that Daniel would be different. He grew so fast, and before long, he would shimmer whenever we shared energy—though he was not in the room. We thought he might be the one to take us to the next level, but it was too soon, too soon."

She shook her head, then turned away and hugged her shoulders.

Liam stepped forward and spoke softly. "Why was it too soon?"

Sister Kathrynne spun to face him. "We were not at fault. How could you expect us to handle the child if Da'an could not? The child was not ready for the next level. He could not absorb the sharing. He reacted . . . poorly. He became defensive. Several of the sisters were injured. We had to discontinue the ceremonies. The boy had to leave, for his safety as well as ours. But if we had known what he would try to do to Da'an, we would have taken his energy, just like we did the others."

Liam frowned. "The others?"

Sister Kathrynne immediately tensed, as if Liam had jabbed her with a sharp stick. She peered at him carefully, her face becoming an expressionless mask. "Yes, why don't you tell us about the others?"

"You were the one who said—" Liam hesitated, thinking as fast as he could. "You already know. I have no reason to tell you."

"Yes, we know, but you don't, do you? I see it in your eyes. That's why you've never visited us before. Not because you were too busy, but because your mind is still too small to understand. You've misled us. You should not be here. Da'an's not coming, is he? If you've harmed him . . ."

Liam did not like the way Sister Kathrynne closed on him. Suddenly this small woman seemed much larger. "I'm his

Companion Protector. I would never harm Da'an. You should know that better than anyone."

"We are no longer sure. Jaridians can assume human facades."

Blue tinged her skin and soft lines of color raced along her arms.

The shaqarava in Liam's palms began to glow, bright white spots of light that he tried to hide by closing his fists and placing his hands behind his back.

"Please," Liam said. "I don't want to hurt you."

"Sisters," she whispered, closing her eyes. "Sisters, I need you."

What was she doing now? Women of the cloister were not telepathic, at least not as far as he knew.

He backed quickly toward the door, then felt behind him for the knob. As his hand closed around the iron handle, his global chimed, but he was not about to answer it now.

Sister Kathrynne's voice came out low and throaty. "No, you will not be leaving us that easily."

She swung her arm at Liam. Glowing brightly now, it blurred as it came at him. Instinctively, he raised his hands to shield himself and was momentarily blinded by a flare of bright white light.

When the spots before his eyes cleared enough to see again, he found Sister Kathrynne on the floor, breathing but unconscious. His shaqarava had reflected the energy back at the woman.

Shuffling came from upstairs and the sounds of footsteps creaked through the ceiling.

Leaving Kathrynne for her sisters to find, Liam fled the house, running until he made it past the iron gate and down the cobbled street.

Several early morning risers, shopkeepers mostly, looked at him curiously. He forced a smile and slowed to a quick walk, doing his best to make it appear that he was late for an appointment rather than running from members of a crazed religious sect who wanted to fry him up for breakfast.

After a glance behind him, he checked his palms. They had returned to normal. Rubbing his hands together, he shivered—and not from the brisk morning air. It had been months since his Ha'gelian heritage had intruded so actively in his normal life. While he recognized and appreciated the particular gifts that parent had left him, he enjoyed being human.

His global beeped once, reminding him he had a message. He pulled the device off his belt and opened it. The message was from Renée.

"Liam, I need to speak with you."

To the point. In messages, Renée was never chatty.

"Renée," he told his global, and waited until her face appeared on the small display.

Her eyes were drawn close together and her lips formed a tight line. "What are you doing in Ireland? Tracing your family tree?"

"Good morning to you, too. Shouldn't you be getting your beauty sleep?"

"Who has time for sleep?"

"I hope I do. That's what I had on my schedule after I made it back to the states—but I suppose you have other plans."

"Of course. I need to see you. Meet me as soon as possible."

Liam switched to the global's locate signal function. His eyes widened and he punched back over to look at Renée. "North Carolina? It's two in the morning there. What's this about?"

"I'd rather tell you in person. Your global already has the coordinates where we should meet. I'll explain everything when you arrive. But don't bring the shuttle. There'll be eyes watching for you."

"I don't have the shuttle. I took a rental car from the portal in Cork."

Renée groaned. "I don't have time for you to drive all the way back there. We need to come up with something better."

Liam grinned. "Well, I do know of a much closer portal, but unless you want my head to arrive on a pole, you'll just have to wait until I get back to the public terminal and jump through there."

Renée did not even ask what he meant.

"Leave the car. I'll send a Doors helicopter to take you to the portal and have another waiting on the other side. The first helicopter will meet you on the east end of Kilnunry in about thirty minutes. The second one will be waiting on the roof of the portal facility in Charlotte. Don't waste any time. This is important, Liam."

"Better be. It's late."

She smiled. "I'll buy you dinner after you arrive. The best cuisine they offer."

"Caviar and Dom Perignon?"

"Not quite. Hurry."

The global switched off. Liam tucked it back into his belt and veered north toward the edge of town.

TWENTY-THREE

Zo'or met Da'an in Foundation Room One. They prepared to enter the Synod Council Chamber together.

"At last," Zo'or said, moving his hands in impatience. "We shall discover the secret information you could not reveal to me alone."

The remark had been meant as a barb, but Da'an simply nodded and closed his eyes, saying nothing.

Zo'or hated Da'an's habit of not speaking. Sometimes having a conversation with his parent more closely resembled talking to himself than to another living being.

They walked into the Council Chamber at the same time but from different directions. Da'an entered on the right, symbolically the direction of divergence. Zo'or entered on the left, the direction of convergence. Of late, these were their usual positions when speaking before the Synod. Today only, Zo'or had been tempted to enter on the right, but to do so made no sense: His policies currently prevailed. As such, he should be leaning toward convergence, but on the matter of the unknown power, he suspected that his position would not align well with the rest of the Synod.

Da'an and Zo'or stopped at preset positions before the five Circles of Power. The two Taelons stood equally close to the circles, or equally distant, depending on one's point of view. For symbolic reasons, Zo'or was prohibited from taking a position in front of Da'an during these meetings, even as leader of the Synod.

Above all else, the Synod reflected consensus. No decision could be made without agreement among all its members—an impractical system for day-to-day decisions. That was why Zo'or, outside meetings, could act as he saw fit as long as he maintained favor with the Synod. It was also why he believed that the long-held tradition of consensus should be abandoned, especially now in time of war.

The Synod had not experienced deadlock in hundreds of years, but only because the minority, after being heard, always conceded to the majority in the interest of the common good. More than that, Zo'or believed that his force of will and unwillingness to change his mind had successfully bullied one or two of the other members to switch sides at decisive moments during the past two years. He had no intention of changing that strategy now.

Da'an spoke first. "A great danger, an old danger, again threatens the Commonality."

Da'an moved his hands in the gesture for complete attention and openness, a gesture rarely used, the human equivalent of shouting into someone's ear while he was soundly asleep, then asking for a hug when he bolted upright in bed. The other members of the Synod, who stood on the Circles of Power in their natural energy state, immediately brightened. Glowing lines danced over their bodies in both irritation and expectation.

Images formed in the air. They were indistinct, more impression than reproduction, allowing Zo'or to see the viewports and the other members of the Synod through them. No, not through them. Beyond them, the way distant objects can still be seen even though one eye is partially blocked by something held very near. By mentally blinking, Zo'or could switch his focus from the reality of the chamber to the pictures being given, without ever losing awareness of either.

Da'an was using the ka'ta'tha'al, the giving. Similar in purpose to what Da'an had done by touching palms with Zo'or, this allowed him to convey his ideas more effectively and dramatically to a larger group, but it also sent ripples throughout the Commonality. All Taelons would feel this disturbance, but most would not understand the sensations. They would need to be briefed when the meeting had ended.

Whatever Da'an had to share, he wanted everyone to know.

In the first images that formed, Zo'or perceived glowing eyes, blindingly bright, with halos of energy radiating from a central point of power, a jewel, similar to the one he had been seeking since the day before.

Zo'or had experienced the ka'ta'tha'al only twice in his life, and both times, only briefly. He enjoyed the sensation and likened it to what he imagined humans felt at the moment of orgasm, but as with all things Taelon, there was no hint of sexuality in this experience.

Da'an's words were spoken aloud, but Zo'or heard them first in his mind, creating a tight echo.

"The Elteena have always been a threat to our species. They hunted Taelons, to feed on our life energy, but Taelons were never easy prey. Most of the time, the Elteena preferred lower forms of life, those that could not fight back. Still, we lost dozens of lives to them every year."

The image that formed showed Taelons dying, not in the blinding brilliance of a Jaridian energy blast but in a painfully slow, wrenching, squeezing way—violent deaths that tore at Zo'or's compassion for his race. A terrifying and long-lasting end, one that did not allow entry into the next plane of existence until the being who had consumed the energy was destroyed.

The fear Zo'or experienced explained why Da'an had selected this method to convey his information. He wanted not only to inform the Synod but also to control them by manipulating their emotions, the same way he had tried—and failed—to frighten Zo'or by showing him the magnitude of the power.

Da'an's voice continued his echoing cadence. "We destroyed the Elteena home world more than twenty-two hundred years ago. A few escaped the destruction. Those, we did our best to hunt down and exterminate, but the war with the Jaridians limited our resources and the Elteena learned that they could avoid detection by entering their dormant state."

Zo'or saw the Elteena as a huge mass of boiling, writhing energy, which gradually closed in upon itself, condensing, pulling tighter and tighter until it became a stone, similar to the one the human, Dr. Waneta Long, had found, the one that had been videotaped by the college news crew and released to the national wire, the one Zo'or could still see in his mind.

But the one Da'an presented differed from the one Zo'or remembered. Similar, but not an exact match. Da'an may have seen other Elteena, but he had not seen the one Dr. Long had taken with her to North Carolina, the one Zo'or would claim for his own.

"I have sensed an Elteena here, on this planet," Da'an said. "It is currently in its dormant state, but I have felt the first stirrings of its coming awakening and metamorphosis into its active form. Once it does that, it will become a powerful adversary."

The images Zo'or saw now were a collage of all that had come before—the glowing eyes, the halos of energy, Taelons dying, the writhing mass shrinking down to become a gleaming jewel of red—fused and overlaid with pain, fear, and energy. But all Zo'or felt was the massive, unfathomable, enticing power.

Zo'or spoke for the first time. "The Elteena could also become a powerful ally."

Da'an's concentration faltered. The images hovering in the air wavered and disappeared, leaving the spell he had woven temporarily broken.

His voice sounded now without the preceding echo. "What you ask could mark the end of our race."

"Or the beginning." Zo'or deliberately moved his hands in a pattern for optimistic excitement. "The power of this creature goes beyond all others. It is immune to mind control and cannot be fooled by any Jaridian device or trick. If we could force it to do our will, it would become our most powerful weapon in our war against the Jaridians."

Zo'or paused, realizing that much more information had come through Da'an's ka'ta'tha'al than he had originally noticed. He now knew all about the Elteena, its history, its weaknesses, its strengths.

Da'an traced out the simple figure for disagreement. "Jaridians do not have a taste that the creature desires. Never before has it sought them out."

"But it could," Zo'or persisted. "It could be trained—"

"What you suggest," Da'an said haltingly, "has been accomplished before. For more than four hundred years, Sha'om kept an Elteena the way some humans keep large and dangerous cats, such as tigers. But like the wild tiger, which can never be truly tamed, the Elteena eventually turned on its master and consumed Sha'om's energy. Since it had lived in captivity so long, it knew our ways and escaped detection for more than eleven hundred years, killing more Taelons than any Elteena before or since."

Zo'or drew the pattern for eager anticipation. "You have just stated the proof I seek. An Elteena can be captured and controlled."

Da'an nodded and closed his eyes, then opened them and tilted his head. "Sha'om spent one hundred years domesticating his Elteena. Most of that time, he kept it in its dormant state. The war with the Jaridians will not last long enough for you to bend this Elteena to your will."

Zo'or could taste the power, fresh in his mind from the images Da'an had placed there. He craved it now more than ever. "Another Taelon could not control the Elteena, but I can.

I have carefully studied the ways of the humans. By focusing their most aggressive tendencies, they often achieve physical dominance over much stronger and more worthy opponents. I can apply the same technique to the mental struggle with the Elteena. I guarantee I shall win."

"A bold statement," one of the Synod members said.

This one felt the power as Zo'or did and would approve his actions, but the others hung back just as strongly. This consensus would not be easily reached.

Da'an moved his fingers in respectful gratitude. "Our time has been well spent, but now I recommend that we separate and consider the issue undisturbed before progressing further."

"No," Zo'or said. "The Elteena has already begun to awake. If I am to control it, I should be given approval to capture it now. When the time comes to act, we can afford no delays."

Da'an nodded solemnly. "What you have said is true, but fear of failure should never be a reason to proceed with undue haste. The only path we can take without deep consideration is the one already known to us—the destruction of the Elteena. Do you concede that this is what we should do?"

"No. The Elteena must be used against the Jaridians. It must be taken alive."

"The matter is settled, then," one of the more conservative Synod members stated. "We shall consider the issues individually and meet again when consensus has the potential to reach its full flower."

Zo'or considered pressing the issue, but he sensed he would fail. He could deadlock them, but he needed a decision, not the lack of one. Why must he be saddled with these traditions of a different age? When he controlled the Elteena's power, consensus would become a relic of the past.

One leader. One vision. One path.

But the Elteena was not yet his.

"I agree." Zo'or said the sacred words but could not help fingering the sign for impatient irritation.

This would not prevent him from acting should the opportunity arise. Nothing would stop him until he had claimed the Elteena for himself.

TWENTY-FOUR

Waneta awoke on a musty bed in the corner of a one-room cabin. Gil knelt close by, light flickering across his face as he stirred the iron kettle that hung in the fireplace. On the table behind him stood a large red ice chest. Beside it sat an empty plastic container, drops of thick, milky sauce clinging to the clear sides.

She sat up and sniffed but smelled only smoke.

Gil had changed clothes. He now wore a button-down plaid shirt and jeans, and his hair, freed from its ponytail, hung loosely around his shoulders. When he turned in her direction, he smiled. The simple expression lit up his face, like something out of a dream she could feel but not remember.

"Good," he said. "I was beginning to wonder if you would sleep right through supper."

She glanced across the room and found the cabin's only window. It stood behind an old hand pump next to a cracked porcelain sink. Night reigned outside, and she did not feel like much time had passed since . . .

Shuddering, she recalled the sight of her great-grand-mother emerging from the trees.

"Did you see her, too?" she asked.

"Who?"

"You must have seen her. She came down the trail from, from her cabin—"

Of course. Her great-grandmother's cabin lay up the mountain, not far from the dig site. They had often walked down the trail to see Gil and his great-grandfather. In those days, it had been a long walk for a small girl. How long would it be now? She did not know. The memories were so fragmented. She saw images of animals, trees, flowers—her great-grandmother naming each in Cherokee as they passed. In another memory, her great-grandmother pulled her through snow on a crudely crafted sled. They were on their way to Gil's for some kind of special dinner. But that was insane: The woman was too old, even then, to be traipsing around the mountain with a little girl in the dead of winter.

Gil scooped beans from the black kettle onto a ceramic plate. "I didn't see anyone, but that doesn't mean much. I was getting the flashlight out of the glove compartment when you fainted."

"I didn't faint!"

He laughed. "Then you must be an expert at playing possum. I could have sworn you were out cold."

Had she really fainted? She had never fainted in her life. Carefully she thought back over those few seconds just before she blacked out.

She could see it so clearly. Her great-grandmother stepped into the glow of the car's dome light, and her body shimmered, becoming semitransparent. Waneta saw branches and leaves behind the old woman. They were visible right through her chest.

Waneta had known that her great-grandmother was dead but had steadfastly convinced herself that the woman she had seen was an imposter, a coincidental look-alike. Now she knew better.

"I haven't eaten all day." She spoke the words as much to herself as to Gil. "I did have a salad, but I skipped supper last night. My blood sugar got too low, that's all."

Gil raised his eyebrows but said only, "I can fix that."

Using his fingertips, he pulled a pan from a ledge by the fire and dropped it on the hearth. "Hot," he said simply. After licking his fingers, he blew on them, then removed the aluminum foil from the pan and set a huge chunk of cornbread on the plate beside the beans. He opened a plastic tub on the table and spooned a thick, white ball onto the plate next to the cornbread.

"Here," he said and handed her a fork along with the food.

Waneta's thoughts remained on her great-grandmother. She touched the crystal in her pocket, which felt warm and smooth. If it really were Taelon, perhaps it was affecting her mind. Gil had not seen the woman. Perhaps she was a hallucination. Waneta could not quite believe that but had no other explanation she was willing to accept.

She looked at the plate. "Cornbread? Ham and beans? Going for the traditional fare tonight?"

"They're leftovers." He grinned and winked before dishing up another portion. "I didn't have much warning or I would have brought along a freshly baked batch of bean bread."

"Bean bread?"

"Sure. Great stuff. Very traditional. But I don't make it very often, and I darned sure don't prepare the cornmeal myself with wood ash lye the way my great-grandfather used to. Too much work. At least the butter's homemade. The ham, too. Not by me—I know a lady who still makes a lot of this stuff by hand. I trade with her for things whenever I get the chance."

Waneta stared at the food. "Why not just go to the grocery store?"

"I do, most of the time, but this helps her out. Besides, I think homemade food tastes better."

She handed the plate back. "I'm sorry, I can't eat this much. My stomach's a little bit jumpy."

"You sure?"

She nodded.

He shrugged and took back her plate, then handed her the other one. It contained about half as much food, but the butter was already melting against the side of the cornbread and the ham had been cooked in with the beans.

After grabbing a fork for himself, Gil sat back on one of the two wooden chairs beside the table and studied her for several seconds before he began to eat.

"Don't worry," he said between mouthfuls. "I've been gobbling up this lady's food for years. I've never been sick yet."

When she still did not eat, he added, "Try it. You might like it."

Normally she would have refused—who knew what kind of unfriendly bacteria might be living in this stuff?—but the aroma from the food wafted up around her nose. Her mouth watered so much, she had to swallow to keep from drooling.

She tried the cornbread first. It was wonderful—not dry at all—and the homemade butter made it even better. The chunks of ham were sparse but exceptionally lean and very salty, a perfect complement to the blandness of the beans.

Before Waneta realized what she was doing, she had eaten every bite and was scraping her fork across the plate.

She stopped when she noticed Gil grinning at her.

"Sure you got enough?"

Silently she nodded and surrendered her plate. The leftovers were gone. She had made a mistake in not accepting his initial generous offer.

After putting the plates and silverware in the cracked porcelain sink, he knelt near the hearth and removed a coffeepot from a metal grate that jutted from an inside wall of the fireplace. The pot looked older than the cabin and was the old-fashioned kind she thought existed only in old cartoons and movies. He filled two cups and handed one to her.

She blew on the coffee for several seconds, then eagerly took a small sip. After the beans and cornbread, she expected something wonderful. Instead, she wrinkled up her face and shuddered. "Yuck!"

Gil laughed. "Sorry about that. I make it way too strong on purpose. It goes better with my flavoring."

He pulled out a pint bottle of black label whiskey and poured a dollop into his cup, then offered the bottle to Waneta.

"No thanks." She longed for a flavored decaf latte topped

with whipped cream and a sprinkle of cinnamon. Instead, she sipped the coffee and forced herself not to cringe.

Perhaps she had declined Gil's offer of "flavoring" too hastily. Nothing could make the coffee any worse.

"Tell me something, Gil." She did not feel comfortable calling him Giliaduh. "When was the last time you saw my great-grandmother?"

"A few days before she died. That was over twenty years ago."

Waneta remembered the day her mother left for the funeral. Dressed in black, she drove off in their old car while Waneta stood beside the neighbor lady and waved.

Her mother had never been quite the same after that.

"She missed you terribly after you were gone, you know."

It took Waneta a moment to realize he was talking about her great-grandmother, not her mother.

"I don't mean when you left the final time," Gil continued, "but when you moved into town. Your mother didn't like living out here with your great-grandmother and having you hear all those old stories."

"I lived with my great-grandmother?" How could she have forgotten something as important as that?

"And your mom. You two stayed out here less than a year. Your mom moved you into town before you started kindergarten. I remember your great-grandmother saying that going into Cherokee to see you was like visiting someone in jail. That's why she almost never did, and your mother never brought you out here again, although she came up often enough. Until you moved, anyway."

Waneta tried to remember more about her great-grandmother, but she could not control the flashes of memory. They came only in response to a sight, a smell, a sound. "What was she like?"

"Your great-grandmother?"

Waneta nodded.

"To know that, you would need to know the story of *Uktena.*"

"*Uktena?*" She frowned. "I do know it, but what does that have to do with anything?"

Gil stared at the fire for several long moments, then shook his head. "No. You don't know the story, or you wouldn't ask the question."

Anger crept into her voice. "I'm a professional archaeologist—I teach a course about Cherokees at the university. Over the years, I've studied the story of the *Uktena* in at least a dozen different forms. I probably know more about it than you do."

"Maybe. But what you know, you know from books. That's like reading about a car accident in the paper."

"So? I still know the story."

"Yes, but it has no meaning, because you haven't experienced it."

"And you have? You're a lot older than you look."

Waneta swallowed the last of her coffee, and a few loose grounds flowed over her tongue. They almost gagged her before she managed to swallow. Gil must have boiled the coffee grounds directly in the pot.

"Listen," Gil said, more adamant now, "books can give you the knowledge, but they can't give you the feeling."

She rolled her eyes.

"Tell me something," he said, his voice growing loud in the small cabin, "why do people go to concerts? Why don't they just buy the music from the store and listen to it in the comfort of their living rooms? The sound quality's much better, it's a lot less expensive."

"You're reading too much into that. People go to concerts the way they go to movies or amusement parks—to have something to do."

Gil shook his head. "No. They go for the experience, the whole thing. From a recording, even a video, all you get is the music, and possibly the images. Going to a concert, you get it all. Being with your friends, the crowd, the lights, the warm-up band . . . all of them are important."

"What? Are you saying you're going to sing the story of the *Uktena* to me?"

"No, but I could." He grinned. "What I'm saying is that energy flows between human beings, not between humans and books, especially textbooks, which claim to be impartial and logical. Compare that to the stories we have. They're handed down, from person to person, and each time a bit of the initial experience is passed on, directly. True, all we have left is a shadow of what once was, but the seed of the original energy is still there. It lives, just as all good stories live and change and grow. But stories must be told often, and told properly. The people who hear them must think about them after the telling is complete, or the stories will die."

She set her empty coffee cup on the floor beside the bed. "I'm too tired for lectures. If you have a story to tell, just do it."

Gil frowned. "I should tell you the whole story—all two hours of it—but I know you won't sit still for that. Besides, you will come to know the tale better than I ever will, so I suppose it doesn't matter. Instead, I will tell you the story the way your great-grandmother told it to me when I was a small child, but you must promise to listen with an open heart."

After a slight hesitation, she nodded. She would listen, if for no other reason than to get a glimpse into her great-grandmother's oral tradition.

Gil straightened on the chair, his expression becoming serious, his eyes distant. "In the old times, before we forgot there were things in the world we did not understand, the Sun sent a sickness to destroy us."

His deep, rich voice resonated in the small cabin. The words he spoke sank deep into Waneta's skin and curled around her bones, penetrating her from the inside out. She felt as if she had entered another time and place—the change sudden and eerie.

Gil continued, "The Sun was great and mighty, even as she is today, so the people knew they must have a great and mighty foe to combat her. The sons of Thunder changed a man into a great serpent called *Uktena*, which means 'brilliant looker' in the old tongue. This great snake was as large around as a tree trunk, with horns on its head and scales that glowed like sparks of fire.

"This great snake failed to destroy the Sun, so the people sent the Rattlesnake instead. *Uktena* then grew so angry and jealous that it began killing men. Warriors were sent to kill the serpent, but they all died, because on the forehead of *Uktena* was a bright, blazing crest, *Uluhsati*, which could burn forests or send forth fire to kill men at a distance, or compel them to him. Even when *Uktena* was asleep, the crystal from his forehead could call people to him. In those cases, it was not the person who took *Uluhsati* who was destroyed, but his family and his tribe."

"I knew it!" Waneta snapped her fingers and pointed at Gil. "When I was in the lab, I realized the stone fit the legend of the *Uktena*, but I didn't remember that the crystal had a name. That's why you asked if I had the *Uluhsati* when you first saw me tonight. You were looking for the crystal from the *Uktena*."

Gil sighed, obviously upset that she had interrupted his story. "I was looking for you."

"You were looking for this."

She pulled the crystal from her pocket and held it toward Gil. Immediately it flared up, although not nearly as brightly as it did when Dr. Messmore tried to take it from her.

Gil threw his arm over his face. "Put it away!"

"Don't you want to see it? This is the crystal from the *Uktena*, what you call the *Uluhsati*. It's the biggest find of my career." Under her breath, she added, "It may be the last find of my career."

Keeping his arm over his eyes, Gil stumbled to the far corner of the cabin and reached into the shadows. He jerked on some kind of bundle. Metal dropped and clanked against the floor as he shook whatever he had found. A moment later, he emerged carrying a large blanket.

No, not a blanket—an animal skin that had been wrapped around some old tools. He held the skin before his face like a shield.

As he grew close, he lifted the hide a little higher, as if he were about to throw it over her head.

"What the hell are you doing?" she asked.

At that instant, he brought the hide down hard across her lap, trapping her in the bed.

"Got it!" Gil said.

Waneta jerked one hand free from beneath the hide and slapped him hard across the face.

His eyes narrowed as he lifted his head to stare at her. "Do not tempt *Uluhsati*. Only the keeper of the stone, who is trained to handle it, knows how to control it."

She thought about hitting him again, but the look in his eyes stopped her.

She did not understand why he had stuck this filthy animal skin on her legs, but it was important to him. Life and death important.

He gripped the animal hide more tightly. "You don't understand the power of the crystal you hold, or the danger it represents. Please listen to the rest of the story and I'll let you go."

She hesitated. What could it hurt? "Fine," she said in an angry voice. "Tell it."

He relaxed his hold slightly but otherwise did not move. As he continued the story, he stared into her eyes.

"*Uktena* is almost impossible to kill. It has only one vulnerable spot. Markings, like those of a snake, decorate its body. Beneath the seventh mark, counting back from its head, lies its heart. Agan-unitsi, a powerful medicine man, killed it by shooting an arrow through that spot.

"After the creature was wounded, it went into its death throes and destroyed an entire mountaintop. Agan-unitsi was saved only because he had dug a trench farther down the mountain and hid there until *Uktena* was powerless.

"Afterward he gathered up the crystal from the creature's forehead, *Uluhsati*. He learned how to control the stone by feeding it blood and wrapping it in deerskin to mask its power. After he died, a new keeper of the stone took his place, but within a generation or two, the elders decided that men were too ambitious and women should watch over the stone. The care of the crystal then passed to an *ahugia*, a wise woman, who became keeper of the stone. So it has remained since anyone can remember, each woman passing on the knowledge of *Uluhsati* to her daughter, or her granddaughter, to whoever had the talent to control it."

He lowered his eyes and looked at the hide stretched across her lap. "You have not been trained. *Uluhsati* is tamed for the moment, because you are of the old blood. It cannot access your life force, nor can it draw the life force from an animal that is already dead. That's why wrapping it in an animal skin or keeping it close to your body confuses it—but when it grows stronger, nothing will be able to restrain it."

"Gil, it's a rock. Granted, it's a special Taelon rock with some unique properties, but it can't be alive. . . ."

His head snapped up, his eyes blazing. "Why can't it be alive? Because that would mean your life has been a lie, that you've rejected our traditions out of hand because they didn't come from a book? You're being silly. What kind of scientist are you, that you ignore evidence when it's right before your eyes?"

She glared at him, then twisted her hand and tugged the crystal free from beneath the hide. She would show him who was the scientist and who was being silly.

The stone flared up again, and Gil jerked backward. He landed on the wood floor, his eyes tightly shut. Quickly he brought both arms across his face.

The crystal warmed in Waneta's palm, as if drawing heat from the fire. It radiated a pale red light. For a moment, she imagined it calling to her in a sweet, seductive voice that she could hear and understand but that contained no words.

Looking at Gil, she knew she could kill him. She had merely to wish it and it would be so. The stone burned in her hand as she stood and stepped in his direction.

The crystal glowed even brighter as she brought it near his arms over his face. Images kept flashing through her mind: Gil exploding, bleeding, dying. Gasping, she backed away and bumped into the stone hearth surrounding the fireplace. Heat warmed the back of her legs as she desperately tried to calm herself by breathing deeply and concentrating on pleasant thoughts—sunshine, green meadows, warm breezes—but the images intensified. The desire to kill grew stronger. She could taste blood in her mouth as she looked down at Gil's helpless form.

Her hands shaking, she forced the stone back into her pocket. For several seconds, it burned against her hip, then cooled slowly, painfully. As the fire disappeared from the stone, it also disappeared from her mind.

She stumbled to the bed and collapsed, shivering. In a weak voice, she mumbled, "It's all right. You can open your eyes now."

Gil lowered his arms. Bright red streaked his face where it had been exposed to the light of the crystal, as if he had lain in the sun for hours. Eyes glazed, he stared at her for several seconds before groggily pushing himself to his feet and fumbling for his cup. His hands were shaking slightly as he splashed in some coffee and topped it off with whiskey. He held out the bottle and grunted, as if too tired for words.

"Please," Waneta said in an unsteady voice.

She held her cup forward. After blinking in surprise, he doled out a generous portion of whiskey, then filled the cup with strong, dark coffee.

Hesitantly, Waneta took a sip. Perhaps her taste buds had

died, but the whiskey seemed to give the coffee a slightly sweet flavor.

For several minutes, she sipped the hot mixture. Gradually, she stopped shaking and leaned back in the bed, glad for the liquor as it warmed her belly.

Gil stared at her as if he were looking into her soul. "You almost lost control of it that time. If you had, we'd both be dead. Don't remove the crystal again until you're ready to put it back in the sanctuary."

Waneta took a large swallow of coffee. "I don't want anything to do with that stone, and I'm damned sure not going to bring it anywhere, for you or anyone else."

"You must—before it awakes and kills us all."

"No. I'm giving it to the Taelons, or to the Eastern Band of Cherokees—anyone who'll take it. If you want the stone to go back to this sanctuary of yours, ask them to put it back."

"They can't. Neither can I. You're the only one who even has a chance."

He stood and set his cup on the table, then sat beside her on the bed. Tentatively, he put a hand on her knee, his fingers light, his touch unexpected but surprisingly comfortable.

"Even after the whites came, even after the Trail of Tears, we've always had a keeper of *Uluhsati* to protect us. Not until your mother took you away was the chain in danger of being broken. You must take your place, just as your great-grandmother did, just as women from your lineage have always done."

"Just because that's the way it's always been doesn't make it right. When we finally get this mess straightened out, I'm going back to the university. I'm up for tenure."

"You don't understand," he said gently. "The life you knew is gone. You must see that."

She closed her eyes, as if blocking her vision could block the truth of his words. Accepting what he was saying would force her to accept so much else—too much. "All I see is that some nut I used to know a long time ago dragged me up a mountain in the middle of the night and won't let me leave."

He sprang off the bed and stomped several paces away, then spun to face her. "You think I like this situation? You think I want to be up here risking my life for someone who doesn't trust me and doesn't understand the danger she's in?"

"Don't you?"

"Hell no!" Snatching the flashlight off the table, he wielded it like a policeman's nightstick, slapping it against his palm as he paced in front of the fire. "Your great-grandmother understood the importance of the work she did. She devoted her life to it, for the good of the people, for the good of everyone on this planet, regardless of what they had done to us. I'm not going to let her down, not after she entrusted me with a task as important as this—and neither are you. You're my responsibility now, and you're going to do what you need to do to set things right again."

"In your dreams. Who appointed you God Almighty? You're not my father. You're not even family."

"I'm the closest to family you've got!"

Waneta and Gil both froze as the impact of his words set in. For several seconds, the popping and crackling of logs in the fireplace formed the only sounds in the small cabin.

"Sorry." Gil hung his head and stared at the floor. "I didn't mean it to come out that way."

"You're not my family," Waneta repeated softly. "And I don't need your help."

He set the flashlight on the table. "Walelu, please."

"My name is Waneta." She lay down on the bed and pulled the blanket tightly over her shoulders.

He sighed and flopped down in the chair. "You've lived among the whites too long."

She jerked her head up and glared at him. "That's a racist thing to say."

"Recognizing the differences between cultures is not racist.

Not recognizing and accepting the differences is. Look, all I'm saying is that I'm not up here for myself. The way I was brought up, I was taught to share what I have with others in need. With you. With the people I work with. With other members of the community where I live."

"I understand all about that Indian way of doing things," Waneta said. "It boils down to nothing more than seeing who can give the bigger gift. But you all know you're going to get something in return. You expect it. You demand it. Where do you think the term 'Indian giver' comes from?"

"Now who's being racist?" He rubbed two fingers against the middle of his forehead, as if fighting a headache. "You may not believe it, but what I do, I do for the good of others. If I expected any kind of repayment, that would not be a gift—that would simply be delayed gratification. All I expect is that some of those I help will help others in return."

Waneta sat up, her mouth open. "What world do you live in? In our society, people don't worry about anyone but themselves. They can't. There's too much competition, too many people. The world you're talking about—where people banded together and helped each other with their daily struggles—that world is long gone. You're living in the past."

Gil finished his coffee in huge gulps, then uncapped his whiskey bottle and held it over his cup but did not pour. Instead, he put the cap back on and set the bottle on the table.

He folded his arms across his chest, and his jaw hardened. "There's nothing wrong with living in the past if it means hanging on to something good. People may behave like you say—in the cities—but this is home. This is where some people, at least, still know how to live."

"It's not my home."

"It could be."

He slid off the chair and kneeled in front of her. Taking her hand in his, he looked up into her eyes. "It's a good place to live, Walelu. Beautiful country. Clean air. There's nothing like waking up early in the mountains before the mist has gathered and looking out over the land where our people have lived for thousands of years. Everything a person needs is here. Good water. Hunting. Fishing. A place to grow a garden."

"Be careful, Gil," she said without any humor in her voice. "It sounds like you're proposing."

He jumped off his knee and turned away. Keeping his back to her, he said, "I just wanted you to know that if something happens to me, you could live here. The cabin's been deeded to what's left of the *gadugi*. They understand your importance. They will help and support you. Also, the land from your great-grandmother is still there. The *gadugi* have been paying the taxes on it all these years, saving it for you." He glanced over his shoulder. "I assume you still own it?"

The *gadugi*? Who were the *gadugi*? The word brought to mind faces of old men, gathered in her great-grandmother's cabin.

Waneta nodded. "I found the deed among my mother's things, but I don't want the land. I don't want to live here. I just want my old life back."

Even as she said it, she realized how unlikely it had become. What if Gil was right? What if she could never return to the university?

She would miss Jill's kindness. And eating lunch with the other professors at the Arena. She would also miss teaching classes. But she would not miss the hoops a person had to jump through to get published, or the endless committee meetings, or the annual evaluations with their trifling raises.

Gil sat in the chair again. "You belong to this mountain, Walelu."

She raised her hands and balled them into tight fists. "When will people quit telling me that? I belong where I choose to belong."

"It will do you no good to deny it," he said firmly. "The mountain will see to it that you go where you must."

"That's easy for you to say. You believe in this stuff."

"I didn't—not until today."

She looked up in surprise. "Are you serious?"

He worked his hands together nervously. "I haven't even thought much about the old stories since my great-grandfather died. Sure, I always knew our ancestors were smarter than the whites gave them credit for. They understood the medicinal uses for hundreds of plants—they could treat diseases modern medicine has only recently learned how to cure. I just never dreamed that some of the more fantastic stories might be true. Like everybody else, I figured the ancient myths were just legends invented to explain parts of nature our ancestors didn't understand. Now I know that at least one of those stories was real."

Waneta nodded. Gil's statement about the plants was factual enough. This intimate knowledge of plant lore had been well documented, not only for Cherokees but for aboriginal people all over the world.

But the *Uktena*? On the surface, that story seemed an obvious fairy tale, but as Waneta reconsidered the facts, the possibility did not seem as far-fetched as it had before.

Gil was right. She was not looking at this scientifically.

When she first examined the crystal in the lab, she thought it was Cherokee. Later, when the Companion Protector showed up with the Volunteers, she assumed it was really a Taelon artifact of some kind.

Perhaps it was both.

Ma'el, a Taelon, had come to Earth thousands of years ago. Plenty of his relics had been found in Ireland and a few in South America. What if the *Uluhsati* were nothing more than a mind-altering weapon that had been left with Cherokees of the Mississippian period?

Perhaps Ma'el had been the original Agan-unitsi. The name did not sound similar, but Waneta did not know Cherokee. Agan-unitsi might simply mean funny-blue-guy-from-the-sky.

The deerskin she found with the crystal had blood on it, but no trace of blood was found on the stone itself, even though the two had lain together in that pottery jar for decades. Since she had not cleaned the stone before putting it in the TMA, the only way for the stone to have no blood on it at all would be if it consumed the blood it was given.

The stone was comprised of elements the TMA recognized but refused to identify. Given that, it seemed likely the crystal came from another world, one vastly different from Earth but known to the Taelons. Who could say what properties such a stone might have? It could alter the minds of those who came in contact with it. It could force them to imagine giant serpents, or even dead ancestors.

As for the blood, it could certainly act as some kind of suppressing agent, although she could not guess how. Perhaps it just gummed up the works of the machinery, or maybe it acted like a sedative. If the crystal really did feed on blood, as the Cherokee legend prescribed, perhaps the *Uluhsati* remained dormant because it was sleeping off a good meal.

Gil's other claim—that her energy and the energy from dead animals confused the stone—could also be valid. She did not understand Taelon technology, but Taelons were energy beings and therefore understood more about manipulating organic energy than humans ever could. Also, she had read articles about how researchers had traced certain genetic markers through hundreds of generations. Perhaps Ma'el had genetically altered some of her ancestors such that their body energy would act as natural suppressants for the crystal.

Whatever the truth, Gil had a point. The ancient Cherokees understood the stone in ways modern science did not.

If she was ever going to get rid of this rock, she would need to trust those ancient stories. That idea did not sit well with her at all, but she saw no alternative. The present Taelons had already shown that they were more interested in shooting first and asking questions later.

"So how do we control this thing?"

Gil looked up, his eyes wide, his mouth working silently for several seconds before he answered. "I—don't know. You're the expert."

"What are you talking about? You're the one who brought me up here. You're the one who knows all the old stories. I don't know anything about this stone."

"You know more than I do. If I touched *Uluhsati*, it would kill me. You handle it like it's no problem."

Waneta raised her hands in the air. "Then how do you know all this legend stuff? Why do you talk as if you live in the mountains?"

"I grew up here, remember? As far as the stories go, I listened to your great-grandmother and my great-grandfather for years. I've probably been exposed to lots more of the old mythology than you have—and you study this stuff. But I'm not some *didahnuwisgi*. I don't sit in the woods and practice spells all day. I work in Nashville as a studio musician."

Waneta blinked several times, then laughed out loud. "You're kidding, right?"

Gil's brow bunched in a pained expression. "No. I play guitar and keyboards, and sing backup whenever I find someone who'll let me. I've been in and out of various bands for years."

Waneta snorted. "And here I thought you were some tough guy. Slipping in under the noses of the Volunteers. Getting us both out. What were you doing? Making everything up as you went along?"

"Not exactly. I served in the army for a time." Gil's face twisted into the same expression he had worn when he spoke of losing friends to the Taelons. "I know how to handle myself when there's a need, but that's not who I am, that's not who I want to be."

"Then why do it?"

"For the same reason you need to take the stone back to the sanctuary. Because sometimes in life, we're the only ones who can."

Gil pulled something out of his pocket. He stroked it with his thumb, as if it were a worry stone.

"When you were little," he said, "you used to take naps in the afternoon. You'd come over in the morning, then after lunch, you'd snooze. Normally my great-grandfather and your great-grandmother would join you, and I'd play outside by myself. But one day, when the rest of you were sleeping, your great-grandmother came out on the porch to speak with me. She was very serious and told me that she just had a dream, one I should always remember. I knew she was an *ahugia*, a wise woman, and whatever she said was important, so I listened closely."

Gil stood up and poured himself another cup of coffee.

Waneta frowned at him, then drained the last of her coffee, which had gone cold. She set her empty cup on the hearth.

"The dream was simple enough. She said that when I got much older, almost when I had forgotten she had ever told me this dream, a time would come when I would be the only one who could help my friend Walelu. She asked if I knew the story of *Uktena* and I answered that I did because *Eduda*, my great-grandfather, told it to me often. She said a day would come when a friend would ask me for a very important favor. On that same day, I would see my good friend Walelu holding *Uluhsati*, the crystal from the forehead of *Uktena*. When that happened, I was to help Walelu put *Uluhsati* back where it belonged."

Waneta studied Gil's face, searching for any trace that he was making up this entire story.

"She also said that when I saw you with the stone, gods like water would come from the sky and that *Uluhsati* would call to them. If the gods took the crystal, our world would die."

Gil rubbed his worry stone nervously for several seconds, as if there were more to the story, parts he was unwilling to share.

Earlier in the car, he said she would remind him of the old ways. He said it in a way that indicated that her great-grandmother had told it to him. What else had the old woman said?

Waneta waited for Gil to speak, but he just stared at the fire for several minutes, drinking the last of his coffee and never meeting her eyes.

Still staring at the flames, he finally said, "Everything has happened as your great-grandmother said it would, as it needed to, for you and me to come together: for me to have the ability to protect you, and for you to have the knowledge you need to put back the stone, whether you realize it or not."

"What is this, Gil? Are you saying we're controlled by fate? By destiny? Does that mean we have no free will?"

"No, not exactly. One of *Uluhsati*'s powers is the ability to predict the future, one possible future, anyway. Your great-grandmother was keeper of *Uluhsati*. She often knew what would happen before it did. She even knew that you and your mother would leave the mountains—she just didn't know when."

Gil looked at Waneta. He had interesting eyes. They had always fascinated her, even as a child, but they had been more joyful then.

He shrugged. "I suppose some things can be changed. I'm no expert, so I don't really know, but I believe I had to bring you here, that it would have happened no matter what I did."

Waneta spoke softly. She was tired and her voice had lost the hostile edge from earlier in the evening. "Things happened the way my great-grandmother said because you accepted her words as fact. That's nothing more than a self-fulfilling prophecy."

The flames shadowed the lines at the corners of Gil's eyes, and he looked much older. "It's true we create our own realities. That's one of the things I learned in the army. They drilled into us that there was only black and white, right and wrong, but pretty soon I figured out there was also a lot of gray in the world."

Folding his hands in his lap, he added, "Maybe I could have resisted my destiny, but maybe not. I just can't believe it was coincidence the Resistance called me instead of someone else, and I darned sure don't believe you just happened to be the one to find the crystal in what was left of the sanctuary rather than some other archaeologist from some other university. It's as if our whole lives have been geared toward bringing us together in this way. But now that we're here, now that we're together, maybe our destiny can be changed. If we try hard enough, if we're careful, perhaps, there's a chance . . ."

Waneta again had the sensation that Gil knew more than he had chosen to reveal. She moved from the bed to the hearth, and Gil quickly lowered his eyes, refusing to look at her, staring instead at the small object in his hand.

Waneta followed his gaze and saw that he was not rubbing a worry stone, but instead was moving his fingers softly over a small figurine, one he had polished smooth from such frequent ministrations. She leaned forward to get a better look at it.

"My statue!"

Gil started, then relaxed and smiled. "Yes, I almost forgot this was originally yours. My great-grandfather made it for you. He was the one who always called me Giliaduh, Puppy, and you, Usdi Walelu, Little Hummingbird. That's how you got the name."

She reached out tentatively and touched the tiny figurine. Cold. Smooth. Parts of it were well worn, but she could still make out the delicate features of the tiny face, could still see the miniature ear of corn attached to the woman's feet, its husk reaching up to caress the woman's legs and curl around her waist and shoulders.

"It looks like me," she said, and the voice of a small girl echoed the words inside her head. Memories flooded over her then, the sudden torrent of emotions so strong that she had to fight to keep the tears from her eyes as she spoke.

"Your great-grandfather carved this from a stone he called an 'old man of the river.' I remember crying when he first told me that, because I knew he had to kill the rock to make this. He told me not to grieve. He said the stone had been placed in the river for him to find, and that the image of Selu had been waiting since the mountains were small for him to set her free."

She closed her eyes and saw a gnarled hand holding forth the tiny figurine. Selu, the Mother of Corn. During her studies, Waneta had always found that myth especially fascinating but had never understood why. Now she did.

The figurine brought to mind other images, other sensations. She recalled standing on tiptoe behind an elderberry bush, straining upward to steal a playful kiss from a tall, dark-haired boy before she ran away, giggling.

"I remember the day your great-grandfather gave this to me. I had been somewhere—perhaps with you."

Gil blushed. He remembered, too.

"That's the last day you were here. We didn't know that at the time, of course."

Gil looked incredibly boyish and cute when he got embarrassed. She smiled as she ran her finger over the figurine again. "Why didn't I keep it?"

"Your mother wouldn't let you, so I took care of it for you. I knew I'd see you again someday—your grandmother had told me—and until then, it helped me remember."

"You've carried this with you all these years?"

Gil scuffed his feet against the wood floor. Staring at them intently, he said, "It's small. Not hard to carry."

Waneta could no longer hold back the tears. Emotions buried for years came roaring back. Now she could remember how much she had loved her great-grandmother, and how upset she had been the day her mother told her they would not be going up to the cabin anymore.

Gil held out the figurine. "This is yours. You can have it now."

She blinked rapidly, trying to focus on the small statue and struggled to find her voice. "I can't take this, Giliaduh. Your great-grandfather made it."

"He made it for you. Besides, it will be a good reminder when—" He paused, then thrust the figurine in her direction. "Take it. I don't need it anymore."

At first, she thought he meant he did not need it because she had come back, but that was not it. Gil was fighting an internal battle, one she did not understand.

"You must believe I'm here to help," he said suddenly. "I don't know how much time we have left before—before things get rougher."

The pain in his voice tore at her. Whatever he was hiding was killing him. She reached out and took his hand. He squeezed it, then turned away, his eyes closed, his fingers trembling.

"Please," he said softly. "You must believe me. You must do what is right."

Inside her pocket, the stone felt cold, and she longed for sleep.

"I no longer know what to believe," she answered, and knew she spoke the truth.

TWENTY-FIVE

Liam met Renée in a truck stop outside Cherokee, North Carolina.

She wore Levi's and a simple blouse. Her hair was pulled back and her earrings looked inexpensive. She bent over her drink like a truck driver over his coffee, except that she was drinking diet soda, heavy on the ice.

Liam held a green-bordered menu in his hand but did not open it. "In disguise?"

"I thought it important to blend in."

She had pushed her plate away, her runny eggs and greasy sausage only partially eaten. Now, sipping her soda, she glanced around the café, her head held carefully still but her eyes always moving.

In a lowered voice, she added, "I'm not the chief executive of Doors International tonight. If any questions are asked, I was never here and we never had this conversation."

Liam turned to see what she was looking at. More than half the booths and tables were empty. Of the people here, most were tired-looking men with tousled hair and wrinkled clothes. Two gray-haired women faced each other, sipping coffee. One table, marked by laughter and loud conversation, held four young men eating an early breakfast.

Liam saw nothing that explained Renée's concern, but he had been here only a few minutes, long enough to receive a menu but not long enough to order.

All he wanted was some toast. Renée's food looked less than appetizing and his stomach was a little queasy. A storm was forming over the coast of North Carolina and the ride in the helicopter from Charlotte to Asheville had been bumpy. The car ride along the up-and-down roads to Cherokee had made him feel worse.

"So why all the secrecy, Renée? Why go to the trouble of having a helicopter waiting for me at the Charlotte portal if it wasn't going to fly me all the way here? Whom are you planning to kill?"

He said the words lightly but knew that if Renée was taking such elaborate precautions, she had good reason. It was exactly this overdeveloped sense of vigilance that had kept her alive when others would have been discovered long ago.

Before Renée could answer, a short, squat waitress huffed her way to the table. "What can I get ya tonight?"

"Wheat toast and a cup of coffee," Liam answered.

"That's all? You sure?"

"I'm not that hungry," Liam answered and handed her the menu.

The waitress tucked it into an oversized pocket of her apron and stomped back to her stronghold behind the counter.

"She's a friendly gal," Renée said.

Liam grunted and rubbed the bridge of his nose with his fingers. "Tell me why you brought me out here at this time of night."

Renée glanced around the room again, then handed him her global. A recorded video showed a dark-haired woman, about twenty, enter the picture from the left. She shoved a microphone into the brightly lit face of a woman several years older. The global's sound was muted, but the jerky camera angle and the roving brightness of the lights reminded Liam of those hasty interviews reporters so often snatched on the steps of some public building.

Renée pointed at the woman on the right. "That's Dr.

Waneta Long, an anthropologist with the University of Tennessee at Knoxville."

When the woman shook her head and lifted her hand to shield her eyes from the glare, Renée paused the video and pointed at an object in the woman's hand. "There."

Liam studied the picture. "What is it? Some kind of ruby? Is that why you brought me out here?"

"Yes, but it's not a ruby. It's Taelon. While we won't understand what it does until we've had a chance to examine it, we discovered evidence of its existence about six months ago. Since then, we've been paying Dr. Long's department to find it for us."

Liam studied the video. "Apparently she has. So what's the problem?"

"We're not the only ones who want it."

Renée repeatedly punched her straw down into her glass, the ice making a slushy crunching sound as she stabbed it.

"Ronny's been making trouble. Last night, a group of his buddies in black gunned down Dr. Long's department head, a true lowlife named Dr. Messmore. They claimed he was a member of the Resistance. Then, just before I called you this morning, *First Edition News* ran a story stating that Dr. Long blew up the building on campus where she works. According to unnamed sources close to the investigation, she was also a member of the Resistance. And to make matters really interesting, she was romantically involved with her department head, recently deceased."

"Any of that possible?"

"No way. Ronny's spin doctors have been putting in loads of overtime on this one. I double-checked with the local cell leader. Neither Dr. Messmore nor Dr. Long was a member of the Resistance—and I guarantee you a woman of Dr. Long's intelligence would never get involved with a dirtbag like Dr. Messmore."

Liam grinned. "You knew him personally?"

"We had our conversations."

She lifted the straw to her mouth, sucked out the ice, then punched the straw full again.

Picking up the global, Liam squinted at the red object in Dr. Long's hand. "So what is this thing?"

"I'm not sure, but the Taelons want it. Desperately. Sandoval wouldn't pull out all the stops unless there was a reason. I want to know what that reason is. Talk to him. I'm sure he'll say he's looking for Resistance terrorists, but he might let something slip that would be useful. Also ask Da'an what's going on. If Zo'or knows about this crystal, there's a good chance Da'an does, too."

The waitress dropped off four slices of toast and an oversized cup of coffee. Liam started on the toast while he thought back over what had happened to Da'an in the theater. At the time, he suspected the boy had caused the problem, and after talking with Sister Kathrynne, he eliminated any other possibility. But what if he was wrong?

"When was the crystal found?"

"The day before yesterday. Probably in the evening, but certainly before dark. We didn't find out about it until late that night."

Liam's chest tightened. The timing matched.

He had been so sure about Daniel, but Da'an clearly said the boy did not cause his illness. Also, Da'an insisted on keeping the shuttle but refused to say what he needed it for. But if Daniel had nothing to do with it, why had Sandoval been snooping around the theater, asking about the boy—especially if he was supposed to be looking for this crystal?

"Liam, what is it?"

He shrugged and tried to breathe normally. "Probably nothing, but I'd like a copy of that video—and anything else you have about the crystal."

Renée nodded and pressed the controls on her global to start the transfer procedure.

After glancing around the café again and seeing no one who

looked out of place, Liam set his global on the table next to
Renée's, so he could watch the progress of the copy operation.

"You may be right about Da'an. I'll contact him in the
morning."

"Good." The corner of Renée's eye twitched.

"There's more," Liam said. "You could have told me all this
over the global."

She picked up the napkin and rolled it between her fingers.
"Doors International sponsored the dig site where Dr. Long
found the crystal. When we heard she had discovered it, we
immediately made arrangements with Dr. Messmore to transfer ownership, per our sponsorship agreement. The Volunteers
killed him before he could deliver it to us."

"Where is it now?"

"I'm not sure."

"And?"

She dropped the napkin and picked up the spoon. "I like to
be careful, so I sent a Resistance acquaintance of mine to collect the stone in case the department head had—how should I
say?—reservations about parting with the crystal. My acquaintance and Dr. Long disappeared about the same time Dr. Messmore was killed."

"Sandoval?"

"At first I was afraid of that, but Ronny's got too many people looking for this woman for it to be just a ruse."

"How do you know that?"

"Cherokees, like most Native Americans, are anti-Taelon.
They feel like they've fought and lost this battle once already,
and they have no intention of losing again. I have plenty of
sources here in town who tell me that every FBI agent east of
the Mississippi is converging on this place. Some have already
started checking the hotels and motels in the area, not to mention the casinos. Two are in a sedan outside. Even so, the main
search won't start until first thing this morning. They don't feel
secure enough in their story to start breaking down doors in

the middle of the night. Plus I don't think they know about the guy I sent in. All published reports have them looking for the woman only."

"Is that how you ended up in Cherokee?"

"Not exactly. I headed here before I knew it was going to become Spook Central."

Liam yawned and rubbed his eyes.

"I hope I'm not boring you," Renée said.

"Sorry. I didn't sleep much last night and I won't get any at all tonight."

Liam had finished half his toast and now took his first sip of coffee. Terrible compared to Augur's, but at least it was hot.

"I don't think my Resistance friend ever intended to surrender the crystal to me," Renée said. "I think he plans to keep it for himself."

Liam frowned. "That seems like quite a jump."

"When this guy looked at the video you just saw, he said two words I didn't understand: *Uckteena* and *Ooluh*-something. Then he said the time had finally come. I didn't know what he was talking about then, but after I hung up, I understood. He's Native American."

"So?"

"So, there're some Native American legends surrounding the crystal. I don't know what they are, but I think he recognized the stone."

"And you think he's going to steal it?"

Renée nodded. "Only, to him, taking it wouldn't be stealing. I'm guessing he wants to return it to where it was found. Probably sees it as his personal quest."

Liam wiped toast crumbs from his mouth and drank more coffee. "Where was this crystal found?"

Renée bobbed her head toward Liam's shoulder. He glanced in that direction but saw nothing except rows of trucks in a dimly lit parking lot.

"The dig site's on the other side of Cherokee. I think he'll take the stone there—if he hasn't already."

Liam considered the possibility. "It doesn't sound like this guy is going to cooperate when you show up and ask for the crystal."

"That's why I brought this."

Renée opened her small handbag and tilted it in Liam's direction. Inside was a small metal box that looked a bit like a silver-plated garage door opener.

Liam chuckled and shook his head. "A taser? Now I know why you brought me out here."

"I don't want to kill the guy." She gave him a half smile. "Besides, you'd be surprised what a taser can do in the hands of the right person."

"If you say so." Liam threw ten dollars on the table.

"Hey. I was going to buy you dinner."

He smiled. "You will. But not here."

Renée put the taser and her global in her purse. Liam kept his global in his hand as he followed her outside. The copy operation had finished long ago, but he had a call to make. He hesitated when he spotted the sedan.

The nondescript brown car was parked in the shadow of a large tractor-trailer. Beyond it, the first gray light of dawn outlined the trees.

Renée stopped in front of her black Porsche. The lights flashed and the car emitted a beep as she clicked off the alarm and unlocked the doors.

Liam laughed. "I thought you were in disguise. Isn't this a little flashy?"

"Maybe they'll just think I married rich. Besides, I chose this car when I was interested in speed, not concealment."

She climbed in on the driver's side.

Liam leaned on the door frame and activated his global.

A moment later, Augur squinted into the display. "What do you want? Some people like to sleep, you know?"

"This is important."

"Everything with you is important, but is it important enough to warrant compensation?"

When Liam did not respond, Augur sighed. "What is it?"

"I need you to track down a Cherokee crystal for me. It might be called *Uck-teen-a* or *Ooluh*-something."

As Liam spoke, he looked back at the sedan. The shadows were still too deep to see into the car. No one was moving in the parking lot except a red-haired woman in a long, simple dress, who had just come out of the truck stop's convenience store.

"That's all you have?" Augur asked. "*Uckteena* and *Ooluh*-something?"

"I'm transmitting a picture of a crystal. I'm sorry I don't have any more, but for someone of your capabilities, I'm sure that's enough."

The red-haired woman climbed into the driver's side of an old green Chevy. A small head popped up on the passenger side, a child with hair the same blazing color as the mother's.

Augur glanced down. "So who's the lady?"

Liam paused a moment—how had Augur seen the woman?—then he realized Augur was talking about the scientist in the video. "An archaeologist named Dr. Long, but I don't think that's going to help you much."

Augur grinned. "Ah, my friend, that's because you focus only on the task at hand. I'm always interested in *broader* possibilities."

Liam watched the Chevy drive away. "Let me know when you have something," he said, still watching the Chevy. Then he punched off the global and climbed into the plush bucket seat next to Renée.

TWENTY-SIX

Both Zo'or and Da'an retired to Foundation Room One after the meeting of the Synod adjourned, but contrary to custom, neither left.

Zo'or remained because he refused to accept the Synod's decision. After Da'an departed, he planned to return to the Synod Council Chamber and demand that they concede his authority to take whatever actions he deemed appropriate.

Da'an remained for reasons of his own. Perhaps he intended to challenge Zo'or's gambit, or perhaps he intended to make his own play for the Synod's attention.

Zo'or could ask, but Da'an would simply evade his questions. Instead, he decided to wait and observe. Eventually his parent would leave or speak. Walking with precise, unhurried movements, he stepped to one corner of the room and assumed a completely motionless posture.

Da'an stationed himself on the other side of the room, still as a statue, and waited in return.

They focused on each other before allowing their bodies to halt all movements, fixing themselves into a perpetual staring contest.

Once set, they remained in place, each battling to see who could outlast the other.

Zo'or could endure this position for days, if necessary, but after several hours of staring at his motionless parent, he realized that Da'an could probably stay at his post for weeks. He had the patience of the universe.

Also, as the hours passed, the power increasingly called to Zo'or. Incredible, undying power. It waited just beyond his grasp, but instead of trying to obtain it, he was wasting his only opportunity to lock in the leadership of his species by staring at Da'an. He had no time for this.

Zo'or broke his stance, then broke his silence. "Why have you remained on the mother ship?"

Da'an held his position for several seconds more, as if wanting to emphasize that he could have easily maintained his place much longer. "It seemed apparent you wanted to speak with me. I thought perhaps you chose to meditate first."

Zo'or stepped forward, claiming the middle of the room. "It is you who wanted to speak with me. Say what you wish, but your actions reveal your true motives."

"I do not understand. Do not everyone's actions reveal his motives?"

Zo'or moved his fingers in mild irritation. "Your attempt to distract my question will not succeed. Why have you traveled to the mother ship in your shuttle instead of taking the portal? Where is your Protector?"

"After I detected the Elteena, I lost the proper balance. I suffered lapses into the la'ras'pa'la. Liam Kincaid stayed with me until I stabilized."

Da'an loved to attach technical names to his actions, as if that made them more important. La'ras'pa'la was nothing more than an antiquated term for the Taelon equivalent of a human swoon.

"Would you not agree that Liam earned a time of rest?" Da'an continued. "Surely I have no need for a Protector while I am among my own species."

Zo'or controlled his vexation and instead made the sign for mild amusement. "Good. You do not want him to know about the power you seek. That is a motivation I can appreciate."

"Do not assign your motivations to my actions. You will always be wrong."

"Will I?" Zo'or ached where he had once felt the power. The craving made him irritable. "If the Synod decides the Elteena must be taken alive, you wish to be the one chosen to confront the creature. That way, you may claim the power for yourself.

"I seek no power."

"Of course you do. That is the true reason you sent your Protector away and traveled to the mother ship in your personal shuttle. That is also why you kept your knowledge of the Elteena hidden from me, and from the Synod."

Da'an gestured in growing anger. "Your perceptions are twisted. It is you who kept the knowledge of the Elteena hidden by denying my request for a full meeting of the Synod. You also failed to disclose the truth when you knew exactly where the Elteena was located. If we had acted together, we could have contained the creature. Instead, you sent Agent Sandoval to retrieve the Elteena for you. Fortunately for all of us, he failed."

Zo'or's body tensed, becoming as rigid as it had been during their staring contest but even less relaxed. He now knew what the Elteena could do. If Sandoval had confronted the creature, he would have died, his life force and the life force of the Volunteers supplying the energy the Elteena needed to begin its metamorphosis.

"I would not have sent Agent Sandoval had you revealed what you knew."

"I revealed enough. I showed you the power."

Zo'or's body locked again, but this time in longing rather than apprehension. He could feel shadows of the energy coursing through him. He must have it. He must!

He struggled for words. "That is—not—the same."

Da'an nodded his head and closed his eyes, conceding the point. "If you could be trusted with the information, I would have given it freely."

Zo'or fought for control. All he could think about was the power. It was as if Da'an, acting as some ancient Taelon wizard, had cast a spell over him, capturing his soul and stealing his mind. Was this what a drug addiction felt like for humans? If so, Zo'or felt rare pity.

"I can always be trusted with information," Zo'or said, his fingers flying in frenzied excitement. "Everything I have done since arriving at this planet has been done to protect the Taelon race."

"As has everything I have done."

Zo'or curled his fingers into scornful amusement. "You and I both know that is not possible."

Da'an remained completely calm, his posture revealing detached interest as Zo'or fought to contain his desperate, overwhelming need.

With precise, slow motions, Da'an drew out the sign for benevolence. "What I know—and you do not—is that the same destination may be reached by many paths. The quickest route is not always the straightest."

Da'an started toward the door but paused just before the exit. "Or the safest."

Then he was gone, leaving Zo'or alone to battle his dreams of glory.

TWENTY-SEVEN

The poker clanking against the hearth woke Waneta. She rolled over and stared at Gil as he stirred new wood into the coals from last night's fire. Every muscle in her body hurt from sleeping on the old, broken-down bed, and her mouth tasted dry and chalky, a leftover gift from the whiskey Gil had added to her coffee. She had been unable to brush her teeth before going to bed—she had no toothbrush—and now that she was awake, she realized she had no way to comb her hair.

Gil had spent the night slouched against the cabin's only door, a blanket wrapped around his shoulders, dozing off and on as he waited for trouble that never came. So how could he be so chipper? Except for the raccoon sunburn on his face, courtesy of the crystal, he seemed completely rested. Perhaps the floor was more comfortable than it looked. Certainly it was no worse than sleeping on the musty lumps beneath her that passed as a bed.

She had never been a morning person, and the thought of going through a day with no personal hygiene items and nothing but Gil's coffee to keep her sanity made her want to go back to sleep, but nature prevented her from doing even that.

Sitting up, she wrapped herself in the blanket. "Where's the bathroom?"

Gil, who stood beside his new fire doing some kind of overly energetic morning stretching routine, responded with a shrug. "Pick a spot."

She squinted at the faint light coming through the dirty window beside the sink, but her brain refused to process anything beyond its most basic functions. "What?"

"Preferably outside." He grinned. "The outhouse blew down years ago, and since nobody lived up here, I didn't see any reason to dig a new one. Just stay away from the stream, okay? That water usually tastes better than what we get out of the pump."

Waneta's eyes widened farther as his words slowly penetrated her morning fog. "I'm headed for Cherokee," she said groggily. "Surely they have a hotel with better accommodations than this."

Gil added another log to the fire, then went back to his stretching. "What do you plan to pay for it with? How are you going to register?"

"I'll figure that out after I use their bathroom."

Gil's jaw tightened the way it had last night when she told him he was living in the past. "It won't kill you to go outside."

Waneta knew that. She had been on enough dig sites in remote locations to realize that a bathroom was not always available. "I'm not like you," she said stiffly. "I don't like being out here. You don't mind living off the land, eating whatever you can kill or grow in the garden. I'm not like that."

"You could be," he said.

She stood up and trudged toward the cabin's only door, dragging the blanket behind her like the train of a wedding dress. "We went over all this last night. I'll put the stone back in the sanctuary. Then I'm going home."

Leaving the blanket by the door, she went outside. She did not go far, and when she returned, Gil was hunched beside the fire, watching over six slices of bacon laid out neatly in an old-fashioned cast-iron skillet. The sizzle of the cooking meat joined the sound of a news broadcast coming over Gil's global.

"How do you like your bacon, crispy or chewy?" Gil smiled at her, as if they were on a camping vacation.

"I don't like bacon," she said.

"Ah, come on. Everybody likes bacon. It may not be good for you, but there's nothing better in the morning than fresh coffee and bacon that's been cooked just right—and I'm one hell of a cook."

The aroma from the fireplace filled the small cabin and Waneta's mouth watered. In truth, she loved bacon, especially old-fashioned slab bacon, the kind Gil was making.

She picked up the blanket and started making the bed. "I thought we weren't supposed to run our globals—something about the new models all coming with locators."

"They do, but normally they give out their position only when they're in transmit mode, not receive mode. But I'm not willing to take even that chance. This global's had its location chip disabled. It has no idea where it is."

When she finished making the bed, Gil handed her a plate with three slices of bacon and scrambled eggs. "The eggs may look nasty," he said, "but don't worry about that. There's nothing better than eggs fried in bacon grease. Trust me."

"I thought you said there was nothing better than bacon and fresh coffee."

He grinned. "That, too."

In another time and place, she might have found him charming. But in the cold gray light of morning, all she saw was the man who had been there when her world came apart. She watched him, feeling trapped and angry. Her life had been taken from her and she suddenly found herself in a world she did not understand and did not like.

She stared at her plate. He was right about the eggs—they were brown and specked with dark flakes—but they tasted wonderful. Eating them, she felt embarrassed. Gil was not to blame for her problems. He had risked his life to save hers, and for that, she owed him more than her scorn and lack of gratitude.

On the global, a man in a tie pointed at a large weather map. His smile was cheaper than his suit. "Yes siree, today's going to be filled with sunshine with a chance for record highs, even in the mountains."

He beamed at the camera, as if he had personally created the clear skies, then turned to a female correspondent. The camera angle widened to include the news desk. "It looks like a continuation of Indian summer. Enjoy it."

"Thanks, Mike," she said sweetly, "it sounds wonderful."

After turning to face the camera, she replaced her smile with an expression deeply earnest and caring, then launched into a description of gang violence on the other side of the world.

Gil finished eating. Dumping his plate and fork into the old sink, he said, "We should be safe here, but *Uluhsati* won't allow us to remain that way for long. I'm going to climb up the ridge and scout around. I'll be back within an hour."

As he put on his jacket, Waneta felt a strong urge to ask him to wait. The idea of being alone in the cabin suddenly frightened her. She wanted to apologize and ask if she could go along but resisted the temptation. She knew nothing about sneaking around in the woods, and while Gil might be a studio musician who lived in the city, he belonged here. By going along, she would endanger them both.

After he left, she finished the last of her bacon. Chewy, with just the slightest hint of sweetness, it was the best she had ever tasted.

How did he do it?

She had definitely been too hard on him. The man could kill, cook, and clean. What more could she want?

Smiling at her own silliness, she put her plate in the sink beside Gil's, then frowned at the mess. After dumping out the rest of the coffee, she used the pot to heat some water. She found a big cooking pot for a wash bin and some gray powder that looked like soap. In only minutes, she had cleaned their few dishes, but her hands stung by the time she finished. Was the soap homemade, too?

As the newscaster on the global blathered about Heisman Trophy candidates, Waneta noticed the frying pan, still by the fire. She picked it up. Although greasy, it remained relatively clean, even though Gil had fried eggs in it. That reminded her of something her mother once said, about how a person should never wash a properly cured, iron skillet with strong soap, and she hesitated to put it in the water. She had caused enough trouble for Gil already; she certainly did not want to ruin his frying pan, especially since it might be older than she was.

Waneta set the skillet on the table—she would ask Gil about it when he came back—and heard the newscaster mention the University of Tennessee.

She assumed that the report concerned football, but then she heard, "Dr. Robert Messmore."

At the mention of the name, she again saw the smoke and the light of the energy blast as it struck his chest. She could almost feel the pain as his arms flailed back and his body collapsed.

The man had been an arrogant ass at times, but he had not deserved to die, and she could not help feeling responsible for his death.

She slumped onto the chair beside the table and stared at the global, horrified to see the exterior of her apartment flash up on the screen. As the view panned across the dingy building, an unknown, unseen voice pried its way into her personal life, twisting it into something evil while exposing it to the world.

"Inside this benign-looking building is the apartment of Dr. Waneta Long, an anthropology instructor at the University of Tennessee. According to information just released, authorities now believe that last night's explosions, which caused more than five million dollars in damage, were set off by Dr. Long."

The story dragged on and on, becoming ever more preposterous, ever more painful. Its scope expanded, showing additional pictures—God, they used her driver's license photo—and providing a special two-minute "exposé" that revealed excerpts from her "personal manifesto."

What manifesto? Would anyone really accept this cock-and-bull story?

Why not? Who had come forward to say otherwise?

They even interviewed her neighbors, none of whom knew her but all of whom had become experts on every facet of her existence.

Lying scum.

Gil was right. She had not wanted to believe, but he had been right all along.

Even if she cleared herself of all charges—unlikely because the authorities had a death to cover up—now she would never receive tenure at the University of Tennessee. She would be lucky to find a job teaching at a two-year college.

Had this rustic cabin become her home? With no money, no possessions, and no way to survive without help, what choice did she have? Last night, Gil had saved her life. Now he would need to go on saving it, protecting her because she could not protect herself. She hated depending on someone that way and swore she would become self-sufficient, even if it killed her.

Suddenly the stone in her pocket moved. She put a hand against her jeans and felt a growing warmth.

"What the hell?" She jumped to her feet. The stone burned hotter and hotter in her pocket. She wanted to dig it out and toss it away, but Gil had warned her not to remove the crystal again. He said it could kill them both if she did.

Boom!

At first, she thought it was a gunshot, but then it came again: Boom!

Someone was pounding on the cabin's old thick door as if using a battering ram.

As she ran to the small window above the sink, hoping she could squeeze through, the boom sounded again and the door flew open.

"Freeze!"

She stopped, then slowly turned around.

One black-clad Volunteer in full body armor stood just outside, half hidden behind the doorjamb. He kept a gun trained on her while another Volunteer darted into the cabin and dropped to a knee, the aim of his gun following his gaze around the room.

"It's her," the one said from his position by the door.

The other acted instantly, swinging his weapon around and pointing it at Waneta's heart.

He was going to pull the trigger. She was going to die.

And with each passing second the stone in her pocket grew ever hotter.

I can save you, it seemed to say. *Trust me.*

She ignored its enticing call. Instead, she raised her hands high into the air, showing she was unarmed. "Don't shoot," she said slowly but firmly, the way she had been taught to speak to rapists or muggers.

"Where's the crystal?" the one on his knee asked, his voice muffled slightly by his helmet and face shield.

"Crystal?"

The Volunteer leaped to his feet and charged her, stopping with his barrel just short of her nose.

"I should kill you," he said.

"Our orders are to take her alive." The other Volunteer stepped inside and closed the door but kept his energy rifle loosely trained in Waneta's direction.

She squirmed. Her leg burned. She had to do something quickly; otherwise she would be forced to surrender the stone. The crystal was giving her no choice.

"I'll get it for you," she said innocently. For good measure, she added, "Just don't kill me."

"We were supposed to locate the subject and call in," the Volunteer by the door warned. "Nothing more."

"Call in, then!"

The Volunteer with his gun in Waneta's face was shaking. She could not tell if it was from excitement or fear, but his jitters were so bad that he had a problem keeping his energy rifle on target. Suddenly he threw it to the floor and ripped off his helmet, which he tossed onto the table. Then he pulled a pistol from a holster on his belt.

"I knew you had it," he said, pointing the gun at her. "I want to see it."

"No!" the other Volunteer called again—just as someone answered from the global.

"Report."

The Volunteer lifted his face shield. "This is unit two-seven. We have the subject in custody. Request additional instructions."

"Stand by."

"We've got to kill her," the Volunteer with the pistol repeated. His shakes were growing worse, but it was the look in his eyes that worried Waneta. Wild, desperate.

"No! Stand by."

The other Volunteer seemed as concerned about his comrade as he was about Waneta. He dipped the nose of his energy rifle, directing it more toward his friend.

Burn . . . burn! The crystal glowed so hot that Waneta squirmed again, but stopped when the Volunteer in front of her tightened his finger ever so slightly on the pistol's trigger.

A man's voice came over the military global. "This is Sandoval. Show me what you have."

The Volunteer with the gun backed away as the other Volunteer faced the global toward Waneta, allowing its microcam to pick up her image. On the display, she saw the face of the man who had been on campus last night, the man who had called her in Gil's car.

Sandoval.

"Excellent. Keep Dr. Long just as she is. Reinforcements will arrive within minutes."

The display went black and the Volunteer sealed the global in a pouch on his belt.

As soon as the global blinked off, the Volunteer with the pistol charged forward and shoved Waneta back against the sink. He placed the barrel of the gun against her neck. His breath stank and sweat trickled down his forehead.

He ran a nervous hand through his hair. "Show it to me."

"We're supposed to do nothing."

He whipped his head around, his pistol dropping and sliding off its aim. "I just want to see it!"

The stone. Just as it had called to Waneta, it now called to this Volunteer. That was why he was bending orders. If she showed him the stone, it would take him completely and they would die. How the crystal could do this she could not explain, but she knew it to be true as certainly as she knew her own name.

A tapping started on the wall behind her, just beyond the window. It worked its way around the cabin, skipping across the front door before it stopped.

When the tapping started, both Volunteers trained their weapons on the sound, their attention following its trail as it moved.

As soon as their backs were turned, Waneta grabbed for the wash bin in the sink.

The closest Volunteer noticed her movement and spun back, bringing his pistol to bear even as she lifted the bin and tossed dirty dishwater into his face.

He screamed and clawed at his eyes, the harsh soap doing its job.

His partner whirled at the noise, his energy rifle ready.

At that moment, the door flew open, knocking the Volunteer forward.

Behind him, Gil charged into the cabin, his hair loose, a high-pitched cry coming from deep in his throat.

The Volunteer recovered and brought his rifle around, but not quickly enough. Gil knocked the rifle aside and drove the base of his palm hard into the Volunteer's nose. The man let out a grunt and crumpled to the floor of the cabin.

The other Volunteer raised his pistol, but his eyes were red and watering. He fired as Gil lunged, getting off three wild shots before Gil knocked him back against the wall. Waneta backed away as the men grappled, pushing and shoving in the corner of the cabin. Gil stumbled over the empty wash bin and landed on the table. He crashed to the floor.

The Volunteer blinked furiously, then raised the pistol for a careful aim.

Gil's eyes went wide, and he felt around until his fingers closed on the handle of the skillet. He threw the pan hard just as the man fired.

The skillet caught the Volunteer in the side of the face and he went down without a sound. Gil jumped on him, then backed away from the limp body, blood on his hands.

Waneta's ears rang from the pistol shots, but they could not mask the voice of the stone, calling to her again. Saliva filled her mouth and she felt an overwhelming need to feed. *Blood. Death.* She slumped back against the corner of the cabin where Gil had retrieved the animal skin. Where was it now? Perhaps it would help.

Gil wiped his hands on the clothes of the Volunteers, then pilfered several ammo clips from their packs and tucked the pistol into the back of his pants.

Waneta crouched in the corner. Burning. Hot. *Feed. Feed!* She clutched at the stone through her pants, willing it to be silent, and looked at the Volunteers. "Are they dead?"

"No," Gil answered but seemed distracted. "Did they call in?"

The stone had started to cool, its fever temporarily subdued, but as its heat left Waneta, she began to shake. Anger, fear, and frustration robbed her of her ability to think. The black-clad Volunteers, lying like corpses on the floor of the room where she and Gil had shared supper and argued before breakfast, brought home a sense of hopelessness even worse than before.

She and Gil were outlaws. They would always be outlaws.

Gil slung an energy rifle over his back and rose to his feet. "Did they call in?"

She nodded.

"Damn!"

His gaze moved from the men to the front door. "We'll have to leave the car."

As he helped her to her feet, she noticed a wet patch of dark crimson soaking through the right shoulder of his jacket.

"You're hurt," she said, dazed.

He glanced at her, then at the Volunteers. "You still have *Uluhsati*?"

She nodded, but could not take her eyes off the growing stain. "We need to get you to a doctor. You'll die."

Slowly he lifted his chin, and in his calm eyes, she saw the depth of his power—like the earth: immovable, unchanging, solid.

"I'm not important. The stone is all that matters."

He looked out the door, his head turning left and right. "Come. We need to hurry."

She glanced back at the Volunteers. "Shouldn't we tie them up or something?"

"We don't have time."

He stepped out of the cabin and trotted away, but she did not follow. She could not move. Her life, everything she knew, was gone. Forever gone. Even after the news broadcast, without realizing it, she had held out a small irrational hope that the events of the past two days were all a bad dream. But they were real. She had felt the stone's power. She had felt its hunger and knew she could not control it much longer.

Gil came back. "Walelu, we need to leave."

He started away again, but when she still did not follow, he said, "I didn't make it to the ridge. Volunteers are everywhere, most headed this way from the sanctuary. They probably have the highway blockaded, and if those two called in, more are on the way. We need to go cross-country and we need to go now."

Waneta swallowed and shook her head. What use was running?

Gil gently touched her face. His fingers were warm and sticky with blood. His or the Volunteer's?

But when she looked in his eyes, all she saw was the little boy, the one she had kissed behind the elderberry bush.

Gil, sweet Gil.

"Don't worry," he said gently. "They have the weapons and the technology, but I have the land. I know this country better than they ever could. If you do exactly as I say, I'll get you to safety, but you have to trust me."

She closed her eyes and nodded.

When she looked at him again, he gently took her hand in his and led her out of the cabin. After a last glance back at what could have been, they headed north down the mountain.

TWENTY-EIGHT

The sensation struck Zo'or again, and he stumbled as he moved down the corridor of the mother ship toward the shuttle bay. In his matter state, the waves of energy felt strange, akin to what humans might describe as pain, or perhaps only discomfort—but they were becoming stronger and more frequent.

The Elteena was awakening.

These sensations were different from those he had felt two days ago. Besides being much more forceful, they came through blind, with no images of any surroundings, but with a texture, as if covered by material of some kind. He also felt a hunger, a need for energy that lay just beyond a thick gauze he could not penetrate. Most important, he knew instinctively where the Elteena was, not in terms of human names, such as North Carolina, but the way a bird knows it is near its summer home after a long migration.

Zo'or tried to walk more quickly, his skin shimmering with each step, the effort to keep his human facade becoming more difficult. He needed to reach a shuttle before he lost control. If the Commonality realized what he was about to attempt, they would stop him—they would take away his destiny.

Volunteers turned their heads as he passed. They would notice that something was wrong, but they would never dare question him. Only other Taelons were a threat, and he made it to his personal shuttle without seeing any other members of his race.

On board, he reverted to his energy state. He powered on all systems and dropped away from the mother ship, rushing at the planet in a controlled descent that would have him in the western mountains of North Carolina within minutes.

Normally he would have entered ID space, even for so short a journey, but he needed to contact Agent Sandoval. He had assumed that the human would take days to locate the woman scientist and had not yet warned him to stay away from her if she were found. Now he felt certain that this latest flurry of activity from the Elteena was triggered by Agent Sandoval or his group of Volunteers.

Before he could activate the communication panel, Zo'or was seized by a sense of frenzied excitement. The Elteena was about to feed but was struggling to do so. For the next several minutes, Zo'or jerked and twitched, the pounding energy shaking him to his core.

Then the emanations from the Elteena subsided, and its hunger, still unsated, lost its anticipatory edge.

Zo'or resumed his human facade and contacted Agent Sandoval.

When the human appeared on the display, he made an obvious attempt to appear relaxed and pleased, but Zo'or had known him long enough to notice the deepened lines at the corners of his eyes and the subtle tightness around his mouth. Agent Sandoval was concerned and worried.

"Excellent work," Zo'or said. "Finding Dr. Long so quickly exceeds even your own lofty opinion of yourself."

"Uh, yes, thank you." Agent Sandoval frowned, then straightened, lifting his chin slightly. "I would have found her last night, but my new assistant didn't finish the analysis of Dr. Long's personal items until early this morning. Turns out the woman owns a piece of ground very near the dig site where the crystal was found. I started our search there. We discovered her at a cabin nearby and have taken her into custody. I ordered additional men to move in for support—but we don't know yet if she has the crystal. Personally, I suspect she's rid herself of it by now."

Zo'or closed his eyes momentarily to feel the energy of the person around the Elteena. "No," he said, opening his eyes. "The stone remains with her. I am certain."

"Certain?" Agent Sandoval wrinkled his brow. "How can you know?"

"That is not your concern."

Zo'or could tell that there were underlying eddies of meaning to Agent Sandoval's seemingly innocent question, but he had no energy available to unravel their mystery.

"Tell your men to surround and contain Dr. Long. At all costs, do not allow her to escape, but under no circumstances allow any of your men to touch the crystal she carries. It would kill them."

"I don't understand. If the crystal would kill my men, why hasn't it harmed Dr. Long?"

It was a question Zo'or should have considered as soon as the Synod meeting ended, but his constant craving for the Elteena's power had robbed him of much of his mental capacity. In truth, he did not know why the woman was unaffected by the crystal. He assumed that the Elteena was using her as its mode of transportation, confiscating her eyes, ears, and legs to take it where it wanted to be for its metamorphosis.

"We have no time to discuss that," Zo'or said. "For now, do as I say. I will meet you outside the cabin where the woman is being held."

Agent Sandoval looked even more concerned than before. It was obvious he did not want Zo'or to come. "Of course. I will send you the coordinates."

If the Elteena had remained more active, Zo'or could have guided himself there. As it was, he nodded, accepting Agent Sandoval's information, then terminated the connection.

A dull ache replaced the emanations from the Elteena as the last of its energy ebbed away. The creature had gone dormant again, but the time for its final awakening approached. It had taken so long to grow active, it must have remained in its diminished state for many centuries, meaning it was much weaker than he had originally anticipated. If he could reach it before it completed its metamorphosis, capturing it would be easy.

Now that the blinding waves of energy from the Elteena had faded, his link to the Commonality reasserted itself. While he could not detect individual thoughts, he could perceive group impressions—and what he perceived most was fear. Many of the Companions must have experienced at least part of what he had, but they had reacted differently. Instead of wanting to seize the opportunity, they were afraid. They did not want him to go, but that was why he would lead and they would follow.

Da'an's face appeared on the communications console. He must have used the override to force a connection, but unless Zo'or activated it at his end, the link would remain one way only.

"You must stop," Da'an said. "Return the shuttle to the mother ship."

Zo'or ignored the request.

"I know you can see my image and hear my voice. I will continue to speak until you activate your display."

Zo'or hesitated, then slid his hand in a short arc across the hovering lights of the shuttle's instrument panel.

"Your overconfidence will destroy you," Da'an said. "Obey the decision of the Synod."

"What decision? They have known about the being for almost half a day and have yet to decide anything. I will contain the Elteena myself."

"You must not pursue this alone. Have patience. The Synod will reach consensus on the best method to contain the Elteena. Then we must act together for the good of all."

"The Elteena will not wait for that. I will do as I must."

"You cannot. By yourself, you lack the strength to control it."

"This one is weak. I do not believe it has the energy for the metamorphosis."

Da'an blinked and his skin flushed a brighter shade of blue. "On what experience do you base this judgment?"

Zo'or did not respond.

"Your ambition has blinded you. One Elteena is more dangerous than all the Jaridians. It is more powerful than an Urod. You do not have the knowledge or the training to contain it."

"I have all I need."

"The creature is preying upon your desires. It has ensnared your mind and robbed you of the ability to discern between its wishes and your own."

"If that is true, then you are to blame. You are the one who showed me the power of the Elteena. You are the one who taught me to long for what it alone could offer."

Da'an stared, unblinking, for several seconds, then slowly closed his eyes. When he opened them, his expression had softened and the bright blue of his skin had faded to its typical shade.

"Your stubbornness endangers both Taelons and humans. If the Elteena transforms and you fail to contain it, the creature could use your connection to the Commonality to take possession of us all. With the energy gained from us and with the humans to feed it, it might reach the level of power necessary to reach across the stars to others of its kind. If so, all life on this planet would perish."

"Your words do not fool me. If you believed as you say, you would never have delayed telling me about the creature when you first sensed its presence. You plan to take the Elteena for yourself."

"I have dealt with . . . an Elteena before."

Zo'or did his best to mask his surprise. While Taelon offspring were born with the knowledge of their parents, there were always gaps in the complicated network of memories and experiences passed on to the next generation. For Zo'or, Da'an's early life still contained many mysteries.

"I have told you the truth. I did not inform you about the

Elteena, because I suspected you would act exactly as you are acting now. Only by joining together and using the power of the Commonality can we overcome the Elteena. I have no motive beyond the safety of us all."

After a moment's hesitation, Zo'or decided. He cocked his head and spoke in a strong voice. "You have misled me before. This is too important for me to trust you now."

"That is why you must."

Zo'or deactivated the console, but the one-way link remained. Da'an closed his eyes halfway and his skin faded to a darker shade of blue.

"Elteenas do not allow second chances. When you find it, do not hold back. Do your best to kill it. You cannot—but it is your only hope for control."

The display winked to black. Da'an had broken the one-way connection. A convenient way to achieve the last word in any conversation.

Zo'or adjusted his fingers, splaying them across the holographic instrument panel, and the shuttle dove toward the tree-covered mountains that concealed the Elteena.

TWENTY-NINE

Liam rode with Renée down the street, the sunroof of her sports car open to the clean, crisp air of midmorning. All around them were signs that Cherokee had become the center of a great search. Blockades were set up on every road leading to or from the small city of 20,000 people, every motel and restaurant was full, and clusters of cars huddled near most main intersections—powwows full of county sheriffs, state troopers, and plainclothes FBI agents.

Earlier in the morning, Liam had tried to get in touch with both Da'an and Agent Sandoval. Neither had been available and neither had returned his call. Now he and Renée were driving around the small town of Cherokee, in part hoping to spot Sandoval, but mostly just getting a feel for the magnitude of the search.

Renée had been right. The Taelons—Zo'or at least—wanted the crystal Dr. Long had discovered, and they were doing whatever they could to find it.

"Ronny must have blown his budget for the entire year," Renée said, smiling, as if Zo'or actually paid attention to a budget.

She showed no signs of being up all night. While she was still wearing her disguise—blue jeans and cheap earrings—her eye shadow and lipstick looked as if they had been applied by a makeup artist, and her eyes remained bright and clear. Her blond hair, made alive by the breeze, caressed her shoulders as she drove down the street in her black Porsche.

Some disguise.

As for himself, he would have liked a couple hours' sleep. He was not used to seeing the sun rise twice in one morning and his thoughts were sluggish. He suspected that he was missing some vital connection between what had happened to Da'an the day before yesterday and the crystal they were searching for now.

"Welcome to the future world of the Taelons," Renée said as she drove past a group of officers. "Look at all of them. They don't even know that Zo'or is the one pulling the strings."

"He may be pulling the strings for good reason. Have you considered that?"

Renée raised an eyebrow as she glanced in Liam's direction. "When have you ever known Zo'or to watch out for the good of humanity?"

"When it's also good for the Taelons."

Renée focused her eyes back on the road, then started singing to herself, so softly and with so little movement of her lips that Liam could barely tell what she was doing. This silent singing, as Liam thought of it, was a new habit. She did it whenever she disagreed with him but did not want to argue.

Liam folded his arms across his chest and leaned back in the seat. "What's your theory? Why do the Taelons want this crystal? From what I saw of it in the video, it didn't look Taelon."

Renée stopped singing. "I don't know why they want it. What's important is that they do."

"So they want it. Why not let them have it?"

Her eyes flashed. "For one thing, we paid for it. For another, it's not nice to go around killing people just because they have something you want. The Taelons don't go out of their way to acquire anything unless it tightens their control over this planet. I'm not about to allow that."

Before Liam could respond, his global chimed. He pulled the device off his belt and peered into the screen.

Augur did not look fresh and ready for the day to begin. He had not shaved, his glasses were off, and he was rubbing his eyes.

"Augur?"

Augur cleared his throat, put back on his glasses, and brightened somewhat. "I have what you asked for, but tell me—when did you start chasing monsters?"

"Monsters?"

"*Uktena* and *Uluhsati*. Cherokee mythology. That was what you wanted to know about, right?"

Liam glanced at Renée, who nodded. "Yes," Liam said. "Those sound right."

"I was afraid you'd say that." Augur shook his head and glanced down. "According to Cherokee legend, the *Uktena* was some sort of huge snake. A real nasty one, too. Big and able to spit poison for dozens of feet. It crawled around killing people until some ancient warrior destroyed it."

Augur grinned. "I know what you're thinking. Real noble guy. Saved his people and all that. But there was more to it than getting rid of an unfriendly neighbor. The snake had a crystal in its forehead—the *Uluhsati*—that gave its owner special powers, one of which was the ability to see into the future."

"Augur, that's—"

"Amazing. Ya, I know. And I got the info you needed in under four hours. Definitely a record. Save the praise. Just send cash, okay?"

Liam rolled his eyes. "Yes, Augur. You're the best."

"Wait. You haven't heard it all." Augur's expression turned serious. "Truth is, the legend of this *Uluhsati* sounds a bit odd for the Cherokee. You see, the warrior who killed the *Uktena* wasn't your normal average Cherokee. In fact, he wasn't Cherokee at all. He came from the Shawano tribe, the Shawnees. But the Cherokees weren't real big on glorifying their enemies. It'd be like a Hatfield bragging up a McCoy."

Augur's face became more animated and his voice grew louder. "To tell the truth, when it comes to this crystal, lots of little details don't make sense. For example, the Cherokees didn't sacrifice animals. Except with this crystal, they did. According to what I found, it needed to be fed with blood every seven days, unless the guy who owned it put it to sleep. The problem there was when the *Uluhsati* woke up, it would need blood and would kill as many people as necessary to get its proper daily requirements of vitamins and minerals, if you know what I mean."

As Augur spoke, Renée's hands tightened on the steering wheel and her face paled. She knew as well as Liam that if the Taelons wanted this stone, chances were good that at least some of what Augur was saying was true.

Augur raised a finger. "I almost forgot. I also checked out that lady you mentioned, Dr. Waneta Long."

"I didn't ask you to check on her."

"Ah, that's a freebie." Augur smiled. "She's one fine lady."

"And?" Liam asked.

"You knew our good friend Sandoval wants her dead, I assume? As usual, you never tell me the whole story. Anyway, she's special as far as the Cherokees are concerned. I checked into her history. She and her mom rejected their heritage and moved into the city when she was just a girl. As far as I can tell, they never returned home. What's interesting about this is that up until her mom left the reservation, all the women on this lady's side of the family were Cherokee wise women, what they call *ahugias*. No written record exists that ties this family to the *Uluhsati*, but it wouldn't surprise me if Dr. Long had seen this crystal long before she dug it up at her field site."

Liam glanced at Renée, who shrugged and shook her head.

"What else have you got?"

"Ah, I see that interests you." Augur imitated Liam's voice. " 'I didn't ask you to check on her.' Aren't you glad now I did?"

"Yes, Augur, you're fantastic."

"The best is yet to come."

A video appeared on Liam's global showing a man with an energy rifle at his side. He stood in front of a building at night, flanked by white columns. After shouting something, he raised the rifle, holding it in one hand and pointing in the general direction of the camera. It was an awkward angle to hold the weapon, and only an idiot would shoot an energy rifle with one hand, but that was what it looked like this guy planned to do. Before he could, an energy blast hit him in the shoulder. He cried out and fell to his knees. When he raised the rifle again, he was shot several times in the chest.

The image froze, then Augur's face returned. "I dug this little tidbit out of the Knoxville police investigation file. According to the accompanying text description, this video was supplied as evidence by the Volunteers after the death of Dr. Robert Messmore, our good lady scientist's ex-boss."

"Yes," Liam said. "I knew he'd been killed, but of course I never saw the video."

"Besides an investigator or two, no one ever will. Wouldn't want too many people to examine it too closely."

The image of the department head appeared again on Liam's global, but this time, the image had been blown up, showing just the man's chest. Augur's voice came over the global, describing the image.

"This video was shot at night. Lots of street lamps and such were around, readily identified as light sources by anybody who cared. Of course, if you have light sources, you have shadows to worry about, but this must have been a real rush job, because our good picture doctors forgot about their moon shadows."

"Moon shadows?" Liam asked.

"Yes. We had a full moon the night this guy was killed. Next to the artificial lights, it cast a dim shadow, one everyone forgot about—except me, of course."

"Of course."

Liam held the global up close to his face, but the sun was too bright on the screen to see the image clearly. He certainly could not pick out any shadow.

"I enhanced the shadow and used it to project what the department head was actually holding. I can't determine any colors, but the shape came out rather nicely."

The image on the screen morphed into a new image, showing the man holding not an energy rifle but—

"An umbrella? They shot a man for pointing an umbrella at them."

"Now you know why your mother taught you not to point—or would have, if you didn't already know everything."

The display showed Augur again, who slumped back on a stool. He had expended his small burst of energy. Once again, he looked as if he had just climbed out of bed.

"So," he said, "what's the connection between the kid you asked about yesterday and our good Cherokee doctor lady?"

Liam frowned. "I'm not sure there is a connection—and I'm not sure there isn't."

Augur shook his head. "Thanks. That clears up everything. Listen, I've been awake for two days straight trying to make a deadline and get my hands on some important incentive cash, and your side trips haven't helped. If you have anything else you want to know, go to your local library, okay?"

Liam smiled. "Thanks, Augur."

"Sure."

The global went black.

Renée pulled into a long line of cars inching forward. The narrow streets were not designed to hold this much traffic.

Liam tucked the global back on his belt. "After hearing what Augur had to say about the crystal, do you still think this stone is something you should keep from the Taelons?"

Renée's eyes hardened. "More than ever."

THIRTY

Branches snapped and bullets whistled through the trees overhead, followed an instant later by the echoing booms of rifle shots.

Gil pulled Waneta to the ground, then dragged her to her feet and slid down into a shallow gully.

Sharp pain lanced Waneta's side with each step, and she fought for breath. Even so, she was doing better than Gil. She could go on. Gil could not.

His face was pale, his cheek smeared with blood where he'd wiped away sweat with his left hand. As he ran, he kept that hand over his wound. Blood dripped through his fingers and soaked down his shirt into his jeans. When they first started away from the cabin, he ran with agility and grace, his only concession to his injury revealed by a wince at each step. Now, panting and wheezing, he stumbled often.

"We've got to stop," Waneta pleaded. "You're killing yourself."

"I'm fine," Gil rasped, then coughed and spat.

At least his saliva was clear. His lungs had not been hit.

Bullets whizzed haphazardly around them. The Volunteers chasing them were shooting blindly now.

The first shots had not been so careless. They came when Waneta and Gil tried to approach the highway about a half mile from the cabin. The Volunteers who spotted them must have been in the trees, perhaps part of the same team as the two who had surprised her this morning.

Waneta had caught glimpses of the black-clad men but could not say for sure how many there were. Even injured, Gil had stayed ahead of them by using the natural terrain to hide his and Waneta's descent down the mountain. Always, he had led them in the opposite direction of the sanctuary. He planned to lose them in the trees, then reach the highway and hitch a ride back up to where they needed to be.

But how much longer could he run? They must have come a couple of miles already, but the constant twisting and turning had left her lost long ago. Now all she could think about was Gil collapsed and dying with Volunteers closing in from every direction. She could almost feel the bullets ripping through her flesh and imagined blood—blood everywhere.

The stone in her pocket warmed and she tried to block her pessimistic thoughts.

They reached the bottom of the gully and darted across a narrow brook. Gil hesitated a moment, checking the narrow patches of sky and the lay of the surrounding hills, then led her into a ravine that snaked up a small rise.

"Come on." He grabbed passing trees with his bloody left hand and pulled himself forward.

Sweat smeared his face, and he kept his teeth clenched, wheezing with each step. As they neared the top of the rise, he began to grunt. The grunts grew louder and sharper until at last he reached the top and threw himself over. As he hit, he folded and rolled into a pile of leaves and sticks gathered at the base of two trees.

Waneta followed, diving in beside him as shots rang out all around them. The sound of bullets and energy pulses hitting the branches and tree trunks reminded her of moths snapping against her car's windshield late at night. Bits of bark and twigs rained down and she lay still, gasping for breath. The shooting continued longer this time, as if the Volunteers could sense that their targets were nearing the end of their endurance. Waneta soaked up every second of rest, building her strength, knowing she would need to run again in moments.

Gil did not move.

Had he been hit again? Her hand trembling, she timidly touched his shoulder.

He rolled over. His hands shook as he pulled the rifle from his back. He checked the energy pulse chamber and cocked the weapon.

"It's up . . . to you," he said in rasping breaths.

"What do you mean? We can make it. You can't give up now."

He winced as he reached out with his clean hand and touched her cheek. "I'm not . . . giving up. They'll be on us soon. We can't outrun them."

"We can't fight, either. There's too many. We wouldn't stand a chance."

Gil took several seconds to catch his breath. "I know. That's why, when they come, you won't be here. I'll hold them off long enough for you to get down the mountain. Steal a car if you have to, but find our people. They'll help."

Waneta swallowed and blinked. "I won't leave you."

"You don't have a choice!" Gil grabbed her arm but immediately let out a small cry and released her, his face scrunched up in pain. "You can't give *Uluhsati* to the Taelons. We've kept it safely for thousands of years, but if you let them have it, it'll destroy our world."

"You can't know that. Maybe those were just stories. Maybe the Taelons know how to control it."

"No!"

Gil gasped and dropped his hand. "Remember what your great-grandmother said—about people from the sky."

"That was just a dream."

Waneta knew what she said was wrong, but if she convinced Gil to surrender now, he would live. Her eyes blurred and she wiped them with her fingers.

"Just a dream." He tried to laugh but coughed instead. Panting and gasping, he gestured toward his bloody shoulder.

"She told me about this. Soon as I saw you holding *Uluhsati*, I knew what it meant. Still do."

So that was the information he had been holding back last night. He knew he was going to die. How could her great-grandmother have told that to a little boy?

"Take the stone . . . back where you found it. Find your great-grandmother. She knows what . . . to do. Listen to her."

"My great-grandmother's dead," she said—but it did not matter. Taelons transferred to a different state of energy when they died. So, too, must humans. Why had that been so hard to accept?

Waneta looked at Gil. She did not see a man, exhausted and bloody, dying from a gunshot wound. Instead she saw a little boy, sunshine bright on his face. A boy she had loved, a man she would love if only she had the chance.

She shook her head and tears fell from her cheeks. "I can't do this."

"Have to. Only one who can."

She lay her head on his chest. His heart was beating fast, struggling against the exertion and the loss of blood.

Listening to the rhythm of his life, she suddenly understood. If their roles were reversed, she would want him to go on, would demand that he do so. As long as one of them escaped, the Taelons could not win.

Pulling away, she tried to smile. "I'll take care of the stone. I promise."

He held her hand and the touch seemed to calm him. His breathing eased and he pointed down the mountain. "Go straight down. Stay in the trees until you reach the road." He grinned feebly at her. "With all the commotion going on up here, even your noisy stomping won't attract their attention."

They stared at each other a moment longer, the finality of that look more lasting than words could ever be.

With a grunt, Gil suddenly reared and fired several shots up the mountain. Return fire zipped past him as he ducked down again.

He grabbed her shoulder and shoved. "Now go!"

She paused for one last backward glance, then ran, following the low points of the land as she had done with Gil.

Shots echoed behind her, but she did her best not to think about them. Instead, she concentrated on what she needed to do to stay alive. She would not fail. Gil had sacrificed too much.

After another half mile, she was winded again, but she spotted the highway and sprinted for it. Her long race down the mountain was finally over. Now she needed to find a ride any way she could and hope Gil was wrong about the roadblocks.

As she worked her way over a bald upturn in the land, a sharp, burning pain lanced through her thigh and she stumbled. Grasping at the pain, she lost her balance and fell just as a tree exploded in front of her and to the right. She hit the ground and rolled. The boom of an energy rifle echoed around her, the sound following the shot. Wood chips fell across her like gentle rain.

She grabbed her leg, afraid she had been hit, but discovered the crystal, burning against her thigh. If it had not activated and made her stumble, she would be dead now. Had it saved her? Or had its ability to see into the future caused it to celebrate her death a bit prematurely?

She did not have time to decide.

Distant gunfire, muffled and distorted by the trees, rumbled far behind her.

Gil was still alive, still fighting.

As for her, the lucky hunter thought he had bagged his deer. That's why he had not fired again. He would be watching the area, searching for movement. When none came, he would bound down the hill to claim his trophy.

She would be gone before he arrived.

Crawling forward, she slithered around the tree. Rocks scraped her skin and pine needles pricked her belly.

She could not see the road but knew she was drawing near. If she could get to its side, she could use the ditch to crawl away. By the time the Volunteer reached the damaged tree and discovered that his prey was gone, she would be down the road and on her way again, her progress hidden by the intervening trees and the rise and fall of the landscape.

The stone grew warm again as she moved along the ground. Perhaps it enjoyed her snakelike progress. She smiled, morbidly amused by the thought.

Suddenly she stopped. Something was wrong. It took her a moment to realize what.

The sounds of gunfire and energy blasts had stopped. She waited anxiously, but they did not return.

Gil's battle had ended.

No!

Tears welled in her eyes and a small sob escaped her lips. She spun back toward the mountain, not sure what she intended but filled with a sudden well of strength she had never known. Her hearing had miraculously sharpened and she picked out the sounds of Volunteers, creeping through the woods.

She could kill them all. In her mind, she saw trees flattened for miles around. With grim satisfaction, she noted the body of each Volunteer, charred and smoking.

Revenge. *Revenge!*

The intelligence behind the stone sang to her, letting her know she had the power to make them pay for hurting Gil.

Gil.

Giliaduh.

Puppy.

The crystal, bright and glowing, was in her hand—but she did not remember removing it from her pocket. It burned, red-hot, but she felt no pain. She was becoming part of the stone, losing herself to it, ruining Gil's sacrifice.

No!

She tried to drop the stone, but it stuck to her hand. Shaking it, she swung it at the ground, but it would not let go, and as she came back to herself, she felt the heat. The crystal burned hotter and hotter.

For several seconds, she ran amok, then threw herself to the ground and rolled, pushing at the stone, straining to make it come free.

Breathless and terrified, she tumbled to a stop by a huge oak tree. From her spot among the fallen leaves, she stared up, following the tree's upper limbs as they reached for the sky. To grow so large, it must have lived for hundreds of years. It had stood on this mountain before the Trail of Tears, before any whites had walked these misty trails. But even before it had sprouted from an acorn, her people had controlled the *Uluhsati*.

"It's in your blood," Gil had said.

She did not know what to do but knew she must not allow the stone to control her. Ignoring the pain, she sat up and focused on the peace around her, on the beauty of the mountains. In her mind, she tasted the sparkling water of the river and listened to the cry of the hawk as it floated high overhead.

This was why her great-grandmother had lived in this rugged country. In the city, the hopes, fears, and frustrations of thousands of people crashed into the buildings and clung to the streets, choking the air and fouling a person's center of balance.

But here, a sense of eternity surrounded everything. Everyday problems still existed, still wore on the spirit, but they remained in perspective.

She could get through this. The stone would not control her—she would control the stone.

Holding it before her like a talisman, she stared deep into the dancing red lights of its soul. *Peace*, she commanded. *Sleep.*

Waneta did not know how much time elapsed before the stone went dark and she could once again release it from her fingers and tuck it back into her pocket.

Blinking, she looked at her hands. No burn marks, but memories of the pain throbbed deep beneath her skin.

She saw a distant flash of black among the trees and thought she heard the crunch of boots.

Rolling onto her stomach, she crawled toward the road. It twisted up the mountain, only a short distance away, but the

Volunteers behind her were close, stalking her, ready to take her life if she gave them the chance.

The stone felt cold against her thigh—it would not warn her again. But just as she had snuffed its power, it seemed to have drained her energy. Exhausted, she hauled herself to her feet beside another old tree, her legs threatening to buckle as she clung to its trunk like a cicada waiting for its wings to dry.

From high above, the roar of a shuttle echoed through the trees. The branches blocked the ship from view, but soon the people inside would spot her movements. They would direct the Volunteers exactly where to find her.

As she hugged the tree, trying to decide what to do, the soft rumble of an approaching motor joined the distant roar of the shuttle. A green car slowly wound its way up the road. It did not seem like the type of vehicle anyone connected with the Volunteers would drive, nor did it move in a hurried manner. It nosed around a curve, almost meandering, as if its driver had no particular place to go.

She crawled forward rapidly, bobbing her head around until she could see the approaching car more clearly. A woman was driving. In the front seat next to her sat a small boy.

The crack of a twig came from Waneta's left and the rustle of tree branches from her right. She froze, listening, but heard nothing more.

Time had run out. Volunteers surrounded her, and she could not run forever. The car was almost even with her now.

If she ran toward it, could she make it? Would she be shot as soon as she emerged from the trees?

About twenty paces to her left, the road cut through the mountain, creating a small, deep hollow.

She scampered toward the top of the cut, staying as low to the ground as she could. To her right, the car climbed along the road. It would pass by before she made it. She straightened and ran the last ten steps, then dove, expecting shots to ring out around her, but heard nothing as she hit the steep bank and rolled down to the highway.

The car's tires made a staccato screech as the vehicle came to a quick stop.

Waneta stood up and stumbled toward the car, willing herself not to run, doing her best to look normal.

A woman jumped out of the car. "Oh, my. Dear, are you all right?"

She spoke with an Irish accent, another tourist taking advantage of the off-season. Waneta brushed past her toward the car.

"Thanks for stopping," she said softly. She kept her head low, afraid that at any instant a bullet would tear through her flesh and end her flight. The cut in the mountain blocked her from view of the Volunteers, but they would have heard the woman's anxious voice and would be rushing to investigate.

Waneta climbed into the backseat of the car without asking. A small red-haired boy peered at her from the front seat, watching her intently with green eyes that shined more brightly than any Waneta had ever seen.

The woman remained on the road.

Get in, Waneta urged her silently. Get in and let's go.

The woman, as if obeying the unspoken command, walked to the car and climbed behind the wheel. She directed the vehicle back up the road, her pace quicker than before, as if she sensed the urgency of the situation.

Fearing that the woman might be taking her to the police station, Waneta quickly explained herself. "I had an accident— up the mountain a ways. Hunters shot at a deer, and it ran in front of me. My car hit a tree."

The woman clucked at her. "I knew Americans loved their guns, but I surely never knew they still shot animals. What a terrible thing. And you. Are you all right?"

"I took a shortcut through the trees. Then I heard your car and ran, hoping to catch you before you made it past. I slipped and fell coming down to the road. Thank you for picking me up."

Waneta's voice was shaky and she doubted her story sounded

convincing, but as long as the woman kept driving, it would not matter.

The stone in her pocket had other ideas. It was heating up again, rebuilding its energy quickly.

Waneta looked out the rear window of the car but saw no signs of pursuit.

"Where are we headed?" she asked, hoping the answer would be anywhere but Cherokee.

"Up the mountain," the woman answered.

The stone burned against her thigh. Reluctantly she pulled it out. It was glowing softly, gradually brightening. She wrapped both hands around it and tucked it between her legs.

"My son and I are meeting someone there." The woman smiled as she glanced in the rearview mirror. "We're late for an appointment. I hope you won't mind coming with us?"

"No, that'd be fine."

Just don't stop.

Waneta bit her lip as the crystal burned against her palms. Ahead on the road, a line of Volunteers trotted down the mountain. They wore body armor and carried energy rifles.

"I'm not feeling well," she mumbled. "I hope you don't mind if I lie down."

The woman did not seem to care. Waneta flattened across the backseat and tried to figure out what she would do if the Volunteers flagged the car over.

It might make no difference. If the stone kept gaining strength at its current rate, it would kill them all before any of the Volunteers had a chance.

Waneta tried to take strength from the land as she had done before, but the woman interrupted her concentration by leaning over the seat, barely paying attention to her driving.

"My name's Triss," she said. "And this is my son, Daniel."

THIRTY-ONE

Zo'or touched down in the small clearing at the coordinates Agent Sandoval had given him. The tiny dwelling nearby looked older than most in the United States. Of an exceptionally crude design, Zo'or recognized its architectural style as that of a log cabin.

After Zo'or emerged from the shuttle, Agent Sandoval greeted him and pointed toward the small building. "Perhaps we should talk inside."

Zo'or noticed the pinched skin around Agent Sandoval's eyes and the way the man refused to look at him directly. "Where is the woman? What has happened?"

Agent Sandoval twitched and stared at the ground. "She has temporarily escaped. The Volunteers who took her into custody were attacked by an unknown male who . . . disabled them, but he won't get far. He and the woman were sighted a couple of minutes ago, and more than twenty Volunteers are in pursuit. I expect to have them both in custody momentarily."

Gunshots sounded and Sandoval lifted his head. "Perhaps we have them already."

Zo'or felt as if hundreds of small magnetic fields were pricking his body. He craved the power constantly now and could not stand to think how close he had come to having it, only to be denied by Agent Sandoval's ineptitude.

"Your confidence is unjustified. Twice you have let the human female slip through your fingers. You will not make the mistake a third time."

Zo'or returned to the shuttle, but before he could power on the ship's systems, a sudden surge from the Elteena struck him in a blinding blast. Instinctively he shed his human facade, but even as energy alone, he experienced boiling, blinding rage. He wanted to lash out. To kill. To destroy.

This was the power he had tasted but never truly experienced. Now, as it soaked through every part of his being, he relished it, drank it in, and reveled in its potential.

But the power did not last. He felt it going, draining away slowly.

The woman. Somehow she was keeping the Elteena from beginning the metamorphosis.

Zo'or clawed at the receding power, lapping at it, desperate to keep just a little for himself, something to sustain him until he could take it all. But like the Elteena, he could not resist the calming effect that surrounded him. Time slowed, then stopped.

His next awareness was of Agent Sandoval, standing just inside the shuttle, his face concerned, his hands folded in front of him.

"Are you all right, Zo'or? Should I contact the mother ship?"

Zo'or solidified into his human facade, and before he could stop himself, curled his fingers, revealing embarrassment. Fortunately the human did not understand the gesture.

"Report," he commanded.

"You have been sitting here, motionless, in your energy state for almost ten minutes.

"I am not concerned with my status."

Zo'or tried to sense the Elteena and failed. Had it returned to its fully dormant state? "Tell me what has happened to the woman and the stone."

"We captured the man," Agent Sandoval said hesitantly. "I believe he is responsible not only for attacking our Volunteers today but also for helping Dr. Long escape yesterday evening. His name is Gil Ledford, a thirty-eight-year-old studio musician from Nashville. I have asked an assistant to compile a full report, but we already know that he grew up in this area and that this property was deeded to his family more than a hundred years ago."

"Bring him to me. I wish to question him."

"My men shot him several times before he lost consciousness. We have a corpsman with him now and I've called for a medevac from Asheville, but I don't expect him to live."

Zo'or cocked his head and turned his palm over gracefully. "Very well. Compared to the woman, the man is unimportant. Where is she?"

Agent Sandoval locked his hands behind his back and rocked on his toes. "She was sighted with Mr. Ledford shortly before he was shot—less than ten minutes ago. That much has been verified. She couldn't have gone far since, perhaps a mile at most. She will not escape."

"Then it is a pity the human male's injuries are so severe. He would certainly know where the woman was headed."

"Perhaps," Agent Sandoval replied, "but she might be running blindly, just trying to escape."

"Which she has done."

Zo'or waved a dismissal before Agent Sandoval could reply. Closing his eyes, he concentrated on the Elteena but felt nothing. If the woman could keep the creature in its dormant state, he would have no way to track her.

"Time grows short. Your delays may have cost us everything. Join me. We will use the shuttle to find and trap this woman before it is too late."

Agent Sandoval nodded. He stepped out of the ship long enough to appropriate an energy rifle from one of the Volunteers. After checking the weapon's power level, he activated its safety, then cocked the weapon and climbed back inside. As soon as the shuttle's cockpit sealed, Zo'or lifted off and headed north, skimming just over the tops of the trees.

From time to time, the Volunteers, in black armor, showed up as shadows below the colorful leaves. Rather than being fanned out in a standard search pattern, though, they were closing in on a single location.

Agent Sandoval pressed his fingers against the tiny receiver in his right ear. Suddenly he frowned and his eyes narrowed, a human expression Zo'or recognized as frustrated anger.

"So," Zo'or said, setting the shuttle's controls to hover in place, "the woman has escaped."

"No. Worse. She's just been shot."

"Sha'bra!" A brief flutter of rainbow lines passed over Zo'or's skin as he moved his fingers in anger. "I gave orders she was to be taken unharmed."

"As I told my men. Whoever made this mistake will pay, I assure you."

Zo'or could not feel the stone at all. If it was starting to bond with the human female when she was shot, what would it do? His knowledge was incomplete. "We must find her. Now."

"I'm having my men triangulate her location with ours."

Zo'or's fingers fluttered in nervous agitation. Without the lingering presence of the Elteena, he suddenly felt unsure of his actions. Perhaps Da'an had been correct. Perhaps he was making a mistake by confronting the Elteena alone.

"They have the location now. Just north of here, along the main road."

As Zo'or banked the shuttle left, he felt the Elteena's presence again, gradually growing stronger. Perhaps the intensity of the creature's last attempt to transform had temporarily dulled his ability to locate it in its less energetic state.

Unless the Elteena had purposefully concealed itself. Was it aware of his monitoring?

That would be unlikely. In its dormant condition, the Elteena had few abilities—and after being dormant for hundreds of years, this Elteena seemed especially weak. It would need to consume an especially strong life to trigger its metamorphosis and become fully active.

Zo'or brought the shuttle over the road. Directly below, a car moved slowly along the highway. Zo'or reached out again with his awareness—and was hit by the full force of the Elteena's presence.

The creature had found its victim.

Zo'or tried to control the shuttle, to bring it down, but the constant pulsing from the Elteena hit him repeatedly, and his fingers would not obey. In defense, he tried to revert to his energy state and failed.

For the first time since he had detected the Elteena, Zo'or felt fear. If the creature completed its metamorphosis, Da'an's concerns might yet become reality.

Zo'or removed all thought from controlling his body. To an observer, it would look as if he just died. His heart would stop, his breathing would cease, and his limbs would go limp. He would also lose all input from his eyes, ears, nose, mouth, and skin. Without any sensory clutter or physical demands, he could fully focus his mental abilities.

Again, he tried to revert to his energy state. This time, he succeeded.

Zo'or could not move, could not speak. All his mental abilities were being used to fight the incredible rush of the Elteena's energy that rolled across him in wave after wave.

Agent Sandoval immediately took control of the shuttle, but Zo'or could not communicate with him. He could not tell him that the woman had escaped from the Volunteers and was now riding in the automobile moving west along the road.

All he felt, all he was, came directly from the Elteena.

Soon, it thought. *Soon it would have blood. Soon it would be free.*

THIRTY-TWO

Renée's black Porsche convertible was six cars from the front of the blockade line when Liam's global chimed. He pulled it open and Da'an's face appeared in the display.

"I will not ask you why you are in Cherokee, North Carolina, and you will not ask why I am ordering you to go to these coordinates."

The new data register lighted on Liam's global. He examined the transmission and mapped the new information against their current location. If they could travel in a straight line, the position lay only a couple of miles to the northeast.

Da'an had been silent, allowing Liam to process the information. Now he continued, "On the way, watch for a Taelon shuttle. It will be Zo'or's. If you see it, follow it to where it lands. It will be near the coordinates I have given you. Report anything unusual to me."

"Unusual?"

"You will recognize the danger."

Liam considered what Da'an had told him. "I need to know more."

"We have no time. I must inform the others in the Synod what has happened, then I will join you. Until then, you must be my eyes and ears. Hurry, Liam. The threat is great—to both our species."

As Liam closed the global and tucked it back onto his belt, Renée said, "If you're his eyes and ears, why aren't you as important as the Synod? He has time to tell them what's going on. Why not you?"

Liam unbuckled his seat belt. "I need to drive."

"Don't you see? Da'an is Taelon. When it comes to the crystal, we can't trust him."

"I'm betting that these coordinates point us to where the crystal is—or will at least get us close. It's where we want to go, anyway. Now let me drive, so we can get there before it's too late."

Renée scowled. "This is my car, remember? Are you saying my driving isn't good enough for you?

"No, it's not, at least not today—and I'm betting the lease says Doors International on it, not Renée Palmer."

"Go to hell." She remained behind the wheel.

Liam lightly touched her hand. "Please, this is important. I know it."

Renée opened her mouth to argue, then closed it.

"Have it your way," she said. Taking her time, she stepped out of the car and leisurely started around the front to the passenger side. Liam hurried around the back and jumped into the driver's seat. He revved the engine and Renée bolted forward and jumped in.

Closing the door, she turned on him slowly, unconcerned, like a cat caught pilfering food. "Thinking of leaving me?"

"If necessary," Liam said and popped the clutch.

Tires squealed and they veered out and around the car ahead, racing toward the front of the line.

Volunteers at the blockade spun to face the speeding car, lifting their rifles and taking aim. Liam pressed the brake and downshifted, rolling to a perfect stop beside the Volunteer commander.

"This is an emergency. I'm on official business from Da'an. I need through at once."

Before Liam could pull out his ID, the commander straightened and shouted, "It's Da'an's Protector. Let him pass."

As soon as they swung the barrier aside enough for the car

to squeeze through, Liam punched the accelerator. The engine roared and the car surged through to freedom.

Renée maintained her mask of calm as they raced along Highway 441, but as Liam downshifted and hit the brakes for their turn, she braced herself with a hand against the dashboard.

"Hang on!" Liam shouted over the wind.

The car skidded sideways on the pavement, then the tires caught, and it sprang across the bridge and over the Oconaluftee River. Liam accelerated across a second bridge, this one over a road. They roared ahead and flashed by a sign saying "Blue Ridge Cutoff." He crushed the brake petal as they neared a sharp left turn.

"Nervous?" he shouted.

"Not if I was driving."

They took the corner hard. Renée clawed at the edge of her seat, then squeaked as her body crushed her arm against the door. She swallowed and closed her eyes until her usual mask of calm returned.

"Da'an is sending you to find Dr. Long," she said over the road noise. "If you do, are you going to turn her over to the Taelons?"

The tires squealed as Liam took the next curve. He hit a patch of gravel along the edge of the road and the black Porsche fishtailed before he managed to straighten it out.

He sprinted up a short straightaway and did his best to pretend the call was not as close as it had actually been, but Renée outdid him. She appeared completely calm, as if she were out for a Sunday drive.

"You didn't answer my question. When we find Dr. Long, we must put her under the Resistance's protection. If we don't, the Taelons will kill her to keep her quiet, just as they killed her department head. What do you plan to do?"

Liam responded by flooring the accelerator.

The engine whined as the grade steepened. Trees, brilliantly colored, whipped by, blocking their view, but Liam's popping ears told him they were climbing quickly.

He took the turns as fast as the Porsche would allow, cutting across each curve, tracing a path that led from one edge of the road to the other. The car groaned and lurched as he worked it between its second and third gears, the engine screaming as he revved it high through the straight stretches of road and roaring like an angry bear through the tunnels.

Surprisingly, they did not pass anyone going in their direction, but they met three cars going the other way. With the first two, Liam jerked the Porsche back to his own side of the road in plenty of time. The third car, a nice Mercedes, crossed his path just as he accelerated out the far side of a curve. He braked and pulled back into his own lane, but the Mercedes had already swerved off the road and slammed into the trees at about twenty miles per hour. Air bags went off all around its occupants like exploding kernels of popcorn.

Until then, Renée had remained quiet, her complexion paling steadily, but now she twisted her head over her shoulder until they lost sight of the Mercedes. "Slow down! You're going to kill someone."

Liam spoke calmly. "Besides the air bags, those folks had their seat belts on. They'll be fine."

"I didn't mean them. I meant us."

The car crossed the highest point, marked only by a curve and a short flat stretch of road, then started down and quickly picked up speed.

Liam downshifted and the motor howled in protest. Tires squealed all the way through each turn, the car in a constant fight with momentum as it sped up after each curve and slowed down before the next one.

They met another car, a green Chevy, but Liam easily swung back to his own side of the road. He glanced in the rearview mirror, then back at the road as they rounded another curve. A group of black-clad Volunteers were running up the road, about a quarter mile distant.

Suddenly Liam jerked the Porsche one way, then the other. The car rocked, twisting violently, and headed toward the side of the road. Spinning the wheel sharply, he yanked on the emergency brake. The rear end rattled and bounced, then caught the gravel littering the edge of the road and slid neatly around so that the front end of the car was pointing back the way they had come.

Liam slammed the gearshift into first, released the emergency brake, and popped the clutch. The car bucked, then groaned as it started another uphill climb.

Renée clutched the door, as if she might jump out. Her eyes were wide and darting. "Where are you going?"

When Liam did not respond, she added, "You've lost your mind! The coordinates Da'an gave you are behind us."

"Did you see that car? The one we just passed? It was an old green Chevy Malibu with two passengers, a boy and his mother."

"First seat belts, now this? Do you make this stuff up? At the speed we're going, you can't see those kinds of details."

"Actually, I see more. Both the boy and his mother had red hair, and the car is the same one I saw this morning at the truck stop."

Renée let go of the armrest long enough to raise both hands in front of her. "So?"

"So, I'm playing a hunch. Da'an said I would recognize the danger when I saw it. Maybe I just did."

Liam accelerated back up the mountain, crossed the highest point on this road, and started down again.

He had spoken with confidence, but even he did not completely understand why he had turned around. He had failed to react at the truck stop when he had first seen the red-haired boy and his mother, but he could not get the idea out of his head that the child was Daniel Shaunessy. Perhaps he had lost his mind, but if Daniel was in the Chevy, meeting him here, so near the crystal, would be no coincidence. The boy and his mother were supposed to be visiting a sick relative, not touring the Great Smoky Mountains National Park.

The Porsche roared ahead, flying into the curving Cherokee Mountain Tunnel. On the other side, Liam scanned the twisty roadway, then repeated the violent spin maneuver.

Renée reached for the door handle and jerked on it as Liam popped the clutch and started uphill again. "Let me out of here! You're crazy!"

"The doors are locked," Liam said calmly.

The car accelerated back into the tunnel. Renée stared at him, her mouth open, until they emerged on the other side.

"Why are we headed this way again? And don't tell me it's because I talked you into going back. I won't believe it."

Liam downshifted. "That Chevy was driving slowly. I would have caught them if they hadn't turned off."

"Turned off? Where?"

They rounded a curve. "Here."

Momentum pushed them against the seat belts as Liam braked hard and cranked the wheel. The car spun onto a gravel siding and bounced up a steep one-lane road.

The tailpipe scraped against the gravel as the car rocked and jolted over the rough road. Liam slowed. On the right, oaks, maples, and hickories rose to a tangle of branches, the base of their trunks above the passenger window. On the left, trees rose up from somewhere far below, their tops branching out just above the car. Between them, the narrow road clung stubbornly to the side of the mountain.

Liam kept the car precisely centered between the gauntlet of trees and thick undergrowth. He did not have room to stray even a foot too far on either side.

"Do you know what you're doing?" Renée seemed to have accepted his decision and was now readying herself for an "I told you so" when things did not work out.

Liam slowed to a stop and glanced around. On his right, a steep rocky face guarded the uphill side of the road. Between the trees on his left, mist-covered mountains rose in the distance like the backs of sleeping dragons after a great battle.

"No," he admitted. "I don't know what I'm doing at all."

THIRTY-THREE

Waneta lay still and prayed that the car would keep moving. The stone burned her palms, and the small red-haired boy leaned over the front seat, watching her, his bright green eyes intent and serious.

What had his mother called him? Daniel.

"Hello," Waneta said from her prone position. "How old are you?"

He did not answer but glanced at his mother.

"He's seven. Big for his age."

Daniel blinked, as if finding out this information for the first time, then pointed at Waneta. "Pretty," he said.

Waneta barely heard him. She certainly didn't feel pretty. Hair clung to her forehead and stuck to the back of her neck, and her clothes were smudged with dirt and marked by bits of twigs and dried leaves. She clamped her mouth tightly shut and gritted her teeth, trying to tolerate the heat from the crystal until she could get it under control again.

What had set it off this time? Would it keep getting stronger, no matter what she did?

She glanced at Daniel's face, and the intensity of his gaze startled her. His keen interest was more like that of an adolescent watching girls at the swimming pool than that of a small boy.

He stretched a hand in her direction, and in a very adult manner said, "May I see it, please?"

Waneta flinched. See what? She glanced down. The *Uluh-*

sati glowed so brightly that it lit up her hands like a jack-o'-lantern. Cautiously, she pulled one hand aside and marveled at the stone. It glimmered and sparkled, like the boy's eyes.

Who was this child? Perhaps the stone was causing her to hallucinate.

A car whizzed by, its engine roaring.

Daniel stretched out his hand again. "Please."

"He's always liked pretty things," his mother said in her Irish accent. "And he's very sensitive."

Was the woman warning her? Even if the boy cried big tears and stomped his feet, prompting his mother to throw her out, Waneta was not about to surrender the crystal, even for a moment. This stone had cost her too much to part with it now.

She closed her eyes and thought of Gil. Much too much.

The car slowed, then bumped and jostled. The crunch of tires against gravel told Waneta they had left the main road. What had the mother said? That she and her son were late for an appointment? Perhaps they had reached their destination and had turned onto one of the long driveways that snaked into the trees and up the mountain. Waneta did not think they had come that far, but the stone had disoriented her sense of time before.

Would she be safe where they were going? Gil had told her to find some of "our" people. Many mixed marriages between Irish Americans and Cherokees had taken place in the mid 1800s; she and this small family could be distantly related. Perhaps they would give her a place to hide, to rest and feel safe—if only for a few hours.

But when Waneta sat up and looked out the window, her mouth dropped open and she stared, blinking in disbelief. She had driven this way so many times in the past four months that she knew every dip, every turn.

They were on the road to her dig site.

The boy and his mother must be working for the Volunteers and were taking her back to Gil's cabin. She would have never guessed.

Still speaking in a manner much older than his years, the boy asked, "Is it time, Mother?"

"Yes, dear." The mother smiled as she drove along.

Suddenly the boy leaned over the seat and grabbed for the stone. Waneta jerked it away, then looked at him in horror. His eyes had become small circles of light and his body pulsated with rainbow lines of color.

Who was he? What was he?

He put forth his hand again, his eyes glowing more brightly. A red spark leapt from the stone to his outstretched finger, then rebounded and struck Waneta hard.

The shock knocked her back against the seat, her head jerking, her hands convulsing as her fingers curled and uncurled.

She lost all track of time, her world shrinking to flashing colors and swaying motions, as if she were on a great ship in a stormy sea.

When she came back to herself, she sat up, blinking slowly. The car had stopped at the edge of the meadow containing the dig site. The boy and his mother were trekking off toward where the stone was found. In the boy's hand, she saw a flash of red.

"No," she said leaning forward. Feelings of nausea twisted her stomach in knots.

She opened the car door and tumbled out into the grass. Crawling after them, she kept wondering, why here? Why had they returned the stone to what was left of the sanctuary? For a moment, she allowed herself to hope that they had taken the stone so they could return it to where it belonged, but she knew that was not true.

The boy was not Cherokee. He was some kind of Taelon mongrel—and she could not help remembering what Gil had said, about what would happen if the Taelons acquired the crystal.

She must get it back. Pushing herself to her feet, she stumbled after them, not knowing what she could do but refusing to do nothing.

The crystal brightened as they walked, blinding in its brilliance, like an impossibly tiny star fallen to earth. The boy and his mother did not seem to notice. Again, Waneta wondered if she were hallucinating. She had been under stress, but she still felt in control of her mind. Outside of the crystal, everything appeared the way it should.

When they reached the dig site, the boy and his mother stopped. They did not look at the squares, still outlined in string, or even seem aware that they stood in the middle of an archaeological site. But surely they had not come here by accident.

"*Uluhsati* won't allow us to remain that way for long." Gil had said those words as if the crystal had a mind of its own. Could that be the answer? Had the stone led them to this lonely mountaintop? It had been kept here for centuries. Perhaps it considered this home.

The boy and his mother faced each other. "I am ready," she said softly.

The boy did not speak. His eyes glowed like molten jade, and his face revealed even more of the lusty eagerness he had displayed in the car.

The boy's blazing eyes and the crystal's brilliance prevented Waneta from seeing the beginning of the transformation. She did not notice what was happening until the distinct outline of the boy's mother blurred into glowing blue. On the Eli Hanson talk show where Waneta had seen Agent Sandoval, a Resistance terrorist had seized control of the program. In response, Zo'or had blurred in much the same way as Daniel blurred now.

The boy's shape also grew indistinct but burned a bright, fiery green, like his eyes. Waneta had never seen—or heard of—a green Taelon.

"I do this for you."

Had the mother spoken the words aloud or had Waneta only perceived them in her mind? She was not sure, but as soon as they were said, the boy's mother flared up like a pool of gasoline kissed by a match.

Waneta squinted and shielded her face with her hand, but

the cool blue of the mother's consuming fire gave off no warmth. The boy's form also brightened, but unlike the mother's, it intensified slowly, building into a brilliant, fiery green that overshadowed the cool blue of the mother's flame.

Her form flickered, pulsing several times, then faded, growing more ethereal in fits and starts until it disappeared.

Waneta stared at the spot the mother had been, unable to believe that the woman was truly gone. Had she died? Or had she merged her essence with the boy's? His form had grown steadily brighter as his mother's light had faded. He had been feeding on her, the way a fire consumes all the oxygen in a room.

The mother, Triss, was dead. *I do this for you.* She had sacrificed herself for her son.

Why?

The brilliant green of the boy's body dulled slowly, his shape sharpening into lines of skin, cheekbones, and hair. He turned in Waneta's direction, the eagerness on his face unchanged, unsatisfied.

Waneta backed away, about to run, but stopped when the boy suddenly clutched himself and bent over, as if racked by severe stomach cramps.

Something you ate? Waneta wanted to ask.

Instead she watched, fascinated, as he twisted and jerked, attacked by an invisible swarm of bees.

"No," he said and twisted again, then said, "I am . . . in . . . control."

He clenched his teeth and his brow sunk low over his eyes. For a moment, he remained motionless, a statue portraying an instant of desperation, then he twisted violently, arching his back and clawing at the sky as if scrambling to find a hold on a slippery ledge.

"NOOOO!" he screamed, his mouth wide open, his bright green eyes blazing like two searchlights through a night sky.

His body writhed and shook, rocked by violent spasms. He glowed again, but with just a flash of darker green that quickly tinted to violet and then to red.

As his color changed, so did his shape. His body widened and lengthened, his shoulders becoming rounded, his neck thickening. His legs snapped together and shimmered, then smoothed into a single limb. He toppled to the ground, grunting, but shivered and jerked, as if struggling to maintain his former shape.

Waneta wanted to run but could not force her feet to move. The horror did not seem real. She viewed it the way she had the scary movie two nights ago, not wanting to watch but unable to turn from the gruesome scene.

The boy raised his head a last time, his face swollen and distorted. Terror showed in green eyes that flickered to red. Hair flattened and fused as the head dropped, and long spikes grew and forked into feelers from what had once been the boy's crown. Shimmers rolled up and down the length of the thick body, and what remained of the shoulders smoothed themselves into the long torso.

When the head rose again, the boy was gone.

In his place wavered a giant serpent unlike any Waneta had ever seen. Rather than scales, gleaming plates covered its body. Rainbows reflected in their sparkling surfaces, and while they overlapped, they did not do so in smooth lines but rather came together in distinct segments.

The serpent wiggled and shifted. Each segment of its body moved together, yet with directions and angles independent of the others. They appeared connected by something similar to a shoulder joint, one that could twist as well as rotate.

Huge unblinking eyes stuck out on each side of the giant head. Convex and set slightly forward, they would be able to see simultaneously in every direction except straight behind.

In the very center of its forehead, embedded in the flesh and looking much like a third great eye, lay the *Uluhsati*. Waneta recognized its red gleaming surface.

The monster turned that cycloptic projection toward her. The *Uktena*, as described in accurate detail within the mythology of her ancestors. She tried to remember the legend, to recall the details of the story and compare them to the reality, but instead all the other stories her mother had told her suddenly came to life inside her mind. All of them now seemed as real and as close as the *Uktena*.

The beast called to her.

That was the only way she could describe what she felt. It wanted her and used its mind to beckon her forward.

She took a step toward the creature, then stopped. Trying to force her gaze away from the beast, she called on a quiet strength deep inside herself she never knew she had. It felt natural, as if it went deeper than her bones, as if it had been a part of her forever. Through it, she felt the beast slowly recognize that she would not succumb to its wishes and felt its growing anger.

The *Uktena* rushed at her in a rustle of grass and snapping of twigs. It covered ground surprisingly fast for such a large creature.

Still, Waneta did not move. She could not outrun it and she could not fight.

Ten paces away, the *Uktena* jerked to a halt and violently shook its head, as if stung. Its eyes flashed green, faded back to red, then flashed green again, less brightly than the first time.

Somewhere inside the *Uktena*, Daniel was still there, fighting to survive—but losing. In a moment, the beast would regain full control.

As she watched the struggle, she remembered a piece of the legend she had forgotten, that the *Uktena* was once a man.

Now she understood how that could be true.

She also remembered a piece of the story Gil had told her last night—that to see the *Uktena* asleep was death, not to the man who saw it, but to his family. Perhaps that was because the *Uluhsati* consumed the man, then killed his family, the way the *Uluhsati* consumed Daniel to become the *Uktena*, then planned to kill her as soon as it finished with the boy.

That thought gave her the strength to wrench her gaze

from the *Uktena,* and once she looked away, she found she could move freely again.

The *Uktena* would soon overcome the last of the boy's resistance, but she could do nothing for him now. She sprinted across the meadow to the old green Chevy and jumped in behind the wheel.

Where were the keys? Where were the damn keys?

She glanced back at the *Uktena.* Its eyes were still shifting red to green to red. If the woman had taken them, then been consumed by her son, who was in turn consumed by the creature, did that mean the *Uktena* had them?

An image flashed through her mind of the *Uktena,* huffing and snorting until it coughed up the keys like a tiny hair ball.

The *Uktena* screamed. A sound unlike any other, it chilled her deeper than cold and more lasting than fear. Again, she felt compelled to surrender herself but easily shrugged off the sensation. It was like a magical illusion revealed; once the secret of the trick was known, it lost its luster.

The *Uktena* charged.

Waneta scrambled across the front seat and threw herself out the passenger door, then crawled away into the undergrowth. As soon as she was out of sight, she cut across to the next switchback in the narrow road, then paused at a break in the trees. Hiding behind a large trunk, she peered up at the old Chevy. If the creature tracked by smell, perhaps her journey through the car would confuse it.

The *Uktena* stopped at the vehicle, but rather than putting its snout to the ground—or even flicking its tongue in the air— it reared its head and looked straight at her.

Great. Another theory ruined by the data.

The *Uktena* left the car and slithered down the road.

Waneta knew it could come through the trees as easily as if they were dominoes set up to be knocked down, but she sensed that it was saving its strength. A great battle was coming.

She did not know if she was picking up the *Uktena*'s version of the future, or if her imagination had finally taken over, but she did not wait around to find out.

Leaving the trees, she raced down the road. She knew she could not outrun the creature, but she damned sure planned to try.

THIRTY-FOUR

As the Elteena's physical distance from Zo'or increased, its effect on him waned. When the shuttle touched down near the highway, close to where the woman had supposedly been shot, Zo'or solidified into his humanoid shape again.

Agent Sandoval looked at Zo'or as if expecting an explanation for his sudden changes of state. Zo'or did not supply him one.

Instead, Zo'or said, "We arrived too late. The woman has escaped and the danger from the crystal has greatly increased."

Upon hearing this, Agent Sandoval asked no questions and made no protests. He spoke into his military global—to confirm the information or to spread the word, Zo'or did not care. Agent Sandoval, as all Protectors, knew that Taelons did not often revert to their energy state in the presence of humans, especially not twice in only a few minutes. He would already understand how serious the situation had become.

Zo'or, in his physical form, was less aware but more vulnerable to the pulsating mental waves emanating from the Elteena. Even without concentrating, he felt the cold from the woman's body and swayed with the motion of the car. As with the first time he felt the power, he picked up images distorted by red prisms. One contained a boy whose face had been among the knowledge he picked up when he consumed the memories of Laura Heward. But most of all, he hungered for the great energy generated by the life force—so close—that had been called to feed the transformation.

"We must hurry," Zo'or said, "but I do not . . . wish to be in physical form when we find the woman, nor do I wish to pilot the shuttle. I will point you . . . in the direction you must go."

"What about the Volunteers? Where do you want them stationed?"

"Have them all . . . converge at this spot . . . where they think they shot the woman. They must not . . . see."

Zo'or struggled to maintain his concentration. Around him, he felt the car turning, felt the creature command its victim to make its move.

"We must . . . go . . . now!"

Agent Sandoval spoke into his global again. Zo'or caught only a few phrases about standard search patterns and securing the area. The power beckoned to him, and it took all his willpower to resist the temptation to give himself up to it. He wanted to control it—not join with it.

Agent Sandoval touched the controls of the shuttle. As the ship rose above the treetops, Zo'or released his human shape and welcomed the freedom of his energy state.

He did so just in time. A numbing burst of energy jolted him—the creature was free of the woman at last. If he had been in his physical form and seeking the Elteena's location, the force of this energy release would have incapacitated him for several minutes the way it had outside the cabin. As it was, he maintained his energy state only by drawing on the strength of the Commonality to support him.

This alerted them to the struggle that would soon take place, but they would not be able to arrive in time to prevent it. Once Zo'or had defeated the Elteena and had its enormous power under his control, no one would be able to challenge his decision to confront it.

But he needed to reach the creature before it completed its transmutation. A dormant Elteena he could handle. An active

Elteena . . . he did not know. If Da'an could be believed, he had no chance—but as always, Da'an kept his own version of the truth.

Zo'or sensed that the creature controlled two of the three humans around it. The third human, the archaeologist, remained beyond the influence that affected the other two and threatened to consume Zo'or.

What was her part in the transmutation? She had carried the creature with her since yesterday morning yet had not been consumed to feed the metamorphosis. His information about the Elteena was incomplete and grossly subjective because of how he obtained it. But he knew that the beast could become active only by draining the life force from other beings.

Earlier it felt as if Dr. Long had restrained the creature, but perhaps that perception had been incorrect. At the university, the musician had helped her escape, but in the woods, after he was dead, surely the Elteena had taken over her mind, allowing her to elude Agent Sandoval's men. If that were true, the Elteena might be holding Dr. Long in reserve. In its depleted state, it might need the life force from two or three beings to complete the metamorphosis.

Whatever her purpose, she would be there to greet the Elteena as it came to life. The being would begin its metamorphosis soon.

Zo'or pointed west and Agent Sandoval swung the shuttle in that direction. They needed to speed up—so little time remained—but he could not risk instructing Agent Sandoval to do so without losing his concentration.

As they closed on the Elteena's location, Zo'or's perception of his surroundings increased. He felt the motion of the vehicle as it gently came to a stop. He heard doors open and felt cool breeze over hard skin. Across it all, he felt hunger. Deep, over-riding hunger.

So close. Soon now.

Then came the awakening.

It started with a taste of what was to come. Sweet—not on the tongue, but on the mind—a smooth caress to whet the palate of burgeoning power.

Then came the recognition.

Zo'or expected the rush, the exhilaration of nourishment after so long without, but he expected the energy consumed to be human. What he felt now—feeding the creature and staining him with its residue—had the flavor of Taelon.

The realization shook Zo'or, breaking his concentration. He reached out blindly for the strength of the Commonality, the way a human climber reaches out as he begins to fall, and found the rope of support slipping past him. He bore down on the link between himself and what remained of his race, scattered throughout the planet, huddled together aboard the mother ship far above, stretching out to the edges of the known universe. His hold caught, but barely. He dangled above the abyss that would mark his plunge into the creature's realm of hunger and lust, then began his climb back to the realm of controlled thought.

By the time the Elteena consumed the last of the energy on which it fed, Zo'or recognized it for what it was. Not Taelon, but human. Zo'or had encountered humans before that could assume Taelon form. He had shared energy with them. The human who had just given her life force for the transmutation had such an ability.

Zo'or pointed down. Agent Sandoval responded by aiming the shuttle toward a junction between a gravel road and the main highway.

Zo'or wanted to tell him to turn more to the south, to aim for the small clearing near the top of the mountain where he sensed the metamorphosis had begun. He pointed again, less downward and more northward, but Agent Sandoval either did not see or did not understand. This close to the source of the disruption, it took all his abilities to maintain control of his energy state and to keep the creature out of his thoughts; he dared not point again.

The Elteena now had the energy it needed to exert greater influence over the reality that surrounded it. Once more, it fed, this time on the tiny human who sought to control it. Zo'or heard the silent cries of surprise and anger, and felt the shock as the human finally realized the magnitude of the power it struggled against. Zo'or felt shock himself as he recognized the energy the beast consumed. More than human, flavored by Taelon, it was further distorted by a band of energy that reminded him of Ha'gel, the only Kimera he had ever known.

How could this be? Ha'gel, the last of his race, had perished. Zo'or desperately wanted to understand, but as the human succumbed to the great power seeking to control it, Zo'or realized he would never discover the answer.

The Elteena's metamorphosis was complete.

THIRTY-FIVE

Steamy wisps escaped from under the hood. On the Porsche's dashboard, a red warning light glowed in the shape of a thermometer.

Liam stated the obvious. "It's overheated."

Renée opened her door but did not get out. "What did you expect? You sprinted up the mountain like you were driving a Formula One. If you wanted a race car, you should have warned me. I would have brought one."

Liam sighed and got out of the car. "You would think that as much as they charge for one of these, it could take a few hills without blowing its top."

"Not with you behind the wheel. I'm surprised it made it this far."

Liam looked over his shoulder. The Blue Ridge Parkway was out of sight, probably a quarter mile back. He had stressed the car on the way up the mountain—that he would admit— but if he hadn't stopped, the car would be fine. Its small fan couldn't cool the big engine by itself. Once the car quit moving, the temperature shot up dramatically. It would take time to return to normal, time they didn't have.

Renée stepped out of the car and shut the door. "So are you ready to explain why it was so important we went sight-seeing up this backwoods trail?"

Liam sighed and leaned back against the car. Why had he come this way? For several seconds, back on the highway, he had felt so sure. The boy, Daniel, and his mother, Triss, were in that green Chevy. The crystal, too. Liam did not know how he knew—he just did. While his Kimeran abilities had decreased with time, he still trusted his intuition. Perhaps this time it had let him down.

He felt nothing now. Had the woman and her son escaped? They may have noticed that he was following them, turned into this drive until he passed, then backed up and gone the other direction.

He swirled the events of the last two days inside his mind, looking for connections. Gradually they started falling into place. "It can't be a coincidence."

"What? That the car quit because your driving could make the AAA's most-wanted list?"

Liam turned toward Renée and waved his hand as if shooing away mosquitoes. "No, the boy, the crystal, Dr. Long, everything."

"Oh, that's clear."

"Listen," he said, leaning forward. "I was in Ireland, because I was trying to find out information about Daniel Shaunessy."

"The dancer?"

"Right. Two days ago, he did a private performance for Da'an. At the end of it, Da'an collapsed. Before I could get him out of the theater, Da'an temporarily reverted to his energy state. Later that evening, the boy and his mother mysteriously disappeared. The stage manager said they received no message of any kind—they just left. A day later, they turn up here."

"I don't understand. How does that relate to the crystal?"

"Daniel Shaunessy's part Taelon, the product of some secret experiment Da'an's been conducting over in Ireland with the help of a cloister there. At first I thought Daniel attacked Da'an during the performance, but maybe I had it backward. In Ireland, one of this cloister's devoted daughters told me how Daniel could have forced energy sharing with Da'an. She said he'd need to transform to his energy state but was surprised he could overcome a Taelon."

"I thought you said Da'an was the one who reverted to his energy state."

"Exactly. You remember last summer? Zo'or shared energy with Sister Margaret right before she started killing other members of her cloister. Maybe Da'an shared energy with the boy and somehow directed him here."

"Uh-oh." Renée was chewing on her bottom lip and refused to meet Liam's gaze. "I, uh, didn't have time to tell you. We knew a lot about this crystal before it was found, enough to have a replica made."

"We? Who's we?"

"Doors International. Joshua."

Liam groaned.

Renée continued, her words coming more quickly. "He's been more hands-on than usual with this project. I wanted to bring you in earlier, when we thought Dr. Messmore might be on the mother ship, but Joshua said he could find out if the Taelons had him. Joshua was also the one who told me the Taelons already knew about the crystal's discovery only hours after it was found."

"Joshua told you that?"

"Hard to believe, isn't it? All this coming from a guy who can't find out if his dry cleaning's ready without delegating the task to someone else."

"Did he say who's feeding him information?"

"No, but obviously it's someone who likes planning. The search for this crystal took months, possibly years. Whoever set this up had a lot of patience."

Renée and Liam said the name together. "Da'an."

From up the road came a cry, far away. It sounded a bit like the scream of a woman or a small boy. Liam pulled his energy pistol from its holster and scanned the road ahead. No birds chirped, no squirrels moved among the branches. Not even the wind dared stir the trees. He was a child of the city, but he could not imagine the great outdoors being so quiet naturally.

Renée stepped away from the car and looked around warily. "What's going on? Did you hear something?"

"Quiet," Liam said.

Renée gave him a puzzled glance, then cocked her head as the distant roar of a shuttle approached from behind them.

They turned in time to watch it descend close by, perhaps over the road. It disappeared behind the trees.

"Zo'or's shuttle," Liam said.

"You sure?"

"I'd bet your life on it."

"My life? Thanks a lot."

He winked. "I'm sure, but I'm not that sure."

Footsteps sounded on the road above them. Liam ran behind the protection of the car and drew his pistol, aiming it at the first bend in the road about fifty yards away.

The footsteps grew louder, scuffled on the gravel as if the person had fallen, then resumed again after several rapid scrambling noises. Whoever was coming was running as fast as possible down a steep, uneven road.

Liam set his gun to its maximum power setting, then took aim again. "Get down!"

Renée walked slowly over behind the car but remained defiantly erect, an easy target.

A woman rounded the bend in the road. Her jeans were torn and dirty, and her arms were scraped and bleeding. When she saw the car, she ran faster.

Her eyes were wild and her hair tangled, but Liam recognized her easily enough.

Dr. Long.

So he had guessed right, turning onto this road, but he did not congratulate himself just yet. Sandoval was probably with Zo'or in the shuttle behind them, which meant that Volunteers would shortly be on the way. In front of them, Dr. Long was running for a reason, possibly fleeing from more Volunteers. All he had accomplished was to put himself and Renée in the middle of a battle zone with no way out.

Dr. Long cupped her hands to her mouth. "Run!"

Liam stood up. He heard a distant rattle but could not identify the sound of what approached. Scraping rather than discrete footsteps, it sounded as if the Volunteers were sliding down the mountain on sleds—and they were getting closer.

"Run!" Dr. Long called again.

Liam watched her sprint past. Her face was wet and flushed with exertion. Winded, she wobbled, obviously exhausted, but she did not hesitate or cast a glance over her shoulder. Sweat soaked her blouse at the base of her neck and across her back.

Renée started after her. "Stop! We're here to help!"

She jogged several steps down the road, then threw her hands up when it was obvious the other woman had no intention of slowing down.

Walking back toward the car, she asked, "What could scare a person like that?"

Suddenly she stopped. Her mouth dropped open and her eyes went wide. She backed a step away, then another step.

"Run," she said under her breath. Then, more loudly, "Run!"

She spun and kicked hard against the gravel as she tried to accelerate.

Liam heard loud scraping behind him and knew that something had rounded the bend, but he was totally unprepared for what greeted him when he turned around.

A large snakelike creature, moving with surprising speed, undulated toward him. At least forty feet long, its body, covered in overlapping hexagonal plates, shimmered with different colors. A huge head, about eight feet off the ground, sported a set of what appeared to be symmetrical antlers—except they twisted and turned, perhaps acting as a sense of smell. Below them, another organ sparkled like a glass eye.

The beast slowed. Red half globes on each side of its head

took turns focusing on Renée's retreating form. The beast bent low and rustled after her, its huge body sliding toward the car like a giant tank heedless of any obstacle in its path.

The *Uktena*. Augur had described it fairly well—Liam even recognized the crystal in its forehead as the one Dr. Long had been holding.

Augur had said that a Shawnee warrior killed it. Only one problem. He did not say how.

Liam raised his pistol and fired at the creature's head.

It paused, stopping with remarkable agility. Twisting its body, it looked down at him. It did not seem hurt.

A prickling started at the back of Liam's skull. He had the sudden urge to lay down his weapon and walk toward the creature. Unlike his earlier intuition, this sensation felt cold, unwelcome—evil. He had never viewed the world in terms of good and evil, but that was the only description that seemed to fit what he experienced now.

Without conscious effort, he stepped from behind the car and started in the creature's direction.

What am I doing?

He forced himself to stop, then clenched his jaws tightly together and slowly backed away.

The creature let out a cry, the same sound he had heard earlier. Close like this, it sent shudders through his whole body.

He raised his weapon and fired over and over. The blasts struck the creature's face, but they just bounced off. The beast seemed to be emitting some kind of energy that protected it the way the Taelons could protect themselves against projectile weapons and explosions.

Although Liam's energy pistol caused no apparent harm, after several blasts, the animal rocked its great head from side to side, like a horse irritated by flies. It bent lower, crimson eyes on Liam, and released another bone-chilling cry. The sound resembled a screeching bird but much louder. The antlers rotated until they pointed directly at him. Once again, he felt the urge to put down his weapon and welcome the animal.

The temptation was easier to resist this time. Rather than stepping toward the creature, he jogged down the road in the direction Renée and Dr. Long had gone but kept his head twisted over his shoulder so he could watch the beast.

The creature reared and screamed again, then rushed forward, right toward the car.

Perfect.

Renée was not going to be happy about this, but Liam needed to use every resource available to him.

Just as the creature reached the car, grinding its way on top and smashing the vehicle beneath its great weight, Liam turned and fired. This time, he did not aim for the creature, but instead sent two energy blasts into the gas tank of the Porsche. The vehicle exploded in orange flames and billows of blue-white smoke.

The blast knocked Liam backward. Heat scorched his face and singed his eyebrows, and the hair along his arms curled into ash-tipped pigtails. Coughing, he stood up, pleased with himself, and waited for the creature to collapse.

Inside the flames, the *Uktena* glowed. Whatever force protected it from Liam's weapon had also protected it from the flames.

It screamed, then turned its crimson eyes on him. He could have sworn it was smiling.

"Oh, hell."

Liam sprinted down the mountain. This time, he did not look back.

THIRTY-SIX

Zo'or resumed his human shape. His form sharpened and his glow faded to normal skin tones as the shuttle came to rest between the trees. After powering down the shuttle, he stepped out onto the small rocks covering this crude human byway.

Agent Sandoval, energy rifle in hand, stepped out beside him.

Zo'or studied the surrounding terrain, then focused his attention up the mountain. The Elteena was on the move. With its metamorphosis complete, it no longer reached out with as much mental force. Instead, it relished the physical sensations provided by its new body, and its focus shifted inward.

Zo'or's agitation showed in his finger movements. "The situation has changed."

Agent Sandoval straightened, as if at attention. "I am ready."

"No," Zo'or said, "you are not."

Agent Sandoval wrinkled his brow, and his mouth worked in silent protest.

Zo'or offered no explanation. Instead he walked away, his steps slow and precise as he climbed the uneven road.

He needed time to think.

The trees to each side of him were filled with color. Autumn in this part of the northern hemisphere had come to fruition. The leaves, which had nourished the trees during the spring and summer, were dying. Soon they would fall away, making room for new buds that would arrive with the spring.

They reminded Zo'or of his people—and of the changes that must take place for them to survive and prosper.

He could no longer pinpoint the Elteena's location, but not knowing its exact whereabouts was the least of his problems.

His words to Agent Sandoval had been an understatement. With its metamorphosis complete, the Elteena could no longer be controlled by any single Taelon. Zo'or would need help from the Commonality. Even then, he would need several more of his own people on site to help focus and guide the energy. But he had no time to call down reinforcements.

He could not subdue the creature on his own, but neither could he leave. As the Elteena consumed lives, its strength would increase and it would soon become too powerful for them to control, even as a combined group. He could not stop it, but he must slow it down, at least enough to give others time to arrive. To do that, he would need to sacrifice himself for the good of his people.

That, he was not yet ready to do.

He was too important to the future of the Taelons to allow himself to be wasted in such an insignificant manner. Still, there would be no future for the Taelons without this planet—and there would be no planet worth having unless they rid it of the Elteena.

To fight or to flee—a difficult choice that was taken from him when Dr. Long, the human they had been pursuing since yesterday, appeared on the road ahead. She was running. Unsteady, on the verge of collapse, she somehow managed to keep placing one foot before the other. Only seconds behind her, Renée Palmer and Major Liam Kincaid appeared, also running, but more energetically, as if they had gone a shorter distance.

Zo'or understood the situation at once and immediately transformed to his energy state.

Beside him, Agent Sandoval raised his rifle. "Stop where you are!"

When none of the humans paid him any heed, he fired several warning shots across Dr. Long's path. Gravel exploded, leaving small black craters. Gasping, Dr. Long stumbled to a halt.

Agent Sandoval reaimed the weapon. "Miss Palmer. Major Kincaid. Freeze!"

Both kept running.

"You must stop!"

Agent Sandoval squeezed off several warning shots that traced in front of them. Tree trunks burst on the uphill side of the road.

Both humans quit their energetic flight.

Renée Palmer, between deep breaths, said, "We don't . . . have time . . . for this."

"I insist you take time," Agent Sandoval said. His eyes studied them a moment, then flicked in the direction of Dr. Long.

As soon as his gaze left them, Renée Palmer withdrew a small silver weapon from her belt and pointed it at Agent Sandoval. Zo'or sensed her movements as much as saw them, but the safety of his Protector was less important than his preparations for the Elteena. He must form a deeper and more powerful bond with the Commonality before the creature attacked, but the other Taelons resisted his call for sarok'palath'ta, the giving over distance.

Agent Sandoval noticed Renée Palmer's movements, but too late. As he spun his energy rifle back in her direction, she fired two rounds of electric stun darts into his chest. He wobbled, the tip of his rifle dipping. His eyes fluttered as he crumpled to the ground.

Major Kincaid grinned.

Zo'or understood the importance of victory but had never grasped the concept of human joy at the suffering or embarrassment of others from its own species.

With a loud screech, the Elteena slithered into view. At once, it slowed and adjusted its course straight for Zo'or. As he expected, the creature ignored the humans. With a Taelon present, they were of no consequence.

Stepping forward, he gracefully raised his hand. He could not outrun a being as fast as the Elteena, nor could he overpower it. The time had come for him to test his control of this reality.

Dr. Long remained in place, but Renée Palmer and Major Kincaid started down the mountain again. Their movement attracted the Elteena's attention. It focused on them and let loose another screech, different in pitch and louder than before. Zo'or recognized it as a mind call. Major Kincaid stumbled but kept running. Renée Palmer came to a halt and turned back toward the beast.

An interesting tactic. With the metamorphosis only recently complete, the creature wanted another life force before it entered into battle. Even without the additional energy, it could have defeated him eventually, but doing so would have left it with little in reserve.

The Elteena was old and cautious, like too many of Zo'or's elders. It should have attacked at once. Instead, by fooling with the humans, it gave Zo'or the chance to complete the sarok'palath'ta. He had fully transformed to his energy state and felt the power of the Commonality surround him.

Fortunately, Major Kincaid allowed his emotional sentiments to overrule his intelligence. Da'an's Protector chased down Renée Palmer and tackled her from behind.

With no chance to feed on Miss Palmer, the Elteena should have taken Dr. Long. Zo'or assumed that it had been holding her in reserve for just this occasion, but while the human leaned on her knees and sucked in great gulps of air, she seemed unaffected by the creature's call for nourishment. Again, he wondered what quality she possessed that protected her. If he knew that, perhaps he could win the battle of wills that was about to take place.

The Elteena attacked first.

With its head held high, it spat. Energy, in large drops of

liquid fire, rained down on him, but he deflected them easily. The weakness of the tactic surprised him until he saw the brightening flashes from the crystal in the Elteena's forehead. The first maneuver had simply been a feint to distract him from the true attack, which came as a focused blast of energy against his mind.

Zo'or staggered back, shocked at the raw force the Elteena possessed. The energy that drove him to the ground carried with it wispy impressions of the Elteena's thoughts. Only now did Zo'or realize how accurate Da'an had been and how incredibly foolish it was to confront a being of this ability on his own—except that the desire to do so had never been his.

The Elteena had affected his perceptions from the start, preying on his innate desire for greater influence within the Synod, using him. It needed Taelon energy to defeat its main foe. But if the Taelons were not its greatest enemy, who was?

And why had Da'an helped the Elteena's purpose? By keeping his knowledge of the true danger secret, by providing tastes of the power, he had increased Zo'or's desire to take the creature on his own. Had that been his intent? Or had the Elteena influenced Da'an's thoughts just as it had influenced Zo'or's own?

Zo'or reached out to the Commonality. The other members of his race were there for him, strengthening him through their bond, but they were too far away, their contributions inadequate.

He was doing his best against the Elteena—and he was losing. In moments, he would no longer be able to hold back the onslaught and would succumb to the creature's will.

The Elteena would then have access to all the Taelon energy it needed. Once that happened, no known force in the universe would be able to stop it.

THIRTY-SEVEN

L iam lay on top of Renée, striving to keep her from slithering away.

"What's wrong with you?" he growled.

"Let me go! I must—ow!"

Liam lost his grip, clawed at her shoulders, missed, and dove on her again.

In front of them, the creature opened its great mouth, baring hundreds of sharp, narrow teeth like those of a piranha. The beast reared back its head and spat. Great globs of liquid fire flew toward Zo'or, who had transformed into his energy state.

The Taelon moved his hand as the flames approached. The globs broke up against a blue wall of energy and spattered around him. At first, they seemed to do no harm, but then the crystal in the creature's forehead began flashing and Zo'or buckled, his form shrinking as if struck by a great weight.

Liam needed to take Renée and run, but he could not carry her, not the way she was struggling. He could try to knock her out, but that was hard to do without hurting her badly.

Leaning close to her ear, he whispered, "Renée, we've got to go. We need to find Zo'or's shuttle and get help."

"No, the Elteena needs me. I must go to it."

"The El-what? What are you talking about? That thing's going to fry us if we don't get out of here."

"We have to save it. The Taelons are trying to kill it, and it won't survive without our help. It's going to rid us of the Taelons forever—can't you see that?"

She twisted, jabbing her elbows back at him. When that failed, she squealed. "You belong to them. You always have. Traitor. Traitor!"

Liam grimaced. The knockout idea was looking better and better.

To their left, Zo'or's energy form crumpled to the ground and the flowing emanations from his body faded to dim colors tinged with blue. The creature was killing him.

"Not on my shift," Liam said.

He found Renée's taser. She had fired both darts, but he dug through her pockets and found two spares. Pressing them into the end of the weapon, he prayed they were charged. He would have only one chance at this.

Bracing himself, he let go of Renée and stood up. He could have more easily stunned her while she was pinned beneath him, but he feared that the shot's force would pierce her skin and hurt her badly.

For a moment, Renée stayed prone, then jumped to her feet and ran for the creature.

"Sorry about this," he said and pulled the trigger.

The first electrical dart struck Renée between the shoulders. She took another step, stumbled, and went down. He tucked the taser into his waistband, then drew his energy pistol.

"Anyone for tag?" he asked and dropped to one knee. Aiming carefully, he fired several rounds at the creature's eyes.

The blasts ricocheted off the creature's protective energy barrier. The head and body stayed motionless and the strange antlers remained pointed at the Taelon. The thing was ignoring him, as if it were in some kind of trance.

Liam aimed again but stopped. Above him, just beyond the trees, came the roar of an approaching shuttle.

Da'an.

The cavalry had arrived.

Liam's global chimed. Keeping his gaze on the creature, he pulled the device off his belt and opened it, then glanced at its small screen. He was gratified to see Da'an's face in the display.

"I am on my way to you," Da'an said, "but I am having problems pinpointing your location."

"I'm transmitting it now, but hurry. Zo'or's down and I'm having a disagreement with the biggest snake you've ever seen."

Liam pointed the global at the creature, then twisted it back around.

"No, not the largest. This one is still growing." Da'an paused, then added, "Do not allow anyone to touch it."

"Right," Liam said. He was more worried about the creature touching him.

Liam tossed the global to the ground, leaving the communication link open, and quickly surveyed the lay of the land.

The narrow road clung to the side of the mountain. Immediately to his right, the ground rose quickly. He could climb that slope, but he would be like an ant climbing a wall—an easy target. On the other side of the road, to his left, the mountain dropped away sharply. A mere ten feet from here to there, but it seemed forever.

The roar of the shuttle increased. Da'an was aiming for the road and bringing the small ship down between the trees—or through them if he misjudged the landing. The Taelon would be here in seconds, but the glow surrounding Zo'or's body was nearly gone. Liam needed to stop the creature now.

Taking careful aim, he fired shot after shot into the crystal on the creature's forehead. Whether it was the sudden appearance of the shuttle or the constant irritant from the pistol, Liam did not know, but the creature suddenly reared its head and let out a hideous shriek that shook him to his bones. Then it turned in his direction and drew back its head to spit.

Liam did not wait for the coup de grâce. He darted left toward the safety of the trees. Only three or four steps, but already the creature's head was coming forward, tracking him as he ran.

He dove for the edge of the road just as the creature let fly its fiery venom.

Tucking his legs to his chin, he hit and rolled, then uncoiled as he slid and tumbled down the mountain on his back, the trees exploding all around him, flaming branches and sparks marking his wake. The energy pistol fell from his hand as he clutched at the passing trunks and dug his heels into the soft earth.

He came to rest about a hundred feet down the mountainside. Immediately he flipped over to his belly and started crawling back up, but he adjusted his course to avoid the thick liquid fire as it slid down the mountain, consuming everything in its path. He only hoped that the diversion had given Da'an time to land and start his showdown with the creature.

The climb was steep. Liam pulled himself up by grabbing branches, but scrambled for traction against the slippery leaves. The entire trek back up to the road took no more than two minutes, but when every second counted, that seemed an eternity.

When Liam reached the top, Da'an was out of his shuttle and battling the creature. At first, he appeared to be doing no better than Zo'or had done, but when Liam looked again, the creature seemed smaller. His perspective had changed, making it hard to tell, but the *Uktena* had definitely shrunk.

He saw Dr. Long, who lay on her belly, pulling on the energy rifle that lay beneath Agent Sandoval's unconscious body. Good luck. He had already shot the creature numerous times and doubted that the rifle's extra firepower would make much difference. He had to credit the woman for her spunk but not her intelligence.

Just then he noticed movement to his left. On her feet again, her jeans torn, her knees scraped and bloody, Renée Palmer shuffled zombielike toward the creature.

"Renée!"

When she did not respond, he reached for the taser, intending to stun her again, but the weapon was gone. Like his pistol, he must have lost it during his tumble down the mountain. After a moment's hesitation, he sprinted across the road, caught Renée by the waist, and hefted her onto his shoulder. Still groggy from being darted, she struggled weakly, but not enough to throw him off balance.

Normally he could have carried her like this for several dozen yards without slowing, but his muscles twitched from his rapid climb up the slope. Trying to turn, he slipped on the gravel and crashed into the bushes on the road's steep uphill side.

Renée's weight crushed the wind from his lungs. As he gasped, she rolled back onto the road and sat up.

Huffing, he scooted toward her and locked his legs around her waist. She pushed against his legs, trying to rise, but he grabbed her wrists and pulled her arms tight across her body, forming a human straightjacket.

She would not be able to move—but neither would he.

He glanced at Da'an. The Taelon lay crumpled next to Zo'or, the light of his emanations barely perceptible. Within seconds, he would be defeated, too. Only this time, there would be no cavalry to rescue them.

THIRTY-EIGHT

Waneta's side ached. No matter how deeply she breathed, she could not get her wind back. She now understood how horses could run themselves to death.

Behind her, the *Uktena* shrieked. Through that chilling cry, Waneta felt its intelligence and its hunger. No wonder her mother had fled. Waneta would jump at the chance to leave all this behind, but she had seen the damage this creature could do. Yet it was the same beast her great-grandmother had controlled for most of her life—and for years beyond. Waneta could not run, but how could she fight?

Like her mother, Waneta had ignored her heritage. How much irreplaceable knowledge had been lost over the centuries to such arrogance? Perhaps a legend had once existed about the Taelons. Waneta did not know of any, but she was not familiar with all the old tales. Before today, they had just been stories— portals into an ancient culture.

But if her ancestors were able to defeat a beast such as the *Uktena*, perhaps they could have defeated the Taelons. Perhaps they did.

The *Uktena* lifted its head and spat liquid fire. Waneta ducked, but she was not the intended target. The glowing balls of venom struck Zo'or, who had walked forward to confront the creature. The Taelon shined a brighter blue but otherwise appeared unharmed.

The fire spattered off Zo'or and rained down around her.

Drops burned and crackled where they hit the gravel, and she backed away, doing her best to get out from between the Taelon and the *Uktena*. She stopped when she smelled burning meat. Smoke curled from a tiny hole in her pant leg, just above the calf. She felt no pain. How could that be? If this stuff fried rocks, what was it doing to her skin?

Her leg went numb, but she managed to hop to the edge of the road before she fell. She was still too near the Taelon if the *Uktena* spit fire again, but the great snake had settled down to a different kind of fight.

Bright shafts of light flashed from the *Uluhsati* and struck Zo'or. The silent beam flickered like a hyperactive strobe light. Incredibly powerful, it had already driven the Taelon to its knees.

She pulled up the leg of her jeans and gasped. The tiny drop of the *Uktena*'s fire had melted her flesh. It looked like a water trail through dust, like a snake crawling along her skin. She reached out to touch the wound, but stopped. This stuff might mutilate her fingers as well. She pulled down her pant leg and stared wide-eyed at Zo'or.

If one drop of the fire had done this to her, how had the Taelon survived the brunt of the attack? The *Uktena* had not spat fire again, but the beam of flickering light poured forth from the *Uluhsati* and pounded the invisible shield surrounding the alien. The Taelon's color grew lighter and lighter. It would not last long.

She had to get away. Lying on the roadside, she looked down. She could slide into the ravine, but if the *Uktena* killed Zo'or and the others, no one would find her at the bottom of such a deep gully, and if her leg did not improve, she would never make it back up the steep slope by herself. Worse, if the wound was anything like a snakebite, she might die from fever before help arrived.

A shuttle roared overhead. Major Kincaid, whom she recognized as Da'an's Protector, had tackled Renée Palmer to keep her away from the *Uktena*. Now the Doors International executive lay sprawled on the roadway, and Major Kincaid, energy pistol in hand, was firing at the *Uktena*, his shots hitting the *Uluhsati* with no effect.

At first, the creature did not respond. When it did, it brought its head back, ready to spit fire. Major Kincaid, amazingly quick, sprinted across the road and dove for the cover of the trees. The crazy fool ran between her and the monster. Liquid fire chased him, spattering and sizzling against the gravel. The *Uktena* spat again at the spot where he had disappeared, and trees exploded with loud pops and showers of sparks.

Waneta ducked and covered her head with her arms, shielding her face. Only after the popping had stopped for several seconds did she dare to look around. Putrid smoke hung in the stale air, but the liquid fire had landed well short of where she lay. Her hands shaking, she ran her fingers through her hair and across the back of her shoulders. Everything felt fine.

Suddenly the shuttle dropped out of the sky like a whistling bomb and hit the ground hard. She turned in time to see its crash bubble flash bright blue, then fade. As soon as it cleared, a Taelon scampered from the ship—not exactly running, but as close to it as she had ever seen a Taelon come.

Like everyone else on the road, she had seen this newcomer on TV. It was Da'an, the North American Companion. When it stopped next to Zo'or and in front of Agent Sandoval, it lost its features and glowed, colorful lines dancing over its skin.

The *Uktena* released an angry cry, then pointed its antlers at Da'an and produced the silent flickering light that had almost killed Zo'or. Da'an seemed better able to handle its attack, or perhaps the beast had used too much energy defeating Zo'or. The great snake shrieked painfully several times, decreasing in size each time it did so.

Even with this apparent progress, the *Uktena* would win eventually. Already Da'an had withered noticeably. In minutes, both Taelons would be defeated and the *Uktena* would kill the rest of them. She could not allow that to happen. In many ways, she was the one who had unleashed this beast upon the world. She must be the one to stop it.

According to legend, the warrior who killed the *Uktena* the first time used a single arrow. Even if Waneta had a bow, she did not know how to shoot one. She eyed a nearby branch that might work as a spear, but she could never throw it hard enough, and the *Uktena* would hardly sit still while she dragged herself within range and plunged a stake into its heart.

She needed a weapon from her world, not one from the ancient Cherokees.

Major Kincaid had a pistol but had taken that with him when he plunged down the mountain. She desperately searched her surroundings and spied the barrel of the energy rifle sticking out from under Agent Sandoval's unconscious body.

She dropped to her belly and inched toward him. Rocks scratched the sensitive skin of her stomach and worked inside the waistband of her jeans. In front of her, Da'an continued to battle. She would need to make it past the Taelon to reach the rifle, but if the *Uktena* spit another volley of fire, she would die more painfully than she wanted to imagine.

It was a chance she had to take.

She crawled forward, almost even with Da'an now. The Taelon had lost most of its color. It still deflected light from the *Uktena*, but where light had once reflected off with no trace, it now surrounded the alien, soaking into the protective barrier like water into a dry sponge.

Her fingernails tore as she clawed at the road and heaved herself forward. She kicked with her good leg but could do nothing at all with the other one.

Behind her, the creature shrieked. The first Taelon, Zo'or, had risen and moved next to Da'an. When the aliens touched, the energy shields surrounding them joined, as if the two were uniting their strength. The *Uktena* twisted its antlers, refocusing its attack. Zo'or crumpled almost at once. The glow from the Taelons faded, flickering, almost gone. In seconds, both would be dead.

She was only a few feet from the weapon. Sandoval's black hair lay mussed and tangled about his head, his mouth hanging open and his hands clenched around the rifle.

Gritting her teeth, she gathered her remaining strength and pushed toward him, but her progress seemed agonizingly slow. In her imagination, she felt the Taelons dying, and with them, her world.

Almost there. Push . . . scrape . . . stretch!

She grabbed the rifle, but she could not pull it from beneath Sandoval. He was not a big man, but she needed more leverage.

Behind her, the creature let out a long cry, like a bugle announcing a victory. She glanced over her shoulder. Neither Taelon was glowing. Were they dead? Or just unconscious?

Renée Palmer had risen and was stumbling toward the creature, but Major Kincaid had emerged from the trees and stood at the road's edge. He had survived; let him take care of the woman.

Putting her good leg against Agent Sandoval's shoulder, Waneta arched her back and pulled as hard as she could. The rifle barely budged. She chewed her lip, then twisted and grabbed its barrel like an oar. Holding tight, she threw her weight backward. The rifle spun free so hard it almost flew out of her hands.

Waneta quickly checked the energy chamber and cocked the weapon as she had seen Gil do. Turning, she saw the *Uktena* slithering toward the Taelons. Would it absorb them the way it had Daniel's mother, Triss?

Suddenly the *Uktena* stopped, its head twisting in her direction.

Damn! It knew what she intended, just as it had known when she was about to be shot.

It reared back its head. She had no time to count the spots but recognized the seventh. Slightly brighter than those around it, it shimmered, its essence wavering as if it did not belong to this dimension.

But she would have only one chance. Major Kincaid had fired repeatedly at the beast without hurting it. If the stories were wrong, if the legend of the *Uktena* had been changed for dramatic effect, she would be dead. For the first time, she had to put her life completely in the hands of faith. She had to trust her ancestors and the oral tradition that formed their legacy. It would be the hardest thing she had ever done.

She aimed and fired.

Bursts of light flew from the weapon and struck their intended target. The creature shrieked in pain. In that moment, she felt the power of her ancestors and knew that the shot from the weapon could not kill the creature by itself. Only the life energy that flowed through her veins, the same energy that protected her from the *Uktena*'s mind control, could put the creature back to rest. The shot from the rifle acted merely as a symbol, a way to focus, to believe in a power she now knew existed. This was why her ancient ancestors could put down such a ferocious beast using only a bow and arrow.

She felt the power flow from her body and strike. Even so, she took no chances. She repeatedly squeezed the trigger, keeping the rifle aimed at the seventh spot, hitting it ten or twelve times.

As the creature writhed in pain, she called to Major Kincaid. "Run!"

He must have learned his lesson from their first encounter, because this time he scooped Renée Palmer into his arms and barreled down the road.

Waneta dropped the rifle and crawled hard for the safety of the ravine. Small rocks scraped her hands and blood smeared her fingertips.

To her right, the beast threw back its head and spat. Its thrashing carved through the gravel and into the foundation rock below, and its tail splintered trees along both sides of the road. Liquid fire spouted into the air and sprinkled the creature. Thick smoke billowed. Screaming, the creature shrank into it.

Pops, sizzles, and shrieks covered Major Kincaid's footsteps as he approached. Waneta did not know he was there until he grabbed her beneath the shoulders and pulled her up.

"It's all right. I'm here to help." He wrapped one of her arms around his neck. "We've got to get to the shuttle."

Waneta did her best to hop along beside him. In front of them, Renée Palmer sat in the cockpit, looking dazed. Waneta did not know whether she should love the woman or hate her. If Ms. Palmer had not hired Gil to find the stone, Waneta would probably be dead—but Gil would be alive.

Major Kincaid helped Waneta inside the ship and dropped her in the seat next to Renée Palmer, then turned to run back.

He never made it out of the shuttle.

In a blinding flash of light and energy, the *Uktena* exploded.

THIRTY-NINE

The instant before the blast struck the shuttle, Waneta thought she saw the two Taelons huddled together, their faint glow parting the oncoming energy wave like a ship's bow splitting the sea. Behind and between them lay Sandoval, partially protected.

The full force of the explosion hit the shuttle, and its protective crash bubble activated, a bright blue shield around the cockpit. The blast shook the bubble, rocking Waneta and tumbling Major Kincaid into her lap. Renée Palmer blinked, as if awakened to find she was still dreaming.

After a few seconds of pummeling, the wave subsided and the rocking stopped. When the protective bubble cleared, Waneta felt as if she had survived a nuclear blast and was looking at ground zero.

Trees were knocked down on each side of the road. Dust and smoke choked the air, and thick acidic blood boiled like witch's brew from dozens of new hollows. Tiny fires burned from several trees, but fewer than Waneta expected. Miraculously, the shuttle had survived. It listed hard to the right and would certainly not fly, but most of it appeared intact. As explosions went, this one must have been relatively cool.

To the right of the shuttle, a bright jewel glowed red in the artificial darkness. *Uluhsati* had survived, just as it had always survived. Waneta wondered if there were truly any way to kill an *Uktena*.

On the road ahead, both Taelons shimmered, apparently alive but unconscious. Agent Sandoval smoldered, his jacket frayed and smoking, his face as sooty black as his hair.

Major Kincaid touched the crash bubble and it dissolved. Putrid smoke filled their nostrils and Renée Palmer gagged.

Major Kincaid, one arm over his face, mumbled, "Come on. We've got to help them."

Waneta could not walk and Renée Palmer did not move to follow him. Instead Ms. Palmer stared off to the right, her eyes changing, her mouth curling into the beginning of a smile.

The expression reminded Waneta of the one on Daniel's face just before he—

"Oh, no!"

Renée Palmer rose and started forward. Waneta dove at her and missed. Pushing hard with her good leg, she lunged again, reaching out blindly, and barely caught an ankle as the woman stepped out of the shuttle.

Renée Palmer jerked her leg free. Waneta slithered onto the ground, then grabbed the ankle again. Ms. Palmer stopped, her head slowly rocking and tilting until her gaze focused on Waneta.

"Release me," she said calmly. Her eyes did not water and she breathed normally. She tried to pull away, but Waneta refused to let go.

Major Kincaid, his back to them, bent over Agent Sandoval and felt his neck for a pulse.

"Help!" Waneta cried, struggling to hold on to Renée Palmer's foot. Though the air was less smoky close to the ground, her lungs still stung with each breath.

Major Kincaid glanced up. He coughed and fanned the smoke away from his face.

"Help me!" Waneta lost her grip, lunged again, but missed. "She's going for *Uluhsati!*"

"What?" He stood up but did not come forward.

Renée Palmer, unhindered, walked briskly to the glowing stone and picked it up.

"At last." She cradled it in both hands and lifted it high in front of her. "We will finally defeat the Taelons."

Major Kincaid understood too late. He ran at her, perhaps intending to tackle her again.

She held out the stone toward him while he was several steps away. A red-tinged crackle of light danced from its center and struck him in the chest. Groaning, he tumbled backward and landed hard against the blackened rock of the roadway.

Waneta crawled toward Ms. Palmer, but she had no real plan for what to do once she arrived. She had been unable to retake the crystal from Daniel, and Ms. Palmer had just flattened a man who was far heavier than Waneta. What could she do?

Renée Palmer grimaced and flinched, much as Daniel had done after his mother's sacrifice, then stumbled toward Major Kincaid.

"I need blood to regenerate."

It was starting all over again.

Suddenly Waneta's great-grandmother emerged from among the jagged tree stumps behind the woman. She walked out of the smoke and the devastation, an angry spirit stepping out of another world to seek revenge on the living.

Renée Palmer spun, then backed a step away. "No. You can't stop me—not this time."

The old woman's voice sounded hollow. She spoke slowly, stiffly, and the smoke did not bother her at all. "You have died and been reborn. My power over you is gone. I am no longer the one who can stop you."

She looked at Waneta. Renée Palmer, controlled by *Uluh-sati*, whirled in Waneta's direction, then threw her arms across her eyes, as if shielding them from a blinding light.

Waneta quickly pushed herself up to a sitting position. Pulling her bum leg beneath her, she did her best to prepare for an attack that never came.

When Ms. Palmer put her arms down, she squinted at Waneta and backed away. "You are unimportant."

She walked to Major Kincaid and bent over him. He

quickly crabbed away from her, rolled backward, and jumped to his feet. His eyes shifted left and right, searching the roadway, but the weapons were all melted or gone.

Waneta's great-grandmother shimmered, like a projection seen on smoke. She walked close to Waneta and looked down. "You can stop her, but only if you are willing to accept responsibility for *Uluhsati*."

Ms. Palmer lifted her hand, and the crystal glowed bright red.

Major Kincaid winced and shut his eyes. He clenched his fists, as if in pain.

"I have to help him," Waneta said. "He saved my life."

"No. *Uluhsati* is at its weakest just after *Uktena* has died. Do not accept responsibility because of what you see around you."

Major Kincaid opened his fists and looked down at his hands. They glowed white hot.

Waneta blinked in surprise. She had thought he was human, but he was neither human nor Taelon. Nor was he like Daniel, who had possessed qualities of both. Major Kincaid had his own special abilities. That was why *Uluhsati* had chosen him rather than Renée Palmer to energize its metamorphosis.

"The power cannot be forced on a person," her great-grandmother continued, "even for the best reasons. It must be taken willingly, and accepted fully, with no reservations. If you choose to walk that path, you will lose all that you have, and gain all that you have not. Never will you be rich in the ways of the whites, but your people will take care of you. It is a sacrifice. It is also a great honor."

Waneta thought of what she had lost: her job at the university, her apartment with its TV and its microwave oven. But she had no close friends. No family. No children. She enjoyed her work, but if she won the lottery, would she still go in every day? Probably not.

What she had wanted most in life was to know the truth and to make a difference.

Her great-grandmother issued a final warning.

"Once the decision is made, it cannot be unmade. *Adado dakanehuh*, the time of binding. For fear of this, your mother fled to the city. The stone will be keyed to you. You will be able to control it, but if you leave the mountain for too long a time, the stone will follow—and your control will be lost. The decision you make now is more important than marriage, more important than religion. This decision is for life. Make it wisely."

Waneta bowed her head. No wonder her mother had run. The responsibility facing her now was like nothing she had ever known—or even imagined.

How could she assume so great an obligation? How could she turn away? In the end, what drove her decision was the same need that had driven her life: the need to know.

She lifted her chin and spoke the words solemnly, defiantly, giving them the weight they deserved. "I accept."

Her great-grandmother smiled and Waneta smiled back. If only Gil could see her now.

Renée Palmer reached out to touch Major Kincaid, but the white-hot light in his palms spread and glowed, covering him, shielding him from the red rays of the stone.

Waneta's great-grandmother bent low, reaching toward Waneta in much the same way Ms. Palmer had reached toward Major Kincaid, but her great-grandmother's touch was gentle, painless. A caress, lighter than any breeze, it anointed Waneta's head and brushed her cheeks.

"Give me your hand," the old woman said.

Waneta reached forward and her great-grandmother brought her own hand down toward Waneta's. Closer . . . closer . . . until their palms met.

Warmth burst at her touch and spread across Waneta in a gushing torrent of knowledge that filled her, then filled her again. It came like a close friend, one she had known yet never known—not in this way. Pinching, biting, clawing, but without pain, without malice. Graced by the weight of ages, it smothered her in its suffocating embrace, then allowed her to breathe new air, cleaner than ever before, tinged with freedom and understanding.

She closed her eyes, drinking in the sensations, shuddering as every part of her being bathed in the warmth of that knowledge. It entered into her deepest recesses and merged with her soul. Throbbing, yearning, she clasped it to her, desperately clinging to its essence the way she clung to life itself.

Gently, the touch subsided. Its parting trailed echoes behind it, emanations that remained with her, leaving her shaken and shivering with aftershocks of comprehension.

Like a newborn after a long sleep, her eyes blinked, then slowly opened.

She knew what to do.

Rising to her feet, her leg suddenly unhindered, she stepped toward *Uluhsati*.

The time had come to put *Uluhsati* back in its place, to return it to the sanctuary—not to a physical location, but to a spot guarded by her spirit and confined by her energy.

Waneta recited a chant handed down from when the world was new. She would not have understood the words only moments ago, but now she spoke them fluently. Her fingers curled, forming the ancient signs, the movements awkward and unpracticed but sufficient.

Neither words nor gestures were the source of the power. Like the weapon used to kill *Uktena*, they were merely a way to focus, a method of teaching, a trigger to unlock instinctive memories that ran in her veins and beat within her heart.

Uluhsati sensed her now. It caused the woman to turn, to release a shriek—a feeble attempt at its mind call.

Waneta unleashed her own form of control. Clouds of icy cold rolled through her. She allowed them to pour forth, their chill reaching out invisibly to surround the stone. Like specters floating through a clear, crisp winter night, they consumed the crystal's energy and allowed her to place a halter on *Uluhsati's* undying hunger.

As the last words of the chant left Waneta's mouth, she

struck her hand downward, twirling her fingers, metaphorically catching *Uluhsati*'s essence and locking it within the stone.

The crystal's glow flickered, struggling, then darkened to nothing.

As the light died, Renée Palmer wavered, her eyelids fluttering. Clutching a hand to her chest, she swooned, toppling over backward and crumpling to the gravel. The stone bounced free and rolled in Waneta's direction.

Major Kincaid ran to Renée Palmer. Coughing, he knelt and felt her pulse, then nodded and turned to look for the stone. When he spied it just in front of Waneta, he rose and started toward her. His face remained calm, with no hint of the eagerness Daniel and Ms. Palmer had shown, but like the others, he wanted the stone. Waneta could not allow him to take it.

He stopped, two steps away.

Waneta stood another moment, then her leg went numb and she sank to the ground.

The stone remained between them. A prize. A dividing line.

But he was looking at her, not the stone. He studied her, as if seeing her for the first time. "Where did you learn to speak Taelon?"

Waneta sat on the ground, her lifeless leg tucked under her. *"Tsalagi tsiwoni."*

The words surprised her. They were Cherokee, and she had understood them. Slowly, haltingly, she forced herself to speak English. It proved difficult at first, as if learning so much so fast had shoved part of her previous knowledge aside. "I don't . . . speak Taelon."

"The words you spoke before, when Renée had the stone, they sounded Taelon." He said it as a comment, not as an accusation. "I couldn't understand their meaning."

"They are Cherokee words, more ancient than our people."

He frowned, his jaw set. His eyes watered from the smoke, but they held no longing—only sadness and determination. "I need the stone."

Waneta looked at him coldly. She bore him no ill will, but he served the Taelons.

Her great-grandmother stepped forward, her form growing more shadowy and indistinct as the smoke cleared. As a young girl, Waneta had called her *Elisi*, Grandmother. That is how she thought of her now.

"Tell him the truth," *Elisi* said. "Now you know it as well as I."

Liam's expression did not change. Perhaps he could not see or hear her. He coughed. "I need to get Zo'or and Da'an to the mother ship as soon as possible, but I can't allow that stone to stay here, unprotected, or this"—he looked around the clearing—"could happen all over again."

Waneta shook her head. "You cannot take *Uluhsati*. It belongs with *Tsalagi*, with the Cherokee. We have watched over this *Uktena* since it first came to our world. Many times *Uktena* has died. Many times *Uluhsati* has brought *Uktena* back to life."

Until she spoke the words, Waneta did not know what she was going to say, but once the words were out of her mouth, she recognized them as her own.

"*Uluhsati* gives great power to those who possess it, but that power must be respected. It must be earned, not taken as the Taelons tried to do. If you wish the world to live, you must allow *Uluhsati* to stay with me."

Waneta casually picked up the stone. It seemed cold, lifeless—but she knew better.

Major Kincaid took a quick step backward, his body tense.

"*Uluhsati* sleeps." She held it forth for him to see. "You no longer hear its voice calling you. I can keep it quiet. You and your friends cannot."

Major Kincaid glanced up and down the road, as if assessing the devastation the stone had caused. "The crystal's too dangerous to leave here."

"We have watched over *Uluhsati* for a hundred generations. We can watch over it a few more."

The smoke was gradually clearing. In places, beams of sunlight splashed against the road.

Beside Waneta, *Elisi* shimmered, then solidified as she stepped back into deeper shadows. "My time grows short, *Sgilisi*, and we have much to do."

Waneta stared up at Major Kincaid.

He looked at Renée Palmer for several seconds, then glanced at the Taelons. "The boy? And his mother?"

"The stone," Waneta said simply.

He shook his head. "Da'an."

After looking at the crystal in her hand for several seconds more, he walked to Agent Sandoval. Lifting aside the man's smoldering suit coat, he retrieved a global. Although the device was melted around the edges, Major Kincaid pulled it open and spoke into it.

"I need transport to the mother ship immediately. Da'an and Zo'or are injured. So is Agent Sandoval. I'm transmitting my coordinates now."

Major Kincaid looked at Waneta one last time.

"Keep it safe," he said solemnly, then turned his attention back to the global.

Elisi moved forward and knelt beside Waneta. "First, we must heal your leg."

For a moment, Waneta understood. She pulled up her pant leg, but the knowledge slipped away. In a panic, she looked to *Elisi*. "I'm forgetting."

"Do not fear. The memories will be there when you need them. For now, allow *Uluhsati* to reclaim the *inaduh* he has given you."

Elisi pointed at Waneta's leg.

Again, Waneta understood. This time, she touched the stone to her fresh scar. She had accepted the power of *Uluhsati* but did not yet feel comfortable with its magic. The ability to heal, to predict the future seemed nebulous and hard to explain scientifically, but where the stone touched, her flesh rippled and flowed, and when she removed *Uluhsati*, her skin was pink and healthy where the snakelike scar had been. She stood and stretched her injured leg. It felt a little stiff but otherwise seemed unaffected.

"Good," *Elisi* said. "Now we can travel. You have a long way to go."

"Where are we going?"

"Knowledge of the stone was yours from the time you were born—you only needed to awaken it to remember—but you have many other mysteries to learn, and we have little time. For too long I have used the power of *Uluhsati* to resist the pull of the Darkening Land, but I am no longer keeper of the stone. My time in this world will soon end."

Elisi shimmered again, but this time she did not step back into the shadows. Through her, Waneta could make out the faint outline of tree stumps and rocks strewn across the mountainside.

The old woman's eyes twinkled. "Before I rest, we must help someone."

Waneta's voice cracked. "Gil?"

Elisi smiled. "It is too soon for him to go to the Darkening Land. You must call him back."

"Giliaduh," Waneta whispered and rose to her feet.

Perhaps magic existed after all.

FORTY

Zo'or turned slowly away from his summoned visitor and stared out the virtual glass of the viewport. Earth rotated beneath the Taelon mother ship, a world just out of reach, a place with at least one mystery left to solve.

Da'an, who had protested being summoned so soon after their recovery from the Elteena, spoke first. "How is Agent Sandoval? Were the regenerations successful?"

"My Protector is well and has returned to his duties. But what of your Protector? He was also on the mountain."

"Major Kincaid was not seriously injured by the Elteena."

"So I have been told. I find that . . . interesting." Zo'or continued to stare at the blue planet, far below. "I also find it interesting that Major Kincaid and Renée Palmer were on the mountain during the Elteena's attack. Tell me, how did that happen?"

"Liam Kincaid is my Protector. When the Synod agreed I should aid you in your battle with the Elteena, I requested he join me, as I should have done."

Zo'or straightened his fingers and glanced over his shoulder. "You had the shuttle, and he could not have arrived so quickly using the portal system."

"Destiny knows more than you or I. Major Kincaid and Renée Palmer were already in the town of Cherokee when I contacted him."

"What were they doing there?"

"I gave Major Kincaid time away from his duties. The

Great Smoky Mountains are a popular tourist area, especially when the deciduous trees have reached the end of their annual growing cycle. Perhaps he was there on vacation."

"And Renée Palmer?"

"You understand human mating practices as well as I."

Zo'or curled his fingers in surprise.

Da'an momentarily closed his eyes and tilted his head to the right, the equivalent of a human shrug.

Turning from the window, Zo'or stretched out his hand and revealed a red stone. Dull, lifeless.

Da'an's hands dropped to his sides, his fingers growing still. "That is not the Elteena."

"Of course it is not. This simple stone was found in the pocket of Agent Sandoval's suit when he was brought to the mother ship for treatment of his injuries. Originally it was taken from Dr. Messmore, the woman scientist's department head. Agent Sandoval believes that the woman supplied this fake to Dr. Messmore rather than providing him the real Elteena. As to how she came to possess this forgery, we do not know, but the man who helped her escape was a known member of the Resistance. These facts imply that the humans knew what the Elteena looked like before it was found—information they could have obtained only from a Taelon."

"Your intentional ignorance of human mythology has led you astray. The man who helped her escape was Cherokee. That group of humans has myths that describe the Elteena's species in detail."

"That may be true," Zo'or said, "but this replica exactly matches the seed of the Elteena you revealed to the Synod during your ka'ta'tha'al."

Da'an remained silent, his hands still at his sides.

Stretching out his fingers, Zo'or allowed the stone to fall to the floor. It bounced and clattered against the deck of the mother ship before coming to rest.

"It does not matter," Zo'or said. "Agent Sandoval will find the woman. The Elteena, the real one, will still be mine."

Da'an's fingers danced in exasperation. "This discussion is meaningless. There is nothing for Agent Sandoval to find. The woman died when she destroyed the Elteena. Major Kincaid has said so."

"Major Kincaid has spent too much time around you; he has mastered the art of half-truths. He did not say the woman was dead. After the explosion, he claimed that our safety was his main concern. He did not search for the seed of the Elteena or the woman, but said she *may* have been destroyed by the blast. Yet no traces of her body were found."

Da'an walked back and forth once, his steps precise. He had been around the humans too long. Taelons did not pace.

"The blood of the Elteena is highly acidic. It may have consumed her flesh. What little was left would be hard to detect amid the rubble. The rain from the night of the attack created a mud slide that carried both the woman's remains and the seed of the Elteena down the mountainside, as well as destroying that section of road. It will take years to excavate such a large area, and even then, we may find nothing. Accept the truth. The woman and the Elteena are gone."

"You do not believe that any more than I."

"What I believe is of no consequence. I am not searching for the woman."

"No. Just as you were not searching for the Elteena. Just as you did not exploit the boy and his mother."

Da'an glanced at Zo'or. "What boy? What mother?"

"The boy who provided the life force strong enough to complete the metamorphosis. The human dancer. You attended his performance the day the Elteena awoke and were in his presence for several minutes. You cannot tell me you did not recognize him for what he was. How naive do you believe me to be?"

"I was ill at the performance, disturbed by the Elteena's influence on the Commonality."

"Major Kincaid told me you were not affected by the Elteena until the boy finished dancing."

"As you have said, Major Kincaid has mastered the art of half-truths. He did not *notice* I was ill until the end of the performance."

Zo'or stepped toward Da'an. "A clever ploy. You send the child to confront the Elteena in your place. If he fails, you have the Synod to help you destroy what you created. If he succeeds, you keep the power of the Elteena to yourself. The greatest reward for the least risk. That is always your way."

Da'an blinked slowly. "Do not accuse me of a scheme only you would devise."

"No. I am sure your plan was much more extensive and destructive than what I have uncovered. The boy had to come from somewhere. What astounds me is your timing. Did you plan for the Elteena to awake during the boy's performance, or was that a fortunate coincidence?"

Da'an moved his hands in a pattern to indicate innocence. "You imply much, but you have nothing but ideas and speculations. I never saw the child until the day he performed for me."

"You cannot hide the truth from me, Da'an. I am not the Synod, which can be misled with good intentions. I sensed the thoughts of the Elteena as it consumed the boy—I know what kind of child he was. You will not take advantage of me."

"You take advantage of yourself." Da'an raised his hands, his fingers undulating in anger. "Give up this quest, Zo'or. You cannot control the Elteena. It manipulated your thoughts and took advantage of your ambitions. You violated the decision of the Synod and walked into its trap without suspicion. You risked everything for personal gain."

Zo'or inclined his head to the right and blinked his eyes once, slowly. "I violated no decision—the Synod made none—and the risk was acceptable for the reward offered. If I had succeeded, Earth would be mine. We would no longer need to worry about the humans and what they might know or what they might do. My power would be complete and the success of our race would be assured."

"And what about Earth? What about the humans? Would our success also be theirs?"

"They are tools. You know that as well as I do. As you so carefully reminded me on my way to the planet, you have encountered an Elteena before. So tell me, how long did you spend planning your return to power? How long did you sense the Elteena buried beneath the soil before you arranged for the human woman to bring it to the surface?"

Da'an cocked his head and performed the gesture of amusement. "You delude yourself in many ways. The Elteena cannot be tamed by a single Taelon mind."

"Unless that mind is yours?" Zo'or traced out a pattern of irritation. "You know I could have controlled the Elteena if I had found it before the metamorphosis began. That is why you asked me to call a meeting of the Synod, because you knew I would not. What frightens you is not how close I came to failure, but how close I came to success."

Da'an's fingers made the intricate movements for a parent reprimanding a child. "You could have called a Synod meeting at any time. Do not blame me for your failure to do so."

Zo'or lifted his chin slightly in a posture of indignant frustration. "You gave me a taste of the Elteena's power, knowing how I would react when I sensed the consumption of the boy. Then you delayed informing the Synod of the danger until they had no time left to reach consensus. That assured that you, rather than I, would be the one chosen to defeat the Elteena. Meanwhile my battle simultaneously disabled me and weakened the Elteena for your conquest."

Da'an closed his eyes but said nothing.

"I warn you, Da'an. Next time you will not succeed so easily."

Da'an's eyes snapped open, and he swept an arm signifying sudden and violent outrage. "There was no success. We almost died. If I had not brought all my experience to bear, if the humans had not helped, Earth would now belong to the Elteena and our race would be doomed to extinction."

"Yes, you miscalculated. You thought pride would cloud my judgment, preventing me from calling on the power of the Commonality before I entered battle. Also, you did not foresee the mother's sacrifice. How could you anticipate that she would willingly surrender her life's energy, improving her son's chances to control the Elteena, but also increasing the power available to it?

"Admit defeat, Da'an. You failed."

Zo'or and Da'an stared at each other, unblinking, for several long moments.

Slowly Da'an turned his head away and indicated resignation with both hands. "If I had done all you say, it is only because you are predictable. You are a zealot, Zo'or. Even now you long for the power of an Elteena that has been destroyed. You seek a woman who does not exist."

"She exists. After she destroyed the Elteena's active form, she recovered its seed and fled."

"How? If available, the woman's life force would have been used by the Elteena to start another metamorphosis."

"If it had wanted to consume the woman, it would have done so when she first discovered it."

"Perhaps. We cannot say how an Elteena thinks. What is certain is that at the end of the battle, you and I were disabled. The Elteena would have known this. It would have stopped at nothing to claim our energies for its own, and it would have taken advantage of any available life force to help it do so. How could the woman resist? Even if she were not palatable, Renée Palmer and Liam Kincaid would have been consumed unless the woman scientist protected them, too. Are you saying that a human—a female human—could control the Elteena when we could not?"

Zo'or walked to the window and stared out. He tried to fill his voice with confidence, but the word came out soft, unsure. "No."

"So. It is settled then."

Earth rotated far below. Zo'or reached out a hand but stopped just short of touching the virtual glass. "For now."

ABOUT THE AUTHOR

GLENN R. SIXBURY has been writing and selling science fiction and fantasy for fifteen years. His credits include science fiction, fantasy, horror, and children's stories published in magazines and international hardcover and paperback anthologies. More than 250,000 copies of his stories exist in print, including international versions in both French and German. He lives in rural Kansas.